NEIGHBORHOOD

WATCH

By

Kevin Kenealy

Chapter 1: Ridgeport

1

When Scott Casey reflected on his time living out his formative years in his parents' Tudor-style home on Forest View Lane in Ridgeport, Illinois, he shuddered as if a chill was running up his spine. As the rain pounded outside his apartment window, he thought long and hard about what he was going to say. At thirty-three, Scott lived about as far away as one could get from Ridgeport: in a one-bedroom apartment in Honolulu. But Ridgeport never moved away from Scott.

Nestled between Naperville and Aurora, Ridgeport was buried on any map. No one outside a ten-mile radius had ever heard of Ridgeport until it made headlines in 2004 for the town's first murder in its 110-year history. After that, it captured America's attention as a town to watch and study under a microscope.

Until that murder, the hearts of Ridgeport's residents seemed to beat as one — synchronized to the same rhythm— and anyone who lived there could feel it. Like most kids growing up in a small town, Scott and his friends knew every shop, business, and street within a half-hour bike ride from one end of town to the other.

Despite its diminutive size, Ridgeport supplied residents with everything they needed. In fact, residents never needed to leave town to do business or be entertained. They never even had to leave the town's borders. A local grocery store stood from the 1960s, and Ridgeporters ventured to that store for all their provisions. A barbershop occupied a lot downtown, along with a women's boutique. Ridgeport Mall, a frequent spot for entertainment in the community, opened in the 1980s with shops, restaurants, and a movie theater on the first floor. The town's parks were well -maintained, and on any summer day, Ridgeport's families enjoyed watching Little League baseball games during the day and adult softball games at night. Fuller Park hosted the annual Ridgeport Festival, which offered a carnival, food vendors, games, and over-the-hill bands. With about 15,000 residents, the town was home to two elementary schools, a private school for grades K-8, and a junior high. Ridgeporter teens attended either one of the area's private schools or Hartville High in Naperville, a top-rated school in the nation.

Scott didn't realize it when he was young, but he lived in a well-to-do area. Many people hired a lawn service, and most moms stayed home to take care of the children. Scott never wondered why the moms of his best friends Matt Norris and Riley Wrobel were always home; he just figured that's how things were. If they really wanted to, kids could play in the streets at three o'clock in the morning, and their parents would have nothing to worry about. But worry, they did.

The mothers in Ridgeport advocated for a crime-free town, a place that was perfect for raising a family, a place like no other. So, when Sue Ellen Norris served as the president of the Ridgeport Historic District, she made it her business to create a Neighborhood Watch group which the entire neighborhood agreed to.

Yes, Ridgeporters loved growing up there. Yet outside of their ten-mile radius, no one had ever really heard of Ridgeport. And those in town wanted to keep it that way.

There is a saying, "Once a Ridgeporter, always a Ridge-porter." Many citizens settled there for life, while others found that the longer they stayed, the harder it was to leave. The town served as a security blanket to many, a place where everyone knew your name and nothing changed. The town Scott Casey grew up in remained the same as he reached adulthood, at least physically.

Ridgeport stood out as an anomaly in Illinois, where, after living with years of political corruption and high taxes, most residents could not wait to leave. When cars entered Ridgeport, the welcome sign read, "Ridgeport Welcomes You," not "Welcome to Ridgeport." It was as if Ridgeport itself was a living, breathing entity. Yet most people paid no attention to the sign as they hurried along to bypass the main two-mile stretch of Coleridge Avenue (named after the town's first mayor) and on to wherever their busy lives were taking them.

Mayor James Coleridge grew up in Chicago in the late 1800s and built quite a reputation working with the city's philanthropic societies - namely Hull House and other centers where working-class people could further their educational and social opportunities. Coleridge was born into a wealthy family, and his charitable nature and personable character propelled him into the heart of the city's mayoral race in 1896, a year that an economic panic swept the nation. Coleridge lost the election to incumbent mayor Wilson Harrison by only a thousand votes, enraging many Chicagoans. Under Harrison's next four years of service, the city plunged further into recession and corruption.

During that time, Coleridge's legion of followers had expanded, and many accompanied him throughout the city to protests for social justice reforms. Several of his followers landed in jail for their actions, but Coleridge often exerted his influence to release them within a day. When the 1900 election drew near, Coleridge's constituents pressured him to run for mayor again, but he had other plans.

As an avid history buff, Coleridge had been poring over the books in his library during the past year, just months before the 1900 election. He was reminded that America was built on ideals, ideas, and freedoms and how immigrants from around the world had come here to practice those ideals. Coleridge asked himself if the once-great nation had turned as corrupt as the lands that those idealistic travelers left behind.

Even so, Coleridge envisioned a future - a future alongside his followers in a place where all the social justice reforms they hoped to achieve had come to fruition. In Coleridge's view, some good remained in the country.

If such a utopia existed, Coleridge was convinced that it was not in Chicago. However, one could cheaply buy acres of land outside the city limits, and in 1900, Coleridge purchased a forty-acre plot of prairie about thirty-five miles southwest of the city in what would later become Ridgeport. Contractors built him a home there, and he soon began advertising his new utopia as a place to escape the city's corruption. At first, several hundred of his followers jumped on board, many of whom were family members. However, two years later, only a hundred of them fled the Windy City for Coleridge's dream community. Many people laughed him off, saying that he'd lost his mind and would die out there in the wilderness. Nevertheless, Coleridge's contracting team built an entire neighborhood full of beautiful Colonial and Tudor-style homes. These, along with a few businesses, became Ridgeport's historic district.

In the fall of 1908, residents elected Coleridge mayor of their new town and established the St. John's Lutheran Church, which was also the site of their town hall meetings. A few months later, in the spring of 1909, Coleridge formally incorporated Ridgeport at one of the first town hall meetings. Residents decided on the name taken from the word *ridge* in Coleridge. The word *port* was taken from their roots in Chicago, which is the largest port in the Midwest.

By 1910, the new town conducted a formal census, counting 150 residents. Three businesses were established: a bank, a hardware store, and a grocer. At the time, plans were in the works to increase the town's size to build a country club, which would attract even more residents and businesses. A police force had not yet been formally established, so a volunteer militia was formed, along with a volunteer fire department. All the workings were in place for a bright future.

And so, it was. A police and fire station began construction that year, and the country club was completed two years later. Thousands flocked to Ridgeport over the next seventy years until the population reached 15,186. The square mileage grew from .0625 square miles to 3.878 square miles. By contrast, in 2019, the surrounding cities of Naperville to the east encompassed 39.24 square miles (and had a population of 147,682), while Aurora to the west took up 45.95 square miles and had 200,000 residents. Even today, many passersby assume they are in one of the two mid-sized cities unless they see the "Ridgeport Welcomes You" sign, which was erected by Mayor Coleridge himself on May 7, 1909, the date of the town's incorporation.

4

Mayor Coleridge served from 1908 until he died in 1940. The town loved him, and he loved the town. He would begin every town hall meeting by saying, "Love thy neighbor" and "Love thy Ridgeport," and the townspeople would ritualistically say it back. When George Stallworth took over as mayor, he continued the tradition in honor of the town's founder. So, when the Great Depression hit, Stallworth created the Public Works Division and the Park District, allowing townspeople to take up jobs to beautify and keep the town running even under the toughest of times. Even as the town grew, residents remained as close-knit as they were when they first moved in. During World War II, several men left Ridgeport to fight overseas, while the women stayed at home to raise money for the home front or to take jobs in wartime manufacturing plants.

But all along, the town contained an unwritten set of values. For example, residents were expected to go to church in Ridgeport. Those who missed church or went to services outside of town were snubbed in public and stopped getting invited to neighborhood outings. So, out of peer pressure, no one missed church. Children were expected to go to school every day and dress appropriately. These were not just school rules; they were town rules. Ridgeporters took the "Love thy Ridgeport" motto seriously, even literally. Following World War II, the school board established a class on the history of Ridgeport. The public library kept records of the town's achievements, and in 1969, to commemorate Ridgeport's fiftieth anniversary, the board of trustees approved the construction of a town museum.

Social decorum was of the utmost importance. Neighbors spent their free time together. While the men hit the links at the Spring Meadows Country Club, their wives sipped afternoon tea or stopped in for brunch at the club's restaurant. Men enjoyed poker nights, and women hosted book clubs. It was not only a bonding experience, but it was a problem for those who could not attend.

5

Ridgeport served as a model community. By 1999, the police force boasted that the town had not seen a murder in its ninety-year history, and year after year, Ridgeport ranked as the safest town in America. When the town's officials were asked why, they always said the same thing, "Love thy neighbor" and "Love thy Ridgeport."

Yet, Scott Casey did remember some scary things from his thirty-three years there, like a few missing person cases. And it was one of those missing persons that led to the town's first murder.

Chapter 2: Ridgeport 1986

In 1986, Scott Casey's family moved into Ridgeport.

Scott's parents, Loretta and John, searched for a good home for the last year while living at Loretta's mom's house in Oswego. They were smitten when they found one of Ridgeport's original Tudor homes in the historic district. Loretta always loved older homes, and John always wanted a fixer-upper. It was perfect.

Their house had that classic front-gabled roof particular to Tudor architectural style, tall rectangular window panes that gave it a medieval feel, a shaker roof, window boxes filled with white petunias to complement the white petunias in the flower bed in the front of the home, a chestnut-color brick on the first floor to offset the snow-white siding on the second floor, and two chimneys jutted out from both sides of the house asking to be used on those cold Illinois winters. A spacious three-car garage sat in front of a long cobblestone drive. The four thousand-square-foot house was an impressive feat of architecture for the time, and the beautiful crabapple trees shone hues of pinks and reds from the parkway. Once Loretta and John stepped foot in it, they knew they had found their home. That day, the Caseys made an offer and took their first steps to become true Ridgeport citizens.

2

On June 27, 1986, the Caseys formally moved to 10624 Forest View Lane. As the movers began unpacking from the moving van, the family noticed a sign planted on their lawn that read "Ridgeport Welcomes You" and a letter inside their door. Jeremy, one of the movers, handed the letter to John.

It read:

"Welcome, Neighbor! In Ridgeport, we have a town motto that we like to go by, which is "Love thy neighbor" and "Love thy Ridgeport." We are overjoyed to have a new member of our family, and we cannot wait to meet you all. Please take the time to peruse through the reading material the town has prepared for you. You will find it on your dining room table. Should you have any questions, please do not hesitate to ask.

Sincerely Yours,
Mayor Sheila Goldman
555-755-3500
"Love thy neighbor" and "Love thy Ridgeport"

Huh. That's quite the welcome, John thought.
"Hey, honey! Loretta!"
Loretta was in the house already, showing the moving men where to put the furniture. Their six-month-old, Scott, stayed at Loretta's mom's house during the move.

In high school, John Casey was of average height but athletic. He did not belong to a clique, choosing instead to taste the variety of high school life: baseball, band, mathletes, drama. You name it; he was in it. He was a smart kid but not particularly popular. Girls considered him handsome if he knew how to present himself. Instead, he had unkempt sideburns and a worn-out baseball cap outside of school. Band merch t-shirts and torn jeans were his outfits of choice, and he was incredibly shy around girls, though they did like him. However, he was too shy to ask anyone out for fear of rejection.

That was until he asked out Loretta Wiley. She had a group of friends, but they were not the popular girls. She was more into writing poetry than spreading gossip or arguing books in class rather than staring off into space. John thought

12

she was wonderful. Loretta came up to John's chin, making him feel less self-conscious about his height. Her wavy, dark, shoulder-length hair swayed like a pendulum as she walked, and she was thin, but not magazine-cover thin. She looked like she would go for a burger on a date and not worry about it. And most importantly for John: unlike every other girl on the planet, he did not feel intimidated to talk to her. In fact, he enjoyed it.

John sat right across from Loretta in class junior year, but she had just broken up with Chad Fizer. He did not have the heart to approach her. When she walked into his AP Lit class senior year, still single, he did not want to blow it. After Mr. Carter explained the partner project for *The Scarlet Letter*, John knew it was his chance to get to know Loretta. He nibbled on his pen cap and swiveled around in his seat to see that no one had asked if she wanted to partner up yet. His face blushed as she gave him a faint smile.

"Hi, Loretta. Would you like to team up for the project?"

John still remembers her smile from that day growing three sizes, showing her pearly whites.

"I'd love to."

And that was the start of their life together. They received an A on that project and started dating immediately after. By May, they were dancing the night away at the "Enchantment Under the Stars" Prom. John held Loretta close and whispered, "I love you" during Eric Clapton's "Wonderful Tonight." It was the first time he had said it. She pressed her soft cheek against his and whispered back, "I love you too. I always will." From that moment on, they were life partners. They went to Eastern Illinois University, which ended up being a solid fit for John's love of journalism and Loretta's love for education. At EIU, the two lovebirds grew in their future careers and in their love for each other.

Following commencement, John walked alongside Loretta, holding hands and diplomas as they made their way across campus to the Old Main Castle for photos with each other's families. Once there, their parents first wanted to take a picture of the two of them together. John wrapped his arms around her with their diplomas in hand, and they gave their biggest smiles. While Loretta was still staring at the camera, John dropped to one knee and removed the engagement ring from his pocket.

"Loretta, will you make me the happiest man on earth?"

The families, of course, were in on it, but they still acted surprised. Loretta paused and then quoted one of her favorite lines from *Pride and Prejudice*.

"Yes, yes, a thousand times yes!" Loretta and John left Eastern Illinois University to graduate to bigger and better things.

When he stepped into the house to find Loretta, he found her sitting in the dining room, staring at the reading material mentioned in the letter. The reading material looked like a copy of *Atlas Shrugged*.

"Loretta, I saw this letter, and it talks about…that… book."

Loretta had a seat at the head of the dining room table. John sat next to her and held her hand. They both stared at it and looked back at each other but could not bring themselves to say anything at all.

3

Loretta turned from the book to stare at John with her jade-colored eyes. John thought how little his wife had changed since high school. Anytime he paid her a physical compliment, though, she told him he needed a new pair of glasses. He swore she still gets hit on whenever they go out somewhere.

"John, this is ridiculous. I mean, look at the size of this thing. You could beat someone to death with this brick of a book."

"I know. I know."

"Well, let's just flip through it. It may be just a lot of pictures and advertising things to do in the area, like a big tourist brochure."

But after looking through the book, John and Loretta discovered questions that needed to be answered and lines that needed to be signed.

"Are they serious? I mean, what town does this?" asked Loretta.

John just sat there shaking his head, trying to make sense of the situation. "I guess they are. Look at the title of the book again, *Ridgeport Welcomes You: Procedures and Guidelines for Happy Living*."

"So? They are just procedures and guidelines. That doesn't mean anything. I think they just want us to keep this on file," Loretta said.

"I guess. I probably should still look this over and make sure."

A couple of movers carried in their Cherrywood Grandfather clock, and Loretta sprang from her seat to motion the men toward the library. John hunched over the book until he was distracted by one of the movers.

"Here's the bill. Just need your signature here, sir," he said.

"Okay, let me just take a quick look around the house first."

"Not a problem at all."

John circled his new home, ensuring the furniture was in order and accounted for. Then he shook the mover's hand, wrote the check, and signed the paperwork. By the time John found his way back to the book in the dining room, it was gone.

He searched the room before looking for his wife to see if she had stored it away. She lounged on the living room sofa with a glass of wine in her hand, staring out the window at the Austrian pines.

"John, come have a glass with me and christen our new home. What do you say?"

"Um, sure, but did you see that book?"

"Oh, I just put it upstairs in your bottom dresser drawer for now. Look at it later. Let's relax right now. Scott is at my mom's. How often do we get this time together?"

John nodded in agreement, forgot about the book, poured himself a glass of Merlot, and parked a seat next to his wife.

"Here's to my beautiful wife and a beautiful life."

"Welcome to Ridgeport. Ha, Ridgeport welcomes you."

"That it does, Loretta. That it does."

Loretta's mom, Mrs. Wiley, stopped by a couple of hours following their toasting of the house to drop off Scott. She also brought over a home-cooked dinner for the two of them – beef tenderloin, mashed potatoes and gravy, spinach, and dinner rolls. She then toured the home with all the furniture in it, grinning from ear to ear for the new family.

"I love that you found a place in a good neighborhood you can call home," she said.

Loretta smiled and considered bringing up the book but decided not to, thinking it might not be all that important. They gave each other hugs and said their goodbyes. The Caseys enjoyed their first meal together in their new home. They put Scott to bed in his crib and fell right asleep after a long day, safe and sound, without a thought or a care in the world.

John enjoyed a week off until he returned to work at *The Naperville Sun.* Loretta spent the summer at home until she started her new job teaching English at Ridgeport Jr. High School. They cherished their time together, as John's job as a reporter consumed much of his days.

The Caseys celebrated a lot of firsts in 1986 – first summer barbeque, dinner party, first Christmas. The morning following the move marked their first as Ridgeporters. Rays of the sun shone through the household, and as Loretta fed Scott his bottle, John shuffled through the kitchen to search for breakfast.

"We forgot to pack food, honey. Honey?"

John felt his stomach rumble and looked like he was about to keel over from hunger as his wife sat, burping his son. He didn't have to say anything. She thought that maybe his idiosyncrasies might be set aside for when Scott came along. She thought wrong.

"Yes, John. We will go out to breakfast."

Loretta rolled her eyes as she carried her six-month-old toward the kitchen. As she rinsed his bottle, she rocked him in her left arm. She'd become an expert multitasker these days.

Shaking her head, Loretta said, "Scott, your father, I swear. I just hope that you don't develop his annoying little habits."

"What was that?"

"Nothing, dear."

At John's suggestion, they made their way to The Ridgeport Egg, a local diner John spotted off Coleridge Ave. on his way into town. As their 1985 Oldsmobile Cruiser station wagon pulled out of the driveway and onto breakfast, Sue Ellen Norris made her way to their doorstep carrying a fruit basket.

The diner offered up a slice of Americana. It featured classic car shows in its expansive parking lot on Friday nights during the summer, and it paraded its American flag garland throughout the place on Memorial Day, the Fourth, Veterans Day, or any other day that was reason enough to be patriotic. Its Jukebox played Elvis, Buddy Holly, and other American rock n' roll stars from the 50s and 60s. If that wasn't enough, Americana customers ordered their steaming apple pie by the gross.

The host led the Caseys over the black and white tiled floor to a red booth next to a picture window. Photos of the town's history decorated each table under protective glass. Nostalgia from the 1950's covered the walls – ads for Coca-Cola, a '57 red Chevy whose front end stuck out of the wall, a picture of Mickey Mantle hitting a home run, and Jackie Robinson sliding into home.

The servers wore Pink Lady outfits from *Grease*, and the waiters donned the T-Bird greaser jackets. A long white and grey bar counter complete with red and grey barstools sat behind a wall of newspaper clippings celebrating the town's history. Just as the popular film *Back to the Future* described, it was as if you had left in the Delorean for 1955. John half expected George McFly to show up at any minute.

Danny, their waiter, gyrated over to the table, menus in hand.

"Thank you very much, thank you very much, everyone," he said, in his best Elvis Presley imitation, swinging his hips suggestively as he handed out the menus.

"Hey buddy, don't you be no square. If you can't find a partner, use a wooden chair!" he said, looking straight at the baby in his mother's arms. He raised his arms over his head, mimicking Elvis' dance moves.

"Everybody, let's rock!"

Then he gyrated over to the table next to him, where a beautiful strawberry blond woman sat.

Dropping to his knees, he sang, "Wise men say, only fools rush in... but I can't help falling in love with you."

He then took her order, still on his knees.

"Rock-A-Hula, baby!" He gestured 'TCBF' with his right hand and shimmied away. He was good at his job, for sure.

Loretta and John checked out the menu while Scott lay asleep next to Loretta in the baby carrier. The menu featured such breakfast items as "Rockin' Robin Eggs," "Unfor-gettable Pancakes," and "I Love Lucy's Waffles."

When Danny came back, though, John did not get any of those things but asked for the "That's Amore Breakfast": three eggs, two pancakes, hash browns, two pieces of toast, and two pieces of bacon.

"And a cup of your Joltin' Joe coffee, please?"

"Ah, yes, sir," Danny said.

Loretta rolled her eyes at her husband and then smiled at Danny before ordering her simple Rockin' Robin Eggs and her cup of Joltin' Joe.

"Nothin' more fun than Rock n' Roll! Be back in a jiff."

Danny grabbed the menus with a smile and made like the wind out of there. Loretta and John held each other's hands as if they were teenagers in love in the 50s.

"Pretty neat place, huh?" Loretta asked.

"Yeah, maybe we should go here after the sock hop."

The Caseys turned their attention to the pictures, and the headlines to the town's history stuck inside the glass of their table. There was a picture of James Coleridge shaking hands with the owner of the country club at a ribbon-cutting ceremony with the headline: "Coleridge keeps promise to open country club." *The Ridgeport News* printed it in 1921. John furrowed his eyebrows, unaware that the town even had a paper. Another photo showed the opening of the diner with the caption: "Several residents gather outside the 700 block of Coleridge Ave. to line up for the opening of The Ridge-port Egg."

Another smaller photo grabbed the far-right corner, but neither of them had a chance to look as Danny arrived with their food. Great atmosphere, great service, and to John's satisfaction, the food was just as great.

"It's fantastic, don't you think, honey?"

Loretta smiled at her husband, took a bite of her egg, nodded, and then watched him gulp down his food like the child she just fed this morning.

After the food and a couple of refills on their Joltin' Joe's, Danny arrived back with the check.

"And uh, here we are, folks. Would y'all happen to have your residency cards?"

Loretta and John looked at each other, unsure if this was part of the act or not.

"No, should we? What is that?"

Then Danny shed his T-Bird voice and talked down to the couple as if he were their elementary school teacher.

"Oh. Well, you will have to read your book then. You can't get one until you read your book. Then you can get discounts all over town. Otherwise, I have to charge you full price."

"Oh, well, okay. Thanks."

And his smile returned, along with his character voice.

"Ah well, shucks. You ah, welcome. And come back anytime. Be sure to bring the little rock n' roller."

The non-resident bill came to thirteen dollars, whereas the in-resident bill would have been just eight. John scratched his head but paid the thirteen dollars, plus a three-dollar tip for the service. Loretta picked up Scott, and John helped his wife out of the booth.

Danny hurried over and thanked them again. Loretta scanned the place one more time and swore she saw numerous faces staring at them. As Danny picked up the bill, it revealed a little picture underneath the table's glass that Loretta and John missed. It was a picture of their house with the three of them out front. The headline read, "New Family Moves In: Ridgeport Welcomes You." It made *The Ridgeport News* this morning. Each morning, the restaurant received copies of all the daily papers and put the front page under the glass inside every table.

7

When John and Loretta left The Ridgeport Egg, they were more than satisfied with their meals and made mental notes to revisit the diner. Little Scotty was in the backseat snoring logs, and as the couple drove home, they smiled at each other realizing just how lucky they were.

As they strolled up to the front door, Loretta spotted the fruit basket sitting on the porch. Enough fruit filled the wicker basket to last for weeks. Mounted on top was an envelope that read "Ridgeport Welcomes You!" John and Loretta smiled at each other in disbelief, and after carrying Scott into their new home, Loretta stepped out onto the porch to grab the twenty-pound basket. The basket covered most of the small kitchen island. All Loretta could think about was the amount of fruit that would eventually be thrown out. Slipping the card out, Loretta tore it open with the eagerness of a squirrel tearing open an acorn. She read the beautiful handwritten calligraphy.

Dear Neighbor:

We are pleased to welcome you to the historic district of Ridgeport. We believe that you will be more than happy with the Ridgeport experience. Please feel free to let us know if you should need anything, anything at all. Enjoy the fruit, and Ridgeport welcomes you!

Sincerely,
Sue Ellen Norris
Historic District Committee President

PS: Do not forget to read your residency book!

"We have to read that book, John."

But just as John went to get it, Scotty awoke crying, which escalated into a temper tantrum. So, the new parents ran to the king of the house. The temper tantrum lasted an hour, and by that time, the book was again forgotten. Loretta tossed the card, and by dinner, they only thought about each other. With Scott's short vacation, the last thing the Caseys thought about was signing documents or reading over Ridgeport's social norms. They spent time playing with Scott, taking walks, and enjoying the new house. No one else needed to be a part of their life right now. No one else needed to until Sue Ellen showed up two weeks later.

8

By the time John returned to work, Loretta had begun making it a habit to walk Scott throughout the historic district. She felt refreshed as she pushed her baby in his stroller over the concrete sidewalk on beautiful summer mornings, viewing the homes of yesteryear. Always the introvert, Loretta had not met anyone yet. Loretta and John focused on Scott and did not even think to introduce themselves to their neighbors. But on July 1, 1986, Loretta ran into her first neighbor, which changed her life forever.

At ten a.m. on a gorgeous seventy-degree morning, Loretta decided to take a different route around the historic district. She usually walked a two-mile loop north, west, and south back home. This time, Loretta turned east and then north. By the time she arrived at Maple Ridge Blvd. at the corner of her east and north loop, Sue Ellen Norris strolled her way.

When Loretta first saw Sue Ellen with her stroller, she thought she was looking at Miss Illinois – a tall, slender blonde in her early 30s, with gorgeous Heather Locklear hair and legs like Cindy Crawford. She envied her tan, wondering if she spent the entire summer in the Caribbean or something. She wore expensive sunglasses and a sundress. Loretta immediately felt self-conscious about being out in her sweats and an old tank top. Scott even spat upon the tank before they left for the walk.

"Loretta? Is that you, Loretta Casey?"

She paused, astonished that this lady she had never met should know who she was. These things had happened in embarrassing situations before, where someone remembered her, and she couldn't remember who they were.

"Yes, yes. Hello?"

"I'm sorry. I never formally introduced myself. I'm Sue Ellen, Sue Ellen Norris. I gave you the fruit basket. I live right next door to you. I meant to say hello, but you weren't in."

"Oh! Sue Ellen! Thank you so much! That was really, very thoughtful of you."

Sue Ellen chuckled and waved off the compliment. Then she shifted her focus to Scott.

"What do we have here? So adorable!"

Scott squirmed in the stroller and exchanged a warm smile with Sue Ellen.

Loretta began to relax at meeting her neighbor, who was also a mother and peeked over at her little one.

"Oh, this is Matt. He's four months old."

"He is adorable too," Loretta said.

Sue Ellen nodded in affirmation, chuckled once more, and bit her lower lip before speaking.

"Why don't you join us for the Historic District Fourth of July Barbeque? It will be a good way for you to get to meet the other families. I would like it if you came."

"Well, yeah, that sounds like fun. Where is it? What time?"

"It's in Coleridge Park, right down the street from your house; festivities begin at two. Come hungry, come happy. You are encouraged to bring a dish."

"Oh, well, will do!"

"Great!"

Sue Ellen stole a look at Scott and rubbed his hair before turning her attention back to Loretta.

"I think these two may be friends one day. Don't you think?"

"Yeah. I think so," Loretta said. She laughed as she said it and threw another look at Matt.

But Sue Ellen turned serious for a moment and just nodded. There was something about Sue Ellen that Loretta wanted to please. She wanted to be on her good side. She wanted, no needed, to be her friend. She lost touch with her high school and college friends since becoming a mom and missed that social aspect of her life.

"Well, I should be going. It will be getting hotter by the minute, my new friend," Sue Ellen said.

"Thanks, Sue Ellen. I'll be there."

After walking a few paces, Sue Ellen turned around and said to Loretta, "Do not forget to read your book."

"Oh. Right, we have, uh, been meaning to…."

But Sue Ellen only turned again and walked on, not allowing her to finish her sentence.

9

Loretta smiled from ear to ear upon meeting her new friend, but her heart raced at the thought of having to make a dish and from the guilt over not having read the book yet. She quickened her pace home, knowing she needed to get to the grocery store. There were things to do, people to please. Once settled at her new home, she transferred the tired six-month-old into the back of their '85 Chevy Astro Van and headed off for Ridgeport's local grocer.

Like the diner, the grocer felt like a step back in time. It was not a chain like the A&P, but the sign shone in fancy red cursive – 'The Ridgeport Grocer – Serving You Since 1962. While it contained ample parking, the store lacked size. The aisles were so tight Loretta felt like she was in a pinball machine the way she constantly bumped into everyone. The sale signs were all handmade – 'Buy One Box, Get Second 50% Off', and the shelves were a teal color while the tiled flooring was red and tan. Employees greeted and assisted customers, all with a smile. Stock boys wore long white aprons with black slacks and white shirts – almost as if they were waiters at a fancy restaurant, while a manager walked by wearing a tie with the same black slacks and a white dress shirt.

Even the customers looked like they belonged in an earlier time – women packed the aisles, and they all dressed as if they were attending a wedding. Some women wore upscale sundresses like Sue Ellen, while others donned power suits and slacks. Loretta even found teenage girls in formal dresses. And gym shoes just didn't seem to exist. High heels completed most of the adult women's outfits, while children sported a pair of flats. Sweats and tanks did not appear like something that women dared wear around Ridgeport. Loretta shrugged off the women's fashion choices and headed to the bakery aisle. She twirled her wedding ring as she inspected the cakes, pastries, cookies, pies, and coffee cakes.

"Bring a dish," Sue Ellen said. She did not want to disappoint her new friend, and in recent years buying a premade coffee cake or cookies seemed to be just fine for family parties. She couldn't remember the last time she cooked.

"Oh my God. I don't know what I'm doing. I think I forgot how to cook," Loretta muttered to herself.

An older, grey-haired woman peeked over at her, set her coffee cake down, and power-walked away from Loretta. But Loretta didn't notice. She was too preoccupied as she recalled recipes before she got married. Loretta continued walking through the aisle, past the bakery, and into the fruit section. She wandered around as she thought, and as she wandered, she talked to herself.

"No, well, I could make that. Yes, no, I guess."

More women slowed their carts and stared her way; a few laughed in her direction. But one man came over to help Loretta with her conundrum.

"Miss?"

Loretta did not hear him at first, as she really was in her own world, searching for something that she did not know she was searching for. The man tapped Loretta on the shoulder and repeated, "Miss?"

Loretta turned around, startled, setting off more contained laughter from onlookers in the fruit section. The man wore a black tie, white shirt, black blazer, black slacks, and of course, kept a white handkerchief in his pocket. Loretta began to wonder if every citizen in the town dressed up or if this was just some special Ridgeport occasion. He stood about 6'2, showed a light stubble, short salt-and-pepper hair, and, Loretta thought, a muscular build.

"You seem a little worried about something, miss."

Loretta blushed. Now she realized that she was raving like a lunatic. Yet this guy had a calming presence.

"Yes, well, I was invited to this Fourth of July party by this woman Sue Ellen, and I'm expected to bring a dish…."

"Sue Ellen Norris?"

"Well, yeah. Do you know her?"

"We go way back. It's sort of a long, complicated story."

"I see."

"So, I take it you're living in Ridgeport?"

"Yeah, just moved in a couple of days ago. We live right next to Sue Ellen, in fact."

"Really? What a coincidence! Small world."

"Where are you…er, I didn't get your name?"

"Oh, I'm sorry? The name is Peter, Peter Barnes. And I live right in Ridgeport, in an apartment on the east side of Coleridge."

"Nice to meet you, Mr. Barnes. I'm Loretta, Loretta Casey."

10

He helped her through the aisles, and together, they decided that spinach and artichoke dip was the way to go.

"Do you think that would be alright for the party?"

"Who doesn't love a good spinach and artichoke dip, Loretta?"

"Ha, you're right, I guess. Hey, let me ask you something."

"Shoot."

"Is it a rule in this town that everyone should dress up?"

Peter laughed and nodded.

"Well, I'm dressed up since I just came from a business meeting, and if you're talking about the women, well, I think they just like to dress up. I don't know what it is with them. But don't you feel inclined to do it. Dress the way you feel comfortable."

"Thanks. That makes me feel better."

"Will your husband and this little guy be going?"

"Yep, you'll get to meet John. What about your significant other?"

"I uh…don't have one.

"Oh? A guy like you?"

"Yep… a guy like me," Peter said and chuckled.

"Well, thank you for your help. You've been most kind. We'll look forward to seeing you there."

"The pleasure is all mine."

Loretta nodded and headed to the cashier for check-out. Before Loretta paid, the cashier asked if she had her residency card. Loretta bit her lip looked away from the cashier and onto her items on the conveyor belt. The cashier shook her head, saying, "You better get one if you want a discount or help to bag groceries." Loretta stood a second, taking in what she said before the cashier turned with her hands on her hips.

"Miss, you need to start bagging your groceries so that I can help out this next lady."

Loretta saw a young bagger, but he shook his head, refusing to help.

"Um, okay."

Loretta bagged each item herself and left, shaking her head. As she walked away, she turned her attention back to the cashier, who smiled while addressing the next customer by name as she looked at her residency card. The bagger immediately began loading the lady's bags.

11

Back home, it took Loretta a frantic few minutes before she found the book. She wanted that residency card. She wanted to feel she belonged in Ridgeport. It was not enough to live there. *You want to be a part of the community!* Loretta thought. She fed Scott and set him inside his playpen with his See N' Say, Chatter Telephone, and Garfield. They would entertain him for at least half an hour while Loretta could get a jumpstart on *Ridgeport Welcomes You: Procedures and Guidelines for Happy Living.*

The book's 510 pages were divided into five separate parts: "History of Ridgeport," "Rules and Regulations," "Activities and Events," "Social Norms," and "Test and Signature Forms." There was also an Introduction from Mayor Sheila Goldman. She had no idea how she could read the entire book by the Fourth and obtain her residency card. She remembered cramming for college tests, but that was when she was single without a baby. She thought about the diner, Sue Ellen, and the grocery store. She began to wonder if she and John had made the right choice in moving to Ridgeport. She thought of the cashier's attitude at the grocery store, but then she also thought about how safe the neighborhood was, what a great school system Scott would have access to, and that she was already making friends. Perhaps Ridgeport did things differently than other towns because they cared, and Loretta was just overthinking things.

Scott played with his See N' Say and tried to pull the string at the side so that the arrow could rotate around to the different pictures. Loretta smiled and wished she could freeze-frame these moments with him. She took a break from the book and helped her son pull the string. He looked up from the toy and smiled. She patted his head and leaned on the playpen, hoping she was raising him right and in the right town. He was happy, and that is all that mattered to her. She settled back onto the couch a few feet away from Scott, opened the book, and began reading.

12

Introduction

Dear Ridgeporter:

If you are reading this book, it means that you are on your way to becoming an official Ridgeport resident. Congratulations. We realize this is a colossal task to read this 510-page book on our town's rules and procedures, but we found it of the utmost importance to continue the way of life that we have established throughout our history. We find that this is the reason Ridgeport stands out as a community in every true sense of the word. No resident is better than the other. We are all equals and work as equals to establish a better town for tomorrow.

In this guide to knowing Ridgeport and becoming a Ridgeport resident, you will need to become comfortable with our history, rules and regulations, activities and events, and social norms, and complete the test and signature form in Part Five. Upon completing this book, you will visit our first-rate village hall building on Coleridge Ave. There, you will hand in your signature forms, test, and complete an oral exam that checks your comprehension of the material. You will receive your score within three hours of the examination. Should you score less than eighty percent, you will not be granted a residency card. You can, however, retake the test as many times as you please.

As far as a little bit about myself, I am a lifelong Ridgeport resident and am proud to say, the first woman mayor of Ridgeport. I am also proud to say that I have added Part Five to this historic book as part of my time as mayor. The board of trustees has applauded the addition of this part since it will bring new move-ins, such as yourself, and a greater appreciation for what we are doing here. If we cannot live as one, we will fall as many.

I look forward to meeting you and seeing you at all our board meetings, as you will read about that in part two of this book. If you should ever need anything, do not hesitate to contact my office.

Sincerely,
Mayor Sheila Goldman
555-755-3507
"Love thy neighbor" and "Love thy Ridgeport"

13

Loretta rubbed her temple. Did I make the wrong choice moving to Ridgeport? A town that requires pages of rules and regulations? I don't know what to make of Sheila Goodman, the addition of Part Five, or what she meant about the "board meeting requirement."

Mayor Goldman said she would find out in Part Two, so she did not want to make hasty judgments about anything until she read it through. She didn't have much of a choice. Loretta already knew the town cared about its history. The Tudor home she lived in was 101 years old, and the townspeople seemed to like holding onto the past. Other than the mall district built in the eighties, the town was historic. While Loretta's subdivision was in the historic district, other parts of town were built between the thirties and sixties. Ridgeport's history made up 152 pages of the text, containing pictures, old newspaper headlines, biographies of influential residents, and stories of important events. Loretta always did like history, and she found this part a fascinating read.

Like most history books, the events followed chronological order, beginning with Mayor James Coleridge buying forty acres of land that later turned into Ridgeport. There were thirty pages alone dedicated to Coleridge and the events of the early developments of the town. Several businesses that are still standing were constructed under Coleridge's long regime – the country club, the grocer in the historic district, the VFW Hall, The Ridgeport Barber, Ridgeport Bank and Trust, The Porterhouse Restaurant, and the First Church of St. John. Coleridge Park was established, along with Coleridge Ave., and of course, all the homes in the historic district. By the time Coleridge passed in 1940, the town had boasted a population of 3,567. Jobs were plentiful, and the addition of the country club and such upscale homes in the historic district drove those with money out of the city and into Ridgeport. By the time of his death, it became an upscale, inclusive community.

Pictures of Mayor Coleridge were taken with the likes of Woodrow Wilson and John D. Rockefeller, Sr. Photos of Coleridge's town reflected his elite status. Loretta flipped through photos of men in top hats strolling down the streets of Coleridge Ave. and women in fancy Edwardian hats coming in and out of the boutique.

Loretta found a photo of the opening of the VFW Hall on March 7, 1922. Ridgeport World War I vets stood in front of the building with Coleridge at the ribbon-cutting. There were a list of all the approximate thirty names of the vets in the photo, along with those who could not be there that day or who gave their lives in combat. One name seemed familiar to Loretta: Steven Barnes.

Could it be? Could it be the same Barnes as Peter? thought Loretta. *That will surely give me something to talk to him about.*

Peter had a resemblance to Steven: similar height, darker skin. At the very least, she thought it a weird coincidence that she should have come across this photo the same day she met Peter. Loretta read on in Part One about Mayor George Stallworth's reign.

The population boomed under his tenure from 3,567 to 8,799. Women went to work for the war effort, taking up jobs in factories in the cities or assembling and sending care packages overseas. A victory parade marched down Coleridge Ave. at the war's end. Patriotism flew to new heights that never diminished. Babies boomed here like

32

nowhere else, and people moved in looking for construction opportunities. Stallworth improved the town's sewer and road systems. Dirt roads became a thing of the past, and he annexed what would become the mall and the modern section of Ridgeport, along with the land on the east side of the historic district. The full map of the town was now set in place. He ordered the old one-room schoolhouse to be demolished to set up the first elementary and junior high schools. The First Church of St. John added a private school that same year.

With the population boom, Stallworth added Parts Two, Three, and Four to the book. "Residents rejoiced!" the clipping from *The Ridgeport News* said. Stallworth served from 1940 to 1960.

By 1960, Stallworth ran for mayor again but lost to progressive Mayor Jim Henderson. Henderson's term brought some scrutiny later over what to do with troubled Vietnam vets experiencing PTSD and peacefully desegregating the school system. While not entirely successful at these issues, he did approve the establishment of the Ridgeport Grocer and The Ridgeport Diner – two staples in the town. He jumpstarted public transportation by adding a bus and rail system transporting residents to neighboring towns and Chicago.

Henderson also had to deal with some tragic events during this time. A nasty snowstorm in the winter of '67 buried Ridgeport in three feet of snow. At the time, the town's government was unprepared with the amount of salt and snowplows available, and it was weeks before Ridgeport was functioning again. Schools closed for two weeks, and the storm caused three reported deaths and four injuries. Following the storm, a February heatwave with temperatures reaching the sixties melted large patches of snow and ice. Several homes flooded from the snowmelt, and Henderson received the blame through it all. Then in the spring of sixty-

33

nine, just as Henderson started his reelection campaign, Henderson's 21-year-old daughter Sue went mysteriously missing. The police saturated the town searching for clues. They even combed the creek that ran through the golf course at the country club but could find no trace of her. Her loss set Henderson's campaign back significantly, and he ended up dropping out of the race. His poll numbers showed that he would have lost anyway.

Mayor Barry Nelson ruled Ridgeport from 1970-1980. For his first order of business, Nelson established the Ridgeport Fair at Coleridge Park, which ran annually every weekend in July. A carnival, bands, and fireworks brought the town together to celebrate the summer and the town's history. He also expanded the number of activities available for residents in the town to the satisfaction of Ridgeport parents. Nelson added the history portion, later becoming Part One to the book. A picture in Part One displayed Nelson holding up the book and giving the thumbs up. Ridgeport completed the massive village hall building on May 4, 1976, and at last, moved out of the old town hall building. The police and fire presence expanded even though crime did not increase, and the village library built a new addition. All in all, Nelson was a pretty good mayor despite needing to raise taxes to construct some of the new buildings. Yet, residents supported his efforts.

The final ten pages referred to modern history from 1980-1986. Mayor Goldman overwhelmingly won the election as the first woman mayor of Ridgeport by reminding residents to "Love thy neighbor" and "Love thy Ridgeport." She vowed to stay true to tradition while making the town a better place for all. She added Part Five to the book, established new housing and condominiums to go with the mall in the new sector, updated infrastructure, and approved the construction of a second elementary school. The last page of Part One showed future town plans that included annexing nearby parcels of land and the benefit of volunteer work from residents. There is a picture of Goldman on the bottom half of the last page giving a campaign speech. She is behind a podium, smiling wide and staring down at her future townspeople.

14

Loretta needed to stop several times to feed Scott, change him, calm his cries, and play with him. She had finished Part One by the time her husband came home around six, and without even asking about his day, darted toward him, shoving the book in his face.

"Look at this thing! Just look at it. Do you know it is required that we read it? I read the intro and the first part. It's over 150 pages, just that much. I'm freaking out, John. I met a friend today, Sue Ellen, and I feel like everyone is pushing me to get this residency card, and...and...."

"Whoa, slow down, okay? I just got home. How's Scotty doing?"

Loretta sighed and nodded.

"He's...he's fine. I'm just a little high strung now, is all."

"I can see that."

John undid his tie and found Scott playing on the area rug in the living room. He knelt beside him and tickled his belly.

"Look here. This is what's important, right?"

Loretta smiled and nodded again.

"So, will you watch after Scott tonight so I can make some more headway on this thing?"

John turned from Scott, confused. He knew something must have gotten under her skin.

"What's gotten into you?" he asked.

"Just a lot. This whole town makes it out like this book is so important."

John stared at his wife, still confused, but consented to her wish.

"I will look after Scott tonight, but just remember what's important, okay?"

"Thank you. I will. Thank you. There is something you should know, though."

John, who started playing with Scott again, was half paying attention now.

"Uh, yeah?"

"We need to go to the village hall and get residency cards."

"Okay, well, that doesn't sound too bad."

"No, you don't understand. We need to take this test in the back of this book, sign these forms, and then take an oral exam at the hall before we can get it."

"Well, can't you just take the exam? Do we both have to do it?"

Loretta had not considered this.

"I...I don't know. I am not at that part in the book yet."

"Well, let me know. Let's do whatever is easiest, okay?"

"Okay, John. Well, I'm going to go upstairs and read."

"Okay. Love you."

"Love you too."

15

John ordered a pizza since there was no food in the fridge. Loretta curled up on the master bed to read about the "Rules and Regulations."

An introduction, written by Police Chief Mark Harrison, welcomed new residents to Ridgeport, urged the importance of the rules and regulations, and celebrated the low crime rate in Ridgeport. Following the intro, Harrison pointed out to the reader a list of duties Ridgeport citizens needed to follow along with practice scenarios that pertained to those rules.

The laundry list of rules on the next page was as follows:

• *All Ridgeport residents are to attend all village board meetings. Residents are allowed two sick days and two personal days from these board meetings. A doctor's note must accompany more than two sick days. Board meetings meet every other Tuesday at 7 p.m. in the village hall board room. Failure to comply with this rule will result in your residency card being revoked and up to a fine of five hundred dollars.*

• *All Ridgeport residents are required to sign up as part of The Neighborhood Watch Committee. You are to see your subdivision committee president for sign-up information. If you are unsure who your subdivision committee president is, please visit the village hall. Failure to sign up will result in your residency card being revoked and a fine of up to one thousand dollars.*

• *All Ridgeport residents of the voting age are required to vote in elections. Those who do not vote will have their residency cards revoked.*

• *All Ridgeport residents are required to make at least a hundred-dollar donation to help advance Ridgeport every year. That donation can go towards one of the schools, the police department, the village hall, the fire department, or charities. If you cannot afford to donate, you can instead volunteer for our "Neighbors Helping Neighbors Program." Ask about that special circumstance in the village hall. Failure to comply will result in your residency card being revoked.*

• *All Ridgeport residents should refrain from gambling, drinking, and smoking in public places. Ridgeport is a dry town, and while we will not investigate what happens in the privacy of one's home (unless there is a disturbance of the peace), failure to comply with this rule will result in your residency card being revoked and a fine of up to five hundred dollars.*

•   All Ridgeport residents under the age of 18 are to be indoors (unless it is a special Ridgeport event, such as The Ridgeport Fair) by 8 p.m. Curfew is strictly enforced. Should children be out past that time, they will be detained at the police station until their parent or guardian picks them up. Their residency card may also be revoked for repeat offenses. We also reserve the right to question parents or guardians.

•   All Ridgeport soliciting is strictly prohibited. Those caught soliciting will have their residency card revoked and fined up to one thousand dollars.

•   All Ridgeport residents should receive their residency cards within two months of moving in. Failure to do so will result in a one hundred dollars fine each month until the card is obtained. If you cannot afford this fine, you will need to volunteer for the "Neighbors Helping Neighbors" program every month.

•   All Ridgeport residents are always to follow the Good Samaritan Law in all situations. Failure to do so will result in your residency card being revoked, along with any other penalty that corresponds with the severity of the situation.

•   All Ridgeport residents must abide by all state and federal laws not stated in these guidelines. Failure to do so will result in not only your residency card being revoked but the appropriate penalty that corresponds with the crime.

Multiple choice questions followed. One such scenario Loretta came across was this:

A 17-year-old was caught after curfew at 8:05 p.m. driving in their car. The 17-year-old said that they were on their way home and could not get home sooner because of a flat tire. Should the teen be brought into the police station?

    1.   Yes. The 17-year-old broke their curfew.

2. No. It is only 8:05, and there should be a grace period.
3. Maybe. It depends on if the kid has had a history of breaking curfew and if s/he did have a flat if there is a spare tire on the vehicle. Also, a simple line of questioning about when and where the kid was should determine their punishment.

Answer: A. The teen is still out past curfew, regardless of the situation or how long it is past the eight o'clock deadline. A formal report needs to be written at the station to remind teens of the seriousness of breaking curfew. The offense will not go on their record if their story checks out.

More situations followed, and Loretta was surprised that such harsh policies were in place. She circled each correct answer in the scenarios section and recalled what Ridgeport was looking for. Loretta made it through all fifty-two pages of Part Two – the intro, the rules, and fifty pages of scenarios, and started to nod off in the comfortable sheets of their king-size bed. She knew the party was only a few days away, but she wanted that card. Loretta needed that card. She tip-toed downstairs, unsure if Scott was starting to fall asleep for his bedtime routine. She looked around at the bottom of the steps and noticed the lights were off. The grandfather clock read nine o'clock. She shuffled to the coffee pot and brewed herself a cup.

16

Loretta rubbed the tired out of her eyes and tackled Part Three, "Activities and Events." The one hundred and twenty-one pages did not faze Loretta. As an English teacher, she needed to scan large chunks of printed materials.

I can finish this in a couple of hours, she thought.

Part Three began with an intro by the Director of Parks and Rec, Sarah Craven.

Dear Soon-to-be-Ridgeport Resident,

If you are reading this book, you are well on your way to becoming a full resident of our well-modeled town. Congratulations! The citizens of Ridgeport are lucky to have eight parks and three facilities as part of our small community. I am proud of the Parks and Recreation Department for maintaining the parks and facilities so the residents may enjoy them year after year. Please take the time to visit our parks and keep them clean for your fellow residents. This community must support each other by attending at least one event per year and bringing your family to the parks. We couldn't do this without you. Love thy neighbor and Love thy Ridgeport.

When Loretta turned the page, she first saw a list of all the town's annual events, organized by month. Underneath each event included a short description with the event's date, time, and location. Events such as The Ridgeport Fair, the Taste of Ridgeport, and Christmas at the Movies interested Loretta. Scott would love the twinkling lights! Following the event list, an extensive number of activities in the town flooded the following pages.

The activities were organized by age group from toddler to adult, and she found every activity she could imagine, from acrobatics to xylophone lessons. Loretta had only wished to have had as many activities available when she was growing up. She smiled when she thought of the future Scott had awaiting him.

17

It did not take long to get through Part Three. She glanced over at her alarm clock, and it was now five minutes past ten.

40

Even as John crawled into bed next to her, Loretta was not ready to call it quits.

"Honey, I want to turn in for the night. Let's call it lights out, okay?" John said.

"Okay, well, I'm going to take this downstairs and at least read Part Four tonight, alright?"

"Can't it wait until tomorrow? You have the whole day off."

"No, it can't, John. Once Scott wakes up, it's not so easy to get stuff done."

John rolled his eyes, yawned, stretched his arms out like a cat, and crawled into bed next to his wife.

"Well, whatever. You do what you gotta do. Good night."

"Thanks, honey," she said. She pecked a kiss on John's forehead, grabbed the book and her coffee cup, and made her way down the stairs.

Part Four elaborated on Part Two, with a list of rules and guidelines to follow. The only difference was these were not officially enforced but were more for social etiquette purposes. More than anything, Part Four did help to explain her time in the grocery store. It consisted of sixty-five pages with a list of what was considered acceptable, followed by social scenarios. Loretta's eyes bulged as she ran her finger down the long list.

All Ridgeport residents should...

- *Dress appropriately when seen in public.*
- *Attend The First Church of St. John every Sunday.*
- *Don't curse in public.*
- *Smile wherever and whenever possible.*
- *Hold the door for each other.*
- *Look at the person who is speaking.*
- *Cough or sneeze with their elbow.*
- *Learn the names of their neighbors.*
- *Be on time.*
- *Clean up after pets.*

- *Always RSVP.*
- *Keep the noise down at home and work.*
- *Shake hands firmly.*
- *Place your napkin on your lap.*
- *Wash your hands after using the bathroom.*
- *Say "please" and "thank you."*
- *Push your chair in before leaving the table.*
- *Ask before bringing a guest to a party.*
- *Wait until everyone has been served before eating.*
- *Be a good dinner guest and a good dinner host.*
- *Remain at home when sick.*
- *Remember their table manners.*
- *Bring food or drink to a party.*
- *Wipe down exercise equipment after they use it.*
- *Bring shopping carts to the corral.*
- *Avoid controversial subjects at parties.*
- *Learn to greet everyone while entering a room.*
- *Return phone calls.*
- *Know that a woman walks on a man's right side.*
- *Cover their mouth when they yawn.*
- *Be silent in the library.*
- *Remove their hat while indoors.*
- *Say "God Bless You" when someone sneezes.*
- *Keep their elbows off the table.*
- *Know that a man pulls a chair out for a woman.*
- *A man asks for permission to marry their daughter.*
- *Leave a fair tip for service.*
- *Don't invade someone else's personal space.*
- *Decorate their homes for Christmas.*
- *Attend at least one social event per year.*
- *Don't overeat in public.*
- *Honor the Ten Commandments.*
- *Read the Bible daily.*
- *Practice prayer.*
- *Remember the Beatitudes.*

- *Always greet others with the town motto.*
- *Not lie, as the Bible says.*
- *Raise children to take education seriously.*
- *Abide by the rules and guidelines in part two.*
- *"Love thy neighbor" and "Love thy Ridgeport."*

Loretta wanted to laugh aloud at the prospect of having to abide by all these points of social etiquette. She shook her head at the religious points.

That's how they legally get away with it. They cannot exactly enforce it, but they can suggest residents are Christian. *I'm still surprised they have not been challenged in the courts*, Loretta thought.

After the long, absurd list of how to behave, the social norm scenarios filled the rest of the pages. Like the multiple-choice questions in Part Two, there were more practice questions in prep for the test in Part Five. Loretta reviewed the norms one more time and then read over the scenarios. One such example was as follows:

Scenario One:

'Mike visited The Ridgeport Diner and ordered: "That's Amore Breakfast." The breakfast includes three eggs, two pancakes, hash browns, two pieces of toast, and two pieces of bacon. He was hungry and finished the meal in a few minutes. Is this an example of breaking Social Norm 41 – overeating in public?

    1. Yes – he ordered and consumed a lot of food in a short period.
    2. No – he only ordered one helping of the meal.
    3. Maybe – it depends on if he was eating with anyone that day.

Answer: B. However, this would violate Social Norm 22 in that Mike did not exhibit the best table manners. Even if no one was eating with him, others could see him scarfing down his food at the restaurant. One should eat more slowly and take their time chewing."

The scenarios were not as easy as Loretta had thought. On Scenario One, she guessed A and had struck out on a few other questions as well. After reading the list, she could only imagine what those women at the grocery store must have thought about her and her outfit. *What did Sue Ellen Norris think of her? John needs to look this over*, she thought. I will not embarrass myself at the party. I will not.

18

She stopped after completing Part Four around 12:30. She could hear Scott waking up on the baby monitor, and she ran upstairs with a bottle. She did all she could to keep from falling asleep as she fed him, rocking him in her arms. Scott was so hungry he drank himself into a milk drunk, and as he fell asleep, Loretta placed him gently back in the crib and slept on the full-size bed next to him.

When Loretta awoke and carried Scott downstairs, John had already left for work. She had so immersed herself in the book that she said only a few words to her husband. Loretta had heavy bags under her eyes and was even more tired than usual, which said a lot with raising a six-month-old. She stared at the book, opened to Part Five on the couch, and looked at Scott, playing on the area rug. She was running a marathon, and now the last part of the race darted her towards the finish line.

Yes, she thought, the morning would be the best time to finish it, as Scott could play with his Winnie the Pooh for minutes on end and be content.

So many rules and regulations. *How I hate that*, Loretta thought. What if I can't keep the rules? For an instant, Loretta thought how much she hated the book and thought about convincing her husband into moving when he returned home, but then she shook the thought from her mind. She did like the idea of the town having a moral fiber, all the activities it offered, and how crime-free it was. *Besides, I already made a friend here*, she thought.

Scott gnawed at Winnie the Pooh's ear and rolled around with him, happy as could be. Loretta shrugged and summoned all her strength to brew another cup of coffee. Then she picked up Part Five and began to read.

It was like reading the closing docs on their home. There were so many pages to sign. Loretta's hand had cramped from signing all the rule agreements and the social norm guidelines. She strained to read all the fine print. For instance, social norm number one talked about appropriate dress. The dress code called for "No bare midriff tops, halter tops, off-the-shoulder tops or spaghetti strap tops that show cleavage; short shorts or low-cut pants that are revealing or show undergarments: swimwear or tube tops (unless worn at Ridgeport Pool and then should be kept to trunks or a one-piece), muscle shirts, pajamas or slippers, any attire that degrades gender, sexual orientation, culture, religion, or ethnicity, and any clothing that advertises tobacco, alcohol, drugs, illegal substances, illegal acts, weapons, or promotes violence. It is strongly encouraged always to dress professionally and in your best clothing, especially on Sundays."

"I might as well be in high school all over again, except this seems worse. Only a one-piece at the pool?" Loretta said to herself.

Reading on, Loretta noticed fine print under social norm number two: "All residents are strongly urged to attend The First Church of St. John weekly. If you cannot make a service, please phone the church secretary and state your reason. If you cannot make it two weeks in a row, please submit a formal letter. The church would require a doctor's note if you are ill. If you belong to a different church, please sign that you belong to a different church. We will contact your church pastor to make sure you are meeting your regular church schedule. If you do not believe in any organized religion, please sign on that line below. You should be aware that you will be asked to volunteer for more town events and/or donate more money to help the town. Should you decline, it could result in you losing your residency card."

There were signature lines for John as well. For some reason, Loretta felt as if she signed her life away, but she shook the thought away. If she wanted to wear a two-piece bathing suit, she could still swim at a neighboring pool in Aurora or Naperville, and if she wanted to wear sweats and a tank-top outside, she could just say that was her best outfit that day, right?

A half-hour later, Scott fell asleep on the floor next to Winnie. Loretta was half asleep herself and thought it was not the best time to sign important documents. Yet then again, she did not care how tired she was. She pressed on, and after about another half hour of forcing herself to stay awake, she completed all forty signature pages. The only thing she had left to do was to take the test.

19

Loretta wisely decided to set the book aside and take a nap as long as Scott was down. She told herself she'd return to the test that night when John came back and had more energy and more time to focus. He needed to sign those pages anyway. She would not be able to get the residency card without those signatures. It seemed like forever before John returned home. Loretta dragged herself up out of bed, groggy as ever, to the sound of the phone ringing. It was John.

"John? That you?"

"Yes. Hi honey. Sorry, I'm not home yet; it's just that a big story came up."

"It did?"

"Yeah. A 17-year-old daughter of one of the Ridgeport trustees went missing last night. She was out past curfew, and the cops never picked her up. Her parents do not know where she is. So, I must get some facts straight and find out some information here."

"That's awful, John," Loretta said, followed by a yawn.

"Are you alright, honey?"

"Just tired."

"Alright, well, I'll see you later, okay?"

"Well, what time do you think you'll be...."

But he hung up, Scott wailed in the background, and Loretta barely kept her eyes open.

It was eleven o'clock by the time John rolled into bed, and Loretta was already fast asleep. She did not dare attempt to take the test in her sleep-deprived state. The party was two days away, and she still needed to complete the test, take the oral exam, and get her residency card if she were to show up to the party as an actual resident. Oh, and she had not made her spinach and artichoke dip.

Loretta left a post-it note on the fridge before she went to bed, hoping that John would see it and sign all the signature forms. To her relief, he did. That was one less thing to worry about. Then while Scott was still asleep at five a.m., she set the test on the kitchen island, pulled up a stool, and faced the biggest test of her life. The multiple-choice portions from the book prepared her for the forty-question exam. Half the test was filled with different scenarios, and the other half were questions based on the town's history. Unlike the A, B, C answer choices in Parts Two and Four, the test followed the usual A, B, C, D answer format.

Loretta needed to flip through the text for reference a few times but felt she would score at least the eighty percent needed for her residency card. She finished the exam in about an hour, just as Scott awakened. *Perfect timing*, she thought. The last page revealed a map of the town and a list of all the businesses, parks, buildings, and schools. Important town numbers for public works, parks and rec, village hall, police, fire, chamber of commerce, and the school board district office were also located in an insert in the back of the book.

With a feeling of triumph, Loretta breathed a sigh of relief and then ventured over to Scott's crib to pick up her fussy baby for his feeding.

20

That morning, Loretta headed over to the village hall to drop off the signature pages and attempt her oral exam. She dropped Scott off at her mom's. She was willing to wait up to three hours in the Village Hall for the test results if she had to.

The Village Hall impressed newcomers with its two-story front that featured two Roman columns extending the length of the Renaissance Revival facade, with a wing on either side of the main building. One wing served as the police station, and the other served as the board of trustees' room. Several Hibiscus and Gardenia trees matched the huge containers filled with purple and white wave petunias with red Tropicana at the hall entrance. Two rows of marble staircases greeted visitors as they approached the glass double doors.

The elderly security guard at the front desk pointed Loretta upstairs to the West Wing towards the Community Development Office. She repeatedly wiped her sweaty palms against her red dress as she ascended the stairs with her documents in hand. Fortunately, the line to take the test was shorter at ten a.m. on the day before the Fourth.

Loretta stepped in front of the wooden rectangular counter with a smile on her face. On the opposite side of the counter sat middle-aged secretary Trina Glasgow.

"I'm here to take the residency test," Loretta said.

Trina investigated Loretta's nervous face and smirked. Trina had seen this look before, the look of those who wanted to become residents but had no idea what they were getting themselves into. Trina loved being part of an elite community and felt those who weren't were beneath her.

"Mr. Paulson will be with you in just a minute," she said with a frown.

"Thanks."

Loretta sat down on a leather seat in the office and continued to wipe the sweat from her palms. Every couple of minutes or so, she glanced up at the hand clock and then over at the office door, thinking that Mr. Paulson would pop out.

"Awfully hot out there today, isn't it, Tina?"

"Uh-huh. That it is," Trina said as she glanced down at her work.

After about fifteen minutes of waiting, which felt like an hour, Mr. Paulson opened the door and said he was ready for her.

Loretta smiled (she remembered that smiling is important), and Mr. Paulson smiled back. He led her down a corridor towards his private office, asked Loretta to have a seat, and closed the door.

"I see that you have brought with you the required signature pages and test there, correct?"

"Oh, yes. Here you are."

"Thank you."

Mr. Paulson set it aside on his wood-grain desk. According to the gold nameplate that shone on his desk, he was the Director of Community Development. Mr. Paulson was the embodiment of a Ridgeport citizen. A degree from

Princeton University hung on the sidewall, along with a picture of a ribbon-cutting ceremony and a bookshelf stacked with law and history books. A photo of his family at the beach stood to his right elbow, and a Princeton pennant hung behind him, along with a large banner celebrating Ridgeport's one-hundredth birthday.

"Princeton? That's quite the accomplishment."

"Oh, well. Yes. It is. I wouldn't have put that up there, but the office wanted us to display where we went to school and all. If it were up to me, I would have joked and proudly displayed my high school diploma. Go Wildcats!"

"Wildcats? As in the Tremont High Wildcats?"

Mr. Paulson smiled from ear to ear this time. Loretta tried to remember if she had a Paulson in class but could not remember him.

"That's right. I was class of '70. What were you?"

"Class of '74."

"I don't think you would know anyone I went to school with then."

"Ha, I think not."

Loretta could feel her hands cooling, her nerves settling, as if of all the offices in all the world, she came into one with a Wildcat graduate.

"Well, I think we should probably get down to business Mrs. Casey. The way this is going to work is like the paper test, only I will ask you a combination of forty history and scenario questions, but there will not be a multiple-choice portion. So, you will be required to tell me how you think that scenario should be handled. Do you understand?"

"Yes. I understand."

Then Paulson opened a huge three-ring red binder with the words "Oral Exam: History and Scenarios" written on the front. Loretta could feel her palms becoming sweaty once again. He flipped through a few pages until he found the right scenario.

50

"Question one. Where did the motto "Love thy neighbor" and "Love thy Ridgeport" come from?

"It came from Mayor James Coleridge saying it at town hall meetings. The townspeople chanted it back, and the motto stuck."

Paulson wrote something down on a separate sheet of paper and then moved on to question two.

"Question two. You are out sick for more than two days and cannot make village board meetings. You could not secure a doctor's note from your primary care doctor. What happens next?

"It depends. If we are looking at this question black and white, my residency card should be revoked with a fine of up to five hundred dollars, but if my primary care doctor was also out for two weeks…." Then Loretta stopped herself and could see that Paulson was not amused with an "It depends on answer." She reverted to her original thought.

"My residency card would be revoked with a fine of up to five hundred dollars. Final answer."

Paulson smiled and marked an answer on his sheet of paper.

Loretta kept this kind of answer in mind, and the smiles kept coming from Paulson. Paulson finished asking questions about an hour later, and Loretta let out a sigh of relief.

"It's always nice to see a former Wildcat," Paulson said.

"Yes, it is. Thank you, Mr. Paulson."

"Please. Call me Ryan. And your results should be ready within the hour. Just have a seat outside, and I'll have my secretary hand them right over to you."

"Oh, terrific. Thank you."

And with that, Loretta left Ryan Paulson's office and headed back to her seat, patiently awaiting her results.

A *Time* magazine with Ronald Reagan on the cover, along with *The Naperville Sun* and *The Ridgeport News*, were stacked haphazardly on the waiting room table.

Loretta remembered her husband's story about the 17-year-old who went missing. She felt guilty for not paying enough attention to him these last couple of days, but what was she to do? Loretta wanted her residency card and was now worried about him getting one, but it was a fleeting thought. She tossed The Ridgeport newspaper aside for *The Naperville Sun* and searched for John's article.

Loretta found John's story buried on page six in an "Inside Stories" column, under the headline, "Teen Ridgeport girl goes missing." Above the story ran a profile picture of a cute teenage girl smiling, wearing a polka dot sundress. She looked like a kid who cared about her education, got good grades, and did not get into trouble. The article did not have much to it, two hundred words or so, yet every word was important to her. She held the paper tight and read.

Police are asking for the public's help locating 17-year-old Emma Ryan, who has been missing for three days.

Ryan is described as 5-foot-6 and weighing 115 pounds. She has dark brown hair and was last seen wearing a Hartville High School spirit wear sweatshirt and torn blue jeans. She also wore a gold necklace with "Corinthians 13:4-8" spelled out on the front band.

Emma's father and village trustee, Patrick Ryan, said she was out at her friend's house in the 100 block of Stallworth Street in the Historic District. Mr. Harper is offering a reward of $25,000 to whoever can find his daughter.

Police Chief Mark Harrison said they are conducting a full-scale investigation in this manner and have already begun questioning families in the area.

Anyone with information on this matter should notify the Ridgeport Police Department at (555)-715-6970.

Loretta could not believe what she had just read. Emma went missing only a few blocks away from their new home. Seventeen years old, and just poof, gone, she thought.

Loretta spent a few more minutes absorbing the article and then turned to the Ridgeport paper. She hoped to find more news about the missing girl there. The story there was on the front page, and the headline simply read, "MISSING" with the sub-head "Can you help Ridgeport find Emma Ryan?"

A news story like this came along once in a blue moon. The rest of the paper ran typical community news: stories about the Fourth of July parade, summer activities, and road improvements.

The same picture of Emma blanketed the front. The same smile. The same outfit. The same innocent look. This time, Loretta saw her picture in color and noticed her polka dot dress contained black and red dots. *How can someone like that go missing?* Loretta wondered to herself. Something does not add up.

Loretta read all about Emma's community involvement over the years and how she volunteered at the VFW hall and the library. She was a National Honor Society student involved in the band, speech, environmental club, and student government. There were several quotes from Ridgeport residents, both young and old, commending the type of person she is.

"She would brighten up our day at the VFW, and we need a little pick-me-up from time to time," said Frank Johnson, a World War II vet.

Her friend Rita Jefferson described her as the "best friend anyone could ever ask for."

"I have no idea where she would have gone, but I wish she would come back. Come back, Emma, come back," said Jefferson.

Village trustee and father Patrick Ryan is offering a $25,000 reward for the person that finds his daughter. The Ryans could not be reached for further comment.

Loretta set the paper down on her lap for a second and could not imagine her parents talking on the matter either if she were in their shoes.

Toward the end of the article, the reporter wrote about how the Neighborhood Watch would be organizing a "Hunt for Emma." The article instructed residents to check with their Neighborhood Watch organizer on where the hunt would begin.

Loretta understood why John could only write so much on the missing girl from a neighboring small town, but she certainly appreciated this detailed version. When she set the paper aside, she felt a slight headache coming on.

Enough was enough. She had crammed for the residency card. She stressed herself enough about the oral exam. She was depressed enough about a missing seventeen-year-old girl. She needed a drink but remembered she would have to do so in the privacy of her own home.

22

Loretta lounged for the next half hour or so, stroking her forehead and glancing up at the clock. She did not try to make any more conversation with Trina, nor did she care to at this point. She wanted her results and wanted to get back to her home.

She temporarily forgot why she was there from her forty-five minutes of waiting. No one went in or out of the office, and Loretta longed for some noise other than the ticking of the clock. She sneezed, and Trina did not even say, "God Bless you." *But weren't we supposed to say that around here?* she thought. Just as she began nodding off to sleep, Ryan Paulson whispered something into Trina's ear at the window. Trina smiled widely and asked politely for Loretta to approach the window.

"Mrs. Casey. Here are your results, dear. Ridgeport welcomes you." And it was the nicest Loretta had seen her all day.

The manila envelope weighed heavy in her hand, even though it only contained a couple of sheets of paper. Her tight grip and sweat added weight to her anticipation.

"Well, go on now," Trina said. "See your results, dear."

Loretta exhaled and quickly opened the envelope. She closed her eyes, and then peeking with her left, saw the prefix "Per." She opened her right eye and noticed it read "Perfect Score." She could not believe it. She had to look at the words "Perfect Score" a few times to make sure it was real and then looked up at Trina, who was still smiling widely.

"Way to go, resident. Now, if you would take your scorecard down to the Residency Card Desk, they will take your photo and print your card. Congratulations."

"Thank you," Loretta said with a smile.

And her joy was likewise reflected in her profile pic on her card. The town's motto shone in bright gold lettering at the top of the card, "Love thy neighbor" and "Love thy Ridgeport," and at the bottom, it read "Official Residency Card." The Residency Card Office explained to Loretta that the card allowed her to receive discounts at businesses throughout the town, access to activities and Ridgeport events, the right to vote in Ridgeport and the ability to hold any political office or committee, discounted membership at the country club and fitness center, and served as the final acceptance and understanding of Ridgeport's way of life.

Loretta signed a final contract saying that she understood the card's meaning, which officially granted her residency.

As the Residency Office clerk handed the card over to Loretta, she beamed with excitement.

"Now remember, keep the card on you at all times," the clerk said with a smile.

"I can't see leaving home without it."

They both smiled, and Loretta walked out of the Village Hall reinvigorated.

23

As silly and frustrating as it was to obtain a card to become a resident, Loretta now felt like she belonged. She had not been a popular girl in high school, and now she felt like she was in a unique clique, an inclusive club that other towns did not understand. John needed to get his card now, and Loretta could not wait to tell him about her perfect score. When Loretta stopped by her parent's house to pick up Scott, she showed off her card. Her parents seemed bewildered that a town would go to such lengths to make someone feel welcome.

"That's great, I guess. Although it sounds like Ridgeport is not exactly as welcoming as you say," said Loretta's mom, Peggy.

But Loretta did not want to hear any more negativity for the day. She rode on her high feelings, and she had no intention of slowing down.

"Well, you just would not understand. Where's Scott?"

Peggy shrugged her shoulders and picked up the playful little guy. Scott smiled wide at his mommy, and Loretta patted the top of his head.

"Hi, baby. I'm so glad to see you. Did you have fun with grandma and grandpa?"

"Oh, he was so good. You have a little angel right there. Please bring him by anytime."

"Thanks, Mom."

Peggy handed over the ever-growing Scott, and Loretta gave her mom the best hug she could with her six-month-old in her arms.

"Love you."

"Love you too, dear."

As Loretta walked Scott out to the van, Peggy looked out the window and waved but carried a worried expression on her face.

24

When John returned home that night around seven o'clock, weary and ready to flop on the couch, Loretta threw her arms around him. She loved having her card, but she hated herself for not spending time with him.

"How was your day, honey? You look beat."

"That's because I am. You don't have to read that book anymore, do ya? It'd be nice if you were around tonight. We could eat dinner together, play with Scott before he has to go to bed."

"I'd like that."

"I made tacos for the two of us."

"Ha, Taco Tuesday."

"Taco Tuesday.

Loretta made John a plate of three softshells and brought him a beer while Loretta poured herself a glass of wine. They placed Scott in his bouncer chair next to them at the table while they enjoyed their dinner.

"It's a shame about Emma, huh?" Loretta asked.

John nodded through a mouthful of taco.

"Yeah, a girl that young. The sources I spoke with didn't seem to know much. I followed up today; no new leads on where she might be, where she might have gone."

Loretta set her taco down, hunched forward, and listened with all ears.

"I read your article. It was good, well written."

John shrugged.

"Pretty straightforward, really. There isn't much you can say with missing children's cases like these, unfortunately. Now, if you find out there's a kidnapping or a murder, heaven forbid...."

"Do you think it's that, John?" Loretta said, eyes widening.

"I don't know," he said and paused. "I don't know what it is."

As they continued eating, Scott almost seemed like he was listening too, moving his eyes from mom to dad.

"They did a huge bio piece on Emma in *The Ridgeport News*."

"Oh yeah? How'd it turn out?"

"It was heartfelt. She was a good kid. Everyone had nothing but kind things to say about her."

"So, I heard."

"John, don't you think there's something off with this whole thing?"

"How do you mean?"

"I don't know. A girl that bright and well-liked just doesn't go missing, does she? I mean, Emma was at a friend's house just before it happened, and her friend didn't let on that there was anything unusual about that night."

John looked down at his plate and used his fork to pick up the remaining pieces of meat, cheese, and lettuce. He scrunched his eyebrows to take in what his wife was trying to say.

"And...well, now that I think about it, she wasn't exactly in dress code."

"Come again?"

"Well, in the book I read, there is a social norms section saying that residents should wear their best outfits at all times. Emma was last seen wearing jeans with holes and a

58

hoodie. Jeans and hoodie aside, it was unseasonably cool Tuesday, but it just doesn't seem to fit the social norm."

"The social norm? I think you're playing detective a little too much here."

"You have to read the book, John. When I went to the grocery store, all the women wore dresses and power suits. And Emma is the daughter of a village trustee. She should know how to dress. Jeans with holes in them are not exactly appropriate dress."

"Well, kids dress like that."

"Yeah, but don't you see? They aren't supposed to dress like that in Ridgeport. Kids at the grocery store didn't."

"So, what are you trying to say? That she ran away because she wanted to dress how she felt like dressing?"

"I...I don't know. I'm just saying that something is amiss. That's all."

John scratched his head and glanced over at Scott. He was staring past them at the window at the setting sun. Rays of brilliant purples and oranges cascaded over the landscape. John bopped his nose, and Scott giggled. Loretta relaxed and giggled as well.

"Anyway, you're probably right. Oh, we got invited to a party tomorrow. It's at Coleridge Park. Aren't you off tomorrow for the Fourth? It's sort of a Historic District Neighborhood party. It'd be nice to get to know the neighbors."

"Yeah. They gave me the day. Sure, that would be nice."

Loretta wanted to mention the book and the residency card to John but figured they should enjoy the remaining minutes of the day playing with Scott and getting him ready for bed. Tomorrow was another day.

25

The following morning, John said that Loretta's spinach and artichoke dip turned out perfect, even if she did not fully believe him. Loretta's nerves had returned. She had to worry about picking out the proper outfit and making a good impression for Sue Ellen and the neighbors. She wanted to feel included.

John, meanwhile, did not care. He never cared, which is why Loretta was attracted to him in high school. John did not care what people thought, but now she wished he did. He lounged with Scott on the couch in the living room, both still in their PJs, watching *Sesame Street*. As Ernie sang "Rubber Ducky," Scott turned to face his dad. It was his favorite tune. Loretta interrupted their peaceful moment on the couch with a tense voice coming from the kitchen.

"What are you going to wear, John?"

"I don't know. It's the Fourth, so something red, white, or blue. The party's not for another three hours."

Loretta marched upstairs like she was going to war and rifled through her closet while John was still sipping his coffee watching TV with Scott.

"Maybe you should wear that nice red polo I got you for your birthday last year with those khaki shorts you have? That seems appropriate?" Loretta yelled from up the stairs.

John rolled his eyes, switched off Sean's favorite show, and carried him upstairs to reality. *You're lucky you're not an adult, kid,* John thought. He sat Scott on his bedroom floor and watched him rock back and forth like a ship on the high seas. John bent down to play with the little guy until only his wife's voice broke their time together once more.

"John! Are you getting ready up there?!"

"Yes!"

John sighed, turned his attention to the closet, and pulled out his American flag tee-shirt with blue jean shorts. When

Loretta saw him a few minutes later, she bristled with anxiety.

"John. I would like it if you went back upstairs and changed."

"Honey, that polo itches, and I'm not comfortable in those khakis. They don't fit that well."

"Anyway, look at the time. We're going to be late if we don't leave now," John said.

"Oh, God. Fine, but it's your funeral," Loretta said, shaking her head.

John stood for a second and then quipped back, "Well, then I suppose I should wear all black?"

"It's not time for jokes, John. Come on, grab Scott and the diaper bag and let's get in the wagon, okay?"

John picked up a crying Scott from the living room playpen and gave him his pacifier. The family walked out to the garage, into the station wagon, and onto the park.

26

The Fourth of July brought a high around 80 degrees, with hardly a cloud in the sky. About two hundred people had already gathered at Coleridge Park. Grills scattered around the park, and neighborhood men fried burgers and dogs under a wooden pavilion. Kids played a pick-up baseball game on one of the two diamonds. A few men moved coolers around and finished setting tents up. A row of well-dressed women prattled away at a wooden picnic bench underneath the pavilion. Several others stood in a circle with non-alcoholic beverages in their hands, chatting. A few kids approached an adult in one of the circles requesting something or other.

As the Casey family moved closer to their first neighborhood party, Loretta spotted the dresses women sported were picnic-appropriate, yes, but also stylish and

61

fancy. These women appeared to shop at only the finest locations and wear only the finest clothes. And they all wore make-up.

"Why didn't I think of that?" Loretta mumbled to herself. "I didn't think to put on make-up."

Loretta shook her head as she noticed the men wearing polos and khakis or short-sleeve button-up shirts.

Two long picnic tables sat side by side for appetizers and main courses, while another table displayed picturesque desserts. Enough food lined the tables to feed all of Ridgeport. John pushed Scott's stroller to the outside of the pavilion and waited for his wife after she finished placing her spinach and artichoke dip. Scott still slept from the car ride and from being pushed up the blacktop trail towards the pavilion. John did not think Scott would last long with all the people there and had a mental time limit for their stay. All Loretta cared about was finding Sue Ellen and making as many friends as possible.

Loretta did not find Sue Ellen, but Sue Ellen found Loretta. Just as Loretta found the one vacant spot for her spinach and artichoke dip, Sue Ellen tapped her on the shoulder, and Loretta whipped around as if she sensed a ghost. When she noticed it was her new friend, she laughed and apologized.

"You startled me. I'm sorry."

"You're sorry that I startled you?"

Sue Ellen ran a hand through her hair and smirked.

Loretta blushed a little but did not reply.

"Nice outfit, girl. You can really clean up."

"Yeah. You like it?"

"Is that a red sundress? That almost looks like the same dress I wore when we met. Are you trying to copy me?"

"What, me? No." But Loretta thought that she was.

"We'll have to do something about you with make-up, though."

62

Loretta touched her face and blushed again.

"Oh, yeah, well, I didn't think to wear…."

"Stop worrying. Are you always this anxious?"

"I, uh, well, no."

And Sue Ellen burst out laughing.

"Where's Matt?"

"Oh, he's at home."

"Ah, is your husband watching him?"

"I'm divorced."

"Oh, sorry."

"Don't be. I'm better off without him."

"So, he's with your mom then?"

"No, with the nanny."

"Oh, I see."

"Yeah, momma's gotta have some fun sometimes, you know? Don't you ever want a break from being a mom?"

Loretta laughed, but Sue Ellen smiled, studying her.

"Where's your man? And where's Scotty?"

"Oh, they're over here. Let me introduce you."

Loretta excitedly grabbed her new friend's hand and led her through the crowd and towards John and Scott. A few people turned to say hello to Sue Ellen. John stood by himself, occasionally looking over at the vast spread of food.

"Here he is. John, I'd like you to meet a friend of mine, Sue Ellen Norris. She lives in our neighborhood, and she invited us here."

Sue Ellen placed just her fingertips into John's hands as if she were a queen. John didn't notice.

"Pleasure to meet you, Sue Ellen."

"Pleasure's all mine."

Sue Ellen approached Scott in the buggy and smiled widely. He lay fast asleep, resting like a little angel.

"He is so adorable. I think he's cuter than when I last saw him."

"Thank you," said Loretta with a smile.

Then they all stood, awkwardly looking at each other for the conversational topic. Loretta's palms started to feel sweaty, and then she finally spoke up.

"John works at *The Naperville Sun*. He's covering that missing child case."

"He does? That's a real tragedy. She was a good kid, most of the time anyway," said Sue Ellen, chuckling to herself.

John looked at her strangely, but before he could get a word out, she spoke up again.

"You know...you should both join the search committee. We'll be meeting tomorrow at my house. You simply must come."

"Well, I can't..." started John.

"I'll be there," Loretta said, interrupting her husband.

"Great! Let me introduce you all to some people."

"Um, no. I should stay here and look after Scott. You two go on ahead," said John.

"Oh, are you sure, honey?"

Sue Ellen looked back and smirked at John.

"Yeah. I'm sure."

He watched his wife spin around and dart off with her new friend like she was her junior high bestie. A few minutes passed, and John gave into his hotdog and chips craving. He never noticed the dress code until one Peter Barnes pointed it out to him.

"Hey, buddy. Looks like you and I are the only two that get it around here, huh?"

"Get what?

"That freedom means you can dress in a tee-shirt and jean shorts if you like," Barnes said. Barnes also donned blue jean shorts and a red tee titled "Freedom." John laughed and felt at home for the first time since arriving.

"The name is Peter," he said, sticking his hand out.

"John." He smiled and gave him his firm shake.

"Where are you eating, John?"

64

"Well, I have my son over here within earshot. I was just gonna stand and eat by him."

Peter nodded and understood.

"Mind if I join ya?"

"That'd be great."

Peter and John talked about Ridgeport, and John brought up how his wife seemed obsessed with the book and making friends lately.

"Oh, the book, yeah. Well, you do want to read it and get your card. There are social norms in there, and a lot of it is just overdone. Women here like to abide by them, and so do their husbands, just to keep their wives happy. Then the single men do it to find a good woman to date. I could care less," Peter said.

John already liked this guy. Here was someone speaking his language. John never cared what other people thought, and he already wondered if he had moved into the wrong town.

"Maybe we shouldn't have moved here. It seems a little uptight."

"Well, in some ways, yeah. But it is a great place to live. It's a great place to raise a family.

There are a lot of activities events; there's no crime, the schools are excellent. The residency card gives you discounts throughout the town. So, the good outweighs the bad."

John considered this and felt more comfortable that these social norms were just a suggestion. After some talk about the White Sox and Bears, Loretta returned with Sue Ellen.

"We met so many…."

"Peter! John, this is…."

"I know. You two know each other?"

Sue Ellen threw Peter a smirk, and Peter nodded and smiled.

"Looks like we all know each other," Sue Ellen said.

"John, I met Peter at the grocery store. I was frantic and could not think of what dish to make, and he helped me find a dish to put together."

Sue Ellen laughed at this and stared over at Peter.

Peter stared back, smiling.

"Oh, gotcha. What a small world."

"Yeah, I'll say," Sue Ellen said and rolled her eyes.

"Peter told me you two are life-long friends," Loretta said.

"Peter's my ex-husband, Loretta," she said, without looking at Peter.

Peter smiled in John's direction.

The awkward silence in the conversation earlier had nothing on the awkwardness at that moment.

"Anyway, I'm glad we all know each other now," Sue Ellen said and walked into the crowd.

Loretta's heart jumped, and she looked towards Peter and her husband before saying, "Excuse me."

"Sue Ellen, wait. Just wait," Loretta said.

Sue Ellen did not turn towards her friend but paused in her tracks and smiled.

Loretta tapped her on the shoulder.

"Did I startle you?"

"Nothing ever startles me, dear. Now, come. We have some more people I want to introduce you to."

And Loretta happily followed the leader.

27

Back at the pavilion, Peter apologized for the scene. He said that he had hoped things would be better between the two. He said he should never have invited himself and attempted to patch things up, but he still had feelings for her.

"I, uh, understand," John said. "But if this is running into a therapy session, I'm afraid I'm not very good at that sort of thing."

Peter laughed and patted him on the back.

"Hey, I got two tickets to the Sox game at the end of the month. I was going to take my dad, but he couldn't go. Do you want to come?"

Peter seemed like a nice enough guy, and John could not think of why he shouldn't, so he shrugged his shoulders and agreed.

"Great. They're box, right behind the dugout. We won't be in front of one of the Comiskey Park beams."

"Well, that's good."

"Well, I should probably head out early in case Sue Ellen comes back," Peter said.

John laughed, and they shook hands again. As Peter walked on, John waited back patiently for his wife.

John's patience wore thin as Loretta ventured off with Sue Ellen longer than John would have liked. He wanted to leave the party about two hours earlier, but she stormed away on her playdate. Meanwhile, Scott began getting restless, and it was all John could do to keep Scott from having an all-out meltdown. John also found the reason for Scott's fuss. By the time Loretta returned, John had already changed a blowout diaper, gave Scott a bottle, and rocked him back and forth to settle him down again.

"I hope we're doing the right thing, son," John whispered. "I hope you're happy here."

John left the picnic frustrated, annoyed with the wife, who decided to spend more time with her new friend instead of her family. On the way home, she talked about her time with Sue Ellen and bragged about how she received a perfect score for her residency card.

"Enough, Loretta! You didn't spend any time with me or your son. Maybe you should start prioritizing what you do around here."

And even though Loretta felt guilty and apologized, she could not wait to go to the search committee meeting the next morning.

28

While Sue Ellen's nanny, Mrs. Stella Greyson, watched over Scott and Matt, Loretta headed out with half the historic district searching for Emma Ryan. They put up flyers with her picture and drove down alleyways and through parks. There was no sign of her. They agreed to meet the following day and search through the forest preserve district. But after a couple of months of searching, the committee and the police department came up empty. Mr. Ryan's $25,000 reward went unclaimed. All signs pointed to a singular conclusion: Emma Ryan, it appeared, was gone for good.

Chapter 3: Ridgeport 1996

In 1996, Scott Casey formed the 'band.' They were not a music band, but a band of brothers: ten-year-old's Scott, Matt Norris, and Riley Wrobel; and his brother Jimmy, aged nine. The band took their first oath on the first day of summer vacation, June 11, 1996. They met in the Spring Grove Forest Preserve next to Spring Creek, spit on their hands, and shook an unwritten agreement never to abandon each other.

"May we band together through thick and thin, and through it all, may we always win!" Scott exclaimed. The group laughed. From that moment on, they were inseparable.

Matt and Scott were friends from the time they started walking. They played GI Joes, Ninja Turtles, and Army Men. They climbed trees, built forts, played sports, and did everything together. As the '80s turned into the '90s, Sue Ellen's nanny Stella watched the boys more and more. Loretta quit her job at the junior high and became a stay-at-home mom. With John's promotion to news editor, the family could afford one less parent employed. The problem was Loretta spent more quality time with Sue Ellen than she did with her son.

John did his best to be there for Scott, but his promotion meant longer and more unpredictable hours. Family time became harder to come by. Scott did not seem to mind, and it was lucky that Stella looked after them both and their education. Scott would realize who he was during that summer, and that served him well in the years that followed.

The band explored Spring Grove Forest Preserve more and blazed trails off the beaten path through wildflowers and thick, overgrown bushes and grasses. They had their favorite spots, such as the Peak, the highest point of the preserve, where you could see all of Ridgeport. They also enjoyed the winding creek over the wooden bridges through the narrow path. There were large stones they could use to cross, and there was even an abandoned picnic bench left in a shallow end, which they used to hold official 'band meetings.'

Scott and Matt stumbled on the hole the previous summer, and Scott jumped right from an oak tree beside it. Matt held his breath, but when the big cannonball splash erupted, and Scott came back up unhurt, Matt jumped in afterward. The band ran there together for the first time on a hot day in May, and it was forever dubbed their spot. On their second official band meeting in the last weekend of June, the group gathered on their bench, and Matt called to order the business of the day.

"This begins the meeting of the band for the last weekend of June 1996," he said solemnly. "On this meeting's agenda, we will talk about ideas for what to do today. Let us first hear from representative Scott Casey."

"Well, I was thinking, we play baseball."

"It's too hot, Scotty. How about we go swimming?" Riley asked.

"Okay, one for baseball, one for swimming. Jimmy? What do you say?"

"I'm down for whatever, you guys."

Scott rubbed his hand through his light brown hair. Sweat ran down his temples. Even through the shade of the trees, the sun seemed to beat down hard.

"Why don't we swim first?"

"That sounds fine, Scott," Matt said.

"Yeah, let's go. I'm ready," Riley chimed in.

"That sounds good," Jimmy added.

"This concludes the last weekend meeting of the band for June 1996," Scott said.

The boys made their way down the narrow winding path that followed the creek. The creek widened to a swimming hole towards the north end of the trail, and that was where the boys spent most of their time swimming.

At about six-eight feet deep, there was enough to cannonball from the trees above. The boys liked the privacy of the water. Most residents in Ridgeport went to the Ridgeport Pool, but the band's parents were too busy to take them, and while Stella often said she would take Matt and Scott, they preferred the seclusion and wildness of the creek.

On that hot day in June, the group played 'Jaws' wearing their tighty-whities. The rules of Jaws were simple: one is the shark, and one is the prey. Once the shark catches the prey and dunks him under the water, the roles reverse. Scared of the deep end, Jimmy wouldn't play and would only swim alone in the shallow end of the swimming hole. As a year younger than Riley, Jimmy was the scaredy-cat of the group. He worried he would get Lyme disease from a tick bite or poison ivy from trailblazing. Still, he always tagged along with the band, and during meetings, he voted, "Whatever works for you guys." He was the group's little brother.

It was on that hot day in June that tagging along almost cost Jimmy his life. While Riley, Matt, and Scott played Jaws, Jimmy cautiously crept closer to the deep end. Ironically, the movie *Jaws* gave Jimmy his fear of sharks and swimming in deep water. He had the habit of taking what he watched and read too literally. He had trouble sleeping for three days when he was ten after watching *War of the Worlds* because he thought aliens had landed outside his house. He could have sworn he heard their heads humming, but it turned out to be the dishwasher every time. He didn't have much in the way of a swim coach, either. His freshman PE teacher passed him despite his refusal to venture off into the deep end. His brother tried teaching him to float but gave up after a couple of times when his legs would sink like a rock. So, each time the band came to the swimming hole, Jimmy waded in the shallow end, watching the rest of the band toss a football, work on their cannonballs, or play Jaws. He always thought about going over, but he hated how he couldn't see the bottom of the water. After all, no one could see Jaws coming, and who knows what was swimming in the deep end? Yet, there was something about that bright sunny day in June that told Jimmy to go for it. Something snapped inside him and threw away his subconscious. He stroked vigorously toward his brothers. He wasn't going to be their little brother anymore.

But just as his confidence was building, he felt a patch of seaweed wrapped around his feet. He was in a grey pool, pulled to certain death. His legs were like anchors. His arms felt like a featherweight, fluttering among the colliding waves. The seaweed encircled him. The water rushed into his throat and down his lungs. It was not until his brother heard him gasping for air that the band started to panic.

"Jimmy! Where are you?" Riley yelled.

The encircling seaweed forced Jimmy under, plummeting him toward the bottom of the pond.

Riley had fifteen extra pounds on his brother, and that day he might as well have had the strength of Hulk Hogan. Riley dove through the murky water grabbed his brother around the waist like a lifeguard, and laid him out to the side of the creek. Matt and Scott followed. With his cheeks puffy, eyes shut, and his bony arms sprawled, Jimmy looked like a beached whale lying in the mud. The three of them stood around him, panicked, shivering, and turned from one to the other.

"Riley, do something!"

Yet all he could do was pace back and forth and rub his temple.

"What am I supposed to do?!"

"You know, like CPR or something, like in the movies? Mouth to mouth?" Matt suggested.

Riley bent down, unsure of exactly what he was doing, but breathed in, and then breathed out, trying to bring Jimmy back to life. He banged on his chest for good measure. Then he breathed in and breathed out again.

Scott teetered back and forth while Matt watched and kept chanting, "Come on, Jimmy, buddy. Wake up. Wake up, Jimmy!"

Riley began crying and sobbing, but after what seemed like an eternity, Jimmy began to cough up water, his body convulsed, and his eyes opened. When he finally sat up, Riley hugged him so tight he did not want to let go. Matt and Scott soon followed. Jimmy gave one more look at the water before looking at his bandmates. Riley wiped a tear from his face. Matt and Scott helped him to his feet.

"Don't you ever do that again!" Riley exclaimed.

"I just wanted to, you know, get over my fear."

"You will, bro, you will. I'll teach you."

The band almost lost a member that day, and they grew stronger because of it.

Just as Jimmy stood up and the boys began to dry off, storm clouds started to form in the preserves.

"We better get outta here, fellas. A storm is a-brewin'," Scott said.

"To infinity and beyond!" Matt said, like Buzz Lightyear in *Toy Story*.

Matt always made pop culture references, and even though they sometimes got annoying, they raised at least a chuckle from the band most of the time. The first bolt of lightning flashed atop the tree canopy, lighting the entire sky. Matt and Scott broke out of a quick walk and into an all-out run. Riley tugged the weakened Jimmy along. Jimmy's body was still limp, but it was just enough to put distance between him and his friends. At one point, Riley could only make out a flash of the back of Matt's shirt as he rounded a bend. Then Jimmy tripped over a fallen tree trunk, colliding head first with the wet trail.

"Jimmy!"

Scott and Matt stopped and turned upon hearing Riley. He lifted his brother to his feet, steered him over the fallen oak, and pressed on. This time, the boys waited for the two to catch up, but as they did, a bolt of thunder pierced that very log they had just escaped. It sent Jimmy's legs into a frenzy like some cartoon character. Crashes of thunder and rain continued to pound through the trees with monstrous force. The boys needed to run a good couple of miles from the swimming hole until they felt concrete. They did not care much about the rain. In fact, it felt good. They cared about the thunder and lightning.

"We gotta get away from the creek," screamed Matt.

"Matt's right. We could be fried green tomatoes before we know it."

Riley rolled his eyes, and the band stretched their legs and made their way up the sloping hills and away from the creek.

Just as Riley pulled Jimmy up the hill, a bolt of lightning struck another tree right next to the creek, only about fifty feet away from them. Scott turned back and froze to watch the single electric current pulverize mother nature, light up the sky in a flash, and then disappear. Matt pushed him along and out of his temporary trance, and the band continued to push higher and out of the woods as quickly as possible. By the time they reached home, the rain had begun to let up into steady drops.

The band headed off into their separate directions home. When Riley reached their household on Cranberry Lane, he whipped past the living room where his parents were snug next to the fire watching a movie and darted up the stairs into his room, still tugging Jimmy along with him like a stuffed animal. Just as he plopped his soaking wet brother on his bed to rest, a knock came at his door.

"Riley...open up the door, please."

Great. What will I tell her? Riley thought.

75

"Jimmy, listen to me, we can't tell mom that you almost drowned. She'll freak out and never let us swim there again. Do you understand?" Jimmy said in a soft but demanding whisper.

But Jimmy only stared at him, blankly.

Riley shook his lifeless body.

"Riley? I'd like to come in now."

"Do you understand, Jimmy?"

This time, Jimmy nodded, eyes wide open.

"Good."

"Coming, Mom!"

When Riley opened the door, and Mrs. Wrobel saw not only that her boys were soaking wet but that her baby had passed out on Riley's bed, she clapped her hands over her mouth.

"What happened here?"

"It's not that bad, Mom, really. We were out playing in the woods, and Jimmy tripped over a big tree trunk. He hit his head bad, is all. And then we got stuck in the storm."

She rushed to his side.

"Oh sweetie, are you okay? Is there anything I can do for you?"

Jimmy nodded his head, but his eyes were half-open.

"Oh, I've told you, boys, that playing in those woods can be dangerous."

"It was an accident, Mom, really. Anyone can trip over a tree trunk."

She frowned at Riley before turning her attention back to Jimmy.

"Let's get you out of those clothes and into something warmer. And then I'll get you some Tylenol for your head. Then, you rest. I'll check on you a little later."

Mrs. Wrobel left the room, and Riley swallowed hard. If she ever found out about his near-death experience, she could forbid them from ever going there again.

In the Norris household, Sue Ellen was passed out drunk on the couch. Stella stopped Matt as he waltzed in, dripping water all over the kitchen floor.

"Where were you?" she demanded.

"In the woods, with the band."

He could tell her anything.

"Hm," Stella said, raising an eyebrow.

"And what happened in the woods?"

"I got wet."

Well, almost anything. Riley didn't think it wise to tell her that Jimmy almost died there.

"I see that. Well, hold still there while I get you a towel, so you don't drip water all over your mom's floor."

Matt waited in his wet rags, shivering. Every part of him was soaked. When Stella returned with the large cotton bath towel, he was glad to be home.

John Casey was still at the office, and Loretta, like Sue Ellen, was taking a late afternoon siesta. After he dried off in the upstairs bathroom, he watched the rest of the rain from his bedroom window. He saw one more flash of lightning from out in the woods before he turned away, and in that sudden flash of light, he came up with the idea that changed the course of the band forever.

2

As the band grew closer, their home life changed. By 1996, Loretta was spending more time with Sue Ellen than she did with her family. Stella watched Scott and Matt when John was not around, so Stella became their unofficial mom figure. The moms paid the boys' way into the First Church of St. John Elementary School signed them up for swim lessons, tae kwon do, and rec baseball. They got top-of-the-line bikes, which they occasionally used, but the boys preferred walking in the woods. They bought chests full of toys, which they played with from time to time. And anytime they bought them something new, the boys smiled and said, "Thank you, Mom."

John, in contrast, made as much time for Scott as possible. He showed him how to play catch, ride his bike, and fix things around the house. Matt always felt jealous that his best friend had a father, but he never showed it to Scott.

However, John's marriage was a different story. John did not know how he lost the woman he married. They both lived in the same house and never talked about divorce, but they never really talked, either. They never seemed to know what went on in each other's lives. John became upset with Loretta from time to time, saying she did not spend enough time with Scott, but Loretta would start crying, saying she was not a good mother. John would always hug her and tell her that she was trying.

For her part, Loretta wanted to feel she belonged in Ridgeport ever since she picked up the book in the summer of 1986. She felt that meeting Sue Ellen was the greatest thing that happened to her. Loretta knew friendship with Sue Ellen made her a better person. On the other hand, John did get his residency card in '86 about a month after Loretta but stayed the same John she knew when she married him. He never cared what people thought, and that feeling never changed. To heighten her sense of belonging, Loretta never left the house without a fashionable outfit or eyeliner and mascara, at the very least. She sprayed on Versace's Bright Crystal perfume because Sue Ellen suggested it. She often ventured over to Sue Ellen's house to "get away from it all."

The day that the band ran into the woods to go swimming was no different. Except it was different for Matt Norris. Matt stood at the edge of the block and was home when he could make out his mother and Loretta saying goodbye to each other on the front steps of their house. The rain had died down by then. He could not see that well from the corner, but he could have sworn he saw them holding hands and kissing. But Matt rubbed his eyes and convinced himself that he did not see what he saw. All he saw, he told himself, was Loretta walking calmly under an umbrella and into the night.

3

A few days later, Peter Barnes phoned John, asking if he wanted to go to the golf range at the country club. Peter had become John's best friend, and aside from his son, he was the only person that made sense in Ridgeport anymore.

"So, I'll meet you in a few minutes then, John-O?"

"Sounds good, Pete."

It was a pleasant 80 degrees, good golf weather. The two of them bought a large bucket, parked themselves under the shade boxes, and set their clubs against the rack.

"Wanna bet I can hit it past the two hundred-marker, John?"

"No. Because I think you can."

"Just got this new titanium driver. The ad says it can swing like the pros. We'll see."

Peter lined up the ball, rocked back and forth, and drove into it, knocking the ball just shy of the two hundred marker.

"Shoulda made that bet, man."

"You'll get it next time."

John pulled out his old wooden driver –the clubs he inherited from his father. He would kill himself if they ever broke.

He always tried to imitate Peter's stance and approach but would always slice. Like Peter, John stepped back and threw a practice swing first, and then stepped back in and swung his hips. He breathed in and out, and keeping his eye on the ball, pulled his arm back tight and released his swing. The ball traveled a sizable distance, but the Titlist had the wrong shape and sliced halfway across the range.

"Well, you just have to straighten out those shoulders. You're dippin'."

"Right."

Easier said than done, though, John thought.

The two forty-somethings said nothing after that for the next few swings. All they heard was the 'swoosh' of the club and the clink of the balls.

"Did I ever tell you about my ex-wife, John?" Peter asked.

"You've never mentioned her since the day we all met her at the picnic. So, I just figured not to bring her up."

"We were married for seven years before we divorced."

John and Peter lined up another tee. This time they used their nine-irons.

"She had an intoxicating personality. It's what made me fall in love with her. I think I fell in love with the idea of her, but I didn't realize it."

"What do you mean?"

"She was always a strong, beautiful woman. She could always get what she wanted. She would never get a ticket, even though she sped like the Roadrunner. She said a few of her professors would look the other way when she cheated. She was an only child and was spoiled rotten. She's used to getting her way."

"I can see how that backfired…."

"Well, yeah. Sue Ellen's not without her good side. She's generous and giving. I'll give her that. But she's manipulative. She makes you feel guilty about everything, even if it's her fault, and you go out of your way just to please her."

John listened but continued to put his ball on the tee and line up his club while Peter had stopped swinging altogether.

"So, it got to be too much. I wanted to see a marriage counselor, but she just laughed it off and said I was weak-minded for thinking that. When I was the one who filed the divorce, she was taken aback. I don't think anyone ever stood up to her like that. I'd never advocate for divorce, but I was worried about what would have happened to her if I didn't."

"What do you mean happened to her?"

"I just mean, she's unpredictable. We once got into a fight over her spending habits, and then she ran up to the bathroom and slit her wrists. I had to run her to the ER and ended up apologizing to her. She ended up okay, and I never gave her a hard time about it again."

"Wow. That's crazy. And that's the person who's in charge of the Neighborhood Watch."

"That's not what I'm worried about, John. That's the person that's already in charge of your wife."

John stopped swinging and turned to look at his friend, horrified.

"But not to worry, she always has had friends, and nothing has ever happened to them. Just be careful is all."

They finished their bucket and then headed to the country club lounge for a burger and fries.

"Sure do wish we weren't a dry county now," John quipped.

"Ha! Me too. We could go back to your place and down a few Millers, though."

"Sounds like a plan, Peter, my man."

The two of them ate their burgers at the non-alcoholic bar and watched the lounge TV – a White Sox game aired to no people in the lounge.

"I do have some good news."

"Oh yeah? What's that?

"I adopted a little girl. The paperwork is all final. It's been something I've been wanting to do for some time."

"Well, that's great!" John exclaimed, patting Peter on the back. He set his burger down and smiled. "That's really, really great. I suppose I should call you dad?"

"Ha, yeah, and she's as sweet as can be. You'll meet her soon. In fact, Josephine is Scott's age, ten years old, I believe."

"Oh, well, I'm not sure how the boys will feel about having a girl in their group, but you never know."

"Ha, well, give them a few years. Why don't we finish these burgers and then see about them beers?"

"Will do, my man. Will do."

4

When the band showed up for its next meeting the following day, Matt was not the one to lead it. The rest of the group sat on their picnic bench, awaiting Matt to call the meeting to order, but Matt sat staring off at the creek, not saying a word.

"Matt? Are you okay, Matt?" Scott asked.

He simply shrugged his shoulders.

The group did not say anything for a minute, but now that the meeting was not underway, they looked to Scott to see if he would run the meeting in Matt's place.

"Well, I called to order an agenda item that I think you all would appreciate."

"You have our attention," Riley said.

Matt still stared off into the creek.

"When I saw that lightning hit the tree some thirty feet from me, I got an idea."

"Yeah, what was that?" Riley asked.

"We should build a clubhouse. But not just any kind of clubhouse, an underground one."

"What? Do you have any idea how much work that would take? How do you intend to do that?" Riley demanded.

"Well, you know how in World War I, they had the trenches. I was thinking something like that. In case we have another storm, we can just dive in. Or, if we get in trouble with someone, we just hide out there."

"What are the chances another storm like that would hit, and who would we get in trouble with?"

But then Matt turned from the creek and spoke up.

"I like it. I like it."

Scott's idea would be put into action now that he had the support of their unofficial leader. Scott relaxed his back and smiled towards Matt.

"Okay, here's what we'll need to do…." Scott began.

Scott told them they needed to dig a trench about six feet by ten feet and place wood on the sides of the hole for support with wood on the bottom for a walkway.

"That's a lot of digging. That could take weeks," Riley said.

Jimmy nodded, agreeing with his brother.

"If Scotty thinks we can do it, we can do it," Matt said. Matt was visibly in a better mood now. "You think we can, right?"

Scott paused but then said, "Yes. With the four of us, yes," and directed his answer towards Riley.

"Fine. I'm in. But this better be the best damn clubhouse," Riley said with his arms crossed.

"It will be. Now we'll need four shovels. And we'll need wood, but we'll worry about that part later."

"So, where are we digging, Scott?" Jimmy asked.

Scott pointed to an area east of the swimming hole in a valley between the hole and a small hill.

"There. It's close enough to the hole where we can hang out, but it's far enough away from the water. I think it's the perfect spot."

Matt rubbed his chin, and Riley and Jimmy nodded.

"Okay, Scott. Let's see where this goes," Riley said.

"May we band together through thick and thin, and through it, all, may we always win!" Scott said, ending their meeting.

5

On the second Tuesday of each month, Loretta made her way to the Village Hall for the board meeting. John joined her for his second required meeting this time, but Loretta had been going to board meetings regularly with Sue Ellen for a few years now. John opted only to go his mandatory three times.

On this meeting night, while they usually carpooled with Sue Ellen, John wanted a few minutes alone with his wife on the way to the hall. He felt a distance growing between them, and he was eager to try to close it. John opened the passenger door of their '95 Chevy Blazer, just like when he and Loretta were dating. He wanted to start remembering all the little niceties that he forgot along the way.

"Here, let me help you in, my dear."

She smiled but did not reply.

Where John grew older, Loretta seemed to stay much the same, at least physically. She was not the easygoing girl he remembered from high school, but he now thought he was going out with a high-class debutante. Ever since she started hanging around Sue Ellen Norris, she's changed. It was not overnight. He left one morning for work and caught Loretta already up, putting on make-up. She asked, "How do I look?" "You look wonderful, honey," he said. She eventually stopped asking. Bags of clothes lay strewn around their room at times, and sometimes Loretta hung them all up while Scott thrashed in his crib, crying. John arrived home in disbelief at times like these. Despite their issues, John didn't believe in divorce. He thought things would work themselves out.

84

Loretta pulled out her compact and dabbed her face in a few places on the five-minute drive to the Village Hall.

"Honey, you look great."

"Uh-huh. I just need a few touch-ups."

John reached over and closed the make-up mirror.

"Why don't we talk anymore?" he asked.

"Oh, well. What do you want to talk about, John? What should we talk about?"

"I don't know...anything. Tell me something I don't know."

Loretta paused and looked out the window. There were a lot of things she could tell him, an awful lot of things – a lot of godawful things. Yet, she decided to go the safe route.

"I'm giving a presentation at the board meeting tonight. I should have told you. I'm sorry."

"You are? Well, that's something. On what?"

She flipped open her make-up mirror again and dabbed her face once more.

"Sue Ellen named me co-chair of the Neighborhood Watch Committee," she said. "The board wants us both to give a quick five-minute presentation on how the committee is doing."

"Oh. Good for you. I'm... I'm proud of you."

"Thanks."

"Why didn't you tell me?"

"I...I don't know. We just never talk anymore, is all."

"Well, I am your husband. I'm all ears." John reached over for her hand, smiling.

Loretta held it like she was holding a stranger's hand, distant and cold.

John slid his hand back and sighed and stared at the road ahead.

"I love you, Loretta."

"I know you do, John. I know."

They pulled up to the Village Hall, and Loretta wasted no time getting out of the car to walk a few steps across the parking lot. She wrapped her arms around Sue Ellen in a great bear hug. John locked the car, watched the pair power walk ahead of him towards the hall, and frowned.

6

Sue Ellen and Loretta looked like twins. Both wore the same purple blazer, white heels, and hair styled in a bob. The only thing separating their outfits was the color of their skirts.

Sue Ellen and Loretta's presentation was first on the agenda following the call to order and pledge of allegiance.

"And now the board will hear from Mrs. Casey and Ms. Norris on their status of the Historic District Neighborhood Watch."

John watched from the front row in the boardroom. The six trustees, along with Sheila Goldman, were all present, sitting atop their sanctum at the front of the room.

Sue Ellen rose from her seat first with the confidence of a woman who had made these presentations before. She motioned to Loretta, and John witnessed a hint of nervousness in his wife's face.

The board set up a projector with a screen facing the left wall. While Loretta prepared the projector, Sue Ellen circled her way around the board members to hand out documents.

Loretta fumbled, trying to turn the projector on and move it to the right location. Sue Ellen had already finished passing out their documents and patiently awaited Loretta's handling of the technology. John bit his lower lip and wanted to help his wife but restrained himself. A couple of board members rocked in their seats, but Mayor Goldman smiled, patiently waiting for someone to begin speaking.

After a few minutes of tinkering with the projector and what felt like forever to Loretta, the projector's light switched on. The title read, "Historic District Neighborhood Watch Update."

"Sorry for the delay," Loretta said.

"Sue Ellen, did you want to get us started?"

But Sue Ellen simply shook her head. "It's your presentation," she said.

"Board members, I have confidence that Mrs. Casey can lead this presentation as I have named her the co-coordinator of the Neighborhood Watch Committee."

John watched his wife gulp as the trustees turned their heads from Sue Ellen towards Loretta. Mayor Goldman still wore a smile. Loretta's mind raced, thinking her friend left her up there to dry.

A moment of silence followed, but then Loretta switched to the next slide and started speaking. She sounded confident and even started talking without looking at the screen. Since Sue Ellen and I joined forces on the Neighborhood Watch, our no-crime initiative has had positive effects throughout the entire town. Crimes previously committed by Historic District residents outside the Historic District have dramatically decreased due to our efforts. Carjackings and burglaries are down thirty percent, and disturbances of the peace calls are down forty-five percent, as indicated by this graph."

Loretta switched slides. Smiles formed on the faces of Sue Ellen and the trustees. As Loretta continued to speak, John's heart swelled with pride for his wife.

"Our residents are also staying in line with the rules and guidelines of the town. According to the town-wide rules and guidelines study last year, the Historic District scored the highest marks in maintaining those rules and guidelines daily. To achieve that, Sue Ellen and I have regularly reminded residents of the rules and regulations."

Trustee George Ladwick asked a question.

"Excuse me, Mrs. Casey, but how have you reminded the residents?"

"We have reminded them through the mail that they need to keep referring back to their books from time to time and have talked to them about the rules and regulations at parties and whenever or wherever we see them."

"Thank you, Mrs. Casey."

Loretta finished her presentation by talking about their plans for the committee going forward.

"We want to take the Watch to the next level this coming year by promoting the Social Norms area of the book. If residents are following the social norms, crime will continue to decrease and stay down. It can only positively influence the town and those who come into Ridgeport. With that being said, 'Love thy neighbor" and "Love thy Ridgeport."

Mayor Goldman responded by saying, "Well done. I think both of you are making healthy strides in the Neighborhood Watch, and we cannot wait to see what comes out of your Social Norms initiative. Thank you both."

Sue Ellen gave Loretta a thumbs up, and Loretta turned off the projector. They both took their seats opposite John, and the meeting continued as usual.

Following the three-hour meeting that concerned sewer and street repair, the Caseys made their way to the parking lot. Loretta and Sue Ellen exchanged a hug while John started up the Blazer.

"You were wonderful in there, Lor'," Sue Ellen said with a huge smile.

"Thanks. Do you really think so?"

"I know so."

"Thanks. I tried my best and...."

"We'll celebrate tomorrow with the ladies. Nanny will watch the boys. What do you say?"

"Sure! That sounds great."

They exchanged another hug, and Loretta hopped in the car with John.

She was still on cloud nine, but John was tired after the three-hour meeting. Nevertheless, he flashed his wife a grin and patted her on the shoulder.

"Hey, kiddo, I'm proud of you. You were great up there."

"What? Oh, you really think so?"

"I know so."

Loretta smiled warmly at John. It was the first genuine smile she had given him in quite some time. She reached out, and they held hands like they were dating again.

"I just have one question, honey."

"What's that, John?"

"What's this 'social norms' business?"

"Huh? What do you mean?"

"I mean, you're not really serious about enforcing that, are you? Say I want to wear jeans outside one day to go to the store. You won't give me a hard time about that, right?"

Loretta yanked her hand away from her husband and stared out at the road.

"Everything I said there, I was serious about."

"Oh, I see."

John nodded and did not say anything the rest of the way home. Loretta chewed her fingernails and looked out the window.

7

Crime really was unheard of in Ridgeport. The Caseys left their garage door open one night by mistake (John had forgotten to close it after putting the lawnmower back). The next day everything was still there, intact. Riley Wrobel left his bike unchained outside Our Lady of St. John's school every day, along with several other kids. No one ever stole them. Michael Gerden, the last employee to leave Ridgeport

Bank and Trust, forgot to lock the door one night. When the employees returned in the morning, no one had grabbed the money. Call it luck, but Ridgeport had to be the safest town in America.

8

Luckily for Matt and Scott, Stella was a great nanny. She might as well have been their mother. She cooked for them, helped them with their homework, gave them chores around the house, and spent time with them. They respected her in a way they could not respect their own moms. But even with all the love and attention that Stella tried to give the boys, they were still out of the house most of the time, especially in the summer.

The boys even shared their idea for the trench with Stella. Stella's eyes would light up as if what they were saying was the most important thing in all the world. The day following the board meeting, Matt and Scott tried to take off from Sue Ellen's house early in the morning undetected.

"Don't you think you should tell your mother you're runnin' off?" Stella asked with her hands on her wide hips.

Matt paused and then shook his head.

"Nah, she doesn't care. Besides, she's still in bed. Can't you just tell her for us, Auntie Stella?"

"Yeah, can't you?" Scott asked.

Stella sighed and slid her old Revue glasses back on her nose. She shook her head and hesitated but gave in to her boys.

"Alright, but you be back for supper. I'm making meatloaf, your favorite."

"Will do! Thanks, Auntie Stella," Matt said.

Stella smiled and motioned for them to get out of there. They darted out, and she blew a grey hair out of her eye and pulled it back into her bun.

She had never outwardly questioned her as a mother in all the years she worked for Sue Ellen, but she did that day. It was 9:30 before she awoke, a full hour after the boys left for their work on the trench. She shuffled into the expansive kitchen, asking Stella to put on her cup of coffee. Sue Ellen settled at the kitchen table and began reading *The Ridgeport News*, but a few minutes passed, and still, there was no coffee. Stella was nowhere to be found.

"Stella? Where are you? I asked if you could get my coffee."

She set the paper down and ventured over to the front room to see Stella sitting in the fauteuil chair and then seemed confused as Stella motioned Sue Ellen to sit down opposite her.

"This is highly irregular. What is the matter? Are you sick?" Sue Ellen asked.

"It's about Matt. You don't spend enough time with him."

Sue Ellen's concerned look soured, and her eyes burned right through Stella's.

"What?" she asked through clenched teeth.

"He left an hour ago with Scott to go dig a trench in the forest preserve. Did you know that?"

"And you let him go?!"

Stella closed her eyes and took a deep breath before continuing.

"He...it... it's important to him, to them."

"I don't care. I don't care! Who made you their mother!"

"I'm sorry, Sue Ellen."

"Call me ma'am, please. Where are your social norms in this house? Do not forget your place!"

Stella hung her head, regretting she said anything.

"Yes, ma'am."

"Never, ever challenge my parenting techniques again. Do you hear me? No one loves that kid more than I do!"

Stella simply nodded and kept her head to the floor.

"Now, make me some coffee. Loretta and I are going to the country club today, and I want to get ready soon."

"Yes, ma'am. I'm sorry, ma'am."

"It's alright. You didn't know. Just don't let it happen again."

"Um, Stella? Make two cups. One for Loretta too?"

"Sure, Sue, I mean, ma'am."

Stella hurried back with two cups of coffee without saying a word. Sue Ellen placed one of the cups on the coffee table and took a sip of the other.

"This is disgusting, Nanny! She threw the piping-hot coffee on Stella's dress, burning through the fabric. Stella cried out in pain.

"Make two different cups. Use a different batch. This must be a bad batch. Then change your clothes. Can't have you walking around here like that. And mop up that mess on the floor. Now!"

Stella did as she asked, and from there on out, Sue Ellen always referred to her as 'Nanny.' Only Matt and Scott continued to refer to her as Stella.

9

The band held no meeting that day since they knew the summer project for the next few weeks. The cool morning weather made for perfect digging, and the boys were eager to start on their clubhouse. They each carried their shovels to the spot east of the swimming hole. Scott remembered to bring a tape measure to mark off the six feet by ten feet, and Matt placed sticks at each side of the trench.

The morning sun shone brilliantly through the canopy of oaks and maples, and the boys looked at each other, wondering who would be the first to dig. Just as they were about to nominate Scott, a gorgeous white-tailed deer strolled out of the brush toward Scott. The rest of the group did not say a word and stood a few feet away from him. The deer did not appear frightened, and had it been Jimmy standing there, he probably would have run the other way. The deer stood only about a foot away. Instinctively, Scott moved forward to pet his fine coat. To the band's surprise, the deer allowed him to do it. The band gave each other perplexed looks. Deer just did not behave like that. But just as Riley yelled, "Man, Scott, let me pet her!" the deer bucked and pranced back into the brush. The band stood there in disbelief. Scott shared a laugh with Matt about how he met a new friend, and with that, the digging commenced.

10

After the boys dug for about half an hour and scratched the surface of what would be the trench, Riley started to complain of the rising humidity. Matt and Scott threw their shovels to the side after hearing Riley complain, and so the band all agreed to take a break in the swimming hole.

But instead of playing Jaws, the band talked Shop. Talking Shop involved talking about pop culture or sports or video games. Anything the boys could talk or debate, they did.

"Hey, you guys gonna go see *Independence Day*?" Matt asked.

"Yeah, I wanna see that!" Scott exclaimed.

"Yeah, but I don't think my mom will let me go," chimed Jimmy.

"Same. Our mom wouldn't take us there on account of it being PG-13 and all," Riley said.

"Can you guys get one of your moms to take us?" Riley asked.

Matt and Scott turned to each other and did not think either of them would be available for that, but knew Stella would.

"Yes. I think we can find someone," Matt said.

"Great. Let's go the weekend it opens– Fourth of July, right?" Riley said.

"Sounds good to me," Matt said.

"Matt, do you think aliens exist?" Jimmy asked nervously.

"Sure do. There must be more than our everyday lives here. Everything is too perfect here in Ridgeport for there not to be some chaos out there in the universe, Jimbo."

"l suppose you're right," Jimmy said.

Then they all turned their attention to the Chicago Bulls and if they thought Michael had it in him to lead the Bulls to another title that year.

They eventually decided to resume digging but only dug for about another twenty minutes before jumping back in the swimming hole. And this is how it went for the next few hours. The band only dug about six inches down into the proposed ten-foot-deep trench. Their arms hung tired, and even though they had taken breaks, their bodies ached from digging. They threw the shovels in the would-be trench and called it quits for the day.

11

The moms rode off in Sue Ellen's '96 midnight blue 3 Series BMW Convertible to the country club. She bought a new car every few years because she got bored of the old one, she said. As she blasted Alanis Morissette's "Ironic" with the top down, the two mothers headed off to their club, acting like high school girls.

Women of high society often met at the country club to discuss their husbands, their kids, or the town over brunch or tea while the men golfed outside or ate in the lounge. They either gathered outside under the white tents with round white tables and white chairs or grabbed a seat in the

Overlook Restaurant above the lounge, which gave views of the course. Today, they made their way to the Overlook.

As one of two fine dining restaurants in town, Sue Ellen's crew visited the Overlook so often they reserved their six-person table. In addition to Sue Ellen and Loretta, there was Margaret Reed, the head of the Neighborhood Watch in the Heartland Ridgeport District, Nancy Harkinson, owner of the Ridgeport Boutique, Vivica Harrison, principal of Ridgeport Junior High School, and Village Trustee Juanita Alvarez, who normally joined them. Even Mayor Sheila Goldman met the group from time to time. When Loretta first dined with the group in 1996, she felt more than intimidated by being part of the elite women in town. She quickly found that she belonged here, though, among like-minded individuals.

You had to be invited to be part of the women's empowerment group. Before Loretta and Margaret showed up, four members sat at the table. The group had talked about adding more when the time was right but seemed content with the six for now. Meetings were informal, but no one seemed to want to miss one.

When Loretta and Sue Ellen arrived, they were the first customers in the Overlook. A gracious male host led Loretta and Sue Ellen to their favorite table in the corner of the room, and they both sat in their usual seats next to one another.

"Is there anything I can get you, two lovely ladies, right now? The breakfast buffet should be up in about a half-hour. You're still a little early."

"Just some water Marco. Thank you," Loretta said.

Marco bowed and walked away. Sue Ellen looked over at Loretta and smiled.

"Speaking up for yourself now, huh?"

"What do you mean?"

"Well, you usually have me order first."

"Ha, what difference does it make?"

"Oh, it doesn't, Lor. It's just interesting, is all."

Sue Ellen grabbed Loretta's hand and looked out at the golfers. Now it was Loretta's turn to smile.

"So, my nanny basically said I'm a bad parent today."

"She what?"

"Yeah. Can you believe that? Can you think of anyone who cares more for their son than me?"

Sue Ellen looked at Loretta for confirmation, and then Marco came by with the two glasses of water.

"No, I can't."

"Right. That bitch."

Loretta gasped at Sue Ellen's lack of decorum but comforted her friend.

"I'm okay, thanks. You're good to me. I'm lucky to have someone like you, Lor," said Sue Ellen.

"Yes."

"You are good to me, aren't you?"

"Well, of course."

"Good."

Sue Ellen swallowed and rubbed Loretta's hand. She straightened up and smiled again. Then she apologized. Another couple of minutes passed, and still, there was no sign of anyone else in the restaurant.

"So, what'd you think of me up there speaking at the board meeting? Really knocked em' dead, huh?"

"Yeah, girl. I am so proud of you. You are growing into your own there."

Loretta noticed that Sue Ellen was still in shambles from the whole nanny thing, so she tried to make her laugh.

"Well, maybe one day I can do what you do, huh? Be a superhero, and run the neighborhood?"

"Run the neighborhood?"

Loretta began to laugh at Sue Ellen's confused face and continued.

"Yeah, and then you could assist me!"

Sue Ellen's expression switched from confused to stonewalled, and Loretta did not notice through her busy laughter.

"That would be the day," Sue Ellen said.

Marco came back to refill the waters, and as he did, Sue Ellen thanked him and asked him for an iced tea and one of his finest special drinks. Marco raised an eyebrow, but Sue Ellen kept smiling, and he hurried off with the water glasses.

Loretta finally stopped laughing and apologized for her behavior now.

"What? Oh no, it was funny. It was a real hoot," Sue Ellen said.

12

Marco returned with the drinks and said the buffet should be ready in about fifteen minutes.

"Do you know what that is?"

"Iced tea?"

"Close. That's a Long Island Iced Tea, Lor.'"

"What? Are you serious?"

"I figured a special occasion to celebrate that hell of a speech warranted a little toast is all. You gotta break some rules occasionally, or you'll go crazy around here. Everyone does it."

Loretta rocked in her seat and rubbed her temple. She could not believe that just yesterday she was preaching social norms alongside this woman, and now she wanted her to break a town rule.

"Where...how did you even get this?"

"Powerful people have their ways. Certain establishments carry alcohol. You just have to be the right person, know who to ask, when to ask, how to ask."

Loretta could not believe what she was hearing. She hadn't had a Long Island Iced Tea in forever, and she did not drink in public since moving to Ridgeport. The devil on her left shoulder was egging her on. The constant need to please Sue Ellen was pushing her forward.

"You're drinking with me?"

"It's a toast, silly. Duh."

"What about the rest of the group?"

"They're not coming today. This is just you and me. So, no one will know."

Loretta nodded and felt a little better. The idea of breaking a rule invigorated her. She closed her eyes and stretched her hand around the tall, cool glass. When she opened her eyes, she saw Sue Ellen smiling at her.

"Here's to Loretta, someone I am proud to call my friend, and someone coming into her own," Sue Ellen said.

Then they clinked their glasses and drank. By the time the buffet opened fifteen minutes later, Loretta had finished her drink filled with Tequila, vodka, Triple sec, and rum. She smacked her lips and felt a buzz coming on. Then, Marco came back and disposed of the evidence.

13

"How was it?" Sue Ellen asked and smiled.

"It was perfect," Loretta said through slurred speech.

"I am so glad that you liked it."

At that very moment, the rest of the group waltzed to the table – Margaret, Vivica, Nancy, and Juanita. Sue Ellen stood up and exchanged smiles and hugs. Loretta's eyes bulged, and her heart raced as she noticed the rest of the group coming their way. Loretta stared at Sue Ellen, flabbergasted that she had lied to her. "But why would she do that?" she wondered.

"Loretta, where are your manners? Stand up and say hello to the group," Sue Ellen said.

Loretta struggled to her feet, swayed, and as she did, she threw up all over Vivica. She started to apologize but then decided to make an awkward run for the restroom.

"She's not feeling very well. I am so sorry, Vivica," Sue Ellen said. "It just so happens that I brought a new dress in the car today, and I think you're about my size. I'll get it, and you can change."

Vivica attempted a smile as bile ran down Loretta's purple sundress and into the carpet. A busboy hurried to clean up the mess.

When Loretta finally did come back, her new outfit hung over her empty chair.

"Well, we're all going to have a good laugh about this one day, aren't we?" Sue Ellen asked as if telling a joke. "Jokes are fun, aren't they, Loretta? So much fun."

Loretta, her head aching and deeply embarrassed, burped and asked if Sue Ellen could drive her home.

"Now? The party is just getting started."

"Please. I am not feeling well," Loretta pleaded.

Sue Ellen smiled and apologized to the group.

"It's okay. You go on ahead. It was an accident, Loretta. Do not worry about it," Vivica said. "Besides, I got a new dress out of it!"

Loretta attempted a smile, and as Sue Ellen got up from the table, she locked arms with Loretta and helped her out of the restaurant.

As they walked out of the place and into the lot, Loretta asked Sue Ellen, "You didn't drink all of yours, did you?"

"No, I did, honey. I just ordered a regular iced tea for myself. You see, next time you play a joke on me like that, expect to be able to take one back. No hard feelings."

And as they left to get into her Beamer, Sue Ellen turned on the radio, and Morissette's "Ironic" played once again.

When the women arrived back at Sue Ellen's place, Sue Ellen helped Loretta into something more comfortable and onto the guest bed for rest. She reminded her that if she had only behaved herself, she would not have to make an example out of her.

"Laughing that loudly in public, Loretta…I mean, really. And at my expense? What are you? A baboon? I named you the co-chair of the Neighborhood Watch Committee, and I expected you to act like it."

Loretta drooped her shoulders and any confidence she had that morning was drained from her. She suddenly felt horrible for her behavior in public and felt guilty for how she treated her friend.

"I am sorry, Sue Ellen, really. I didn't think about what I was doing."

Sue Ellen ignored her for a moment but tucked the covers tightly around her.

"Sue Ellen, are we good?" A single tear started to form out of Loretta's right eye.

Sue Ellen sat beside her on the bed, smiled, gave her a peck on the forehead, and lightly rubbed her short hair.

"Oh, darling. Of course, we're good. Just learn from your mistakes is all. I've been a resident here longer than you have. You'll always be my student. And I'll always be your teacher. You remember that."

"Well, you're a good teacher."

"Okay, now get some rest, student."

Sue Ellen left the bed, but she blew Loretta a kiss before she closed the door. Loretta opened her hand to receive it and smiled as she did so.

"Now, get some rest."

"Okay."

Sue Ellen stepped downstairs to find Matt and Scott coming in the door. The frustration she felt that morning returned. Sue Ellen's fists clenched in a tight ball, and she gritted her teeth. She did all she could to not stomp down the stairs towards the boys who did not ask for her permission to run out of the house in the early morning hours.

She caught them by surprise. Just as they bent down to remove their shoes, Sue Ellen stood right beside the two. They both jumped back when they turned around, knowing they were caught. The boys nearly tripped over their own shoes and fell back headfirst into the doorway. They did not expect Ms. Norris home this early, and now they knew they were dead meat. Her lips twisted into a snarl, and her face beat red as the sun. They knew they were in for it.

"Matt, you are grounded for a week. You will not see your friends. You will stay in the house and will not be allowed to play with any of your toys or watch TV. You will have to do chores and reread the book. Is that clear?"

"But…"

"Is. That. Clear?"

Matt hung his head before looking up at his mom and said, "Yes. All clear."

"As for you, Scott, I can't send you home since your mother is not feeling well. Plus, your dad is working, so you both will be grounded for the rest of the day. But you will not be spending time in Matt's room. Oh no, that would be cheating since all his toys are in there. You will both be grounded to the basement. I know how much you two love the basement."

Scott and Matt stared at each other and felt a chill run down their spines. They always sensed the basement might be haunted. Houses this old carried with them leaking noises, cold cement walls, dusty old furniture, and odd smells. Ms.

Norris never used the basement except to store antiques and holiday decorations. These antiques consisted of an old doll collection and old signed photographs. There was nothing to do down there except feel the cold, damp air and feel creeped out the entire time. Scott tried to change the subject to delay the inevitable.

"What's wrong with my mom? Is she okay?"

"She's fine, dear. Just a little cold is all."

"Can I go see her?"

"I'm afraid she is resting. You can't disturb her right now."

"Well, shouldn't you ask her what my punishment should be?"

Sue Ellen laughed at this and said she was sure she would agree on this matter.

"Enough of this. To the basement, both of you."

She led the boys to the basement and said that she would bring them both down bologna sandwiches.

"Bologna? You know we hate bologna!"

"I know you do," Sue Ellen said. "Eat it, or go hungry."

The boys hung their heads, and the two of them felt their palms begin to sweat as Sue Ellen opened the squeaky door that led to the place they would spend the rest of the day.

"Down you go."

They hesitated but finally descended as if going to their ultimate demise. In the boys' eyes, they thought that they were.

As the door shut and locked behind them, they knew there was no going back.

16

When Matt and Scott did not return from lunch to meet Riley and Jimmy at the trench, Riley sat in the six-inch deep hole next to Jimmy and looked through the tree-line, expecting to see them. As each minute passed, Riley grew more restless. And as Riley grew more restless, so did Jimmy.

Sitting in the hole led to pacing, and pacing led to yelling about how stupid the project was in the first place.

"What now? Do they think they can just run off and leave us here to do their dirty work? Well, I don't think so, Jim. I don't think so one bit. If they're not here tomorrow, I ain't comin' back."

"But what if something happened, Riley?"

"Oh yeah? Like what?!"

Riley was getting madder by the second and was now not even looking through the tree line. He was hoping that they would not come just so he could stay mad.

"Nah, they want us to do this, and then they can just enjoy it. Don't you see?"

"Yeah. I guess so."

Riley nodded and threw his shovel in the hole. It landed spade first and wiggled back and forth like the sword that pierced the ground in *Braveheart*.

"All right, Jim. Let's get outta here. If they're not here tomorrow, I say don't do this stupid digging again. Deal?"

"Sure, Riley."

And with that, Riley nodded again and led his brother out of the woods and towards home.

17

The boys tried a light switch at the bottom of the stairs but were not surprised when the bulb burned out.

A late 1970s model orange cotton couch with a white line pattern sat in front of a rabbit-ear television. The two boys parked themselves there. Dust sprang up from the cushions as they sat down.

"Gross," Scott said. "Think there are rats down here?"

103

"Let's try not to think about it, okay? But yes, there are rats down here."

The boys gulped and looked at the old grey Phillips TV. Matt hopped off the couch and turned the knob but was met with static. He turned the knob again and again, but there was nothing but distorted horizontal lines up and down the screen.

"This sucks, Matt."

"Tell me about it."

Scott looked at the TV's grey lines scrolling up and down like a conveyor belt and remembered that Riley and Jimmy were waiting for them at the trench.

"What will Riley and Jimmy think when we don't show?"

"Relax. We'll be there tomorrow."

"But your mom said you're grounded all week."

"Pff. She's never around. I'll be out of here by tomorrow."

The boys looked around the huge expanse of the dark basement. The sound of drops of water on a lonely pipe filled the room again. The doorway upstairs seemed so far away now.

"We need to do something, Matt, to, you know, keep our mind busy. We're going to be down here awhile."

"Agreed."

"Let's explore this place."

"Now you're talkin'."

18

Using their hands to guide them, the boys found their way into the utility room. A small beam of light shone from a dusty window. Their nerves settled from the creepy drip noise as they found the leaky pipe coming from over the water heater. As soon as Scott started to laugh, he thought he felt a rat run past his ankle, and he nearly jumped out of his skin. The two darted out of the utility room, and Scott slammed the door behind them. With his heart still racing, he admitted to Matt, "Rats are my number one fear." Matt chuckled and put his hand on his shoulder.

"It may not have even been a rat. It could have been a mouse. You just think you saw one."

"I know what I felt…I…I think it was a rat," Scott panted.

"Okay. Whatever. So why the fear of rats anyway? I mean, there are scarier things to be afraid of."

"Well, you ever see that movie, *Ben*?"

"Nah."

"See that movie, and you'll see what I'm talking about. It's like *Gremlins*, but with rats."

Matt laughed again and assured him they would not go back to the utility room. He asked if he still wanted to explore or if he preferred staring at the broken TV.

"No, let's see what else is in this creepy basement."

"Just as long as we don't find any more rats."

19

The boys stumbled across a room on the opposite side of the basement that was shut tight with a combo lock. They had never noticed this room. Scott and Matt nodded and smiled at one another. They had to figure out the code for the lock, and from the small amount of grey light coming in from the adjacent egress window, the boys had just enough to make out the numbers on the lock.

"It's probably my birthday or something. Try 2386 Scott."

Scott turned the combo, but it would not budge.

"Okay, try 8623."

Once again, he tried the combo, and it would not open.

"Try my mom's birthday. 3858."

Scott shook his head no, and the boys started to look frustrated.

They tried (5838), combinations of Stella's birthday (9226), Loretta's birthday (4354), John's birthday (5553), and even Scott's birthday (7786). Nothing cracked the lock.

"Maybe we can get something to, you know, pry it open."

"Pry it open? Are you nuts? She'll know we did that, Scott."

"Right."

"Well, are there any other combos you can think of?"

Above the door was a wooden sign with white lettering. It read "Love thy neighbor" and "Love thy Ridgeport." Scott looked at it with interest for a minute, rubbed his chin, and then looked back at the lock.

"Scott, what's the birthday for Ridgeport?"

"May 7, 1909."

"Try it."

Scott turned each number 5,7,0,9 in anticipation. Matt stood behind, hoping that would do it. On the first tug, the lock did not budge. Matt hung his head, but then Scott readjusted the number 9 and tried pulling at it again. The lock clicked and broke free. He yanked it off the latch, and the door squeaked open.

A lone pull string light hung in the middle of the room, and Matt switched it on. The boys circled the room in wonder.

20

A giant map of Ridgeport decorated the center wall, with each part of the town ---colored green, yellow, and red. A red binder laid propped open with a list of names in it on the wooden desk in front of the map. At the top of the list, read "Ridgeport Master List." The boys noticed the names, like the map, were also highlighted in green, yellow, or red. Scott found that his mom's name was highlighted in green, but his dad's name was in yellow. Matt turned the page and saw his mom's name was also green. Some of the names, such as Emma Ryan, were crossed out.

"What do you think these colors mean, Matt?"

A picture hung on the east wall of Sue Ellen shaking hands with the mayor, smiling for the cameras. A newspaper clipping about the missing Emma Ryan girl framed the spot next to it. A small bookshelf housed a few books, and one of them contained an extra copy of *Ridgeport Welcomes You: Procedures and Guidelines for Happy Living*. A book about anger management and one on social etiquette were stacked on top of each other. The book that Matt pulled out though was a scrapbook with the binding titled "Memories."

The two of them huddled around it, and instead of the scrapbook being loaded with memories about the family, it contained photos of different people from the town. They flipped over a picture of Emma Ryan with the newspaper headline "MISSING: Can you help Ridgeport find Emma Ryan?"

On the back of her page in the scrapbook was a handwritten listing of all the social norms and rules she broke in her time in Ridgeport. There was a surprising amount:

- Stayed out past curfew
- Did not dress appropriately in public
- Cursed in public
- Caught smoking in public
- Did not wipe down exercise equipment after use
- Did not renew residency card
- Did not greet people with the town motto
- Did not always attend church
- Did not attend at least one social event per year
- Did not smile wherever and whenever possible

A confusing list of signatures from the board of trustees and mayor Sheila Goldman followed. Emma's father and village trustee Patrick Ryan was mysteriously absent from the signatures.

The boys' eyes caught a photo on the following page of Sue Henderson with the headline "Mayor's daughter Sue goes missing." Then once again, on the back, the board of trustees filed at least ten grievances against her. There were other pages from different years. One page was for Steven Barnes, circa 1922.

"Do you think he's related to your dad's friend, Peter?"

"I...I don't know Matt."

The boys started to flip the pages again. They spotted a few residents they remembered: Michael Ivery, a kid in their third-grade class, and Sarah Johnson, a teenage lifeguard. Their yearbook photos highlighted their pages with activities they were involved in.

"I remember them. Michael's mom took him out of school and had him homeschooled. And Sarah stopped working at the pool in the middle of the summer a couple of years back. Remember?" Matt asked.

On the back of their page stated their violations, which numbered nine for each of them. Signatures followed.

The boys heard the basement door open and dropped the book mid-read. They jetted out of the forbidden room, quietly bolted the lock back, and flew back to the couch just as Sue Ellen made her way down the stairs. Sweat dripped from their hands and temples.

"I brought you, boys, a couple of bologna sandwiches and water. If you eat them, and you don't make any noise down here, I just might bring you some pudding cups."

"Oh boy!" Scott said under his breath.

But Matt nudged Scott in the side, and Scott remembered the investigation and that they may not want to be interrupted anymore – even if it meant eating pudding cups.

"Um, we're actually not that hungry. The sandwiches are fine."

Sue Ellen gave the boys a strange look as she handed them their plates.

"No pudding cups? Say, why are you boys sweatin'? It's not that warm down here, is it?"

"We uh, we were doing jumping jacks, Ms. Norris," Scott said.

Matt nodded, hoping she would bite the lie.

"Yeah, we were pretending we were in the military."

"Uh, whatever. Just don't let me hear you upstairs. Your mom is trying to sleep."

"Will do, Ms. Norris."

And with that, she smiled, turned, and headed back upstairs and out of sight.

The boys wiped the sweat from their palms and foreheads and breathed a little easier. Matt took one bite of his sandwich, and if he were not so hungry, he would have fed it to Scott's rat. The water she gave them was lukewarm, but they happily downed it to get the taste of bologna out of their mouth. They hated bologna more than any other food. After choking their sandwiches down, they made their way to the room, unlocked the combo, and snooped around once more.

21

Just as Matt entered the forbidden room, Sue Ellen returned through the basement door and down the stairs. Only this time, he did not hear her. Matt continued to rummage through the room, looking for anything else out of the ordinary.

Meanwhile, Scott looked up from the dusty couch to find Sue Ellen coming toward him. He froze, and his mind raced to think up a lie as to where Matt could be.

"I came down to collect your plates. Where's Matt?"

"Oh, he's in the utility room."

"The utility room? Doing what?"

"Matt!" Sue Ellen yelled.

Matt froze in front of the door. It stood open a crack, and he was pretty sure the combo had fallen on the floor.

"Matt! Why are you in the utility room?"

"He's uh, well, we saw a rat. We think we did, and he's just making sure."

"A rat?"

Sue Ellen made her way to the room, but Scott shook his head. He realized he messed up with that lie. He grabbed the glass plate he was going to give back to her and instinctively threw it down on the cement floor. It broke into a million different pieces.

"What the hell! What is wrong with you...you little brat!"

"I'm sorry. It was an accident."

Sue Ellen glared at him.

"I'm going upstairs to get the broom and dustpan. When I get back, you will pick up every piece of that plate. You hear me?"

"Yes, ma'am."

She grunted and made her way back upstairs. Once Matt heard the basement door close, he bolted from the secret room. He picked up the lock, but it slipped out from his sweaty palms. He breathed out and tried again. He turned the combo, locked the door, and sprinted back toward the couch. Sweat dripped down his shirt and under his armpits.

"Thanks. I owe you one," Matt said.

"Don't sweat it."

"Ha, good one. I guess I am a sweaty mess."

The boys lounged on the couch, just as they did when they first arrived in the basement. They did not say anything for a second but tried to calm down from what had just transpired. Before they could get a word out, Sue Ellen descended with the broom, dustpan, and small garbage bin in her hands.

110

"Matt. There you are. Find the rat you were supposedly looking for?"

"No. But we did see it. We did."

Sue Ellen raised an eyebrow but then could see that they might be telling the truth.

"Well, I suppose this is an old basement. Maybe I should get pest control down here."

She handed the broom and pan to Scott. "Clean," she commanded. She waited, tapping her foot next to the broken pieces. Matt sat by, enjoying Scott's Cinderella moment. Once he finished, Scott handed her the cleaning materials and responded to her one-word demand with one of his own, "Done." Sue Ellen scanned the area, grunted once more, grabbed Matt's plate, and marched back upstairs.

22

They both itched to return to the room but decided it was enough excitement for the day. And then Matt remembered the pair of Walkie Talkies that Stella got them for Christmas and knew that they would come in handy in times like these. Matt and Scott agreed to communicate via their Walkie Talkies while Matt served his sentence in the basement. He wanted to stay at least a day down there and find out what else was in the room. They shook hands on the deal, and Scott commended Matt for his bravery. They used their imagination to ease their anxiety during the rest of their time in that dungeon together.

The boys played War and pretended the basement was being infiltrated by Nazi soldiers. They hid behind the couch and fired their machine guns, or their fingers, at incoming forces approaching from the southwest, or the utility room. Occasionally, Matt or Scott would fling a grenade over the couch and imitate a whirring noise as they tossed it over. Then they crouched down and covered their ears. They rushed down the hallway when the coast was clear, pushing the Nazis back. After a while, Sue Ellen returned, and their fun departed. The war was over.

"Scott? Your mom is awake. She wants to take you home."

Scott nodded but turned back Matt's way. He acted like he had a Walkie over his mouth, and Matt reciprocated. Sue Ellen took no notice, and that was the point.

23

As Loretta walked Scott back home, she did not say a word. She was trying to forget about how she had embarrassed her friend, and now she tried blocking out the news that Scott ran off with Matt without permission. Once inside the Casey household, they kicked off their shoes in silence. Loretta, never the enforcer, stared at her son.

"Just wait until your father gets home and hears about this! Now, go to your room! I'm not leaving the house or letting you out of my sight!"

Scott slumped his shoulders and scurried away upstairs. Loretta failed to remember that John had his poker night once a week at Peter's, so he would not be home until late. She'd just have to wait a little longer for Scott's punishment.

With John out working the next day and Loretta still in bed, Scott saw it as his perfect opportunity to take off for the Wrobel house to work on the trench. He picked up his red and white Dino bike with chrome handlebars and his raised seat in the backyard, perfect for pulling wheelies, and shot off for the Wrobel's home at around 8:30. Scott planned to explain their absence yesterday, and when they found out the news about the room, Riley and Jimmy would hang on to his every word.

The morning sun already baked Scott's pale skin. The humidity first thing in the morning made Scott brush the sweat from his forehead just a few minutes into the bike ride. After about fifteen minutes of sweaty pedaling, Scott arrived at the Wrobel's front porch. He set up the kickstand, rang the bell, and put on his best smile for Mrs. Wrobel at the front door.

"Hi, Mrs. Wrobel. Are Riley and Jimmy home?"

Unlike Riley's pessimistic personality, Mrs. Wrobel was all sweetness and optimism. Scott and Matt figured he got his tough shell from his old man. Nonetheless, the boys loved Riley anyway.

"Oh, I'm sorry, dear. Riley and Jimmy already went over to your house to find you. You can wait here if you'd like for when they get back?"

Scott had not thought of this possibility. Just a day after he was caught out of the house, he would be found out again. At least this time, it would not be by Sue Ellen. At least he hoped that it would not.

"It's okay, Mrs. Wrobel. Tell them to meet me at the trench."

"The trench?"

"They'll know what that means."

"Oh. Well, okay. Are you sure you would not like to come in for a minute? You look like you could use a glass of water?"

Scott shook his head and politely declined. He said that he had brought a backpack with water and snacks. Mrs. Wrobel smiled and nodded and then waved him goodbye before closing the door.

24

He figured that he might be grounded for life at home, but he tried not to think about that now. All he wanted to think about was digging the trench and telling Riley and Jimmy about their adventure in Ms. Norris' basement yesterday.

There was something about the woods that helped Scott forget about all that. He wished he could live here, safe in the trench. Scott wanted to create a new home for himself, and with each dig, he felt more independent and closer to his sense of accomplishment. Scott did not wait for Riley and Jimmy to make their way to the trench but began digging where he left off. He already wanted to jump headfirst into the swimming hole, but he needed to make way on the trench.

He dug at a fever pitch and did not even look up from the dirt for at least ten minutes. Dirt flew from the hole. He could feel his muscles swelling up and sweat pouring from his forehead. It was not until Riley and Jimmy arrived that he threw the shovel down, opened his backpack, and pulled out his water bottle. Nothing beats a chug of ice-cold water on a hot day. He learned later as an adult that the simplest things in life are truly the best things, like the first cool sip of water after working hard outside. Riley pulled up on his black BMX bike, with Jimmy holding onto his back on the pegs. He threw the BMX down to the side of the trench, and per usual, he did not waste any time getting right to the point.

"So, what gives man? Where were you and Matt yesterday? Is he coming today?"

"Yeah, is he?" echoed Jimmy.

Scott smirked, and the brothers looked at each other, confused.

"Is something funny? You left the two of us out to dry yesterday, Casey."

"We were found out, Riley. Ms. Norris grounded us."

Riley's eyes went wide, mouthed a silent "Oh," and nodded. Jimmy looked around at nothing as if he were embarrassed.

"We're sorry, man. We didn't think about that. So, you're not grounded anymore?"

"Not exactly."

114

"Not exactly? You skipped out of the house?"

"Yep."

"Dude. That's awesome."

"Didn't my mom say anything about that?"

"She didn't answer the door. Must have been asleep."

Scott breathed a little easier and shook his fist triumphantly in the air.

"And Matt? He's still grounded then?"

"Oh. Oh yeah, big time. All week."

The brothers started their way towards the shovels, but Scott stopped them.

"There's something you two need to know, though."

"What's that?"

"We found something...something that might be important."

Scott proceeded to tell them about the forbidden room with the strange map, the list of names, and the memories scrapbook. He took the Walkie Talkie out of his pack and explained that Matt would stay connected if he found anything else out of the ordinary. As skeptical as Riley usually was, Scott realized this was something he believed.

"So, what do you think this means, Scott?"

"Not sure. I just know it's weird. Who keeps a locked room full of this stuff in their house?"

Riley rubbed his chin. Jimmy looked from his brother to Scott.

"We'll just have to wait for Matt to tell us more. He's supposed to snoop through the room today."

The brothers nodded. They hung on Scott's every word and said they would keep their ears open for any transmission. Then they all agreed to get to work on the trench. Riley did not even complain about it, not once.

25

Matt never felt better to be grounded. He had an excuse to snoop around in the basement. Besides, once he felt confident that he searched every corner of that room, he would break out of the house anyway. That morning, though, his mom decided to act like a mother. Before he had the chance to run down the basement steps, Sue Ellen stopped Matt and asked him to sit on the loveseat in the front room with her. She patted the seat next to her and attempted a smile. Matt saw this as a new development. Was he ungrounded? For once in his life, Matt wanted to be sent down to the basement. He did as she asked, and she smiled at him again before looking out at the window. A distant silence followed between the two.

"When did you grow up so fast, Matty?" She turned to face the window as she said this.

Matt never saw his mom like that before.

"Mom? Are you okay?"

She turned his way and found her holding back her tears. Matt shifted in his seat but put his arm around his mom.

"It's okay, Mom."

"Is it? I lost track of my little boy along the way somewhere."

Sue Ellen pulled a few Kleenexes from her pants pocket and began wiping her eyes.

"You can do what you want. You're growing up so fast. You just don't listen. I'm just not a good mother for you."

Matt felt a pang of guilt and hung his head. At the same time, he wanted to tell her that it was true. She had not been a good mother for him. She was never around, so of course, he grew up a lot faster.

"Maybe we should start spending more time together."

"Sure. I would like that, Mom."

Matt really did like that. He wanted more attention from his mom, but he had no idea what he agreed to.

She dabbed the rest of her eyes and set the Kleenex back in her pocket.

"Good, so why don't we start with today? Let's get some ice cream at that new Wally Cone that just opened outside the mall. What do you say?"

"But I thought I was grounded?"

Sue Ellen frowned but put her arm around her son's shoulder.

"I decide when you're grounded or not. Now, do you want ice cream, or do you want to spend time in that dusty basement?"

"Well, ice cream, I guess," Matt said with a chuckle.

Sue Ellen's smile returned. She told him to get ready. She said she did not want to miss another moment with her son.

She allowed Matt to switch on the rock station as loud as he wanted, and Pearl Jam's "Alive" blared out of the BMW. Neighbors stared at Sue Ellen and Matt, but she could have cared less. As the Neighborhood Watch Committee president, she could get away with a little disturbance of the peace if she wanted to.

Matt had not had ice cream in some time and had heard Wally's was pretty good from Riley and Jimmy. His mom let him order whatever he wanted – not bad for a kid who was supposed to be grounded. His order of a triple chocolate fudge sundae with sprinkles and a cherry on top was bigger than his head. Yet Sue Ellen was good about straying away from any unhealthy foods and ordered a skinny strawberry smoothie. Sue Ellen wanted to know more about Matt's friends, and Matt asked about his mom on the Neighborhood Watch Committee. It was everything he wanted out of a mom. It was everything Matt saw from other moms. He had forgotten about the basement, about the Walkie, about the room.

They both happily ate their frozen treats, and everything was right in the world. At one point, Matt's triple fudge chocolate had smeared all over his face. Just like a mom, Sue Ellen wet a napkin and brushed it off in front of everyone. He was glad to have a mom who cared for him once. Just as he was settling into his ice cream coma, Sue Ellen threw her son a Grinch-like crooked smile.

"I know you and Scotty were in my room in the basement."

Matt froze. He searched for a lie but was caught, deer in the headlights.

"Know how I know? Go ahead and ask me. Go ahead."

But no noise could come from Matt.

"The combo numbers were not in the exact location that I placed them in when I locked it. The devil is in the details, son."

Matt forgot about the rest of his ice cream. He felt sick to his stomach, and he was not sure if that was from all the ice cream or from being caught.

"Find anything interesting?"

Matt shook his head and grew more scared of his mom than he ever thought he could be.

"I can assure you that it's only information for mommy's Neighborhood Watch Committee. That's all."

Sue Ellen finished the last few sips of her smoothie.

"Oh, and I did change that lock. You need a key to open it now. It was silly of me to think a combo would be sufficient. I do suggest you never try anything like that again. Are we clear?"

Matt nodded.

Sue Ellen's warm smile returned, and without asking if Matt was finished, she got up and began walking out. Matt wiped his face and obediently followed his mother.

26

A few hours passed, and the boys did not hear a word from Matt. It was time for Scott to check in. Riley and Jimmy took a break and grabbed a seat near the swimming hole.

"Scott to Matt, Scott to Matt. Come in, Matt."

Scott waited, but there was nothing but static on the other end.

"Scott to Matt, Scott to Matt. Come in, Matt."

Again, he heard nothing.

Scott tossed the Walkie Talkie on top of his pack and joined Riley and Jimmy beside the water. They lay in the grass, their arms throbbing from all the digging.

"Are you guys going to the Fourth of July Party at the Park?"

"We have to go, don't we?" Riley said.

"Yeah, I guess so," Scott said.

"We should see that movie, *Independence Day*," Jimmy said.

They glanced his way and nodded at the idea. Scott picked up a few stones and skipped them across the water. They hopped a few times before falling in. Riley crossed his arms over his eyes. If it were not so quiet, Scott didn't think he would have been able to hear his Walkie Talkie.

"Scott. Come in, Scott. This is Matt."

"Come in, Scott."

Scott jumped up from his spot and ran toward it. Riley and Jimmy joined him.

"Go ahead, Matt."

"I think I found something."

27

The boys held on to every word as Matt relayed his message, not about what had transpired between him and his mom at the ice cream parlor but about what he had found in the basement later that day.

"It's a poem."

The rest of the band fell silent, trying to figure out how this was significant.

"It's 'The Road Not Taken' by Robert Frost. Remember, we read him in Mrs. Glick's class?"

"Oh, yeah," Scott and Riley said.

"So…so what?" Riley asked, confused.

Well, it's right beside the door, written on a sheet of paper. Ms. Norris must have dropped it when she was changing the lock."

"Changing the lock?"

"Yeah. That's the other thing. She knew we went into the room, Scott."

He proceeded to tell them about the ice cream incident, how she found out, and how getting in the room would be virtually impossible now. Scott felt a cold chill run down his spine.

"Are you still with me? Scott?"

"Yeah. Still here."

"Well, I don't know why, but I think it might be important."

"A poem is important?" Riley butted in.

"Don't you remember what Mrs. Glick was telling us about it?"

"No, I don't, Matt. What?"

"It's about making wise decisions. It's about choosing your path in life or something. And he talks about being in the woods, like us."

"Oh, come on. It's a frickin' poem, Matt."

"Well, I still think we should look into it."

No one said anything, so Matt continued.

"Fine. I'll go to the library and read the poem again. If I can't make sense of it, then I'll drop it, okay? Okay?"

"Sounds good," everyone said.

"Alright. I miss you guys. See you soon. Over and out."

"Over and out," Scott said.

28

Loretta made it her business that Scott never left the house after that. She grounded him an additional week, and when Loretta and John were not at home, she left him with Nanny, with strict orders never to let him out of her sight. Sue Ellen likewise ordered Matt not to go anywhere for an additional week on account of his breaking into the room. When the brothers found out that they were both grounded, they vowed to continue digging, but that vow only stretched as far as a couple of hours for a one-day dig for that entire two-week period.

When Scott stayed at Matt's, they served their time in the dungeon together again but did not find the place as thrilling as before. There was no way into the room now. They needed a key, or at least a bobby pin or something. There was nothing like that in sight. They managed to get over their fear of the basement, but now they were fighting its boredom. There were only so many times they could play War. They yearned for fresh air, to go on their bikes, and to go back to the woods. To be locked down there in the summer was torture.

Matt and Scott kept reviewing the Robert Frost poem. Their last and only clue connected all the weirdness that was Sue Ellen's secret room. Matt wondered if the poem came out of the secret room. He wondered if his mom did not want the poem in there anymore. The two of them hunched over it like they were looking at an important map, dissecting every word on every line. Sue Ellen would come down the stairs at times with bologna sandwiches, and one of the boys

121

would stash the poem in their pocket or underneath the couch's cushions.

Scott brought over a pencil from his house one day, and they annotated the entire thing, line by line. Matt took the first stanza:

"Two roads diverged in a yellow wood,
And sorry I could not travel both
And be one traveler, long I stood
And looked down one as far as I could
To where it bent in the undergrowth;

"Two roads diverged? What do you suppose diverged means, Scott?"

"I think it means split off, like two different paths."

"Yellow wood? Like the woods are yellow? Like fall, maybe?" Matt asked.

They paused and looked at each other, scanning the words – undergrowth, bent, traveler, wood.

"Do you think this is about our woods?" Scott asked.

"This is an old poem. I don't think so."

"Yeah, but why does my mom have it?"

"I don't know. Let's keep reading."

"Then took the other, as just as fair,
And having perhaps the better claim,
Because it was grassy and wanted wear;
Though as for that the passing there
Had worn them really about the same,"

Matt scratched his head, and Scott reread it, trying to make sense of the words. They tried to remember what Mrs. Glick had said about this poem, but that seemed like ages ago now that it was summer.

"I'm guessing whoever this person is in this poem took the harder of the two paths, the grassy one? What do you think?" Matt asked.

"I...I think you're right."

The boys read on.

"And both that morning equally lay
In leaves no step had trodden black.
Oh, I kept the first for another day!
Yet knowing how way leads on to way,
I doubted if I should ever come back."

This stanza served even more problematic for the boys, as the only line they seemed to understand was the last.

"Whoever went on this path did not want to go back?" Scott questioned.

"Or they thought that they couldn't," Matt said.

They both nodded, and by now, Matt and Scott started to get a headache from trying so hard to figure something out from nothing. They pushed on and finished the poem.

"I shall be telling this with a sigh
Somewhere ages and ages hence:
Two roads diverged in a wood, and
I took the one less traveled by,
And that has made all the difference."

Matt and Scott reread the last stanza a few times. They figured the "Two roads diverged in a wood" was important, or it would not have been repeated. Of all the stanzas, they understood this one the best.

"So, this person took the path that was the harder one and…." Scott began.

"It was worth it," Matt finished.

"Right. Telling this with a sigh, though? What do you think that means?"

"Don't know. They are happy they did it. Or sad. I'm not sure."

The two shrugged their shoulders, and Matt rubbed his forehead in frustration. It was all they had to go on. There was no getting in that room, at least in the foreseeable future, and they were looking at anything that made any sense. They agreed that it was a good poem but did not see it as a map to some significant place or explain what those colors by the names meant. They thought it had to do with their woods, but that could have been a stretch.

"What other poems did this guy write?" Scott asked.

"I don't know. That was the only one we read in school."

"What if there are other clues we're not seeing?"

A light bulb suddenly turned on in Matt's head.

"Maybe there is a link. This is just one piece of the puzzle," Matt said.

Scott nodded, and for the first time in their lives, they got excited about poetry. They wondered how they would get their hands on the rest of Frost's poems while grounded, and then Scott had an idea. He would ask Loretta to go to the library and check out Frost's poems, so they had something to read together.

"I'll say that we really got into his poetry ever since Mrs. Glick's class and would like to read some more since we're grounded. She would have to say yes," Scott said.

They both agreed that it was a good plan, and they looked forward to finding some sort of clue to what Matt's mom was hiding in that room.

29

Loretta was pleasantly surprised to know that her son was interested in something other than running around in the woods. She checked out *The Poetry of Robert Frost: The Collected Poems, Complete and Unabridged*, and Loretta felt like she connected with her son in a way that she had not in quite some time.

He smiled widely when she handed it to him, saying, "Wow. Thanks, Mom. I love you."

It was the first time he'd said "I love you" in about a year. Loretta had not said it in about three.

Scott made sure he equipped himself with a notebook and two pencils, along with the book for his study session with Matt. He also made sure he kept all this stuff in a backpack. He did not want to take any chances should Sue Ellen see him with a book about Robert Frost. He felt like a detective. Mrs. Glick would be proud, but Scott also wanted the police chief to be proud as well. He envisioned himself before the chief with a ribbon pinned to his chest.

"And here is your ribbon of courage, Scott Casey, for finding the reason for this secret room. You and your friend Matt Norris will receive the key to the town of Ridgeport. Everything you want is yours."

Scott stared off into space for a second before forcing himself back to reality. The book of poems weighed heavy in his hands. He did not realize this poet wrote so much. He knew it wouldn't be a quick read, but he figured even if they read a few more, they could start to notice some sort of code or something. The two of them looked through some of his most famous poems: "Stopping by Woods on a Snowy Evening," "Fire and Ice," and "Acquainted with the Night," making notes and writing down words on the notebook paper that stood out.

Scott liked the two lines "And miles to go before I sleep" in the "Stopping by Woods on a Snowy Evening," and Matt wrote down how the poem "Fire and Ice" related to the Bible, where God first destroys the world by water in the great flood and then by fire in the book of Revelation.

"He seems to talk about the woods a lot," Scott said.

"He does. In the poems, he is also lonely, like one person is walking or talking," Matt said.

They tried to connect themes to Frost's other poems. They did not think the poems were exactly happy, but something was calming about them. They liked the idea of being in the woods, and it made them miss their woods even more. After reading a few poems and taking a few notes, the boys still did not know what this meant. Upon hearing Sue Ellen stepping down the basement stairs, Matt threw the book and notebook in Scott's backpack. They agreed to share the information with the brothers once they 'got out of jail' to see if they could come up with any answers.

30

By the time Scott and Matt's 'prison sentences' were up, it was already July 3. Riley and Jimmy had already gone to see *Independence Day* without them. They told them that they just couldn't wait any longer, and their dad had agreed to take them.

As they had discussed, Scott and Matt were upset with the brothers for not waiting to see it with them, but they quickly got over it when they mentioned their findings with the Robert Frost poems. They showed the brothers the notebook containing similar themes, words, and clues of what might be in the room. The band relaxed beside the swimming hole, trying to make sense of what was in the notebook, but the Wrobel brothers scratched their heads, just as Scott and Matt had over the last week. Unlike Scott and Matt, Riley shrugged his shoulders at the book.

"I see a bunch of poetry notes and two guys who had a bunch of time on their hands," Riley said.

Riley and Jimmy laughed together and handed the notebook back to them. Scott and Matt were not amused.

126

They tried to explain that they thought this was all connected and may even be a conspiracy of sorts.

"A conspiracy? Have you ever thought that your mom might just like Robert Frost? Have you ever thought of that? No. You two just went a little nutso in that basement. That's all."

"Nutso? Nutso? What about the room? Is that nutso? If the poem was on the kitchen table upstairs, then sure. But it was beside the door, Riley. It was beside the door," Matt said.

Riley rolled his eyes and suggested they go swimming. Jimmy stood there awkwardly, waiting to see what everyone else would do. What everyone else was doing was not getting ready to go swimming. With a dismissive gesture, Matt waved Riley's suggestion off, shaking his head in disgust, then stormed off. Scott turned his back on the two of them. They hopped on their bikes and rode like the wind out of there. Riley huffed but removed his shirt and jumped in. Jimmy looked on and followed his brother into the water.

31

That weekend, the annual Fourth of July party marked the next time the band saw each other. Three days passed between the incident in the swimming hole and the party, an eternity considering they made it a point to see each other every day. Their unofficial meeting at the annual party would be their last together that summer.

Peter Barnes brought his adopted daughter Josephine with him that day, and for the first time in a while, Peter gained some attention from his fellow neighbors. One neighbor was Sue Ellen. She darted over to her ex-husband with Loretta by her side like a Siamese twin. Peter laughed and ate a burger with John. Josephine stood next to them, with a plate of her own, looking awkwardly around the adults. Peter and

John were turned the other way and did not even notice Sue Ellen.

Sue Ellen felt all sorts of things as she approached Peter: anger, frustration, curiosity, and even a mild attraction. She shook off the last thought and tried to pull herself together. Here was this beautiful little girl with short black hair, green eyes, and a lovely red summer dress. She figured she was about Matt's age. She wondered where Josephine's mother was. Peter nearly choked on his burger as Sue Ellen tapped his shoulder. John turned around to see Sue Ellen and Loretta with similar smirks on their faces as if having fun at a party was some crime.

"The kids are playing at the playground," John said.

Sue Ellen ignored him and looked right from the silent Josephine and up to Peter.

"So, I see you have a daughter now?"

"Sue Ellen, this is Josephine. Josephine, Sue Ellen."

Josephine curtsied just like she would if she were addressing royalty. Sue Ellen was even more impressed with the little girl.

"Josephine, why don't you run along to the playground and let the grownups talk, okay, sweetheart?"

"Yes, Daddy."

Peter and John watched her walk towards the playground and towards the band. Loretta and Sue Ellen kept their focus locked with the men.

"So? Are you going to answer my question, Peter?"

Peter smiled and shook his head. John did the same to his still smirking wife.

"There you go again. Why don't you have a burger with us and I'll tell you all about it? Relax, Sue Ellen, it's a party."

"I. Am. Relaxed. Peter. I just want to know what you are doing with a young girl that looks about Matt's age? Were you seeing someone when we were still married?"

Watching Sue Ellen and Peter, Loretta started to feel uncomfortable. Her smirk faded, and she started toward her husband to make a getaway. But Sue Ellen held onto the back of her dress.

"It's okay, Lor. We can all hear this. This should be good."

Peter laughed a deep belly laugh, and his plate shook.

"Josephine is adopted. She knows, but I don't like to mention it in front of her. It's just not something you talk about in front of an adopted child, you know? She never met her father, and her mother was a cocaine addict who overdosed right in front of her."

Sue Ellen loosened her stance, and Loretta shifted uneasily at hearing the news. She liked Peter even more than she did that day at the grocery store ten years ago.

"Oh. I'm…"

"Sorry?"

"Yes. I'm sorry, okay, Peter?"

"Thank you."

Sue Ellen bit her fingernail. For once, she was not the poised, confident woman that she presented herself to be. She had not seen this coming. Of all the emotions she felt, feeling stupid was not one of them. She felt like that more than ever now.

"Well, then, I suppose I shall be seeing you two around. Enjoy your food," Sue Ellen said. She shook her head in embarrassment and blushed once more as she walked away. Loretta did not follow her at first, and Peter smiled at her. John grabbed his wife's hand. Sue Ellen turned back and told her friend to come on. Loretta apologized but did as she was asked. John let go of her hand and frowned.

"I told you to watch out for that woman. She's got Loretta wrapped around her little finger," Peter said.

John kicked the dirt in front of him and nodded.

"Yeah, I know. I don't even know who Loretta is anymore, Peter. She's not the woman I married. That's for sure."

32

Sue Ellen led Loretta away from the men and towards an empty picnic bench at the other side of the tent. A few people tried to get their attention, and Loretta started to reply, but Sue Ellen pushed her along. Once they were seated, Vivica Harrison walked up to their table with a plate of food. Sue Ellen told her they were not interested in her company right now.

"Sorry, Vivica. Loretta and I need some privacy right now."

Vivica looked confused but nodded and turned to leave.

Everyone around the table was laughing, engaging in friendly conversation, eating a plethora of good food, and overall enjoying their time. And then there was Sue Ellen, resting her head on the wooden table. Loretta looked concerned but felt helpless all the same.

"What's wrong, Sue Ellen?"

She did not respond right away but instead remained silent and cuffed her hands around her ears. Loretta searched the area to see if she could get up to leave. Her plan came to an end when Sue Ellen began venting.

"He says I'm impulsive. I am. I am! He is such a good man. He always wanted kids. I never did. And do you know why? I didn't think I would be a good mother. And then I have a one-night stand with this guy from Chicago, and there comes Matt. Figures, right?"

Loretta sat there too shocked to say anything, so she just listened. Sue Ellen reached out and held her friend's hands. Sue Ellen's hands felt sweaty, but she needed comfort. Sue Ellen rubbed her sweaty palms all over Loretta's until they both were filled with sweat.

"What do you think of Peter? I mean, if you weren't married to John…you know, would you?"

Loretta stared at her friend. *She would*, she thought. Yes, she most definitely would pursue him.

"You skank. That's my ex-husband I'm talking about. You want him, don't you?" Sue Ellen asked through a wry smile.

"What? Sue Ellen, I…"

"Well, you can't have him. You have John, and you have me."

She continued to rub her hands and now ran her fingers through Loretta's hair.

"You would never do anything to double-cross a friend, would you?"

For all the people talking and having fun around them, suddenly the party shrunk, and things became eerily quiet around their table. Loretta was surprised at the line of questioning. Of course, she would never do anything to double-cross her. What was wrong with her?

"Definitely not. No. Why do you ask?"

Sue Ellen shrugged and covered her face with her hands. When she released them, Loretta saw she was beet red.

"I think I have a crush on Peter. When I saw him with that beautiful little girl, I was so impressed with him. It's like he moved up in the world, and I didn't. It shows maturity, you know?"

A family came over to sit down next to the ladies, but Sue Ellen was not as polite this time in asking for space. She glared at the family and demanded some privacy. They backed away carefully like they were punished in school.

This was a side of Sue Ellen that Loretta had not seen before. She jumped in her seat when her friend barked her order at the sweet family. Just as fast, Sue Ellen turned around and warmly addressed Loretta.

"So, I don't know. What do you think?"

Loretta did not know how to respond. She was not sure what the question meant.

"What do I think about what?"

Sue Ellen rolled her eyes in frustration but continued.

"What do you think about me asking Peter out?"

"Oh. Will I lose you?"

Sue Ellen smiled and held her friend's hands once more.

"Honey, I will never lose you."

"Well, then, I guess it would not hurt. As long as you have feelings for him?"

"Yes, I think I do."

Sue Ellen smiled for the first time since they got to the party, and Loretta sighed with relief. She would ask out her ex-husband. She never thought that she would see the day.

33

As the band played American Gladiators at the playground, they almost forgot about their argument. The goal was to start at the swings. You had to jump off the swing at its highest point, then run up the climber steps, over the shaky bridge, onto the trapeze rack, onto the second bridge, up the stationary steps, and down the curved slide. Two members of the band competed at once to see who could finish first. It was a simple game, but then again, the nineties were still simple times.

Riley had continuously beat out Jimmy, but Matt had continuously beat Riley. Scott beat Jimmy all but one time, but everyone thought he let Jimmy win to make him feel good. Any girls who came to the playground typically stayed to play 'nice' on the swings or did not swing too high. They goofed around in the playhouse or built something in the pit. They used the equipment but were never seen playing American Gladiators. That was until Josephine arrived.

Everyone said that the only time Scott lost to Jimmy was because he let Jimmy win, but Scott later said it was because he was distracted by Josephine sitting alone on the swing.

He made it down the slide for the win but saw this pretty girl he had never seen before. He then paused just long enough to look at her, allowing Jimmy to slip ahead of him for the win. After Scott did go down, everyone congratulated Jimmy. Scott shook his hand but then made a bee-line to sit next to Josephine on the swings.

34

Scott grabbed the open swing next to Josephine, who hung her head and was just barely scraping her feet across the dirt pile underneath the swing.

"Don't ya know how to swing?"

Josephine looked up at Scott for a second, smiled, then looked back at her feet.

"Yeah. I do, but I just don't know anyone around here."

"Oh. Well, that's okay. I'm Scott. So, now you do."

Now she looked up. Her smile returned, and she was grateful to meet someone other than adults.

"Wanna swing with me, uh, what's your name?"

"Josephine. Just call me Joe."

"Joe? That's a boy's name."

"Well, then call me Josephine."

"That's okay, Joe. I like it. It's different."

She smiled again, and as Scott started into his swing, so did she. He egged her on to swing faster and higher. He was amazed at how good a girl could be. Around this time, the rest of the band came by to find Scott swinging next to a girl.

"Hey, Scott! What are you doing? We were about to start another round of American Gladiators over here!"

"Okay!"

He slowed the swing down, and so did Joe. Before getting off, he waved goodbye, but as he started to get off the swing, he asked Joe if she would like to play a game of American Gladiators with them.

"It's kind of a boys' game, but you know. It could be fun."

"Well, I have a boy's name, Scott."

Scott smiled and was happy she agreed to join in. The band looked confused that he allowed a girl to join but did not seem to mind. Despite her feminine summer dress, she was surprisingly good at American Gladiators. She beat out Jimmy and Scott, although some of the boys thought Scott had let her win. She was not so good that she could beat out Riley or Matt, but she was good enough to compete, so that was something. Jimmy felt more than defeated that day but kept saying that at least he beat Scott. The boys kept rolling their eyes and laughing each time he would mention this. It would be a running joke with Jimmy for the next couple of years.

When the band grew tired running around the course, Matt thought it would be good to get some more food to refuel. All five of them made their way to the tent, picking apart brownies, snack cakes, and chocolate chip cookies. None of them bothered sitting down but ate as they walked. When Matt decided to go back to the playground, Scott told them to go on ahead. He wanted to spend time with Joe instead. Riley shook his head and pushed his brother along, but Matt told him just to meet them up when they were ready. Scott never came back. He spent the rest of the party with Joe, and the two of them became inseparable for the rest of that summer.

35

Sue Ellen almost did not ask Peter out. Loretta informed her that he was already getting into his car to leave when like a madwoman, she ran out to the parking lot and blocked his car by putting her hands in front of the windshield.

"Peter! Wait! Just...wait!"

His eyes opened wide, and Joe furrowed her brow in confusion.

She closed her eyes and breathed out slowly before crossing over to his driver-side window.

"I wanted to…."

"Yes?"

She was flustered, and she was not used to being flustered. She did not want to be turned down. She was not used to being turned down. She closed her eyes again and decided that she would say it quickly.

"I wanted to ask you out on a date. I want to try this again."

Peter paused, surprised. Sue Ellen opened her eyes and smiled at Peter, but he smiled back before she could say anything else.

"It's a date."

"Wow. Really?"

"Yeah. I never really lost feelings for you. I always hoped things would work out for us."

Now her eyes glowed, and her heart leaped a beat.

"How about I pick you up tomorrow night, say seven? Are you busy?"

Sue Ellen shook her head, and that was that.

"Then I will see you at seven."

"I'll see you at seven, Peter," Sue Ellen smiled.

As he drove away, she waved and smiled. Joe felt good for her dad but mostly felt good about meeting Scott. The two of them will be meeting up tomorrow, too. Joe was starting to feel comfortable in her new hometown. She met friends and maybe a new mother, too. This was what Joe had always wanted.

36

It was all Scott and Joe from that point on the rest of that summer of '96. He saw Matt from time to time, but Riley and Jimmy were not included in that circle. The trench went unfinished and would not be worked on again for some time. It was the beginning of things, but in many ways, that summer ended their childhood.

Chapter 4: Ridgeport 2003

On a beautiful Saturday in September 2003, Peter and Sue Ellen were remarried at The First Church of St. John. There was not a pew empty, as family and friends from Ridgeport occupied every square inch of the church to celebrate the holy occasion. Loretta served as matron of honor, and John served as best man. Stella, Matt, and Scott sat in the front row. Riley and Jimmy sat a few rows back with their parents.

Joe walked down the aisle ahead of Sue Ellen, carrying a small bouquet to match the bride's arrangement. She bowed her head at first. The boys waved their arms furiously to get her to look up and smile. She smiled at them and walked tall down the aisle.

The stained-glass windows displayed the different saints, and the sun's soft light beamed onto the long, carpeted aisle that led to the altar. A wood carving of Jesus Christ hung on the Crucifix at the center of the altar and watched the bride as she elegantly walked toward the altar. Underneath the traditional wooden gable roof, the organist played Lohengrins' "Wedding March." All faces watched Sue Ellen on her special day. She even wore the same dress when they first married – a lacy, strapless ball gown style. Yet when Peter got his second first look at his bride, it was as if he was getting married for the first time.

Sue Ellen gave Matt a nod, and he smiled wide. He had seen a fundamental change in her since she started dating Peter. She even treated Stella like a human being and began calling her by her real name, instead of Nanny, over the past year.

The traditional church service began with hymns, readings, a sermon, and communion. Sue Ellen's Aunt Ruth read the Old Testament Reading of Proverbs 3:1-6, the same verse that was read at their first wedding. Peter's cousin Matt read the New Testament Reading out of Corinthians 1:4-8, a verse Peter picked out because of the words "I always thank my God for you." Father Ritter extended the verse found in Proverbs 3:1-6 by talking about the importance of staying to the true path of the Lord. He finished his sermon by referencing Mark 12:31, "The second is this: 'Love your neighbor as yourself.' There is no commandment greater than these." Somehow, he had found a way to echo the town's motto of "Love thy neighbor" and "Love thy Ridgeport" into the wedding sermon.

They did not write their own vows, deciding to remain traditional. Father Ritter began, "Looking like newlyweds as they anxiously and lovingly gazed into each other's eyes, waiting to become husband and wife once again."

And with the "You may now kiss the bride," Matt and Scott diverted their eyes to the floor, embarrassed. Seeing his mom and his best friend's dad kiss was a little uncomfortable. But their eyes turned back up once Father Ritter announced, "I now pronounce you husband and wife." The congregation applauded as they clutched their hands and raised them in the air. The organ music started up again, and they made their way to greet friends and relatives before lining up for the first of many photographs.

2

The couple never seemed happier than that night, at one of the country club's banquet halls, in the same place they had celebrated their first reception. It was unfathomable to anyone that Peter and Sue Ellen ever got divorced in the first place. The band sat together alongside Stella, Mr. and Mrs. Wrobel, and Joe, who had been welcomed into the band. They shared their first date eating brunch at the country club and thought it the perfect spot to get married.

It was the first wedding the band had been to, and for their first one, they were impressed. Ridgeport residents dressed in black tie, and the women wore their most expensive evening wear, complete with diamond jewelry. Anyone who was anyone in Ridgeport was there, and even Mayor Sheila Goldman showed up. Wait staff served hors d'oeuvres as guests stood around sipping cocktails and glasses of fine wine. Since weddings were private events, alcohol was allowed. The hall must have seated three hundred people, and the dance floor looked as though it accommodated all three hundred at once. A large crystal chandelier hung above the floor, sparkling elegantly for its dancers. The jazz band echoed this elegance, and even they dressed in black tie.

Just as the guests passed the dinner rolls around and the Caprese salad was being served, John grabbed hold of the microphone for his best man's speech. Scott set down his half-eaten piece of bread. He knew his father was a good speaker and always had a way with words. Whenever he spoke, Scott listened. He seemed so calm up there and did not even read from a piece of paper. Scott did not know how he would perform in front of so many people.

"Well, these two love birds love each other so much, they just had to get married twice."

As John paused, laughter followed. *That one took guts*, Scott thought. Although, Sue Ellen did not look too amused.

"In all seriousness," and now John turned his head toward Sue Ellen, "I am overjoyed that we are here celebrating the union of Peter and Sue Ellen." That put at least a small smile back on Sue Ellen's face.

"Peter is the kind of person who will do anything for you. He gave me a new Driver when I...broke mine at the course. He didn't let me borrow one. He gave me one. And then he proceeded to give me golf lessons."

There was more laughter. John was good at this sort of thing.

"Peter is the kind of person that will show you what it means to enjoy life. Whenever I got stressed covering a story for *The Naperville Sun*, Peter was there asking if I wanted to go for a round of golf or get a burger at the clubhouse. I would let go of my stress unless I broke a club."

As more laughter ensued, Scott looked from the crowd to his father and couldn't be prouder of the suave person he was.

"Peter is the kind of guy who is always there for you, through thick and thin, and I just can't say enough good things about my best friend. When I saw you and Sue Ellen together at the Fourth of July picnic three years ago, I knew there was that spark again. When he told me how well that first date went, I could tell that it would lead to this night. Sue Ellen, I can see how happy you make Peter; I have never seen him as happy as he is tonight. Thank you, Sue Ellen."

Scott swore he saw her blush this time and nodded in affirmation.

"So, if we can all raise our glasses and bless Peter and Sue Ellen and their family for many years of love and happiness."

"To Peter, Sue Ellen, and Josephine, who make their family complete."

All the guests, including the band, raised their glasses in unison and clinked together. Peter raised his glass toward John in thanks and intertwined his glass and arm with Sue Ellen. They drank deeply, looking into each other's eyes.

Then it was Loretta's turn, and out came a wrinkled piece of notebook paper. She seemed more nervous than her husband and did everything she could to compose herself.

"Well, Peter, you are getting quite a woman. You are getting the whole package. And Sue Ellen…"

But Loretta paused, and a tear was already forming from her right eye. She blushed a deep red, and for a second, it looked as if she might not get through the speech. The guests waited awkwardly. Sue Ellen did not react but waited patiently for her friend to continue.

"I... I can't do this. You're perfect. I love you. I love you, Sue Ellen. That's all. Peter, you're a lucky man."

Tears streamed down her face. Another bridesmaid stood up to comfort her, and a couple of guests yelled out, "It's okay, go on." Loretta crumbled up her speech in her right hand, and her right hand was shaking. Scott could not believe what he was seeing, and Joe held his hand tight underneath the table. The rest of the band looked over towards him and then around the table in silence, before staring back up at the train wreck of a speech.

Loretta then went over to hug Peter. He then smiled over at Sue Ellen, who forced a smile.

"So, let's raise our glasses to a wonderful couple and the wonderful life they will have together," she said between tears.

Glasses clinked, and as she sat down, claps were few and far between. Loretta wiped the sweat from her forehead. The same bridesmaid that consoled continued doing so, but Sue Ellen did not so much as look her way.

3

After the toasts came the wedding dinner, which was nothing short of heavenly. The band would have been just as happy with mac and cheese, but after eating their Caprese salads, they admitted that the steak and sea bass were delicious. Joe laughed at Scott for eating around his asparagus. Scott poked fun back that he was saving the worst for her.

As he became known, Bottomless Pit Riley was a beanstalk but could eat the band under the table. His brother had a similar build, but he was a very picky eater for a more realistic reason and often only finished half of his meals. Matt looked like he was most likely to be the professional athlete of the bunch, with Scott looking the most' average.' He was not skinny or fat. He was not built, but not out of shape, either. And he believed Joe was a beauty queen. All the band wanted her but would never admit it. She had grown into quite a young woman – she grew a few inches over the summer, and the boys noticed that she filled out in 'all the right places.' She was a nerd, one of them, but she was also undeniably hot. And the band wondered how much longer in their high school careers she would hang around with them.

Mrs. Wrobel attempted conversation with the group.

"How's high school going?" she asked. Stella smiled, listening attentively while Mr. Wrobel gobbled up his steak, just like his son Riley. Matt was the first to speak up, as usual.

"Aw, it's okay, I guess. I'm liking this year okay."

The mother of two looked over towards Joe and Scott next to see if they were willing to add, but they were too busy talking to each other.

"And Scott...Joe? What do you think about being juniors now?"

"Huh? Oh, well, it's good," Scott said.

"Yeah, it's good. Really, good," Joe said and nodded as she spoke.

Mrs. Wrobel smiled and took another bite of her mashed potatoes. Stella spoke up next.

"Well, what is good about it, Mr. Casey?" She only used his last name when she thought he was being disrespectful. Scott had not been called 'Mr. Casey' in a while now, and his face flushed a bit when she said it.

"Oh, well, I'm getting all A's for one, and I'm having fun writing for the school newspaper. The teacher says that I have a real knack for reporting."

143

Stella smiled and seemed satisfied with the answer. She looked over at Joe, expecting another such response.

"Oh, well, I have Scott in one of my classes. So, that's exciting. And I have all A's too, and someone said that I could be the lead in the school play, and my counselor thinks I can take AP courses next year."

"Well, that's wonderful!" she exclaimed. "Joe is a keeper, Scott."

Joe's hand wrapped so tight around Scott's that it cut off his circulation, and even when he tried to let go, he was not able to. She did not like being put in the spotlight like that.

To protect Joe, Scott jokingly threw the light back on Riley and Jimmy.

"Riley? Jimmy? How's school for you this year?"

They stopped chewing and cast an annoyed glare in Scott's direction, one that their parents and Stella did not see.

"Yeah, thank you, Scott. How is it going, guys?" asked Mrs. Wrobel. Mr. Wrobel was still eating, unaware of the conversation, until his wife nudged his shoulder to wake him up to his surroundings. Riley spoke up first.

"It's…" He looked from his parents and over to Stella, whom he knew was expecting more than just an "It's good" answer.

"Well, you know I didn't make the golf team, so I was going to try out for track in the spring. The gym coach says I'm one of the fastest runners he's seen," Riley said.

"Uh-huh. What about your grades, young man?" Mr. Wrobel asked.

Scott and Matt looked at each other and now felt sorry for Riley. He got good grades, but he struggled in math, and they all knew it. The last thing he wanted to tell his folks was that he was failing algebra.

"They're good. Can't complain."

144

He looked like he was walking on eggshells, though, expecting Thor's hammer to come down on him from his father. But instead, his dad patted him on his head and ruffled his hair.

"Atta boy."

"Jimmy, sweetie. How is it being a big sophomore this year?"

Jimmy hated it when he felt second-best compared to his brother or the rest of the band. He cringed when he heard the words "big sophomore."

Jimmy remained much the same as he had when the band was formed four years ago: quiet, following in his brother's footsteps, trying to fit in. He would not exactly find out who Jimmy was until later in high school. He shrugged and murmured something under his breath.

"Jimmy, honey, I can't hear you."

"It's good, Mom. It's good. School just started, so I don't have anything to report, okay?"

Stella gave him a disapproving look, but Jimmy hid his face from her. Mrs. Wrobel frowned at her son but did not press him any further. With the food about gone, the band wished they had the table to themselves. Adults always mess everything up, they thought.

4

After dinner, Sue Ellen and Peter cut the cake and then dancing followed. The happy couple cut into an impressive black and gold six-tier behemoth filled with strawberry buttercream, vanilla buttercream, Devil's food cake buttercream with Reese's peanut butter cup buttercream, and chocolate buttercream. Peter aimed with a piece of frosting at Sue Ellen's mouth, and Sue Ellen recoiled in laughter. The photographer and videographer captured the loving moment.

Their 'second first dance' was the same song as their first dance from their first wedding – "And I Love You So" by Elvis. They gazed into each other's eyes like actual newlyweds. It was indeed a beautiful testament to the love they shared. At that moment, Loretta got up to use the bathroom. She did not return to the reception for quite some time.

5

Sue Ellen and her father Glenn danced to Louis Armstrong's "What a Wonderful World." Glenn did not move so well anymore, but he was overjoyed to share the moment with his daughter. Peter slow-danced to Rod Stewart's "Forever Young" with his mother, Dorothy. It was sweet, and aside from the awkwardness that was Loretta Casey, it was a wonderful wedding all around. And with that, the lead singer fired up the guests. And then, Sue Ellen, Peter, and Joe had a 'family dance' to "We Are Family," by Sister Sledge.

"Alright, let's get this party started! All of you love birds out on the dance floor."

Then they broke into "Wonderful Tonight" by Eric Clapton. Husbands and wives, boyfriends, and girlfriends made their way, slow dancing with their arms around their waists and their arms around their necks, swaying to the lyrics.

Mrs. Wrobel dragged her husband out on the floor, leaving Stella to watch the band. Scott shifted uncomfortably in his seat, feeling like he should ask Joe to dance. Joe appeared uneasy, too. They looked around the table from Riley to Jimmy to Matt. After being friends through the years, they developed a sort of ESP and, at that moment, knew what each other were thinking.

"Stella, would you mind if we stretch our legs? We'd like to walk around the porch, get some fresh air."

146

Even though Stella knew better that they would not just be going out for some fresh air, she allowed them to take off anyway.

"Well, I suppose this music is a little dated for you anyway. Don't wander too far."

"Thanks. You're the best, Stella," Joe said.

"Yeah, you are. Thank you, Stella," Matt said.

"You're welcome!" she said, with a warm smile and a barely detectable wink.

As the Clapton classic continued, the band headed out of the hall and onto the porch. It was a gorgeous night at the tail end of summer. They strolled to the iron railing on the balcony just outside the hall and looked out over the golf course. Golfers ran the course all day here, but now it was one large empty park. Music blared inside, but the crickets played their own tune around the course.

Riley leaned over the railing, aiming for a perfect shot, and in the vernacular, hocked a loogie. He arched his back and shot it, like Leo DiCaprio in *Titanic*. Jimmy took notice and was the first to follow. His didn't travel as far as Riley's.

"Hey, Riley, man. Impressive," Scott said.

Scott tried, and Matt followed suit. A fountain of spit flew in all directions over the balcony. Joe rolled her eyes. Never to be outdone, she pushed them aside.

"Please. This is how it's done, boys."

Joe waited until a couple walked out of the club. She snorted, threw her back in it, and let a huge wet loogie fly. It landed right on the old gentleman's head. He whirled around, angry, unsure of where the wetness came from. Realizing the damage, the band sprinted from the railing, and just as the man glanced up when he heard the noise, the woman ushered him along.

As he walked away, the band roared with laughter. They had more fun in that one moment than they had at the entire wedding.

"Joe, that was awesome!" Matt yelled.

Scott patted her on the back, and Riley gave her the band handshake – two bumps followed by a shake, followed by a flick of the fingers. Jimmy rested against the handrail and smiled. Joe stood back and performed a curtsy, acting like the perfect woman after the perfect unwomanly act.

"Man, did Stella ever stare Jimmy down in there for 'not reporting' to his mom," Scott said.

Matt snickered. "I guess you're happy that you're not staying with her at my place tonight."

Jimmy shook his head and stared out at the course.

"Yeah, wait, what? You guys are staying with Stella? What about your folks?" Riley asked, butting in.

"They want their own rooms at the hotel tonight. They need some 'alone time,' is what they told us," Scott said.

Matt snickered again. "They've had alone time from us their entire lives."

Scott nodded in agreement, and Joe reached out and grabbed his hand. A moment of silence ensued before Jimmy spoke up.

"So, what are we gonna do now?"

The boys looked at each other's faces, waiting for the next idea, but Joe stared at the course. No one else was out on the porch, and no one else was walking out of the clubhouse below. Not a single headlight beamed from the cars in the parking lot. Scott looked skyward and thought he saw a shooting star, but then Joe broke the silence.

"I got an idea, that is, if you're all man enough for it," Joe said.

They all chuckled.

"What is it, Josephine?" asked Matt.

She turned her attention back to the band, and a sly smirk began to form from the corner of her mouth.

"Gentlemen, I say we make this an opportunity to indulge in our first adult beverage!"

This idea threw the band a curveball, pitched with mixed emotions. Jimmy looked around to see if anyone had heard her. Riley nodded, Matt smirked along with her, and Scott bit his lower lip. None of them wanted to chicken out from her dare, but they were split on her plan. Riley and Matt embraced it while Jimmy and Scott felt less than enthusiastic. But it did not matter what they thought. Jimmy did whatever the group did, and Scott did not want to seem like less than a man compared to his girl. They were doing this. They were going to sneak a drink, or drinks, from the reception.

"And how do you not get caught?" Scott asked.

Matt interjected. "Most of the guests are already out on the dance floor. We can break up and make our way around the tables snatching the excess alcohol. They would, of course, have to keep their eyes on their mothers and Nanny.

"It's pretty much mission impossible," Riley chimed in.

"Oh, come on, don't get your panties in a twist, Ry. No one will even be paying attention to us," Joe said.

Everyone laughed, even Jimmy, until Riley glared his brother's way.

"Alright, well, let's do this then."

They took a couple of steps, paused to collect themselves, and walked back into the hall. Joe was right; most of the guests were on their feet and rocking out to "Brown Eyed Girl." A few tables sat empty, and the ones that weren't were filled with guests that looked so tired they did not care what was going on around them. When the band hit the hall entrance, Joe directed the boys where to go.

"Act casual. Don't draw attention to yourself, but don't look like you're not trying to draw attention to yourself," Joe said. "Let's get in and out. So, try to be out by the time this song is up, got it? We'll meet back at the iron railing," Joe said.

"Ha, ha. Fly casual?" Matt butted in.

"What?" Joe asked, confused.

"Han Solo, *Star Wars*?" Matt questioned.

"God. You guys are such nerds."

"You're a nerd too, Joe," Scott said.

She smiled but then pointed towards the tables and like a general, gave the order to move out. It was unusual for anyone besides Matt to lead a project, but with this being her idea, it fits. Each band member maneuvered their way around a section of the hall. Riley and Jimmy found their way up the middle, Scott and Joe took the left flank, and Matt ran around the right side. Despite being distracted by Matt's nerdy allusion, the band followed Joe's orders, and by the time "Brown Eyed Girl" finished, they arrived back at the railing with adult drinks in hand.

Jimmy power walked out of there a good couple of minutes after the rest of them. He panted by the time he hit the balcony, and the two drinks he carried shook in his hands.

"Did anyone see you? What took you so long?" Riley asked.

"I...I don't think so," Jimmy said.

"Don't think so, or know so?" Matt followed up.

He thought for a second, still panting.

"No. No one saw me."

"Good. Did anyone see any of you?" Matt asked.

They all shook their heads no.

150

"Well, then, this calls for a…wait a minute. Jimmy, is one of those drinks a Shirley Temple?" Matt asked.

"What?" he asked, looking at the drink.

Joe laughed, inspecting the drink. She took a sip and confirmed.

"It is! Jimmy here went out of his way to steal some kid's Kiddy Cocktail!"

They held their stomachs as they heaved laughter. Jimmy blushed and hung his head. He was not one to get angry. He was much too shy.

"It's okay, Jim. We're just messin' with you," Riley said.

"Yeah. You can act like you got a buzz," Matt said.

More laughter followed, and this time Jimmy walked to the other side of the fence. The band joined him, and they all patted him on the back.

"Don't be so sensitive, man. What's this other drink you brought here?" Joe asked.

Joe peered at the brown liquid filled to the top of the crystal glass. Jimmy sniffed it and liked the smell. He said it smelled like some sort of wood. He passed it around, and they all gave a whiff and agreed that it indeed smelled like wood.

"That ain't no Kiddie Cocktail, Jimmy. You got Jack Daniel's Whiskey there," Joe said.

"Man. What are you, like a bartender?" Matt asked.

The band looked at her waiting for a response.

"My dad, my real dad, used to drink these. He used to drink a lot of these. So, I'll always know what these are," Joe said.

"Oh. Joe, I'm sorry," Scott said.

"For what? I'm fine. Really. Now, I say that we make a toast," Joe said.

"Yeah. I like the sound of that," Matt said.

"What are we toasting?" Scott said.

"We toast to us, and this moment, and to being together, forever."

They looked down at their drinks once more. Joe raised her glass first, followed by Matt, and then eventually the rest of the group followed, clinked together, and drank their poisons. It was just the start of a wild night.

8

The band showed mixed reactions after they 'lost their virginity' to alcohol. Jimmy spit out what was left of the whisky. Riley set his hands on his knees, Matt nodded, Scott breathed out slowly, and Joe smiled. Later in life, they would find out that Riley downed a fireball shot, Matt slurped a Jack and Coke, Scott tried a Vodka Tonic, and Joe helped herself to a Long Island iced tea.

"I think I'm going to be sick," Riley said.

Riley stumbled forward toward the ledge of the balcony and hurled over the top of it, careful not to ruin his suit. As the rest of the band watched, Joe rushed to his side and patted him on the back.

"It's alright, Riley. Get it out."

He paused, dry heaved, and spewed again. Chunks of sea bass fell out the side railing and onto the concrete below. Luckily, no one came out of the club at that moment. Joe continued rubbing his back as the band just watched, holding their drinks. Riley clutched the railing, waiting for the next round, but nothing came out this time. He waited some more, but he felt his stomach start to settle.

"You okay now?" Joe asked.

Riley nodded and turned, trying to wipe the leftover fish from his lips.

"Ew man, gross," Joe said. "One of you, go get him a napkin and some water."

"Sure. I got it," Scott said.

Jimmy and Matt approached Riley.

"You okay there, big fella?"

"Yeah, you okay big brother?"

Riley furrowed his eyebrows at Jimmy and Jimmy looked down at his shoes.

"Yeah. I'm good now. Thanks for not helping, guys. Thank you, Joe."

A few minutes later, Scott returned with some napkins and a glass of water, which Joe took and handed to Riley.

Riley wiped all the gunk off his face, took a swig of water, and spit out some more bile.

"Gross man. Just gross," Joe said again.

"Sorry. Thanks for the napkins and water Scott," he said.

"Don't mention it."

"Maybe you should take a break from drinking tonight," Joe said.

"Yeah. I think that's a good idea."

The four of them then patted Riley on his back and turned their attention to Joe.

"What's next, Joe?" Matt asked.

"Next?" Scott questioned.

The band minus Riley continued to sip on their drinks, feeling their bodies go loose and their cares falling away. Riley joined them, but water would be his drink of choice for a while now.

"I think Scott should pick this time. Scott?"

The band looked at Scott, taking another sip of his Vodka Tonic. He looked out at the golf course, and not wanting to be outdone by his girlfriend, suddenly came up with a crazy idea.

"Who's up for a round of golf?" he asked.

"Huh? Are you nuts? The course is closed, dude," Matt said.

Scott knew his dad golfed with Peter often, and his dad told him of an unlocked maintenance shed where they kept spare clubs and balls. Perhaps it was still unlocked?

"I know how we can play tonight. That is if you're up to it?"

They all continued to drink, and as they continued to drink, they would have said yes to anything.

"Sure, boyfriend. Show us how to play this golf game," Joe said.

"Just follow me."

9

Scott led them out of the country club and onto the golf course. No one had noticed their drinks, or so they thought. And if they did, they were already too buzzed to care. They stumbled past the lights and onto the dark fairway, hole one. He turned them to the left of the first hole and towards the driving range. At the far end of the range stood a wooden shed, and it swung half-open.

Without hesitation, Scott pulled the creaky door. He found a light bulb attached to a chain, but Joe reached out and yanked on it before he got the chance. There were all kinds of groundskeeping tools – rakes, shovels, a Rototiller, and so on. But Scott's dad was right – in the corner leaned a golf bag filled with clubs.

"Jackpot. What do you say? Who's up for a round?" Scott asked.

Joe whooped and hollered while Riley and Matt gave Scott the band's handshake. Jimmy just took another swig of Whiskey.

"Now, who's going to carry 'em?" Matt asked.

"Not it," Joe said.

"Not it," Scott said.

"Not it," Riley said.

"Ha, that leaves you caddy, Jimmy boy," Matt said.

Jimmy held tight to his glass and frowned, but Joe spoke up.

"We can all take turns, guys. Don't tell me you all are too weak to carry some clubs."

"Fine," Matt said. "We can give Jimbo a break," and he playfully punched him on the shoulder.

And it was around this time their speech started to slur, but none of them seemed to take much notice.

"Well, wait just a minute here. We're going to get caught, aren't we, Scott? I mean, won't people, won't…people see (burp) us if we start on one hole?" Matt asked.

Scott threw his hand on his friend's shoulder and smiled wide.

"Matt, my friend, we are start going to on hole nine. You, see? We just walk there now."

Jimmy started carrying the golf clubs, which weighed as much as he did. Inebriated, he did all he could to keep from falling over. It was at least a mile hike to hole nine on the other side of the course, so Scott suggested that the band just hit the balls from the range and call it a day.

"We just ball here and then put the bag back like nothing happened. That way, no one must carry nothing," Scott said.

The band liked this idea, and they each grabbed a club. Scott unzipped the bag on the side to find boxes of balls. There must have been enough for them to hit at least ten balls each. They each took their own tee in the range, and lucky for them, no one could see the range from the porch. After the first couple of clumsy swings on his three-wood, Jimmy miraculously straightened it out and hit one at least two hundred yards straight. The band gathered around Jimmy in awe. It was the confidence boost he needed that night, and in a way, it was a turning point for the youngest band member. He won a golf scholarship his senior year, and by that time, shy Jimmy Wrobel had turned into a confident young man.

As memorable as Jimmy's swings were, Scott's last swing may have been more memorable. By this time, Scott was barely standing up, and he knew that people were talking to him, but he was not sure what they were saying. He blamed these reasons for what happened to his driver on that last swing.

All he heard was a bunch of laughter mixed with the sound of a large thud against the driver's mat. It took Joe shaking him out of his drunken stupor to alert him that he had broken his club on the swing. The club's head had traveled further than the Titleist. Scott's eyes grew two sizes, and Joe pushed him back towards the shed. Matt picked up the clubs and that concluded the band's nighttime golf outing. The groundskeeper got his clubs back minus one and may have had one or two balls left of the fifty or so he had kept in the bag's side pouch. Jimmy also left his signature. He vomited all over the entrance to the shed just as they were leaving – the same Jimmy who just moments before looked like he never took a sip of alcohol. The band paused for a moment and then helped Jimmy up and skedaddled out of there.

10

The group staggered back towards the reception hall, trying their best to carry Jimmy. By the time they reached the green on hole one, the sprinklers had turned on, and the entire band got soaked. Most of Jimmy's vomit ran off at least, but it would be hard to explain now why the five of them were dripping wet from head to toe.

"We could just ditch the clothes and go back to the reception naked," Joe suggested through laughter.

The rest of the boys' faces blushed, but Matt shook away the idea.

"We have to get to a room with bath. We will use the dryer in there," Matt said.

Riley nodded. Riley and Matt were the only two halfway coherent members now that Jimmy and Scott were entirely out of it.

"Hm. Not as good as the naked plan. But it'll do," Joe said and tossed her hair back.

They moved as fast as they could, as they did not want to get caught. The band made their way back into the club and found restrooms on the bottom floor. It was like they had walked home in a downpour, and so it was some time before they could even pass as halfway dry. The adults were also drunk and would take no notice, they thought.

Scott and Joe came out of the restroom first. Scott leaned back against a wall while his girlfriend of two months walked out the door. Even with his blurry vision, he knew that she was the most beautiful girl in all the world. Joe did not hesitate. She pulled his head close to hers and kissed him long and hard. Even though her breath stank of all kinds of liquor, Scott's body went stiff, and his arms held back as if he were about to go into flight. It was the first time they had kissed. It was the first time Scott had kissed anyone. It was not just a peck either, it was an open mouth, and of all the great moments in his life thus far, that was the greatest. He had not felt a thing the last hour or so, but that was like the kiss that brought him back to life. He wanted the kiss to last forever, but as soon as Matt walked out of the restroom, the kiss was over.

11

When they found their way back to the reception hall, the band pounded out its last tune, "Goodnight, Sweetheart, Goodnight" by the Overtones. The remaining guests formed a circle around Sue Ellen and Peter as they shared one last

157

dance before sharing their first night as a married couple once again. Joe did all she could do to keep Scott standing up straight, and Riley kept checking in on his brother for signs of another puke session. Matt spotted the Wrobels swaying next to some couple they did not recognize but could not figure out where Stella was. They reeked of alcohol, but if there was such a place to reek of alcohol, it was there, where half the guests also smelled like it was their first and last night to drink in their lives.

As the band watched the guests belt out the "Do-do-do-do's," Stella snuck up behind them, and after tapping Matt on the shoulder, he about fell over. He knew it. They were found out for sure. Nothing ran past Nanny. Nothing. The only difference between Nanny and Sue Ellen was that Nanny showed compassion now and again.

The band turned as a record upon Stella's tapping Matt's shoulder. Joe did her best to make Scott look alive, ala Bernie from *Weekend at Bernie's*. The 84-year-old woman did not tower over them like she once had, but she still had that hold on them. Stella served as the primary caregiver in Matt and Scott's lives and influenced the rest of the band. She did not have to say anything. Holding her hands tightly to her hips and her lips tightly wound across her face said it all. Matt sighed, but Nanny did the talking for them before he could speak.

"I'm disappointed in all of you. Drinking like that."

They were caught. And if Nanny knew, who else did?

"Do you realize how much trouble you could have all gotten into?"

They were too drunk to lie, so the members who weren't ready to pass out just nodded. Stella frowned and relaxed the arms from her hips. She looked over their heads to the circle on the dance floor. The jazz band pushed out its last few notes, and the crowd sang its last "Good night." If Nanny was going to keep the conversation private, now was the time to wrap things up.

"I was about your age when I did what you did. There's a time and a place. And you are neither in that time nor place. I found out the hard way in my life. Trust me. Now, I trust you feel guilty enough from our conversation today. Learn from this. I love all of you. Just try not to let them find you out."

Stella smiled that kind, grandmotherly smile before brushing past them to speak with the Wrobel's. The band turned around and breathed a sigh of relief. She was not going to snitch. Their hearts slowly stopped beating out of their chests. They were safe, for now.

12

The band avoided their parents to the best of their ability at the end of the reception. She instructed them to remain close to her until they left and did not dare breach the contract of the woman who both knew their secret and the one who they trusted not to break it. Besides, had they run off again, that same trust just might be broken.

When the Wrobels approached their children, Stella planted herself in between them. Mrs. and Mr. Wrobel were as drunk as their children and did not seem to notice what was going on. Mr. Wrobel even reached out and tousled Jimmy's hair. Jimmy did all he could from vomiting all over his father's shoes. If it had not been for Riley clutching his arm, he might have.

"So, we'll pick them up in the morning sometime, Stella," Mrs. Wrobel said.

"Take your time, dear."

"You all behave now," Mr. Wrobel said.

Then Mr. Wrobel grabbed his wife's hand, and as they turned, the Wrobel children noticed Stella reach down and squeeze their hands. They saw her give them a small smile before moving the band along to find the next parent.

They found John next, but Loretta was not by his side. Since her awkward speech, no one had seen her. Always the reporter, John noticed something off about the five of them, but Stella spoke up.

"They'll be in good hands with me tonight. I trust you will be at our house in the morning, John?"

"Oh, oh yes. Is there something wrong with all of you? Is that alcohol I smell?" he asked.

"They're fine, John. Relax. This whole place reeks of the beverage. You don't think that I would let these children out of my sight, now do you?"

Before John could respond, a groomsman approached him, congratulating him on his stellar best man's speech. Stella took advantage of the diversion and motioned the band onwards toward Peter and Sue Ellen with instructions to follow closely behind her.

They shook hands with their departing guests and with their backs to Stella and the band, which remained behind Peter and Sue Ellen, as instructed.

"Well, I must be going, dears. I am so happy for you both," Stella said, shaking their hands.

Peter glowed and gave her a hearty handshake while Sue Ellen gave her a genuine smile. Just as Stella was about to turn around, Sue Ellen's smile faded and asked that her children come out from hiding behind them. Stella tried not to look embarrassed and stepped back so that the band could come forward.

"Aren't you all going to give us a hug? Congratulations are in order, I believe?" Sue Ellen asked.

Stella knew that everything Sue Ellen did was for a reason. Sue Ellen pulled her 'two boys,' Matt and Scott, in for a bear hug. She must have noticed something off about them, but she did not say a word if she did. Peter followed suit and held his arms out for Joe, who reluctantly wrapped herself around the big man. Riley and Jimmy stood looking at each other through it all, feeling awkward as ever. When the love fest was over, the two of them stood back and exchanged their congrats.

"Well, we must be going then? I suppose you two would like to be going? I should get these kids home. It's been a long day for them," Stella said.

"Oh yes. I know," Sue Ellen said as she stared down at all of them before turning her face to a warm smile.

"I...love you, Mommy," Scott blurted out.

Joe and Stella laughed nervously. Sue Ellen chuckled and rubbed Scott's hair.

"I love you too, sweetie."

Stella waved goodbye to the couple and flew with the band, past the remaining guests and out of the country club. Sue Ellen did not take her eyes off them.

13

No one spoke a word on the way home. Stella borrowed the Casey's Chevy Blazer, so there was enough room to seat all six of them. Scott and Jimmy were passed out by the time they arrived at the Norris castle. Riley nudged his brother awake, but Joe was not as subtle and planted a wet willy on Scott, causing him to pop his eyes open and jump out of his seat. Joe almost cried from laughing so hard.

Stella led the band up the sidewalk and into the house. Without her, they might have wandered the whole neighborhood until the wee hours of the morning. Ever the caregiver, Stella gathered the group into the kitchen, where she forced them to drink water and prepared some eggs to coat their stomachs.

The band didn't say much at the kitchen table, and Jimmy did all he could to stay awake. While Stella grabbed her seat at the head, and while she was still plenty upset with them, she loved the five of them dearly. They ate without so much as taking their eyes off their scrambled eggs, which Stella said is supposed to help a hangover. Matt thanked Stella for helping the band out after a few minutes into their meal, and Stella said she would do anything for them.

"Stella, would you like to be our manager?" Matt asked.

The band all looked at him, confused, and so did Stella.

"What do you mean, child?"

"You know, every band needs a manager and figured you could be like...our manager?"

"Oh, I don't think, um...." Stella started.

"Let's take it to a vote then. Who is all in favor of Stella as the manager?"

Except for Jimmy, whose head was now planted firmly on the table next to his plate, hands unanimously jetted straight into the air.

Stella smiled and thanked them for including her in the band. She asked what her duties were, but Matt said that her duties involved making sure they always did the right thing.

"You know how to do the right thing. You don't need me to tell you that," Stella said.

"We did tonight," Joe said.

"Yeah, we did," Riley chimed in.

"Ha, yeah. Look at Scott there," Matt said.

"I love you, Mommy!" Joe exclaimed in his direction.

The band laughed, and even Stella started to laugh before she caught herself.

"Now, that's alright. Ms. Norris has been there for him through a lot of years," Stella said.

"What do you think of my mom Stella?" Matt asked.

Stella hesitated and noticed that all eyes were on her now.

"I think she is a lovely woman."

Matt rolled his eyes and took another bite of egg. Stella knew that she had lied but could not bring herself to speak

162

ill of his mother. Stella would never tell Matt about when she poured piping hot coffee all down her dress. What good would that do?

"But Matt?" Stella started.

"Yes?" he asked, his eyes still on his eggs.

"Do what she asks, but don't be afraid to do the right thing either."

Matt gave her a funny look at that last part, and Stella shook her head as if trying to forget what he said.

"Well. Can I take your plates? I think we should get you all to bed."

14

Stella set the band up in the living room with their sleeping bags, except for Joe. She said she did not feel comfortable with a girl of that age sleeping with her boyfriend and a bunch of boys, so Joe was in the guest bedroom. Joe handled her alcohol better than the boys and climbed the stairs with as much vigor as a Sherpa. Meanwhile, once the boys struggled with their sleeping bags, they hit their pillows like rocks. Joe's separation meant very little in the grand scheme of things aside from what she found in the guest bedroom.

15

Joe was the first to awaken the following morning and noticed that Stella's door was open a crack. Joe, still in her pajamas, paused in front of the door. She could see Stella was still asleep and started to walk down the stairs. But something stopped her. Stella would have been up by now. Knowing she had the band here, she would typically prepare breakfast downstairs.

"Am I just getting spoiled?" Joe asked herself. "Maybe. But let's wake her anyway. I'm starved."

Joe turned at the front stairs and knocked lightly on the cracked door before entering. Stella lay asleep, showing no signs of getting up. Joe thought once more of turning back and meeting up with the band, but her hunger pangs drove her once more.

She tapped Stella on the arm, no answer. Joe whispered in her ear. No answer.

"Oh, God. What am I doing? Am I this selfish over food?"

She heard her stomach growl this time.

"Yes, yes I am."

She violently shook Stella, this time like a kid eager to wake their parents on Christmas morning.

"Stella! Wake up! Stella!"

No answer.

Joe paused, and as hungry as she was, her hunger was replaced with fear.

She shook her again, harder this time.

No answer.

Then Joe did what she had hoped she never had to do: she checked her pulse.

No answer.

16

The usually cool and confident Josephine Barnes let out a blood-curdling scream. She screamed so loud the rest of the band came running up the stairs and into Stella's room.

"What is it? What happened, Joe?" Scott asked.

"Yeah, what happened?" Matt asked.

Joe held her head in her hands and wept uncontrollably. It took her a minute to lift her heavy head and look them in the eyes.

"She's... she's dead, Matt. Stella is dead."

Scott reached Joe and Stella, while Matt rushed to the opposite side of the bed. Riley and Jimmy hung around by

Stella's feet. Matt rechecked Stella's pulse just to make sure.

"I already did that!"

"Well, maybe you didn't hear it!" Matt yelled.

Matt waited and waited, hoping to hear…anything. But after a minute, he collapsed his head on the sheets, overcome with grief, lying next to the closest thing he had for a mother.

Riley, who usually found the right thing to say in any situation, could not utter a word. Jimmy couldn't either. Joe sobbed uncontrollably, and Scott put his arm around her, trying to do his best to comfort her while trying to keep it together himself. The group stayed close, coming together for a group hug. They needed each other now more than ever. They lost their manager, their best friend, their mother. There would never be another Stella.

"We let her down last night," Joe said through tears, "And she still forgave us. She still forgave us."

"She did," Riley said.

"What are we supposed to do now?" Jimmy asked.

"What do you mean?" Matt asked, lifting his head from the floor.

"Don't we...call the cops or something?" Jimmy asked.

"No. Let's just wait until an adult gets here. They'll know what to do," Matt said.

The band did not eat breakfast that morning and did not leave the room until there was a knock at the door. None of the band wanted to leave the room until Matt volunteered.

Standing at the door were the Wrobels. Matt tried to wipe the tears from his eyes, but they could see that he looked upset. His face was beet-red and tearstained from crying. He could not speak but led them up the stairs to Stella's room.

When the Wrobel adults saw their sons, they looked as if they had all their life drained from their faces. Mr. and Mrs.

Wrobel wrapped their arms around the two of them in a great bear hug.

"I love you guys," Jimmy said.

"Me too," Riley echoed.

"And we love you," Mrs. Wrobel said, holding back tears.

The Wrobel boys had calmer expressions but wilder hair when they finally let go. Joe suppressed a laugh at Riley's disheveled hairdo post hug. Mrs. Wrobel made her way around the band while her husband stood staring at Stella's lifeless body in the doorway.

"Come here, Matt, it's okay," Mrs. Wrobel said, with her arms outstretched.

Matt turned from Stella's bedside, wiped another tear from his eye, and fell into Mrs. Wrobel's arms. He felt that he would have jumped into any stranger's arms that day. He just needed comfort. The band leader who went out and partied the night before was now someone who needed an adult more than ever. *Thank God for Mrs. Wrobel right now*, he thought.

"It's okay, Matt," she said again.

Mrs. Wrobel patted him on the back and held him close as if she were Riley or Jimmy. Matt started to cry and then sobbed in her arms. Mr. Wrobel did not take his eyes off Stella, and the band could not take their eyes off Matt.

"I...never...got...to tell her...that I loved her before...she passed," Matt said through tears.

"She knew Matt. She always knew," Mrs. Wrobel said.

She hugged Matt for what seemed like a good five minutes. When he let go, the rest of the band jumped and surrounded Matt with love. Mrs. Wrobel, in turn, hugged each of the band members in the same way she comforted Matt.

The band couldn't believe that Stella was dead. For them, it seemed like she was the same age she was when they were young. They knew that they had grown up, but it seemed like

166

she never did. Matt, and to a certain extent, Scott, felt cheated out of a mother. They realized they were holding on to something imaginary and realized now more than ever what horrible mothers they had all these years. It made Matt cry even more, and it made Scott retreat into consoling Joe, forgetting his feelings.

There was another knock at the front door. The Wrobels stepped out of the room this time, and there was some talk down below, but the band did not hear what it was about or who was at the door. John walked in, with the Wrobels waiting outside to allow enough space in the already cramped room. His heart dropped upon seeing a dead Stella surrounded by the dead-inside teens. Scott released his grip on Joe and ran over to clutch his dad tight. John reciprocated and kissed the top of Scott's head.

"I'm sorry, Scott. I know how much she meant to you," John said.

"Where's Mom?" Scott said as he pressed his face against his dad's chest.

The two of them let go of each other, and John looked at his son sympathetically.

"She... she's not feeling well, son."

"Oh. Is she okay?"

John nodded, and Scott gave a little half-smile before returning to Joe to comfort her. Within another few minutes, there was a final knock at the door, and this time, Peter and Sue Ellen walked inside.

17

Sue Ellen wailed when she heard the news and rushed up to the crowded room. Peter was right behind her. Her eyes darted to each member of the band before settling on Stella's lifeless body, and she rubbed her temple, hyperventilating.

"I need some space! Get out! Get out!" Sue Ellen yelled at everyone in the crowded room. Mrs. Wrobel, who was standing closest to her high-pitched scream, nearly jumped off the floor. The band gave one look at each other before solemnly walking out the door. Mr. and Mrs. Wrobel followed suit.

Peter stopped on his way out.

"Do you want me to stay or…

Sue Ellen glared at her new husband, and he shriveled like a frightened turtle. He bowed his head obediently and followed the others.

"And Peter, close the door."

"Yes, dear."

Sue Ellen closed her eyes and took a deep breath. When she allowed herself to relax, she approached Stella and pressed her ear against her chest, almost expecting a heartbeat. It was as if Sue Ellen did not believe the others when they said Stella was dead. And then, when she did not hear one, she let out another dramatic wail. She threw herself onto her still frame.

"Why'd you have to go and die? Just...just why?" Sue Ellen lifted herself from the bed and paced around her room. She noticed a picture of her with her deceased husband, Henry, on her dresser. She let out a rare tear, a tear that turned into tears, tears that turned into sobs.

Peter motioned for the rest of them to move downstairs and out of earshot of Sue Ellen's grieving. He hugged Joe and Scott, who were still embracing while moving them downstairs.

"Let's head down to the living room. I'll get us some coffee," Peter said.

As they made their way downstairs, they could still hear Sue Ellen wailing.

"But you went and died. You had to go stirring up trouble. You knew exactly what you were doing. Didn't you? Didn't

168

you? You should never have gotten so involved with those brats! They weren't good for you or your heart, Stella. You know you had a condition. But you did it anyway. Well, you can rot in hell for it now. I'm sorry. I'm just so upset with you. How could you throw your life away with them like that? You were supposed to be their nanny, and then you were giving me mothering advice. Me?"

Sue Ellen stopped pacing and sat next to her on the bed. She grimaced at her and shook her head. Then she closed her eyes and breathed in and out once again.

"We had good times, sure. You were good to me. There's no denying that. I wouldn't have had any other housekeeper. The house was always clean; food was always on the table. Matt was always...Matt was...taken care of. What am I gonna do? How'd you take care of that kid? That kid and those wild things he runs around with? What about Joe? How? How am I supposed to handle them? You just weren't hard enough on them. Yeah. That's it. They wouldn't be the little menaces they are...poking around in my stuff, going out in those woods, running around the golf course, if you didn't always make excuses for them. And if you didn't always make excuses for them, you wouldn't be lying here dead. Serves you right."

Sue Ellen wiped her tears and dried her eyes with her sleeve. She got up from the bed but turned to look at Stella one last time.

"I'm glad you're dead. Ridgeport is better off without you."

Sue Ellen calmed down after ranting to Stella. Drying her tears, she started to appreciate all Stella had done for them. Some of the memories of Stella made her smile. When she went downstairs, she was still smiling.

"So, are we having coffee?" she asked the same group she just yelled out of the room.

"Um, yeah, I got it, ready, dear," Peter said.

Matt drooped his head upon seeing his mom. He wasn't sure, but he could have sworn he heard her rant upstairs.

18

Matt, Scott, and Joe sat close to each other on the leather couch, staring blankly at the TV. Riley and Jimmy took up the lodge chairs on either side of the sofa. Nothing was on, but they didn't care. The adults sipped their coffees, making small talk. Scott held Joe's hand in his lap while Matt fidgeted with his hands. He tried convincing himself that what his mother said wasn't true. He tried convincing himself that he didn't hear her at all. He wondered if anyone else heard her, but if they had, they pretended not to notice. Sue Ellen left to grab some more coffee, and when she returned, she made a beeline for Matt.

"How are you doing, son? I know this is tough, but we'll get through this."

Matt stopped fiddling with his hands, looked up at his mother, and shook his head.

"I have to go. I need to see her again."

"Um, sure. Do what you have to do, Matty."

She turned her attention to Scott and Joe and smiled widely.

"If there is anything I can get for the two of you, you let me know, okay? Can I get you something to drink?"

Joe shook her head at Sue Ellen but added a look of disgust. Her feel-good attitude really got under her skin.

"I'm going to go check on Matt."

Sue Ellen whipped her around and glared at the girl before taking a breath and sitting next to Scott. She reached her hand out and grabbed hold of his. Scott shifted awkwardly in his seat and looked for his dad to help, but he was busy sipping his coffee and talking to Peter.

170

"Scott, you have always been like a son to me. You know that?"

Scott's hands felt clammy, and he wished he could just let go and check on Matt being left staring into space.

"Um, I have?"

"Yes, my dear boy. You've always been there for Matty. And, Joe. Now that Stella is gone, I'm going to have to pay all of you extra special attention. I'll have to be more involved in your lives. I know I've been absent, but I want to change all that. I want to get to know you better, who you are, what you do, where you go."

"Where I go?"

"Oh yes. That's what good mothers do. They worry. And like I said, I've always felt like one to you. Haven't you always felt like a son to me?"

"Um, well..."

"Haven't you?"

Sue Ellen tightened her grip on Scott's hand until Scott felt like she was squeezing his bones.

"Ow...yes...yes. I have."

"Good. I'm glad. Now, how about that drink, my son?"

"Well, actually, I was thinking of checking in on Matt."

"How about that drink?"

She started to tighten her hand around his again.

"Oh, sure, sure."

Sue Ellen loosened her grip, and her smile returned once more.

"Good. Don't go anywhere. I'll be right back."

Upstairs, Joe found Matt in prayer next to Stella, and Joe joined in, holding Matt's hand while Matt led the prayer.

"Oh Lord, please take care of this wonderful woman. She wasn't a real saint, but she should have been. She was the best person I ever knew, and I think we can all say that we are better people because of her. Thank you, Lord, for bringing her into our lives. In your name, we pray. Amen."

171

"Amen," Matt and Joe repeated.

"That was beautiful," Joe said.

"Thanks."

Joe rubbed Matt's back, and they just stood there for a second, taking in the quiet of the room. They thought it comforting to be there without all the people crowded in there with them. Then Matt went stiff as a board, and Joe squeezed his hand, seeing he was on the verge of a breakdown.

"Matt, what's wrong? What's wrong, Matt?"

"I... she…"

Joe wrapped her arms around Matt. He immediately started bawling.

"She was...yelling at Stella. She...said, 'how'd you take care of that kid?' And...and...she told her to 'rot in hell!'" The sobs continued.

Joe patted him on the back and held him tighter. She held him a good five minutes before the tears subsided, and he loosened his grip.

"You okay?"

Matt breathed out. "Thanks. I'm okay as I'll ever be."

"Matt...if it makes you feel any better, I heard her too."

Matt swallowed. "You did?"

Joe nodded.

"I'm not scared of much, but I'm pretty sure I'm scared of that woman."

Matt chuckled. He didn't know how else to respond. Joe chuckled back.

"Come on. I guess we should go back downstairs. You sure you're good to leave the room?" Joe asked.

Matt sighed but said, "As good as I'll ever be."

As they were about to leave, Joe noticed that the window was open and turned around to close it.

19

By the time they reached the living room, the band and the parents had migrated into the dining room. Sue Ellen was busy preparing bacon and eggs for all of them. For Joe, it reminded her of how selfish she had been that morning, but she also reminded herself that Stella would just laugh at her for being too hard on herself.

For the moment, everyone tried to focus their attention off Stella and talked about the wedding the night before. The band, however, did not want any adults poking into their whereabouts into the latter part of the evening. Yet, no adult did prod. Instead, they ate Sue Ellen's bacon and eggs, though they were mediocre at best. The band really missed Stella, especially her cooking. The band would have eaten cardboard just to have a moment's distraction from her death. They ate in silence, and no one spoke of funeral plans. They could not think about moving on. Not just yet.

20

When the ten of them had finished eating, all eyes turned to Sue Ellen. As the one closest to Stella, the band thought it was her responsibility to manage funeral arrangements. Sue Ellen sensed what they were waiting for but forestalled it by hurrying back to the kitchen.

Excuse me, won't you? I'm going to put another pot of coffee on," Sue Ellen said. She jumped up from the table and rushed to the kitchen.

Peter wiped his mouth and stared at everyone for a second.

"I guess I'll go join her."

Sue Ellen hung her head with one hand on top of the pot and one covering her eyes. Peter stopped at the kitchen island before moving around and placing a hand on his wife's back.

"Honey? You, okay?"

"No. Do I look okay to you, Peter?"

"Well, I mean, I know this must be hard…."

Sue Ellen's back stiffened, and her hand squeezed the coffee pot.

Peter stepped back for a second and thought about retreating to the table and finishing his breakfast. Instead, he rubbed Sue Ellen's back. Her tightness and her grip on the pot relaxed.

"Thanks, dear. I'm sorry. I'm just…this whole thing is too much for me, you know?"

Peter just continued to rub her back.

"And I know we have to make funeral plans. I do. I know everyone out there is wondering what the next step is. Ms. Neighborhood Watch Leader will tell them what to do, but I don't always have the answer, Peter. I don't."

Sue Ellen turned around to see her husband's worried expression on his face. She smiled and pecked him on the cheek.

"You're a good man, Peter. Thanks for calming me down."

Sue Ellen straightened her hair and walked back into the dining room.

"Kids, why don't you go into the living room for now?" suggested Sue Ellen. "We need to work on the funeral arrangements."

21

When Sue Ellen sat down at the head of the table, she leaned back, covered her eyes, and then ran her hands through her hair. Peter and the Wrobels remained silent. When she removed her hands, her hair was in disarray, and she carried a worried expression on her face.

"I don't know what to do. Does anyone have any ideas for arrangements?"

Stan Wrobel looked down toward the table. Peter looked toward Sue Ellen but then looked toward Stan. Peggy Wrobel fidgeted with her hands.

"We could hold it at that funeral home in Naperville, Smith Funeral Home? They took care of my uncle, and they did a good job, I think."

Sue Ellen nodded and looked toward Peter.

"Honey, Peter, what do you think?"

"I think whatever you want is fine by me."

Sue Ellen rolled her eyes. Peter spoke up again after seeing his wife's reaction.

"This Smith Home sounds nice. We visited my aunt Helen there. They're affordable too."

Peggy perked up with this and smiled toward Sue Ellen.

"Uh-huh. Naperville? Naperville."

Sue Ellen noticed the "Love thy neighbor" and "Love thy Ridgeport" art plaque sitting on her dining room buffet and knew the answer.

"We'll make the arrangements at Ridgeport Funeral Home, and she'll be buried in our town, at Hope Cemetery."

"Okay then. It's settled," Peter said.

Sue Ellen raised a glass in a toast. "Love thy neighbor" and "Love thy Ridgeport."

22

The obit in *The Ridgeport News* on September 11, 2003, read:

Stella Whitmore, 84, beloved wife of the late Nathaniel, loving daughter of John and Dorothy Abram, the cherished nanny of Sue Ellen Norris, and survived by her brother Harry, her brother-in-law Frank, her many cousins and

many friends - 3:00 to 9:00 p.m. Visitation Saturday,
September 13, Funeral Services Sunday, September 14 from
11:00 a.m. to 12:00 p.m. at Ridgeport Cemetery. For more
information, call Ridgeport Funeral Home, 708-499-3102.

It was hard, to sum up, the special kind of person Stella
was in an obituary. Scott thought unless you're a celebrity,
it only gives the reader a snapshot of someone's life – who
they married, who they're survived by. But it does not tell
the whole picture of who Stella was. Their Stella – the
woman with the grandmotherly smile, the woman who
would stick her neck out for you even if that meant
jeopardizing her job. She was a friend and a mother. She was
someone who could never be replaced, and now she was
gone. Scott shook his head, blinking back fresh tears.

23

The first chill of Autumn came the day of the wake. The
leaves had not yet given way to yellow, but the humidity
over Ridgeport all summer had finally broken. The sun
shone brightly, and there was not a cloud in the sky, but the
cool, crisp air called for Scott to wear his blazer over his
black shirt and tie as he headed out the door with his parents
to the funeral home.

Not one of the Caseys spoke on the short ride. Loretta just
stared out the passenger-side window. When John returned
with news that Stella had died, she slept the rest of that day.
When Loretta finally awoke, she acted as if nothing had
happened. This annoyed Scott, but he just avoided his
mother, like she had avoided him the last five years. That
was three days ago, and she was acting as if she were still
avoiding him.

They arrived at the home right at ten. Only a few other
cars were in the lot. One of them turned out to be Sue Ellen's

Porsche, which was the family vehicle of choice now even though Peter had the more sensible Jeep Grand Cherokee. Scott remembered thinking that everyone in the world should turn up for Stella's wake. Everyone in the world should have known the woman who was the closest thing he had for a mother. And yet, cars continued to pass the home like any other day. She was gone, and all that Ridgeport had left of her was her 85-word obit in *The Ridgeport News.*

It was only the second wake in Scott's life. His uncle's untimely death to liver cancer was first, but Scott was in second grade. He didn't know his uncle all that well. At that wake, the only thing he remembered was playing *Donkey Kong Country* in the basement of the funeral home while the adults paid respects upstairs. He would later think it strange that a funeral home would have a Super Nintendo in the first place, but then again, nothing is stranger than death. The Ridgeport Funeral Home was quiet. The director pointed the Casey family towards Room Two with a sign that read "In Memoriam: Stella Whitmore." He felt his stomach drop, and his mouth went dry. He knew his mentor and friend, Stella, was there at the front in the casket. She would never breathe again, he thought, tears again welling in his eyes. He wanted to run. He wanted to scream. But he kept stumbling forward, like the walking dead.

Floral tributes to Stella greeted the family as they went inside. Flowers of all shapes and colors splashed the front of the room, while old photos decorated the left and right sides of the walls. Rows of chairs sat empty in the middle, but there were no names in the guest book yet. The Caseys were the only ones there for the moment, and Scott had never felt more alone in his life.

24

John put his hand on Scott's shoulder as Loretta gasped upon seeing Stella's body lying in the casket. Scott squirmed out from his dad's hold, looking for Matt or the Wrobels. When there was no sign of anyone making their way through the room, Scott made his way over to the wall of photos along the right side of the room. John put his arms around a hysterical Loretta, who was sobbing so loudly she could be heard throughout the room.

There was a tap on Scott's shoulder. To his great relief, it was Joe. He needed Joe now more than ever. He felt alone, so terribly alone. Joe wrapped her arms around Scott's delicate heart. For the first time in their relationship, Scott shed a tear, albeit one he dared not let his girlfriend see.

"Where's Matt?" Scott asked, trying to stay composed.

"He's coming with the Wrobels," said Joe. He needed to get out of the house where Stella died, and his mom said your mom was too hysterical to have him over."

Although frustrated, Scott chose not to say anything and just hugged Joe tighter. Loretta wriggled out of John's embrace when Sue Ellen arrived. Sue Ellen rolled her eyes and patted the top of her friend's head.

"There, there. Loretta. You are all torn up, dear. You're making your face look like a raccoon, you know?"

But Loretta continued sobbing, and after another fifteen seconds, Sue Ellen decided she had enough 'consoling' her friend. She unhooked herself from Loretta's grip and said she had to freshen up in the restroom.

"Oh, I'll join you!" Loretta exclaimed.

"Oh, honey. Why don't you wait for me on one of the couches here and collect yourself first, okay?"

Loretta nodded, while Sue Ellen smiled, turned, and strolled to the restroom. Peter and John took no interest and instead took to having a deep conversation about the

Chicago Bears' recent loss to the Packers and if they had what it took to make the playoffs.

Joe and Scott likewise paid no attention to the drama between the two women. Joe's slender hand clutched Scott's sweaty palm as they walked by a timeline of 'Stella through the Ages.' Black and white photos mixed with grainy technicolor shots from the sixties and seventies to crisp, modern images. Most showed Stella smiling, and they were not 'fake, smile for the camera smiles.' They were the genuinely warm smiles that the two of them remember. It was the smile she carried with her every day of her life. Stella was a happy person, and she brought joy wherever she went. There was a black and white of Stella with her brother Harry, playing in the yard at their old home on the Southside of Chicago, a photo of her in nurse's uniform, and one of the band posing with Stella. Peter had taken it only weeks before her death.

"Aw, remember that day, Scott! We all came over to wish her a happy birthday and got her a cake, and Sue Ellen had gone out for the day. Then Peter thought it would be a good idea to take us all up to her room to get the picture of all of us. It's the only one of all of us together."

"Yeah. I do. I love that picture. Even Riley and Jimmy look halfway normal."

"Hey...I heard that!" Jimmy shouted.

Joe and Scott turned around to see Riley and Jimmy standing with Matt.

"Shush. Keep your voice down," Scott said.

Riley elbowed his brother and shook his head.

"Yeah, show some respect, little bro."

The band was back together now, and at least for the time being, the world was okay anyway. They formed a circle and conducted the secret band handshake, just like they had four years prior. Some things never die, and they needed something that never died in this time of need.

179

The five of them gathered around the photo. Joe picked it off the display.

"Joe, what are you doing?" Scott asked.

"This is our photo. No one else deserves it. Stella would want us to have it," she said.

"Yeah, Joe's right, but who gets to keep it?" Matt asked.

"Well, I think we should keep it in a wallet, and we can see it anytime. We can each hold onto it for a certain amount of time, and then the next person can get it. It will be our good luck charm, like Stella is still with us," Joe said.

They nodded in unison.

"Well, who keeps it first then?" Riley asked.

"I vote Joe. She came up with the idea," Scott said.

"Sounds good to me," Matt said.

Riley and Jimmy did not say anything for a second but finally raised their hand to confirm the vote.

Before stuffing the photo into her wallet, Joe noticed that Stella's window was closed, and something jogged her memory.

"Guys. Her window is closed in this photo."

"So? Her window was always closed. She never wanted it open. I don't think it could open," Matt said.

"But that's just it. It was open when we found her," Joe said.

"Are you sure?" Scott asked.

"Scott, I closed it."

The group looked at the photo as if thinking the window might open.

"Well, maybe she got hot," Jimmy said.

"I don't think so. Stella hated having it open. She liked the heat," Joe said.

"You think someone opened it?" Scott asked.

"I don't know," Joe said. "It's just…odd. That's all. It shouldn't be open."

180

They looked at the photo one last time before Sue Ellen approached, and just before she caught the photo, Joe stuffed it into her wallet and out of sight.

25

Stella hardly resembled herself, dressed in her Sunday-best green and white-spotted flock dress and white pearls. The mortuary cosmetologist did their best to bring Stella back to life, but it made her look more like a lady of the night than the sweet woman the band remembered. When Scott approached the bench to give his final respects to the woman who had taken care of him the last fourteen years, he knelt to begin to pray, but nothing came. It was Stella who had taken him to church. It was Stella who had taught him the importance of prayer, of reading his Bible. But at that moment, even though he knew that Stella had lived a long, fulfilling life, Scott felt slighted by God for taking the closest person he had to a mother. So instead of paying his respects, he made a beeline to the parking lot. No one outside of Joe had noticed him leave.

Seeing Scott take off in such a hurry, Joe hesitated at the bench, crossed herself, and made his way to the back. By that time, a few more townspeople had filled the room. Running to catch up with Scott, Joe's jet-black hair waved behind her as if taken up in a violent windstorm.

"Scott! Scott! Where are you?!"

There was a path next to the funeral home. Darting her eyes to and fro, Joe saw Scott's blazer dangling from a tree branch. Joe made her way through the thick tangle of overgrown bushes and down a beaten path. The bottom of her black dress ripped, and she gritted her teeth in frustration. She hiked deeper into the woods, and a good thirty minutes passed. There was still no sign of Scott. It was eerily quiet, and no walkers, runners, or horseback riders made their way

181

on either end of the path. To the right of the path, Joe noticed a valley that appeared to have a trench dug out of the soil. It was the clubhouse the band set out to complete but never finished. That meant the swimmin' hole would be nearby.

"Scott! Are you down there?! Scott!?"

Joe attempted to run through the mud pit, stumbling as she ran, sliding onto her stomach on the sloppy mud like she was running a slip n' slide. Her hands slick with mud, she peered into the trench and noticed a shirt followed by a pair of underwear. It was Scott's shirt and his underwear, she was sure. There, in the nude, was Scott.

He had his back to her, and she could not believe she found him, skinny dipping. She thought he would be sulking on a log a few feet into the woods. Joe chuckled to herself, impressed. At that moment, Joe forgot about Stella and the reasons Scott had run from the funeral home. Her grief over Stella and worry over finding Scott evaporated at the moment. If this is the way Scott chose to express himself, she was with him, all the way. What had Stella taught them, after all?

Before she could say a word, Scott turned around, not embarrassed to be naked in her presence.

Joe found herself blushing this time.

"Hey there! Are you going to join me?"

He trod water, calm and confident.

Joe hesitated. She had never gone skinny-dipping before, and even though she acted adventurously, she checked that side of her at the edge of the water. Scott motioned with his arm.

"The water's fine!"

Despite her resolve, Joe was still tempted to turn around and leave. She bit her lip, and in one motion, she threw off her muddy, torn dress and hesitantly tugged her bra. Slowly, she rolled down her panties. Joe climbed the dead trunk overlooking the hole. It was a weird way to see his girlfriend naked for the first time, Scott remembered thinking – climbing a tree like a chimpanzee. But she was striking nonetheless – it would be an image that would stick with him his entire life. When Joe took the leap and hit the cool water near where Scott was still treading water, she screamed so loud that birds flew out from the trees.

"Holy shit Scott! It's cold in here!"

Scott laughed and splashed her in the face.

"What the hell? You go and splash me!"

Then there was nothing but silence, and the two backed up from each other to take in the forest while they kept treading water.

"So why are you out here? I was worried sick about you."

Scott said nothing, scanning the forest preserve as if he did not hear her.

"Scott?"

"This place calms me. It always did. I don't have a mom, Joe. Loretta hasn't been my mom in years. And...and..."

And Scott began to cry. It was the first time Joe had ever seen him cry. Instead of waiting for him to continue, Joe swam over to him and slipped her arms around him. He buried his head in her shoulder, letting his tears flow freely down her back. In the light, with their bodies fused, it was the most intimate moment of their young lives. It transcended sex. It transcended friendship. As he cried, Joe held him in her firm, athletic arms, giving him the strength and comfort he needed. Scott tightened his grip around her waist. They stood like this for what seemed like an eternity, saying nothing but communicating like never before. It was a magical moment.

"I don't know what I'm going to do now, Joe. I don't have a mother."

"I know," she said and continued to calm him in a warm embrace in the cool water.

"If it makes you feel any better, I don't have one either."

Scott turned his head from her shoulder and looked into her eyes. It never occurred to him that Stella meant to her just as much as she meant to him.

"I'm sorry too, Joe."

Joe shrugged her shoulders.

"Don't be. Peter's a good man. And a good father. Plus, we got each other, and Stella is never really gone. She's inside of us all."

Scott nodded and continued to search her eyes. He knew if this was a time to kiss her, this was it. Instead, Joe rested her head against his. Her lips must have been inches from his at this point. Scott closed his eyes and took in the moment. When he opened them a minute later, she pushed off and started to swim back toward the shore. She flashed him a half-smile as she did so.

"You're leaving?"

"I'm getting cold. Besides, they're going to start wondering where we are. Don't you think we should head back?"

Scott knew he missed his opportunity. Still, it was a moment he'll never forget. Feeling his lips so close to hers was almost better than any kiss.

"Sure. You're probably right."

26

An icy wind cut through the trees and up to their spines. Scott convinced himself it was the only thing that could stop their perfect moment. That gust of wind reminded the two of them of just how cold water felt by mid-September. A cloud strolled over, blocking out the sun with it.

Without a warm summer sun to dry off, their dirty clothes provided their only warmth. Joe's dress was covered in mud and torn at the hem. She shook her head as she hesitantly picked it out of the mud pit, but just as her frustration flared

184

over her ripped and dirty dress, she took one look over at Scott buttoning his shirt and smiled. She would remember this moment forever.

The cloud pulled back, and the sun shone once more on their old swimmin' hole. The pair walked towards the pond. Scott reached out his hand to Joe. She took it, intertwining their fingers as they looked across the pond together. It took on a whole new meaning for them now.

After a long moment, Scott finally said, "Well, let's go, Joe."

"Okay, Scott," Joe said, with a smile meant for Scott alone.

27

Scott did not want to leave the woods. He could have stayed there forever. There was a crazy thought that ran through his head to finish building the trench and live out the rest of his days right there, in the comfort of the woods where they could make their own rules and live their own lives. He smiled at this idea but decided not to share it. It sounded too good to be true, like George and Lennie's dream of the farm and the rabbits.

"Whatcha smilin' for?"

"Huh?"

"What's the smile for? You just smiled and were looking off into the distance."

"I...I was?"

Joe laughed and rolled her eyes. She let go of Scott's hand and rubbed it on his shirt sleeve.

"Man, you got all sweaty, Smiley. You were smiling, though."

"Oh, well, I was just thinking about us. It was a good day, wasn't it?"

"It was Casey. It was."

"But that's not what you were smiling about."

"It was!"

"Come on. Tell me! I know your looks. You were deep in thought."

Scott looked down at Joe and reached out to grab her hand again. He looked around and noticed a chipmunk scurry in the brush.

"I was just thinking of Stella, is all. I'm gonna miss her. I don't exactly have a mom, you know?"

Joe grabbed Scott's hand tight. Scott kicked a pebble on the trail, and had it not been for their wake attire, they would have had no idea that civilization was at the other end of those woods.

"I didn't think about her ever dying, you know? Why did she have to die?"

"I know, Scott."

The pair continued to stroll through the woods at a leisurely pace. They were in no hurry to head back to the funeral home. They walked in silence, letting the touch of their hands do the communicating for them. Then, Joe spoke up.

"I have a weird feeling that Stella didn't die of natural causes, Scott."

"Because of the window?"

"Yeah, because of the window."

"What are you implying?"

"What if there is something else to this?"

"Something else we're not seeing?"

"Like what?"

"Like, like…"

And at that moment, a barn owl swooped through the trees. They both saw it and craned their necks left to right to watch it jet from the sky to branch. The owl landed on a tall tree and stared down at them as if the bird had picked them out. Joe glanced over at Scott to see if he saw what she was seeing and noticed that he appeared reassured. All the nerves she had seen in him on the walk had vanished.

"The owl came to tell me Stella's okay. She's okay, Joe."

Joe hugged Scott. They stood there until the owl flapped its gigantic wings and moved on. Joe tugged Scott's hand along the path and back to reality.

28

When they returned to the funeral home and met up with the other band members, the rest of the band performed a double-take at Joe's muddy, ripped dress alongside a blushing Scott.

"Well, well, well, what happened here?" Matt asked.

"We…"

"Scott, I'll field this, thanks," Joe said.

The band circled the two. No one else in the home seemed to pay them any mind as they were busy prattling away with other adults.

"Maybe we should step outside, just in case someone hears us," Joe said.

The band nodded and brushed past a couple of people they didn't recognize and out toward the exit. The cool air welcomed Scott and Joe with a good memory, and Scott wished he could just retreat into the woods with her. Joe stole a look at Scott and smiled, and Matt took notice and wore a confused expression on his face.

"So? What's up?" Riley asked.

"What's up is that Scotty boy here decided to go for some skinny dipping."

"Ha, you what?" Riley asked.

Scott looked at Joe and blushed again before scanning the band's faces for another response.

"Well, alright!" Matt exclaimed and reached out for a high five.

"Ha, thanks," Scott said, hi-fiving back.

"And, that's not all," Joe said. "I went in with him."

"You what? You skinny-dipped with him?" Matt asked. It was Matt's time to blush now. Joe nodded, smiling.

Riley, Jimmy, and Matt let out a collective smile and patted the two on the back.

"Alright, well, look at you two. Skinny dippin' on the day of a funeral," Riley said. Jimmy nodded with a grin.

"Sounds like somebody's jealous they weren't in the pool with us," Joe quipped back.

The ordinary quick-witted Riley had no real response for this, aside from, "No, I just...just...oh, never mind."

Joe chuckled, and Matt patted Scott on the back again.

"So, is that how your dress got like that?" Matt asked.

"My dress got like that because I fell into a mud pit. Not my most gracious of moments."

Matt looked at the dress and laughed. Joe laughed along with him, and then the rest of the band jumped in. Another cool gust of wind blew through, and Joe recommended they go back inside.

"I didn't say I was going back in. I just think you should. If anyone asks where I am, just say I'm out here, and that I couldn't handle myself. It's probably not a good look for a girl with a muddy dress to stay inside the home."

"Ha, good idea," Matt said. As the band made their way back inside, Scott hung back. Joe raised an eyebrow at his staying behind.

"What's up? Do you want another round there, Casey?"

"Uh-huh, just surprised that you told them."

Joe gave that half-smile again that she flashed him in the pool.

"You wouldn't have told them eventually anyway? You wouldn't have told Matt that you went skinny dipping with me?"

"No...I...well...I"

"That's what I thought. It's okay. I don't care if they know. I mean, if I knew you didn't have to tell your friend everything, it'd be nice, but I get it."

"Hey, I don't have to tell him everything. I don't."

Joe nodded and smiled.

"Uh-huh. So, if I kissed you right now, you wouldn't say anything?" Joe asked.

"No. I wouldn't."

Joe scanned the parking lot, but just as she was about to lean in for a kiss, Sue Ellen came walking out of her car and toward the doors. Joe pulled back. As Sue Ellen walked past them, she eyed Joe's disheveled look up and down but only said, "Joe," and nodded.

Joe gulped and responded, "Sue Ellen."

Sue Ellen did not so much as look at Scott, and as soon as Sue Ellen made her way inside the home, Scott knew his moment for a kiss had expired once again.

29

Loretta did not even notice that Scott had run off. Scott saw his normally mild-mannered father rip into his mother that night. He had never seen his father act like that. He resembled a bear rudely awakened from its slumber. Words spit out of John Casey's mouth with the firepower of an M-16. All Loretta did that night in the kitchen was tremble at a spot by the back window, like a single leaf still attached to a tree in late November.

Scott had tried to leave the corner couch with a view of the kitchen, but each time he so much as sat up, John barked at him to sit down.

"Stay here, Scott. I want to make sure your mother knows where you are!"

What started as an argument about Scott's disappearance from home that day morphed into much more as the berating continued. Years of John's bottled-up frustrations with his wife poured out of his mouth.

"You're not there for him, and you're never there for me. You only care about you and her next door. That's it. It's just like when I went to support you at your board of trustees speech. You didn't care that I was there. You only cared that she was there."

Scott shifted awkwardly in his seat. He watched Loretta quiver, helpless before she broke down in tears. He could not help but feel sorry for the woman, even if everything his father said was true. What Scott wanted at that moment, more than anything, was Joe. He closed his eyes and pictured her in the swimmin' hole. A brief smile flashed across his face until he came to from the sound of curse words flying out of his father's mouth.

Scott ran to his bedroom this time, not caring what John wanted of him. He could take no more. He heard the shouting continue for a good twenty minutes, and then when his father knocked on his door about an hour later, Scott pretended to be asleep.

"Scott? I...I just want to talk. Scott?"

John peeked inside but saw that the lights were turned off and that his son lay under the blankets with his eyes closed.

After the door closed, Scott opened his eyes again. He did not hear another noise in the house until Joe threw a rock at his window.

30

"Joe?"

"Hey! Come out and play with me!"

"Shush! My parents are sleeping, and my dad is kind of crazy tonight."

Joe laughed that kind of flirtatious laugh that drove Scott crazy. Her carefree laugh matched her pink pajama pants and white hoodie, which were against Ridgeport's dress code. She could really get in trouble if anyone saw her dressed like that out in public.

"What are you doing out so late? It's past curfew!"

"Whatever. My new mom is the curfew police. I can do what I want. So, are you going to come out, or do I have to throw rocks at your window all night?"

As much as Scott wanted to go, he hesitated for a second. Should he get caught up past curfew with a scantily clad girl, he could wind up in a heap of trouble. Then again, he thought, he would be up past curfew with a scantily clad girl. His girl, Joe.

"I'll be right down!" he whispered loudly. He closed the window and thought about dressing up but rushed out in his shorts and t-shirt. If she was going to break the dress code, so was he. They were a couple. Besides, what are pajamas compared to what they did that afternoon?

31

Certain days remain in a person's memory, and for Scott Casey, the day of Stella's wake was one of those days. It was one of those days, not just because of Stella, but because of Joe. In the quietest of moments, he would smile. And the night that Scott Casey decided to break curfew and run off with his girlfriend was one of the last purely happy moments he would have for some time.

Scott crept down the stairs and out of the house with the moves of a cat burglar. His heart sank into the pit of his stomach when the bottom step creaked, but there was no stir in his parent's bedroom. There was nothing but darkness outside, except for the reddish glowing cheeks and white hoodie Joe wore. A howl of wind pushed under Scott's jacket and up his back. Their crabapple tree danced vigorously against the black sky. There were no lights on in any of the neighboring houses. Joe's teeth were chattering, but she managed a smirk nonetheless.

"Bout damn time."

"I'm here, aren't I?"

Scott looked left and right like a kid crossing the street. Joe threw her hand on his shoulder and laughed.

"Relax. No one's gonna catch us. My folks are all in bed, and I'm pretty sure we live in the dullest neighborhood in the country."

"Right. I know. I'm just making sure."

Joe rolled her eyes this time and motioned for him to follow. Scott hesitated but did as instructed.

"Where are we going?"

"No questions."

Into the woods, their woods, they disappeared. They didn't look back. The entire neighborhood was asleep except for Sue Ellen. She sat in her French armchair overlooking her street, with an Amaretto Stone Sour in her hand, and her eyes shot in the direction of Scott and Joe.

32

Joe's dark hair flung from side to side as she grabbed Scott's hand and led him deeper into the woods. Leaves fell from side to side, and Scott heard them crunch underneath their feet. The outside world seemed so far away now, but then again, everything seemed far away anytime he was with Joe.

"Here," Joe said, and with a tug of Scott's hand, he came to a halt and nearly fell over.

"What are we doing here, Joe?"

She pointed to a campsite to the right of Scott where there were old tree trunks set up around a rock pit. A couple of old empty beer cans someone left behind were strewn around the rocks.

"You want to have a fire?"

192

"Smart boy. Now, why don't you gather some firewood for us, huh?"

"And what are you gonna do?"

"I'll save our seat!"

Scott couldn't help but smile at her. He thought of how eventful a day it had been. It was odd that he had never felt more alive on the day that he attended Stella's wake. Joe was his spark. It was all about Joe. Scott dressed the wood in a log-cabin structure, with the kindle stuffed inside with the bigger logs squared around it. When he finished and stepped back, he crossed his arms, showing his satisfaction with his work. Joe stood from her seat and pecked him on the cheek.

"Now, you'll have to light it for me."

"You don't have a lighter?"

"Nope."

Scott ventured off to find two strong sticks to rub together, but as he did, the fire started to burn. He looked back, and there was Joe with a wide grin. She held up her lighter.

"You goof," Scott said.

"Did you really think I was going to make you light the fire?"

"I don't know. You made me get the wood and build it."

Joe sat back down and patted the spot next to her on the tree trunk. Scott complied, and they stared at the fire, hypnotized as the flames ate the kindle and moved onto the logs around it. Neither of them said anything. He awkwardly placed his arm around her shoulders. Joe leaned into him, but out of the corner of Scott's eye, he could see her pull something out of her right pants pocket. It looked like a bag.

Before he could explore, they heard a rustling sound in the forest, startling him. Scott shot up like a prairie dog, but she ignored him when he turned his attention back to Joe. The wood was not the only thing blazing now. Joe pulled a joint out of her pocket, lit it up, and took a long toke. Scott's mouth dropped open. If anyone were to catch them, it would be time in jail for sure.

"Want some?"

Joe puffed the smoke in Scott's face and smiled. And all at once, he forgot about Ridgeport. He wasn't in Ridgeport anymore. He was in the wild. There were no rules in the wild.

"Yes. Yes, I do."

33

It would be the first, and the last time Scott would light up. By the next morning, he would find out that grass would be something he would rather walk on than smoke. But in the meantime, it was great. Though, it was only great because it loosened them both up enough to be close in a way that didn't involve skinny dipping.

"You were going to tell me something earlier today, but I couldn't get it out of you."

"I was?"

"Yeah. It was when we were walking out of the woods. Remember?"

"Oh, yeah."

"What was it?"

"Well, I…"

Scott took another drag on his joint, stared at the fire, and watched the sparks fly majestically into the night sky.

"I like it here."

"Ha. Me too."

"No, I mean...I want to live here, Joe."

"Yeah, right, me too."

Scott shook his head, stood up, and began to pace this time.

"No, I mean like, Ridgeport is all bullshit...you know? I mean, it's all do this, and do that. Don't do that. No one is like that. We're not robots, Joe."

She nodded in agreement and continued to stare at the fire.

"Remember the trench?"

"Yeah, so? You want to build a clubhouse and live here?"

"I...I don't know. It'd be better than living at home, in a house that's not even a home."

"So, this is all about Stella dying?"

Scott turned his back and looked out at the woods. He jumped up again and thought it was something coming toward them.

"You pretty jumpy there? That stuff is supposed to calm you, buddy."

"Thought I heard something coming."

We should finish the trench."

"You're kidding?"

"No. We should. We started it. Why not finish it?"

"Because we're not twelve. We're in high school now. We went skinny dipping today. The rule is when you see each other naked, you can't go back to t-ball."

Scott didn't say anything after that for a while but instead sat back down and snuggled next to Joe. The temperature dropped an easy ten degrees overnight, and he was cold and hungry.

"Aren't you hungry?"

"Lucky thing I brought s'more stuff."

Joe pulled out a Hershey chocolate bar, graham crackers, and marshmallows out of her sweatshirt pocket.

"You had all of that in your front pouch?"

"It's a big pouch. I'm a kangaroo!"

"You don't happen to have skewers in there too, do ya?"

Joe smirked and pulled out foldable skewers from her front pocket as well. Scott nodded, impressed.

As Joe handed Scott his skewer, their hands met, and then their eyes locked. Scott knew that this was his moment. Scott moved closer to Joe and kissed her like it would be the last time he would ever kiss her. Some moments in life you know right away that you'll remember forever. This was one of them. That first kiss with Joe he didn't fully appreciate on account of their being half out of their minds, but even though he was high, he at least felt that he had his wits about him. When Scott finally let her go, she looked at him for a second, breathless and spellbound. It was a perfect night. The fire crackled under a blanket of stars. Their only neighbors were their familiar trees, and their only concern was for each other. Joe smiled widely and kissed him back. *Maybe it wasn't just the fire keeping their bodies warm by now*, he thought. It felt like they kissed forever, even if it was only five minutes. When they took a second to catch their breath, Scott decided to go for it.

"Joe, I...I love..."

"Shush," Joe put her hand to his lips. "Do you hear that?"

"Nah, I wanted to tell you that I…."

"It's coming from over there by the tall grasses."

Joe was the one standing up now, and Scott was the one to pull her down. He brushed her hair aside and kissed her again. They embraced, warmed by the fire and emboldened by the lawlessness of their actions. This time, Scott and Joe felt the intense love between them.

The last thing Scott remembered from that night was taking his first bite of s'mores. When he awoke, it was dawn, and he was lying face down in a meadow, far from the fire pit. Joe laid asleep on his right, with her arms flailed out. He noticed she had cuts on her arms and a gash on her forehead. His stomach was churning.

As Scott tried to get up, the world spun as if Scott had just jumped off the Tilt-a-Whirl. The brilliant indigo and black-eyed Susan flowers danced in the early morning light and off his swirling vision. Then, after taking a step, he threw up whatever was left of the s'mores all over the patch of meadow. Some chocolate dripped down his sweatshirt and into the grass below. Joe stirred but stayed asleep like a baby.

The vomiting brought him to. The vertigo had passed, and he could see Joe once again. She looked like she had the shit beat out of her. And she was still the most beautiful girl he had ever seen. Scott knelt beside her, and while stroking her luscious dark brown hair, he whispered for her to wake.

"Joe?"

Nothing.

This time he shook her whole body like shaking a parent awake on Christmas morning.

"Joe! Wake up!"

That did it. One eye slowly opened, and Scott breathed a sigh of relief.

Joe let out a monstrous yawn and stretched her arms as far as they would go. She slyly smiled at the boy she shared experiences with that would last a lifetime.

"Joe...you look awful."

"Well, thanks. You don't look too good either. What did you throw up or something?"

"Uh. Yeah. You may want to watch where you step."

They helped each other up and tried to figure out where they were. They were in a part of the wood neither of them had seen before. There was a giant oak in the middle of the field, but other than that, only tall grasses and flowers swayed in the wind.

"Do you remember what happened last night?"

Joe felt the cuts along her arms before touching the flesh wound on her forehead. There was evidence of a trail of trampled grasses to their right that spanned a good distance. Since having known her, Scott saw that Joe looked worried for the first time. She was supposed to be rebellious, devil-may-care. But she looked worried. She rubbed her arms frantically, and periodically felt her forehead. Her eyes moved from Scott to the trail that led to where they stood.

"I remember...running."

"Running?"

Joe continued to rub her arms but nodded her head in confirmation.

"Why were we running?"

"I... I don't know."

"We were running from something. We were running from people...from bad people."

Scott looked Joe up and down to take in the severity of what happened overnight. The last thing that he remembered was eating s'mores.

"And that must be how you got so banged up."

But Joe just nodded. A hawk circled overhead as if thinking Scott and Joe were prey.

"Who do you think was after us, Scott?"

"Well, we did break a lot of rules last night. Do you remember hearing a rustling in the woods, Joe?"

"Um, I think so. Maybe, yes."

"Do you suppose?"

Joe bit the tip of a fingernail but didn't respond. The two noticed that the dawn colors began to fade, and the purple and reds slowly turned to blue.

"We need to get going. We're outdoors, and we have a funeral today. We could be in deep shit if anyone finds out we're not home."

"I think we're already in deep shit, Scott. Someone tried to catch us last night for something. It must have been bad enough for me to hurt myself like this."

Scott nodded but grabbed her hand and began down the trail and out of the meadow. Before they broke into a run, Scott noticed something in the grass. It was a little dirty, but Scott saw it was a silver necklace with the name of the verse "1 Corinthians 13:4-13" engraved on the front. Even though he felt a pang of guilt for picking up something that didn't belong to him, he also wanted something to give to Joe to remember their special night together. He put it in his pocket to give her when the time was right.

35

Amazingly, Scott returned home when the rest of the Caseys were still asleep. The clock said nine o'clock in the morning. Dripping with sweat and out of breath, Scott tip-toed up the stairs and into the shower. He reeked of bonfire, pot, sweat, and dirt. By the time he came out, he had smelled coffee downstairs and footsteps in the kitchen.

All he wanted to do was sleep. But, sleeping in a prairie after one of the craziest nights in his life did not give him energy. But it was 9:15 now, and the funeral started at eleven, which meant there was no time to sleep. Scott threw on some sweats and a t-shirt to eat before getting formally dressed in black. As he pulled out a box of Cheerios from the pantry, his dad called from the living room.

"Scott!" John called. "Come in here, please?"

Scott rolled his eyes, thinking he just wanted to make it through the day without any more surprises. He begrudgingly set the box on the kitchen island and moved to the other room. His mom and dad were seated next to each other on the living room sofa, smiling at him between sips of coffee.

"Scott... I'm sorry for how we acted last night," John said.

"It was really out of line, dear," Loretta said.

Scott frowned but then remembered how out-of-line he had been, running off into the woods.

"It's...okay. We all do stupid things sometimes."

"Great. Glad you understand, bud," John said.

And as Loretta rubbed John's hand, Scott shook his head in disgust and turned to go back to his cereal. He liked it better when they fought.

36

Scott and Matt served as pallbearers, and there was nothing worse than carrying Stella's body to her grave, but they agreed to do it out of respect for her.

Stella was buried at Hope Cemetery in Ridgeport, next to her late sister Nora, who passed away when she was just 21. The pastor read a passage from John 14: "Do not let your hearts be troubled. You believe in God; believe also in me. My Father's house has many rooms; if that were not so, would I have told you that I am going there to prepare a place for you? And if I go and prepare a place for you, I will come back and take you to be with me so that you also may be where I am. You know the way to the place where I am going."

The guests gathered around the casket. There was nothing more to see now. It was just a box lowered into the dirt. The funeral director passed out roses. Scott and Matt threw theirs in together. Their eyes filled with tears as the casket was lowered to the ground.

Stella was not the only one out of sight that day. Joe never showed. Matt said she had a 102 fever and was at home resting. But when Scott and Matt came back home to check on her, she was gone.

Chapter 5: Ridgeport 1983

1

In 1983, Sue Ellen and Peter divorced. It was also the year that Sue Ellen created the Neighborhood Watch. They married in 1980. They started with great heat, but after '82, something lit a match that sparked the kindling, which ended up raging into a wild dumpster fire of a marriage by July of '83.

Peter decided he was ready for kids in the spring of '82. Sue Ellen laughed it off and told Peter that he'd married the wrong girl. She wasn't the motherly type. He thought she might come around, but when she refused to give up taking birth control, things turned south in more than one way.

"You said you wanted kids when we were engaged!" he'd cry.

"I don't remember saying that," she snapped back.

As the months dragged on, Sue Ellen became more controlling of her husband. In fact, Sue Ellen controlled her husband like a puppet. She was Pavlov, and he was her dog. Peter objected to this control at first but eventually just gave in. He knew that it was not worth fighting for.

"Remember, I'm going out with a couple of friends this Friday night, dear," he said.

"Oh yeah, no, I think it's better if we attend that aerobics class together, I've been talking about. They have one every Friday at the gym."

"This Friday? But I've been scheduling this with the guys for weeks. Can't we start the class next Friday?"

Sue Ellen flashed a look at Peter that said a firm "no," and Peter hung his head obediently.

"Yes, dear. I'll call them up and say I'm not going."

Sue Ellen smiled widely and said, "Perfect. You'll have a great time."

About a year later, Sue Ellen suspected Peter of cheating, despite having no evidence. She thought because he kept late nights, something was off. Sue Ellen once followed him to his job because she suspected he was having a fling with a coworker. She was wrong. Instead of finding Peter flirting with some floozy, she walked into his office and saw him lurched over his computer, typing away.

"Peter! There you are."

"Um, Sue Ellen? I'm surprised to see you here."

"Oh, well, I missed you silly. I just thought I'd drop by."

"That's very sweet. It's good to see you."

Sue Ellen smiled, but Peter tapped his finger on his desk, looking from the computer and back to his wife.

"Honey, I'm sorry, but I have an awful lot of work to do. If I can finish a few things up here, though, I'll do my best to get home early today, okay?"

"Oh, sure, sure."

Peter smiled at his wife, and Sue Ellen smiled back. Before heading out to leave, she scanned the room for any good-looking women. She didn't see any, not any, as beautiful as herself at least. She felt so much better than she had before she walked in until this one walked into the building as she was leaving. She was younger and at least just as pretty and dressed in a scandalous low-cut top. Her heart sank, and she began to ponder all over again if this could be a girl Peter was having an affair with. *Is that why he ushered her out so quickly?* she thought. She shook the thought, but it would only keep resurfacing as the weeks and months passed on. She kept seeing that young girl walk into that office building. She confronted him about it one day, and she could have sworn she saw him blush.

"Peter, are you having an affair at work?"

"What? Are you insane?"

"Well, are you? I know there's at least one attractive girl who works there."

That's when she thought she saw him blush.

"You mean Sarah? Sure, but she doesn't light a candle to you."

"So, you admit that she's attractive. I see."

"Hey, you said it yourself first. I also said that she's not as attractive as you. What do you want me to say?"

"I wanted you to say that you didn't know of any attractive girls who work there."

"Fine. I don't."

"But you already did! I got the answer I wanted."

As time went on, and Sue Ellen's rants and accusations became more outrageous, Peter found himself often apologizing for things he never did. As she became more abusive and accusatory, Peter started to believe he was at fault. They divorced in the weirdest way, and ironically, Peter was the one who left with the upper hand. Sue Ellen came home and noticed that Peter was watching a program on TV.

"Turn that off. I want to watch something now. Aren't you going to make dinner for me?" is what Peter remembers her saying.

"I want a divorce," he said.

"Say that again?" Sue Ellen said, stunned.

"You heard me. I want a divorce."

Sue Ellen froze in her spot, started to tremble, and then the tears began to fall. As soon as Peter rose from the couch and made his way to comfort her, she pushed a hand out in front of her, blocking his advance.

"Get away, Peter. Stay away."

"I was just going to…."

"Stay away!"

Even though Peter backed up a few steps, she continued to holler at him.

"Stay away! Stay away! Stay away!" She screamed so loud the neighbors heard. Not knowing what to do, Peter put on his shoes and made his way toward the door.

"I'm going for a walk. I'll let you calm down."

"Yeah, you go! You go!" As he was about to head out, Loretta picked up their clay table lamp and heaved it in his direction. He ducked and closed the door behind him. It smashed against it and broke into several pieces. Sue Ellen screamed once more before sitting herself next to the couch and breaking down into tears once more. She could not believe that he was the one who was divorcing her. No one had ever stood up to her, and now here she was, powerless and without a husband.

2

Sue Ellen didn't take to single life all that well. Without having Peter there to control, she felt helpless. Before they formally filed their divorce paperwork, Sue Ellen pleaded with Peter to take her back, but he firmly stood his ground.

"Honey, I know that I was too hard on you all these years. We can work on it, we can. I'll let you go out and see your friends sometimes."

Peter almost bought it too.

"Sometimes. Let me?"

"I don't need you to let me do anything, Sue Ellen. I'm my own person."

"No, that's not what I mean. Oh, we can work this out. I know I can be a little nut. It's just because I care about being with you."

Peter shook his head, pausing to sign the papers for a second, and looked into her eyes. Sue Ellen smiled wanly.

"I still care for you, but this just isn't working out. I don't think it will do either of us good to stay together."

Then Peter signed the divorce papers and, as he did so, added, "Who knows? We'll see each other again one day and get along just fine. Anything can happen."

Later that night, Sue Ellen drank herself into a stupor. She visited Kenlawn Liquors in nearby Woodlawn, buying two bottles of cheap chardonnay. She didn't even bother with a glass in the kitchen but drank right from the bottle. Lifting the first bottle to her lips, Sue Ellen found she had company.

There was Stella.

When Stella took notice, she tried to console her at the kitchen table.

"Go to your room you! Can't you see I'm busy!" Sue Ellen yelled out.

Stella did as she asked. It was the first time Sue Ellen lashed out at her. It would be the first of many.

There was no noise in the kitchen other than the hum from the fridge and the ticking of the clock. Time passed as Sue Ellen drank deep draughts from the bottles…from eight to nine to ten. By ten p.m., Sue Ellen had a bottle and a half in her and was feeling woozy. But she was knocked back into semi-sobriety, or at least, consciousness, at five past ten. Sue Ellen heard a scream coming from a parked car down the street out of the open window. The high-pitched scream pierced through the night and through Sue Ellen's bay window. Sue Ellen stumbled toward the window and noticed a girlish figure with a man leaning toward her. The thought of calling the cops raced through her mind, but then she remembered that she was drunk and didn't want to call the cops drunk. She would have Stella do it! Yes, Stella would call.

"Stella! Stella, are you there?!"

But Stella was fast asleep, so Sue Ellen yelled a few times up the stairs before Stella collected herself and rushed down to the kitchen.

"Yes, ma'am? What is it?"

Sue Ellen glanced out the window, but by this time, the car was gone.

"Nothing. Thanks for nothing. You're too late. Go on to bed."

"But what happened?"

"What did I say?"

"Yes, ma'am."

Feeling exhausted and defeated, Stella turned back up the stairs and into her room. That was the night that gave Sue Ellen the idea for the Neighborhood Watch.

4

Sue Ellen passed out at the kitchen table moments after her stakeout of the neighborhood. A half-bottle of cheap chardonnay was cradled in her right hand, and her right cheek pressed hard against the tablecloth. She laid there an hour before waking with a crook in her neck and dragging herself upstairs to her bedroom.

As daylight broke, so did she, with heavy bags under her eyes and knots in her stomach. She made frequent trips to the bathroom where Stella could hear her gutturals echo through the home. Despite how Sue Ellen treated her maid turned nanny all those years, Stella did everything in her power to be there for Sue Ellen. Stella saw her pain and felt sorry for her, and she understood that what had happened between her and Peter had wrecked her.

It's not that Sue Ellen was always bitter toward Stella. She had better days—the day after her self-pity party was one of them. Self-pity party, day two started that day, but Stella made sure to put a stop to it early. When Stella walked into the living room and saw that Sue Ellen was watching a soap with a bag of potato chips and candy by her side, she flicked the TV off, picked up the junk food, grabbed a glass of water, and threw it into Sue Ellen's face. Sue Ellen froze, and for a second Stella was worried she might be fired, but when Sue Ellen burst out laughing, all was well.

"I guess...I guess I had that one coming!"

"Well, you needed something to get you off of that couch."

Water dripped off her face and hair and onto her shirt. She wiped her eyes with the bottom of her t-shirt.

"Here, let me help you off that couch. Then why don't you go shower and get into some clean clothes? I'm going to go to the grocery store. You want to join me? It might do you some good to get out of this house."

"Well, seeing as how you thought I needed water splattered on my face, that's probably a good idea."

They both laughed this time. It was one of the few moments that Stella and Sue Ellen would ever share a laugh.

5

Sue Ellen hadn't gone grocery shopping for herself in over a year. She did not need to, now that Stella went for her. But it was refreshing to go back. Strangely, such a mundane task gave her a sense of purpose again, even if it was as simple as picking out the freshest fruit.

Stella didn't dare bring up Peter and instead focused the conversation around dinner that night and food she needed that week. Stella navigated the aisles like a veteran and picked up ingredients for grilled tilapia to make for dinner. It was Sue Ellen's favorite. They even stopped at the florist for an arrangement of annuals to brighten up the house. Stella could have sworn that Sue Ellen wore a smile on her face at checkout, and as they walked out to the parking lot, she even said, "thank you."

"So, where next?"

"We're going home, Sue Ellen."

"Right, but after that?"

"Oh. Well, I always go to the village board meetings on Tuesdays. You're welcome to join me."

"Right, tonight. I've been meaning to go."

"Okay, let's go then," said Stella.

And that night started Sue Ellen's infatuation with everything Ridgeport. As the rules stated, "Love thy neighbor" and "Love thy Ridgeport."

6

Little did Sue Ellen know that night's village board meeting led her life in a whole new direction. For the past few months, she refused invitations to parties and made excuses to avoid seeing friends. Only Stella remained by her side, and deep down, Sue Ellen enjoyed her company. Right now, she even enjoyed it outwardly.

"Thanks for bringing me here, Stella. I needed to get out of the house."

"You're welcome, dear."

Residents packed the hall. Sue Ellen's mouth dropped to the floor. The board voted on approving Mayor Sheila Goldman's Social Norms Policies that night. When Goldman ran, she promised to not only modernize Ridgeport but also stay true to Ridgeport's historic values and traditions. She hinted at this policy in her 1980 campaign, but a formal plan did not come to fruition until earlier this year.

All the seats were filled, but Stella and Sue Ellen remained standing. Several other residents stood with them along the back and sidewalls. Following the pledge, the Ridgeporters recited the town motto, "Love thy neighbor" and "Love thy Ridgeport," and then the meeting began.

Following the call to order, public comment concerning the town's potential new social norms initiative commenced—a line formed down the middle of the room in a haphazard, single file. Residents grumbled, and the words "ridiculous" and "outrageous" filled the room.

"What's the matter?"

"You'll see."

Perplexed, Sue Ellen scanned the room as if she had seen it for the first time. Some Ridgeporters appeared calm. Others looked as if their cat had just died. And all this time, Sue Ellen knew nothing about what was going on. Her ugly divorce and subsequent reclusiveness forced her inward, away from the outside world.

Joe Henry stepped up to the podium, the first in the lengthy line of impatient citizens. *He must be at least ninety*, Sue Ellen thought. With puffs of white hair that remained around his ears and a thick white mustache, he looked like Waldorf, that short old crabby man from the Muppets that was always cracking one-line jokes with his taller friend Statler.

"I think we ought to do away with these social norms. I, uh...I don't like it," he croaked hoarsely.

When he spoke, he sounded like his voice could go at any second. It was as if this would be the last speech he would ever give.

Henry pulled a wrinkled piece of paper from his pocket and placed his reading glasses over his nose. Joe Henry was a legend at town meetings. He had attended every board meeting for the last fifteen years, and he always made sure to get a comment in, no matter the subject.

"It is not right for a man, or a woman, I suppose, to have to fit under a set of rules of what you say is proper and what isn't," he began. "I didn't fight in WWI just to come back to this country and have my freedoms limited."

Joe Henry rambled for another few minutes, pontificating on the social norms initiative infringing on the rights of every resident in the room and on every American's freedom. Half the time, it seemed like he was telling old war stories or losing his place. One trustee, Joe Kendall, drummed his fingers against his desk after a couple of minutes. However, mayor Sheila Goldman remained upright in her chair the entire time, with a slight smile on her face. She took in what he was saying and nodded every couple of minutes. Joe had seen this same type of response from the board before - tapping on the desk, fighting to stay awake, and the smile and nod from the mayor. The board hardly took anything seriously from everything he proposed or complained about in his fifteen years at the podium.

After Henry had finished speaking, Mayor Goldman thanked him for his comment, and Henry stuffed his paper back in his pocket, returned his reading glasses to his front pocket, mumbled a few frustrated words, and stepped aside. Déjà vu hit him again at the podium. For Henry, he trudged away unsatisfied, just like last week and the week before that.

"Stella? What is this social norm initiative? I haven't been paying too close attention."

"They want to regulate what everyone can wear or can't wear, how people should properly behave."

"Oh, I see."

Some rules wouldn't be a bad idea, Sue Ellen thought. Peter cheated on me with that slut in the low-cut top. Then that bulky man raped that innocent girl in the car last night. Sue Ellen stared at the disgruntled faces in the line. A few of them wore sagging sweatpants to match the saggy bags under their eyes. She wondered how people could leave the house like that. She wondered if the people from last night were in the crowd. Sue Ellen gasped but quickly covered her mouth with her right hand.

"Are you alright?" Stella asked.

"I...I think so."

"Do you need to go and get some fresh air?"

"No, it's okay."

211

Sue Ellen's eyes scanned the room again, just as she had when she arrived and settled on a group of women, beautifully dressed in the front row. One of the women she recognized was her neighbor, Joanne Mitchell. They sat ramrod-straight, adding a couple of inches, and their make-up appeared professionally done. Unlike the complainers in line, they sat smiling. *They wanted the social norms initiative*, Sue Ellen thought.

Stella noticed Sue Ellen staring out at the crowd.

"Are you sure you're okay?"

"Yeah. I'm just thinking."

Sue Ellen eyed the goddesses in the front row one last time and smiled. "Should I say something?" she muttered.

7

The line moved forward following Henry's exit. The rest of the townspeople weren't quite as long in their comments. Just as the line came to the last speaker, Sue Ellen rushed to speak her peace. Stella cocked her head to the side, interested to see what Sue Ellen had to say.

After the man in front of Sue Ellen said "Thank you" to the board, Sue Ellen stepped to the podium. Her mouth felt like dry cotton candy, and her hands were like oily fish. Just that morning, her day consisted of watching soap operas and eating junk food, but now she looked out on board members, who had just listened to twenty speeches from the community about why the social norms initiative should not pass.

The trustee who drummed his fingers on the desk started up again, and another was yawning. Sue Ellen felt the crowd looking toward her and heard murmurs of "What's going on?" and "Is she going to speak?"

She thought about turning around and leaving. She abhorred public speaking.

212

"Miss? Do you have a comment for us?"

Mayor Goldman appeared confused and frustrated. The clock read 7:45, which meant the public comment portion had dragged on for an hour. Sue Ellen glanced back at Stella, who flashed her a smile. It gave her courage to go on. She gave the best speech of her life.

8

"I get the feeling that some people around here are not comfortable with the social norms initiative," she began.

Sue Ellen heard chuckles from the crowd. Even Mayor Goldman formed a half-smile.

"Well, I say to those people, have you no decency? Have you no belief in what is right for the common good for Ridgeport?"

Stella's jaw dropped open, unsure of where this new development started for Sue Ellen.

"When I was sixteen, I saw a woman in a short skirt walking down the street. I thought it was the coolest thing. I wanted a skirt like that, one that showed off my long legs. I asked my mom for a week if I could have one. Finally, she gave in. 'As long as you don't wear it to school, she said.' Well, I didn't, but I did wear it to a September Friday night football game at school. I wanted to look good for my date that night."

The crowd started to understand where this was going but stayed quiet to hear her out.

"Well, my date did like it. He liked it a lot. He kept saying how good I looked, and by halftime, he said that we should 'get out of there.' So, we did. Like a perfect gentleman, he opened my car door for me and helped me inside. I asked him where we were going, and he said he wanted to take me to a place where we could look at the stars. It all sounded very romantic. When he pulled into the driveway of a closed-

213

off forest preserve, nothing but darkness surrounded us. 'We should see some good stars here, huh?' I asked. But he didn't have stars on his mind. He ran his arm up my leg, and well, I tried to leave the car," Sue Ellen said, tears filling her eyes. "But he was a lot stronger than me. He didn't let me leave. He...he…"

If Stella's jaw were any longer, she would have tripped over it. She decided it was best to comfort Sue Ellen. But Sue Ellen brushed off her hug, and Stella stood by her side. A single tear dropped from Sue Ellen's cheek. Mayor Goldman intervened, saying that she didn't have to continue, but Sue Ellen shook her head and did anyway.

"I was raped that night. A sixteen-year-old girl. Raped. And if I hadn't worn that godforsaken short skirt that I begged my mother to buy me, I probably never would have been." Sue Ellen dried her eyes with her sleeve. Her story shook the boardroom to its core. Even the grumblers hung their heads in sorrow. The Ridgeport community came together for Sue Ellen at that moment.

"I don't want that to be our town. What's our saying? 'Love thy neighbor" and "Love thy Ridgeport?" Well, if it takes some guidelines to do that, why not? I think we should start a Neighborhood Watch program so all the Tommys of the world can know they have no place here. To have freedom, you need to give a little up. That's why we have street lights. We all love to hit the gas pedal, but we don't want accidents. I am for the social norms initiative. And I think you all should be too. Remember: 'Love thy neighbor' and 'Love thy Ridgeport.'"

A hush fell over the room. Mayor Goldman's face looked as if it was going to burst from her empathetic smile. Then someone started clapping, and in a second, the whole room stood in a round of applause. Several skeptics and former speakers jettisoned the room with disgruntled huffs, but most residents stood with Sue Ellen. In one day, she transformed from a lazy person to a crowd-pleaser. The tears that streaked her face just a moment before washed away and were replaced with joy.

The social norms initiative passed that night by a measure of 7-0. The initiative called for informal guidelines to be implemented that dictated how Ridgeport residents should act to better the town, and it would be tied to residents getting and renewing their residency cards.

Mayor Goldman asked if Sue Ellen could talk following the meeting.

"We're all going to the country club for some drinks. Why don't you join us?"

"Oh. I thought…"

"Thought we don't drink?"

"You're right. We don't drink in public."

"Oh. Well…okay then."

Sue Ellen blushed, and the mayor smiled.

9

Stella broached the subject of Sue Ellen's impromptu speech in the car ride home. She hoped and prayed for weeks that the social norms initiative would not pass and showed up at every board meeting and read every newspaper article she could find to stay current on the proposition. Over the last couple of weeks, enough of a minority rose in Ridgeport that Stella felt confident that the initiative might not pass. Her hope ballooned when she saw the long line of protesters giving angry speeches against it in the aisle. And then, out of nowhere, Sue Ellen decided it was time to turn the vote. She never even heard that story, much less anything else about her private life. Sue Ellen protected her life in a locker, for her eyes only. She only shared superficial things. She never told Stella the details of her divorce or anything about her parents or what she was like growing up. So, Stella felt both slighted and empathetic for Sue Ellen. Slighted because she had no problem telling an audience of strangers what was one of the most private moments in her life, but empathetic because she carried so much pain with her.

As Stella drove, her thoughts continued. At one moment, she wanted to hug Sue Ellen, and the next, she wanted to yell at her.

"Stella, are you okay? You seem like you're going to have a nervous breakdown."

Stella said nothing, staring out at the road ahead.

"Stella? Anyone home? Stella?"

"What?! What is it?!"

"Woah. Take a chill pill. I only wanted to see if you were feeling okay. I know you're stressed out about something."

Stella took a deep breath to gather her thoughts before she spoke again.

"It's just...where did all that come from? You're a private person. So, what made you want to go up there and talk?"

"I'm just really passionate about social norms. I think it would be good for the community."

Stella nodded and kept driving. She noticed a man in sweatpants out walking his dog. *Little does he know that he may get in trouble for that very soon*, she thought.

"And that story? What made you decide to share that story with all those people?"

"I made that up. Tommy never raped me. It was consensual."

Stella nearly slammed on the brakes, and her jaw dropped once more.

"You...made that up? But, how could you? A story like that?"

"I was an actor in high school. I guess a part of it never left me."

"So, you've never been raped then?"

Sue Ellen stared out the passenger-side window.

216

"Yes. I have."

"Oh. I'm so sorry, dear. You can talk to me if…."

But Sue Ellen withdrew within herself, and if this was acting, Stella thought she was doing a damn good job.

Sue Ellen once more looked out the window, thinking back to how Mayor Jim Henderson made seven-year-old Sue Ellen show him 'things.' As a friend of her dad's, he made frequent visits to their house and agreed to babysit from time to time. He said because he was the mayor, she could get in a lot of trouble if she said anything about their secret playtime. So, she didn't. She never said a word to anyone.

10

While Stella stayed home to contemplate the events earlier that evening, Sue Ellen made her way to the country club. She thought it strange that she should go to the country club at ten p.m. on a Tuesday. When she pulled up in her Lexus, she only noticed about a dozen cars huddled closely in the lot. *Most of those cars are the board's*, she thought.

The lights outside the club were off by then, and the sprinklers on the golf course were on. Sue Ellen thought this was a joke. Those cars belonged to the waitstaff. So, when she reached the door and saw it was locked, she wasn't that surprised. She turned around, ready to walk back to her car, when a man approached the door.

"Excuse me, miss, but we're closed for the night."

"Yeah. I see that. I was just supposed to meet some people here, is all."

The man was a host for the country club. He wore a white shirt button-up with black pants.

"Oh. My apologies, then. You must be with the Goldman party?"

"Yes. Yes, that's it! Yes."

217

"My name is Michael," the man said. "I'll escort you."
He opened the door and led Sue Ellen by the hand and up a
flight of stairs.

11

Sue Ellen heard laughter from the restaurant as she climbed
the stairs with Michael. He directed her into the lighted room
and toward the back, near a window overlooking the golf
course.

"Hi there, Ms. Norris. We were beginning to think you
wouldn't show," said Mayor Goldman. She grinned, holding
a drink in her hand.

"We don't drink in public," Sue Ellen remembered her
saying. Sly, very sly. Did they invite her into their secret
government club that seemed to be dancing around the rules?
I think they did, Sue Ellen thought. And Sue Ellen grinned
back.

"Sue Ellen, I'd like you to formally meet the board. You
never got to meet them, have you?"

"No, I haven't."

"Everyone, this is Sue Ellen. Sue Ellen, everyone."

And one by one, all the seven members (John Farrell,
Mike Rivera, Jane Fizer, Dr. John Peterson, Jack Anderson,
Eugene Williams, and George Leak) approached and shook
her hand. A few even thanked her for her speech earlier that
day.

12

A bartender stood at the ready while Michael doubled as a
waiter asking board members for refills.

"What can I get you, Ms. Norris?" Michael asked.

Sue Ellen noticed Mayor Goldman strike her a glance.

"Um...I...do you have any white wine?"

218

"We sure do."

"Any Riesling?"

"One glass of Riesling…."

"Make it a bottle," Mayor Goldman insisted.

"Oh, I don't know."

"Honey, it's for the table. Please."

Sue Ellen blushed and nodded.

"Yes, Mayor Goldman. One bottle of Riesling coming right up."

How weird all of this was. Every board member delighted in their poison as if it was as socially acceptable as before the proposition passed.

Sue Ellen arrived about a half-hour late, but one or two of them already appeared to have a buzz going. She thought how none of this would have happened had it not been for Stella getting her out of the house, for seeing that long line, for taking the risk to humiliate herself, and for accepting this invite. She thought an entire initiative passed because of her. She transformed. It was as if the sleeping pupa woke into a beautiful and free butterfly.

Michael carried over the large bottle of Riesling, and as he set it down in the middle of the table, Mayor Goldman nodded with satisfaction.

"Hey, that was some speech, Sue Ellen. It took a lot of courage for you to get up there like that," said Jeannie with a smile.

"Thanks," Sue Ellen said.

She felt like a light bulb in an Amish town, a little out of place. Yes, she gave a great speech. But what else did she have in common with these people? Did it matter? No other Ridgeport resident cozied up next to the mayor with a bottle of wine that night.

"It must have been hard for you to tell that story. I had a sister that was raped and…," said George. But Jane cut him off before he could finish his story. Sue Ellen found George to be a few drinks in already.

"Don't mind him. He doesn't always think before he speaks, dear."

George grumbled and left the table for the bar.

Mayor Goldman rolled her eyes and nodded at Jane for cutting in.

"I think we should all have a toast," Goldman said.

The members raised their glasses, but Sue Ellen hesitated.

"That means you too, honey. You're in on this too."

Sue Ellen grabbed her glass of wine and held it in the air.

"To Sue Ellen, for, without her, the social norms initiative may not have had the support of the community. Cheers, Sue Ellen!" exclaimed Mayor Goldman. And the glasses clinked.

Goldman winked at Sue Ellen, and after a few sips, Sue Ellen began to relax. She still stayed quiet but found the talk on government affairs and community gossip quite entertaining.

"And Joe Neeman is cheating on his wife?" asked Jack. "Are you sure? They were always so chaste."

"I saw him. He was walking out of the flower shop holding a young thing around her waist, and he had a bouquet of roses for her."

"Oh. Wow. Do you suppose his wife knows?" Mike asked.

"Not a clue. Saw the two of 'em at Jimmy's little league game together. They looked as happy as can be."

"Poor woman," Jane said.

Sue Ellen nodded, thinking about her recent divorce.

The night drew late, and half the party needed to go home in Jane or Eugene's car. Sue Ellen started gathering her things, but Goldman squeezed her hand to hold her back.

"We're not going anywhere just yet. We have a business to talk about."

The board members said their goodnights, and at two a.m. Sue Ellen and Mayor Goldman sat alone at a table at the country club's restaurant, drinking Riesling.

13

Two nights in a row, Sue Ellen stayed up late hugging a bottle of wine. She feared she might be turning into an alcoholic, but last night's drinking and this night's drinking meant a world of difference. Last night's drinking was just sad. This night, well, meant something. She heard a bottle of wine a day was good for you. Wasn't that the saying?

She dreamed this? It seemed like a dream - sitting alone with the mayor, drinking wine at two a.m. at the country club restaurant. She'd wake up tomorrow and have a good laugh. Stella will find her on the couch again, forcing her outside. But right now, it's reality, and the reality is that Mayor Goldman wanted to talk business.

"You said in your speech that you thought we should have a Neighborhood Watch."

"Yes."

"Tell me more about that."

14

Sue Ellen calmed down a bit. She relaxed, just as she had relaxed after her few initial sips of wine.

"I think that if we are to enforce the social norms initiative and keep the neighborhood safe, we need a Neighborhood Watch program, where all the neighbors enforce the initiative and watch for those who break it or watch for any unsafe activity."

Mayor Goldman nodded, taking a notepad out of her purse. She began scribbling down a few notes.

"What are you writing?"

"I'm just recording what we're saying."

"It's a business meeting, remember? We have to take minutes."

"Oh. Okay."

Sue Ellen wondered how hard the mayor worked for the village. She didn't seem the least bit tired. She wondered how much sleep she got or how much time she took off.

"Sue Ellen, do you have any leadership experience?"

"Have I been a manager? Is that what you mean?"

"Doesn't have to be..."

"Well, I was the president of my student government and vice president of my sorority house."

"Really? So, why did you have trouble starting your speech then? You seemed nervous. Usually, leaders have no trouble speaking in front of people."

Sue Ellen almost fell off her chair. She almost forgot how nervous she was, and now that the mayor pointed it out, that embarrassment came spiraling back.

"Are you alright?"

"Yeah. Well, I don't know. I guess when I got divorced, I lost a lot of my confidence."

"Oh. I'm sorry to hear that, but I was glad to see you went through with the speech. That's why you're here, you know?"

"I had a feeling."

"I want you to lead the Neighborhood Watch. We'll say that you just lead it in your subdivision, but you'll really oversee the town. Of course, I'll pull the strings, and you report to me. But you'll be like my watchdog. How does that sound?"

"That sounds great. But what do you want me to do, exactly?"

"With the people who are breaking our social norms, keep a list of them. I want to know who they are and what norms they're breaking."

"Oh. Okay. Sure."

Sue Ellen took another sip of white wine. She noticed that she had just about drained the bottle. She knew a massive hangover was coming.

"What are you going to do with the list?"

"Don't worry about it. Just produce the list, and I'll handle it from there."

"And, pardon me, but what's in it for me?"

Mayor Goldman laughed heartily, but the laughter turned to a smile and nod.

"You'll get all the benefits that you saw here tonight, plus monetary, of course. Each time you bring me an offense or a name, you'll see a reward."

Sue Ellen knew that the decision she would make there that night might influence the town's future. She thought back to those standing in front of her in line and those women in the front row in the boardroom in flattering yet conservative dresses. Sue Ellen considered what she wanted the town's future to look like - one filled with drunken sloppy, sweatpants-wearing idiots or one filled with polite, educated, and well-groomed individuals. She chose the latter. And so, Sue Ellen shook Mayor Goldman's hand.

"This calls for one last toast. To the future of Ridgeport," Mayor Goldman said.

"Love thy neighbor" and "Love thy Ridgeport," Sue Ellen said.

Chapter 6: Ridgeport: 2004

<u>Part One</u>

1

In 2004, panic turned to hopelessness for the band. They, along with the town, had searched since the day of Stella's funeral for Josephine, known to all as Joe. There were no traces of her anywhere. They combed the forest, set up missing person signs, checked *The Ridgeport News*, stopped by the police office several times a week, and asked Pastor Denton to pray for her at church. They even posted a blog on their Myspace page entitled "Save Josephine Barnes," and although it got several comments, none were helpful in their search. As 2003 turned to 2004, the band's spirits were all but broken.

2

Scott took the loss especially hard. That was his Joe, his girlfriend, his soulmate. His grades dropped, and he was in danger of failing English and math - two subjects he would need to graduate from Ridgeport High School. His teachers said he showed no motivation in class. It didn't help that Joe sat next to him in his English class. Joe's empty seat was an everyday reminder that she wasn't there. John received frequent phone calls about his performance, but he just shrugged his shoulders and went to his room when he confronted Scott. They tried taking away his video games TV time and grounding him. But he welcomed the grounding. He only came out of his room to eat. When John or Loretta tried talking with him about Joe, he always muttered the same response, "I don't wanna talk about it."

Three weeks into Scott's grounding and seeing no improvement in grades, John decided to try a different approach. He invited Matt over, hoping he could get through to him. John had always liked Matt, seeing him as the more mature one of the group. If his parents couldn't get through to him, his best friend could.

It was a typical Saturday for the Caseys, and Scott had locked himself in his room once again. Matt knocked on his door.

"Go away!"

"Scott? It's Matt."

Silence.

"Just a second."

Scott opened the door. It was one o'clock, but he stood in his PJ's and his hair uncombed. It was clear he hadn't showered.

"You may enter."

"Wow. Thanks."

John peered from the lower steps. He had tried everything he could think of. Well, he thought, at this age, kids listened more to their friends than they did to adults.

3

Matt looked Scott up and down. "You look like garbage. Absolute garbage," he said.

Scott smiled. It was the first time he smiled in a couple of months. He lifted his arm and noticed he smelled rancid.

"Okay. I smell like garbage too."

Matt chuckled and sat on Scott's unmade bed. It looked as though it hadn't been made in weeks. Matt noticed a handwritten sheet of poetry that lay askew on Scott's dresser and couldn't stop himself from picking up a sheet.

"What's this?"

"Oh, that, well. You don't have to read that."

"The snow falls outside,
But it's colder in my heart
Warm me, cup of Joe."

226

That's beautiful, man."

"Thanks. It's a haiku."

"Ah. Like *Wayne's World*?"

"Huh?"

"You know when Garth says, 'We're looking down on Wayne's basement, only that's not Wayne's basement. And then Wayne is like, 'Garth, that's a haiku."

"Yeah, something like that...."

Matt set the poem back down on the dresser and looked back at his friend. Even though Scott was happy to see him, Matt could tell there was a pain in his eyes.

"We all miss her. There's not a day that goes by that I don't think of her too, Scott, but she would want us to live our lives."

Scott buried his head in a pillow and shook his head.

"I can't. It hurts too much, man."

"Yeah, but look at you. Is this what you want to be? You don't even leave your room. She wouldn't want you to be like this. You know that."

"Yeah, I guess."

Matt stood up and looked out the window. It was as warm as a January day could be in Chicago - thirty-five degrees and sunny. The icicles were melting outside Scott's window.

"Why don't you say we head down to the forest and take a walk or something, just like old times? It might do you some good to get out of the house?"

"I can't. Grounded. Remember?"

"I think your dad might let this one slide."

Scott pushed the pillow aside and moved toward the window next to Matt. The day did seem quite inviting.

"Alright. I'll go. Maybe I should shower first?"

"Nah. Shower when you get back. Just throw something other than PJ's on," Matt said and chuckled again.

Scott smiled once more and nodded. And just like Matt said, John had no problem with Scott leaving the house. In fact, he felt pretty relieved.

4

Matt had bought himself a used 1996 Saturn SC1 Coupe with money he saved working a job at The Ridgeport Grocer since last year. Scott had yet to buy a car, but he also had yet to get a job. Riley's car crapped out on him most of the time, so Matt's car served as the primary vehicle for the band.

He imagined his Saturn as a sports car since it was a coupe and contained a Performance button, which was nothing more than a button that gave extra rotation to the tires, but he liked to think of it as his boost in horsepower. "Maybe the Saturn's one hundred horsepower might get an extra ten from that button," Scott often said, teasing him. Matt was never impressed.

The car ride to the forest was about five minutes, compared to the thirty-minute bike ride it used to be. But no matter the distance, Matt had to blare music wherever they went. He inserted Pearl Jam's *Yield* cassette tape.

"This is a highly underrated album, Scott."

He was always giving side notes about the music as the songs played away. It was both interesting and annoying.

As Eddie Vedder mumbled "Brain of J's" lyrics, "The whole world will be different soon/The whole world will be relieving," Scott and Matt tried to mumble along with it.

Just into the second song, "Faithfull," Matt pulled into the forest preserve parking lot. He turned off the tape, turned off the car, and they hopped out, ready to explore the woods that came to mean so much to them over the years.

5

The brisk January air was welcoming on Scott's face, and as he walked toward the path, he started to feel invigorated. The sun glistened against a few inches of snow, and in other places, snowmelt made the path wet, but the boys didn't mind since they had their boots on. Scott hadn't walked the woods in a month and only left the house to go to school or take out the garbage.

"Do you still come here, Matt?"

"Yep. Sure do. Come here at least once a week. Keep thinking I'll see her."

Matt led him down another path he found about a month ago. It was off the beaten path and led out of the forest and into a grassland.

"I like it out this way. There's an open plot of dirt in the center, and you can see the entire forest from there."

Scott remembered this path. It was the same path Joe, and he had run to, slept in, and ran back from months before. It was the same place Scott told no one about. In fact, he didn't tell anyone he was at the forest preserve that night with Joe. He was too nervous, breaking so many town rules, and too upset to relive that night with anyone.

When Matt reached the dirt circle where the high grass sagged in all directions, Scott knew it was the same spot they spent the night in.

"Pretty cool, huh? You can see everything from here."

Scott nodded and looked around. It was true. You could see everything from there, in the winter at least, when the grass was more thinned out, and the flowers had died.

"Matt, there's something I need to tell you about this place."

"Yeah? What is it?"

"This was the last place I saw Joe."

Matt cocked his head, confused. This seemed like a big secret to hide for a friend who confided everything in him. Scott hung his head in embarrassment. Of all the places in the forest preserve, he hadn't expected to end up there. He hadn't expected to reveal the truth today. He thought he might tell it one day, but he wasn't counting on that day to be at that moment. After he said it, he knew that information may have been vital to the authorities finding her, but he knew police combed through that area anyway. He was with them when they did.

Matt turned around and took a good, hard look at the trampled grass. Scott could see his heavy breaths puff against the cold.

"I'm sorry for not telling you, Matt. I didn't know how."

"Really? You didn't know how?"

Scott hung his head once more. He looked down at the trampled grass. He wished he could have that night back. It was the best night of his life, but he also blamed himself for Joe's disappearance. He thought their night was the reason men were after them that night…scary men.

"Listen, Matt; you have to understand something about that night. It was both wonderful and scary at the same time. It's one of the reasons I've been such a train wreck."

"You're not the only one who's been a train wreck. You just chose to go shut-in."

Scott kicked the dirt but decided to go on.

"Don't you want to know what happened?"

Matt didn't say anything for a long minute. Scott was about ready to drop the subject when Matt turned around.

"Yes. But this better be good."

Scott told Matt the entire story from beginning to end, starting with how Joe came to his window, urging him to come outside.

"And these men chased us through the woods."

"Did you get a good look at them?"

"No, not really. I think they dressed in all black. That's about all I know. And they were big, like NFL-linebacker-big."

"And by the time you came here, you were safe?"

"Yes. As I said, we slept here for a while, and when we awoke, we realized it was dawn, and we had to head back."

"Huh. That's it?"

"Well, come to think of it, Joe was scratched up pretty bad. She thought she might have tripped or something."

"Really?"

Matt looked towards the path that led back into the woods on the opposite side toward the swimming hole and the trench.

"I think we should keep walking. Let's retrace your steps from that night."

"Already did that about a million times, Matt."

"Eh. Let's do it one more time. Can't hurt, can it?"

Scott sighed, shrugged his shoulders, and walked over the trampled, tall grass and down the makeshift path he had created with Joe.

Matt and Scott scanned the woods, thinking Joe might pop out behind a tree and give them a good scare. All they saw now was melting snow from the barren trees and gray sky. There were no signs of life, but Matt tried to keep Scott's hopes up.

"Still makes for a good walk, doesn't it?"

"I guess."

Scott couldn't help but feel responsible for Joe's disappearance and had blamed himself ever since she went missing. The path broke off into the main trail, and Scott led them to the campfire spot. Ashes spilled over in a pile in the middle of the pit, but everything else was gone. No graham cracker crumbs or marshmallows had been left behind. They were eaten by an animal or blown away by the wind. Scott shook his head. He knew he had seen this exact scene before but hoped for something different. He remembered so vividly that night - the laughter, the intimacy. How could such a perfect night turn south so quickly? Matt scratched his head and placed an arm around his friend. It was like being at Stella's funeral all over again.

"Maybe she's really gone, Scott, and we're not sure why."

"No! She's not! She can't be. She's out there somewhere. And I'm going to keep looking!"

Matt nodded but started to think it was a lost cause. Joe had been missing for four months now. If she could have returned, she would have come back by now, wouldn't she?

"I'm sorry, Scott. I know how much she meant to you. She meant a lot to all of us."

"I...I need to walk some more. Can we just walk some more?"

"Yeah. We can do that."

Scott led Matt in the direction of the trench. Scott looked at the project they started as kids. He stumbled down the little hill and onto the trench. Matt hesitated but followed. Scott walked around the clubhouse.

"We gave up on this too soon. We should've finished it."

"Yeah...well."

"I want to finish it."

"Okay, but it's winter. The ground is too hard."

232

"I want to finish it."

Matt laughed, but he knew Scott was serious.

9

Matt and Scott stared at the unfinished project. The gears in Scott's head were turning, and he rubbed his chin with his forefinger. He tried to think about how he would dig past frozen soil.

"I think we got a blowtorch in the garage."

Scott's eyes opened wide, and he patted Matt on the back for his insight. Then he rubbed his hands together and nodded.

"So, this is happening. Good," Scott said.

Matt didn't even ask why. He knew he needed something to get his mind off her. Even if it was childish, it was something to do. He supposed his friend could find a job somewhere instead but decided not to suggest that at this point. Let him have this.

"You'll help me, right?"

"Well, sure. I may not be here all the time, with work and all, but I'll come as much as I can."

Scott nodded again and looked toward the plot. He remembered carving it out. He remembered how cool it would be to finish it, and now it would finally come to fruition.

"You think Riley and Jimmy might help too?"

"I don't know. I can't speak for them. You'll have to ask them yourself."

Scott brushed some snow away from the trench and smiled. He looked right in the direction of the swimming hole. So many good memories were made at this spot. He wanted those memories to last.

"Well, let's head back. It's starting to get cold," Scott said.

A gold chain hung from Scott's back pocket, something Matt hadn't noticed before.

"Hey Scott, what's that?"

"Oh, I found this in the meadow that night Joe and I slept there. I was going to give it to her."

"And you've kept it with you all this time?"

"I told you. I'm going to give it to her."

"I understand," Matt said. But he shook his head as Scott turned around and continued his walk back.

10

Scott looked like a whole new person as he entered his house that evening. He had something he lacked earlier that day: purpose. John agreed to remove his grounding restriction if his grades improved, which they did in a hurry. He had eight assignments missing in one class, and Scott made sure to make every one of them up. He didn't want anything to stand in the way of digging the trench.

It took three weeks for Scott to bring his grades up to a B, John's minimum requirement to lift his grounding. He turned all his work into his teachers, and they even allowed him to retake his assessments. Those three weeks involved a lot of late nights and staying after school in the homework lab. He vowed never to slip that far behind again.

11

A cold February deep freeze blanketed Chicagoland. Scott's school closed for a week due to record cold temperatures. Meteorologists advised people to stay indoors. Unlike most of his classmates, Scott was devastated. His parents again strictly enforced their rules; this time, it was not to go outside in the Antarctic to prevent frostbite.

234

"They're saying you can get frostbite within fifteen minutes, Scotty," Loretta said.

Scott rolled his eyes at this and mumbled under his breath.

"What do you care? You'd probably be happier if I weren't around anyway."

Loretta didn't hear him, though, and was already on her way back to the living room to relax in front of the fireplace.

Just like when he closed himself off before, Scott marched up to his room and closed the door. Frost snaked up his windows. *No chance to work on the trench*, he thought. He sighed and lay on his bed.

Scott looked around his room. It hadn't changed much over the last few years - a Frank Thomas poster, White Sox, Bulls, Bears, Blackhawk's pennants, and a Beatles poster decorated his walls, a bookshelf with a random assortment of books stood tall opposite his window, and odds and ends collectibles dotted here and there. A couple of finished Lego sets sat on the floor in the corner. There was a closet with sliding glass mirrors that reflected the entire room. His HP computer that sat on his computer desk was visible from these mirrors. Scott moved from the bed and onto the chair in front of his computer. He remembered instant messaging Joe late at night for hours. Joe. He couldn't shake her from his mind.

He clicked the Internet Explorer icon and visited Ask Jeeves. From there, he typed in Josephine Barnes. He had already read every article he could find on her, but why not reread them all? He'd find something he hadn't seen before.

12

He started with the latest article dated two months ago from *The Ridgeport News*, "Barnes Girl Still Missing." It said that despite all community efforts, Josephine Barnes had still not been found. It went on to say that if anyone had any idea of where she might be, to contact Peter Barnes at 815-555-9087 or 1-800-843-5678, which was the hotline for Missing and Exploited Children. Earlier articles contained stories from the major papers as well - *The Daily Southtown*, *The Chicago Tribune*, *The Chicago Sun-Times*. Scott did not notice anything different in any of the articles he read.

John's voice called from downstairs, "Scott! Dinner is ready!"

"Alright! be right down!"

Frustrated, Scott sighed once more, and as he stood, he frowned as he took another look at his frost-covered windows. Then he backed away from his computer, ran out his door, and rushed downstairs for dinner.

13

Loretta and John patched up their marriage as best they could since their fight the night before Stella's funeral. Loretta still saw Sue Ellen, but it wasn't as regular as before. She was too embarrassed, following her botched wedding toast, and Sue Ellen canceled plans with her sometimes at the last minute. Sue Ellen lost some interest in her special friend following Joe's disappearance and Loretta's lack of confidence and mental breakdown at her wedding. The silver lining in their time apart was that they spent more time with their families, something they hadn't done for most of their lives.

Scott still felt distant with Loretta, and even though he could see she was making attempts to get to know him, he found the attempts forced. Besides, his mind wandered back to Joe most of the time.

John served his personal favorite - Shake N' Bake pork chops. Scott hated pork chops, and John always made them on Thursday nights when he got home from the office. The

236

only thing that made them bearable to eat was if Scott poured half a bottle of Sweet Baby Rays BBQ sauce all over them. Usually, the side of applesauce wasn't bad, but it wasn't enough to counter the taste of the pork chops. Scott learned to stop complaining. It did not go well. So, he just resorted to eye rolls or dramatic sighs. John noticed that Thursday evening.

"I saw that young man," John said.

"Alright. I'm sorry."

John set the kitchen table, and they all sat around, and like the perfect family, John led in grace.

"Come, Lord Jesus, be our guest, and let thy gifts for us be blessed."

"Amen."

"Amen," echoed Loretta and Scott.

A few bites into digging in, Loretta spoke up first.

"Scott, honey. How is everything going? Are you enjoying your time off from school?"

"Sure."

One-word answers became commonplace for Scott over the last few months. He had no time for a real conversation with his parents when his head was stuck on Joe.

Loretta felt defeated and looked over at John for help. She knew she failed as a mother for so long, and talking to her son became foreign territory.

"Scott, what are your plans this week? We could watch a movie tonight. You can pick one out."

"I don't have any, and I'm not much in the mood for a movie, thanks."

Scott was picking at his food by then. He already shoveled in the applesauce and forced in a few bites of the pork chops. The plate made a sort of slew of BBQ and applesauce mix. It looked like paint smeared on a palette.

"May I be excused? I'm full," Scott said.

Scott had no idea yet what it meant to work a full day, come home to cook for three and engage in a friendly conversation with the family. All he saw was pork chops he didn't like and did not care about anything but Joe. All he cared about was what mattered to him, in his world. He would grow to regret this time he blew off, but it would take time.

John frowned but agreed.

"Yes, you may be excused." Loretta bit her lower lip before saying, "I love you," as he got up to leave.

Scott turned before he walked away and mumbled it back under his breath.

14

Back in his room, Scott stared at the computer screen once more. He already hated being home from school. He hated the deep freeze and not being allowed to go out. His eyes grew heavy. He laid down to rest. Then he had one of the weirdest dreams of his life.

15

Scott dreamt that he was playing hide and seek with Joe. They were in the forest, and Scott counted from ten. He heard Joe rustle through the leaves. When Scott opened his eyes, she was nowhere to be found. No matter how much he called, she didn't answer. That dream segued into the next, where he was sitting in school looking out the window. He spotted a cute girl walking in the parking lot, but it wasn't Joe. She was mesmerizing, the way her ripped jeans hugged her waist and her golden blond hair waved in the wind as if she were a mermaid. He hesitated. Where was the girl walking? She left the lot for the sidewalk. Little by little, the girl vanished from view. Scott took one look at his teacher and then at Joe's empty seat. He jumped up, opened the classroom window, and leaped out onto the grassy plain adjacent to the parking lot. He ignored the screaming from the teacher and the laughter and cheers from the students. He ignored all common sense in favor of following the mystery girl. She walked a few paces ahead, and Scott broke into a run, but no matter how fast Scott ran, she remained a few strides ahead. She looked like a metronome, keeping perfect time with the swaying of her hips.

The residential block fell away, and the mystery girl strolled into the forest. Scott continued after her. She never turned around, never seemed to notice he existed. She led him to the trench and stopped. Then she turned, and her face was just as pretty as her back – azure blue eyes, full rounded lips, tanned skin. She sported a gray hoodie, and around her neck hung a necklace - it looked like the same necklace Scott found in the forest.

The mystery girl walked within lips reach of Scott. He wanted her, and he didn't even know her. She was beautiful, but he could now see that she appeared sad. There was something hidden in those eyes, something lost.

"Find me, find Joe," she whispered in Scott's ear.

"What?" Scott was startled.

"Find me, find Joe," she said again. This time she arched her back and faced him directly. She looked like she was going in for a kiss, and just as Scott leaned in, she evaporated into a thousand little pieces. A rain of sparkling confetti rained down on Scott, and he heard it once more. It echoed throughout the forest.

"Find me, find Joe."

And that's when Scott woke up. He shot up, panting. Sweat dripped off his forehead and down his shirt as if he had just run a marathon.

16

Scott grabbed the notebook on the nightstand next to his bed and scribbled down as much as he remembered from the dream:

Hide and Seek with Joe in the forest...running after a cute blond girl into the woods...she wore a sweater with ripped jeans and had that gold necklace around her neck - was it my necklace? She told me if I found her, I would find Joe. If I found her, I would find Joe. What the hell does that mean? Find her...find her where? Find her how? Who is she?

Scott's necklace sat next to his notebook. He picked it up and examined the verse. It did look the same. Or, at least, he wanted it to be the same one. His eyes were drawn to the name of the verse, "1 Corinthians 13:4-13." He had heard that verse somewhere before - at Sue Ellen and Peter's wedding. He grabbed his NIV-Version Bible from his bookshelf and turned to the verse. "Love is patient; love is kind. It does not envy; it does not boast; it is not proud. It does not dishonor others; it is not self-seeking, it is not easily angered, it keeps no record of wrongs. Love does not delight in evil but rejoices with the truth. It always protects, always trusts, always hopes, always perseveres. Love never fails. But where there are prophecies, they will cease; where there are tongues, they will be stilled; where there is knowledge, it will pass away. For we know in part, and we prophesy in part, but when completeness comes, what is in part disappears. When I was a child, I talked like a child, I thought like a child, I reasoned like a child. When I became a man, I put the ways of childhood behind me. For now, we see only a reflection as in a mirror; then we shall see face to face. Now I know in part; then I shall know fully, even as I am fully known. And now these three remain: faith, hope, and love. But the greatest of these is love."

It truly was beautiful. Scott understood why so many decided on this verse for their wedding. He read it again and again, looking for any sort of sign or hint as to how to find the mystery girl. He must have read it ten times before tossing the good book aside on his nightstand and rubbing his temple.

Maybe it was just a dream. *Just a crazy dream*, Scott thought.

He once more looked out his frost-covered windows. He frowned at the thought that he now could be working on the trench. The trench...the trench. That was in the dream too. She turned around at the trench.

Scott looked at the verse once more, and his finger ran over, *"When I was a child, I talked like a child, I thought like a child, I reasoned like a child. When I became a man, I put the ways of childhood behind me. For now, we see only a reflection as in a mirror; then we shall see face to face."* His eyes bulged, and his heart leaped a beat. He knew what he had to do.

17

Scott raced downstairs like a kid on Christmas morning. He knew he had a present waiting for him, but he didn't know what it was or who it was. John and Loretta idled in front of the fire, drinking hot chocolate. When Scott ran in behind them, John nearly spilled his drink.

"What's the matter, son?"

"What's wrong, Scotty?"

Loretta had gotten into the habit of calling him Scotty now as if she had always called him that.

"Can I go to Matt's? It's important. I wouldn't ask if it weren't."

"Scott, we talked about this. No going outside in this weather," John said. Loretta nodded in agreement.

241

"But it's just next door, and I need to get out of the house. I would just go over there to sleep over? Please."

John and Loretta looked at each other. They did like the idea of having the house alone for the night, and he did make a good point that the house was right next door.

"Well, okay. But stay at Matt's. And only if Sue Ellen and Peter say it's okay."

"Yes. Thank you. Thank you so much."

Scott grabbed the phone out of the kitchen and called Matt. He picked up on the third ring.

"Yeah. What's up?"

"Tell your mom and dad I'm coming. I'm sleeping over."

"Okay. Hold on."

Scott held the phone away from his ear and heard Matt yelling.

"Mom, Peter! Scott is coming by to sleepover."

"Alright, you're good."

"Great. See you in a second."

Scott hung up the phone and even hugged his parents.

"Love you too, buddy."

"Love you, Scotty."

Then he headed upstairs, dressed in layers, and walked next door as fast as he could. He hadn't felt this good in weeks, and this sleepover was just what he needed, although Scott had no plans to sleep. He knew anytime he and Matt got together, it meant something would happen. It meant anything but the ordinary.

Matt answered the door and laughed at his layered, Pillsbury Doughboy frame before welcoming him in.

"Thanks. It's not like it's cold out or anything."

Scott closed the door. The grandfather clock chimed eight o'clock, but the night had just begun.

242

18

The coat rack wobbled from the four layers Scott removed. Matt chuckled before steadying it just as it was about to come clunking down on his friend's head.

"You know, you wouldn't have gotten frostbite from walking to my house."

"Ah, well, just in case."

Matt shook his head and smiled. He, too, was glad Scott decided to come over. He spent much of the day doing housework (his mom's orders) while she and Peter watched the *Star Wars* trilogy. She had never seen them. Peter decided to take the day off work to watch them in order.

"Better to stay warm and avoid Planet Hoth outside," Peter told her.

She looked at him confused, which made him tell her to make sure she paid extra close attention to the first part of *The Empire Strikes Back*. Matt wanted to watch too, but Sue Ellen tasked him with mopping, vacuuming, dusting, and cleaning bathrooms. Without Stella, Matt now assumed many of her roles until Sue Ellen could find a suitable replacement.

"What do you want to do?" Matt asked.

"I have to tell you something."

"Okay. What is it?"

Princess Leia choking Jabba the Hutt could be heard from the living room. They had reached *The Return of the Jedi*.

"Well, let's go somewhere else. Your room, maybe?"

"Alright. That's fine."

For as clean as Matt made the rest of the house, his room was a mess. His bed was unmade, paperback books and comics lay strewn next to the dresser on the floor. Clothes of all kinds blanketed the carpet around the bed. The blinds faced at an angle covering the window. One corner of his poster of Pearl Jam was peeling from the wall, and his TV was still on with PlayStation games set haphazardly on top of and next to the system.

"What happened here, Matt? It looks like a tornado ran through here."

"Yeah, well. Ever since Stella died, I gave up caring about keeping things tidy in here. She refused to clean up after me, so she pushed me to clean my room. Now I'm not motivated to do it. My mom is trying to do it for me, but as long as she doesn't nag me about my room, well, you see how it is."

Scott understood but shook his head nonetheless. He could never live in such filth. Matt turned his PlayStation on, and on came *Crash Bandicoot*. Matt pushed his blankets away and found a spot on the edge of the bed. He pulled his controller within arms-reach and started the game.

"When are you going to get the PS2? The graphics are much better, and you can play all your PS1 games on there, Matt."

"Eh. I spent all my money on my Saturn, so when I have the money for it, I'll get it. You wanna buy me one?"

Scott watched his saved game. He got far. He was at the Boulder Dash level, where a giant boulder chased Crash throughout the level as he tried to get as many boxes as possible. Scott watched as Matt twisted and turned his controller like a madman. He ran into the helpful Aku Aku mask that allowed him to kill anything in his path without harm.

"Yes!" he roared.

Scott paced and watched as Matt easily beat the level.

"So, what is this you want to tell me?"

19

Scott didn't hesitate but spelled out every detail about the dream he had.

244

"Yeah, and she stood right over the trench and said, 'Find me, find Joe.' I think it's a sign."

Matt listened the entire time, rubbing his chin, and then said, "That's pretty messed up, man. Weird dream."

Scott hadn't expected this reaction. He expected something more. He expected him to say, "We have to figure this out."

Instead, he said, "That's pretty messed up. Weird dream." And then he proceeded to start the next level of *Crash Bandicoot*.

Scott turned the game off before he had a chance to start.

"Dude. I didn't get a chance to save my last level. Not cool, man."

"Oh. Sorry."

Scott grabbed the controller from Matt's hands. He came over here to share this wild story. He didn't want to watch Matt play the rest of *Crash Bandicoot* all night.

"Matt, she was standing in our trench. The Bible verse said…."

"I know. The Bible verse said, 'When I was a child, I talked like a child, I thought like a child, I reasoned like a child. When I became a man, I put the ways of childhood behind me.'"

Scott started to wonder if Matt was right. Wasn't this just a crazy dream that he should let go of? Scott could see it in his room. Now, he could see it on his face. Scott seemed to be at an impasse with his friend - his friend he had not been able to hang out with since that day in the woods. Matt was right. He did have to let this one go. Scott turned on the PlayStation to power back up Crash.

"Can I play too this time?"

"I guess that's alright," Matt said.

20

The boys played into the night. They started at level one together. Scott was no slouch at Crash either. It was the modern-day Mario, and if you didn't play Crash, you really can't consider yourself a gamer. One level turned into the next, and they were halfway through the game before they knew it. Sweat ran from their fingers and onto the controllers, and their eyes grew heavy from hours of playing.

"I'll grab us some Mountain Dew. We'll beat this thing in one sleepover."

"Sounds good, man," Scott said.

Scott looked at Matt's alarm clock - 11:30. They had been playing for about four hours. He took his eyes off the game and refocused them on Matt's window. The frost-covered it so thick blinds wasn't even necessary. Frost. He remembered why he came, and it wasn't to beat *Crash Bandicoot*.

Matt walked into the room with four cans of Mountain Dew.

"Got a couple extra for the long haul."

"Matt, I gotta go. I have to go dig the trench."

21

Matt froze as still as his window pane. He hung the Mountain Dew cans from his hands like icicles, and his face hung just as expressionless. Like the tin man, it took him a minute to get the words out.

"You're kidding?"

But he could see in his eyes that he wasn't.

"Scott, it's colder out there than Antarctica today. That's what they said on the news. Ant-frickin'-Arctica."

"I don't care. Did you see how many layers I wore?"

"Why don't we think this through."

"Are your mom and Peter still up?"

"No, but..."

"Perfect. Now, if you'll excuse me."

Matt tried to block the door, but Scott brushed past him. Matt swore under his breath and chased him down the stairs. He knew stopping him at this point was a lost cause, though. Scott was doing this thing, with or without Matt.

22

Once again, Matt blocked Scott from leaving through the front door. Scott threw clothes on like the Tasmanian Devil, and it took Matt stealing his coat, gloves, and winter hat to get his attention.

"Come on, man. Give me my stuff."

"How are you going to dig out there, genius? The ground is frozen solid. And what do you have to dig with?"

Scott didn't think any of this through. In fact, his real intention was just to go there. He thought he might see the mystery girl, and she might lead him to Joe.

"I...I don't know."

Matt frowned but continued. "This really means a lot to you, going out there. Doesn't it?"

"Yeah. It does."

"Well, I'd better come with you. Don't want you killing yourself."

"Are you sure? You...you don't have to."

"You owe me. Plus, it's past curfew. If my mom finds out about this, well, we're just going to have to be real quiet getting out of here. No one can know. Understand?"

Scott nodded. After running out with Joe that night, the last thing he wanted to do was break the law. But he would break any ridiculous Ridgeport law if it meant finding Joe.

"Alright. Here's the deal. We need some supplies - a couple of shovels, an ax, and a couple of thermoses of hot chocolate."

"Right. So how about making those hot chocolates? You know where everything is. I'll get ready. Don't make a sound down here. Peter's a heavy sleeper, but my mom's not."

"Got it."

Scott considered how grateful he was to have Matt as a friend. Who else would go out in sub-zero temperatures to dig a hole with him? Matt, that's who. Scott thought of his dream again, of mystery girl, and of Joe. His hopes were high, and he hoped his dream wasn't just a dream.

23

The two boys looked like they were about to hike Everest with the layers and supplies they brought. Matt filled a bookbag with protein bars, two thermoses of hot chocolate, and a big bottle of water and then headed to the garage to grab the two shovels and the ax.

The two Sherpas tiptoed as quietly as they could from the garage back to the front door. Scott hit a loose floorboard in the foyer that creaked, and they both held their breath before looking upstairs to see if anyone noticed. Scott breathed a sigh of relief when no one had. Then they threw their ski masks and gloves on, opened the door, and headed out to Matt's car. There was no turning back now.

24

The cold hit them instantly, even though they wore half a closet's worth of clothes. The brutal thirty mph wind gusts hit them like a brick of ice. Scott stayed focused, though. No wind or cold was going to deter him from his mission.

"The door won't open," Matt said.

"Huh?"

"Frozen shut. I got some WD-40 in the garage."

"Okay; well, hurry up. It's freezing out here."

"Really? You're gonna be the one who's going to be the one to complain it's freezing?"

"Sorry. Just get the thing."

Matt shook his head and opened the door to the side of the garage. When he came back out, he held the can of WD-40 in one hand and a blowtorch in another.

"Good thinking again with the blowtorch."

Matt nodded. "Well, let's just hope it softens up the dirt."

Then he handed the torch to Scott and sprayed some WD-40 on the door handle. Matt pulled, but still no luck.

"Try pouring a little more."

Matt smothered the handle this time. Scott yanked the door like it was a game of tug and war, and after the second spray, the door swung open.

"Okay. In we go. This should be fun," Matt said.

It took a few turns of the key for the car to start. With their ski masks and multiple layers on, they looked like burglars about to rob an igloo. Matt skidded on some ice backing out of the driveway but then straightened out once they were on the street.

"You owe me big for this, you know."

"I know," Scott said.

25

The parking lot was closed off at the preserve, so Matt parked right in front of the rope. They had just hoped none of the forest preserve police would still be there. They took their chances that no one wanted to go out in the weather if they didn't have to. Matt nearly slipped on the ice getting out of the car and swore at Scott when he thought he was going down. Scott didn't say anything. Truth was, Matt could call him all the names he wanted. He braved the deep freeze with him over an impulsive need to dig the trench. That was a true friend…a brother, even.

"Sorry, Scott. It's just this cold."

"It's alright. We should get going, though. It's not going to warm up anytime soon."

The last time Scott and Matt came to these woods, winter looked more like a postcard - snow clinging to trees and sprinkled on the trail. The woods seemed so peaceful. They were what they always were - a place of escape, of freedom, of revival. Now, they seemed so uninviting. The wind whipped through the naked branches, and their limbs shook as if having a seizure. Matt and Scott paused in their tracks as they heard the howl of a coyote. Scott remembered seeing a band of coyotes on top of the hill overlooking the preserve parking lot a few years back. There must have been five or six of them just staring him down, daring him to enter their woods. He didn't that day. But that was a different day at a different time.

Scott stepped back at the howl, but Matt tugged him toward the main trail.

"Come on. I didn't come out here to stand in the parking lot," Matt said.

26

Some of Scott regretted leaving the comfort of the house, playing *Crash Bandicoot*. Every step into the icy wind told him that, but he clung fast to his dream. He marched on to the trench, hoping to find anything that would lead him to Joe.

Carrying all that equipment in frigid temperatures was no easy task for the two boys. On any other day, it took the boys about a half hour to reach the trench, but that day it took them double the time. Their arms ached from carrying the equipment, and neither of them was sure that they'd have the strength to dig a hole in frozen ground. When they reached the trench, Scott looked around every angle, thinking he might see the mystery girl. Would she walk up out of the swimming hole like in *Beloved*? He shook the thought away. The swimming hole was an ice rink.

"Well, now we have to get the blowtorch and wait for it to do its job," Matt said.

Scott nodded, and Matt pulled the trigger on the torch over a large area in the middle of the trench. Scott shivered as he paced back and forth, with his arms wrapped tightly around his stomach.

"Sounds good."

Matt pulled out one of the thermoses and handed it to Scott but left the other one in the bag.

"Aren't you going to have yours?"

"Nah. Not yet. We might be out here a while. I'm meaning to save it."

"Will it stay hot that long?"

"No, but I'd like to think it will. It's at least keeping me warm right now."

Scott stopped shivering after the first couple of sips. Not only was it warm, he now had something else to concentrate on besides the cold.

Matt pulled out a lighter and played with the flame.

"I'll be right back."

"Where are you going?"

"Gonna gather some firewood."

"Oh. Good thinking."

As Matt walked off into the darkness, Scott heard another howl from a coyote. He turned in all directions but did not see any sign of a coyote. He tried to convince himself that it was just the wind and took another sip of hot chocolate. Matt came back carrying a few broken branches and kindling.

251

"The branches are wet, but the kindling is dry. We'll have to make sure that enough airflow gets through to heat those branches."

Matt set up a pit, carefully placing the kindling on top of the branches. Then he kissed his lighter and lit the kindling. They both watched as the kindling fired with ease, but then a couple of minutes later, the fire died out as soon as it hit the wet branches. Matt twirled the lighter in his hand and said he'd be back with more kindling. He ventured back and forth three times before he got the fire to catch. But when he did, it was glorious. Not even the tundra could stop two best friends.

27

"Doesn't this remind you of that Jack London story we read in English class?"

"Maybe? I didn't pay attention in English class, remember?"

"Well, the main character keeps trying to build a fire in the bitter cold. He eventually dies, and his dog sits by the fire he built and ends up eating him. I think that's how it ended anyway…."

"That's messed up if that's true. Total Donner Party stuff Scott."

"Yeah. Well, don't get any ideas."

Scott couldn't see a smile but did see Matt shake his head. The fire felt satisfying in the otherwise brutal night. It reminded Scott of the fire he and Joe had built months earlier, only that one was more for recreational uses.

The woods meant something different to Scott than they had before, especially at night. They were once a place of refuge. They were a place of trauma but also one of guidance. He thought of the lyrics from "Amazing Grace," "I once was lost, but now I'm found." He hoped that was true of Joe. It sounded good to say. He liked when people sang it in church. *That was because everyone is lost or was lost at some point*, he thought. But they could be found. *That's my hope for Joe*, he thought. Scott shook his thermos and noted that his hot chocolate was almost gone. He told himself to save some for later. Matt stared at the fire and stretched out his hands for extra warmth.

"What do you think happened to Joe, Scott?"

"Honestly?"

"Yeah."

"I think those men in the woods got her."

"You said she made it home."

"Doesn't matter. They found her. Some way."

Matt paused to think about this. Matt loved playing detective, and anything having to do with puzzles or scavenger hunts always appealed to him. He said that he wanted to become a cop after high school, and Scott said he would be the finest cop Ridgeport ever saw. But Matt said he wanted to serve somewhere as far away from Ridgeport as he could. He wanted to start over.

"Matt, do you remember that room we found as kids in your basement?"

"Sure do. Can't forget a thing like that. Why?"

"Well, do you remember that book of names we found with the names crossed off?"

"Yeah...I do."

"Do you think Joe's name was on that list, you know, crossed off?"

Scott could see Matt staring hard into the fire now. He removed his ski mask, and he rubbed his chin. He was lost in thought.

"Matt?"

"I don't know. I don't. I mean. We don't even know what that list meant."

"Yeah. It's just strange, though. Don't you think? And those signatures from the board members and the mayor on them?"

Matt forgot about the signatures and nodded as he said this.

"Is that door still locked?"

"Oh yeah. I tried a couple of other times. You couldn't open that thing with a lock cutter now. She got a fancy electronic one. Forget about getting in there."

Scott sighed. He thought that was a long shot anyway. Matt couldn't quite tell if the soil was any warmer than when he set the torch on the trench.

"Well, should we try to start digging? The night's not getting any younger or warmer," Scott said.

"We can try."

Matt and Scott grabbed their shovels and kept the ax at arm's reach just in case. Matt gave Scott the honors of digging first since it was his idea. But Scott couldn't move much in his many layers. To move, he took off his coat.

"We're next to a fire now anyway. I'm fine."

When he brought the shovel down, a jolt ran through his arm like a bee sting. The ground was still frozen solid. He looked at the tip of the spade, surprised to see there was no dent or scratch in it from the impact.

"Well, we probably should torch the ground a little more," Matt said.

The boys threw their shovels down and sat next to the fire, trying to soak up as much warmth as they could, and Matt warmed the hard soil once again. Scott gathered the shovels. Scott's shoulder still ached from his jab into the frozen dirt on his first try but stabbed at the ground once more. This time, the shovel scraped through, but barely. At least Scott didn't feel a sharp pain through his shoulder. Digging past the first inch or so became problematic, though.

Matt reached into the backpack and pulled out what was left of the hot chocolate in his thermos. He poured it all over their digging ground, much to Scott's disbelief.

"Matt. You didn't want that? You might get too cold."

"Pff. I'm by a fire, dude. I'm fine."

The hot chocolate softened the top layer of dirt, anyway, and the boys were able to dig a little deeper. Dirt flew in all directions. When it got too clumpy, one of them brought out the ax and broke up the soil. Scott knew something was going to happen. He just didn't know what. He had to finish the trench first. The mystery girl was coming back. Whatever it was, something was going to happen. It had to.

28

Matt played along with Scott for a good hour before calling it quits. He threw his shovel down and picked up the backpack.

"Well, we should get back. We want to make it home in time before the sun gets up."

"Right, okay. Just another minute."

"Scott, I came out here on this selfish, impulsive field trip of yours in the blistering cold. Now you can grant me a favor and go back."

Scott knew he was right. He had been selfish and impulsive. It would make a good story to tell in years to come, but still. It was selfish and impulsive. He was tired and frustrated too. He wanted to believe in the dream, but Matt was right. He was just looking for a way to bring Joe back. And Joe wasn't coming back. Not ever.

Scott brought the ax down like Thor's hammer in one last swing of frustration. It struck something. Something hard. The familiar jolt shot through Scott's arm. They had softened up the soil enough where a swing from the ax shouldn't have been that hard. He picked up the shovel and threw some dirt to the side.

"I'm leaving in five minutes. With or without you!" Matt yelled, sitting by the fire now.

"Uh-huh."

There was something down there. It was something yellowish-white, a rock. Scott kept digging, and after he scooped out a few more piles of dirt, he gasped as he dropped the shovel.

"Um, Matt?"

"What? Are you ready to go?"

"Matt. Come here. Matt?"

"What? What is it?"

Matt reluctantly stood up from the fire and crossed over to the excavation site. He was tired and wanted nothing more to do with the trench. Not now, not ever.

"Is that a...?"

Matt's jaw dropped too.

"Yep. That's a skull. That's a skull, Scott."

29

The two boys glanced at each other and then down at the skull.

"What if it's?"

"Joe?" Matt answered.

"Yeah."

"I don't think she would turn into a skeleton that fast."

"Don't think so?"

"I don't think so. I think I saw something on the History Channel about that. I mean...I could be wrong."

The fire was dying down, and they could feel the biting wind once more.

"What should we do with it? Do we leave it here?" Scott asked.

Matt hesitated. He kept his gaze on the skull and then looked around to make sure they were the only ones around.

From a distance, there was that howl of the coyote again, only closer this time.

"Let's go. Grab the skull."

"What? Really?"

Matt dug some dirt around it, grabbed it, and then threw it in the backpack. The fire was dying, but as Matt looked over his shoulder, he could see something over in the distance - a band of coyotes was approaching.

"Run! Run, Scott, run!"

30

But just as the boys started to break into a run, the coyotes came out from a pack of bushes and greeted them head-on. The boys froze to the spot, only about five feet away from the angry beasts.

"Um, Matt... what do we do here, Matt?"

The coyotes gnashed their teeth, and their hair stood on end. Matt held his arms out and began backing away slowly. Scott did the same.

"Nice coyotes. Good coyotes," Matt said.

But they just growled and gnashed their teeth even more and began inching toward them.

"Scott - toss them the rest of our food."

Scott was fixated on the leader, who seemed fixated on his face.

"Now, Scott, do it."

Scott shook out his trance and pulled the rest of the protein bars from his pocket. He tossed them at the coyotes' feet. The coyotes looked to the boys and then looked to the bars. Much to Matt and Scott's luck, the band of coyotes converged on what was left of Matt and Scott's food. They fought over it like it was the first thing the animals ate in days. The boys continued backing up slowly and, once they felt like they were a good distance away, broke into a run. They left behind the two shovels and the ax and ran as fast as they could against the howling wind. They could still hear the gnashing of teeth as the coyotes devoured the food.

The boys ran as fast as their layers of clothing would allow them. Even though he knew the coyotes were far behind them by now, they heard the occasional howl. They didn't want to take the chance of another ambush. So, they continued to run at full speed. Scott's side began to hurt. He wasn't the athlete Matt was, but he wasn't about to be another dead body out in these woods. Mind over matter. *Isn't that how marathon runners make it in their last stretch?* he thought.

Scott hit a rock and almost fell, but Matt pulled his hand up. The wind made it feel like they were running on a treadmill. The coyotes continued to howl, and they imagined them touching every branch and leaf. Neither dared look back. Scott and Matt saw that they had reached the clearing, the opening to the parking lot. As the boys entered the lot, Scott peered over his shoulder and witnessed a few more coyotes standing on top of the hill on the other side of the trail, staring them down. The boys jumped the rope blocking off the forest preserve like track stars. Matt and Scott spun out in Matt's Saturn so fast they almost forgot they had the skull with them.

31

They were panting like dogs in heat. The only silver lining was it made them forget all about the cold. Matt turned on some tunes. This time it was his Foo Fighters *One by One* cassette. The title track came on, and as Dave Grohl sang, "All my life I've been searching for something/Something never comes never leads to nothing/Nothing satisfies, but I'm getting close/Closer to the prize at the end of the rope." Scott listened and thought about how crazy this night was, how crazy these woods had become. He looked over at Matt, but he just hummed along, driving. He wasn't sure he connected the lyrics to what was happening, and something was happening.

The clock above the tape deck read 4:30 a.m. They could have beaten *Crash Bandicoot* by now, but this was an adventure that even Crash himself might have had trouble maneuvering.

If his night in the woods with Joe changed the course of his life forever, this might have been a close second, Scott thought.

32

When the boys returned home, the familiar sight of a home with heat and a bed was heaven. Matt was careful to park in the same spot he had before, and they made like cat burglars into their home, without a sound.

By the time they successfully made it up to Matt's room, undetected and de-layered, they felt like they hadn't slept in years, but the boys also felt like they were on the brink of hypothermia. They each took turns soaking in a hot bath after what seemed like forever in the tundra. Scott felt the chills subside and thought about the crazy night, about the coyotes, about the skull. When they had finished their soak, Scott walked into Matt's room with a yawn.

"What should we do with the skull?"

Matt shrugged and said that the bookbag should be kept in the closet for now.

"Good idea. Hey, do you think we should call the police about this?" Scott asked.

"I think we should get some sleep. It's been a long night."

"Right."

259

And so, they agreed that it was bedtime. Scott stared up at the ceiling, thinking about the night, and his mind always drifted back to the skull. He wondered what the next step was now. He remembered the dream.

"Find me, find Joe."

Is the skull the mystery girl? Scott thought.

Scott rubbed his forehead and turned to his side, looking out at the frosted window. He remembered looking out at his frosted window just yesterday when everything seemed normal. Now here he was, with a skull in the closet of his best friend's house. He thought about what to do about it before his mind turned to the homework he had for the week. He still hadn't done any of his English, or math, or science for that matter. Mr. Lorenz always gave a lot of science homework, but he didn't mind. He liked him, and so did all the kids. He...Mr. Lorenz? Scott thought for a second. He might know what to do about the skull. He told us that he once wanted to go into anthropology. He might know something about this. Scott forgot all about his homework and concentrated on a new assignment. He was going to ask Mr. Lorenz about this skull. His heart beat rapidly, and he did all he could do to calm himself to go to sleep.

33

The remainder of the week seemed to drag. Matt decided it would be better to show Riley and Jimmy the skull than to tell them about it over the phone. He was also paranoid about anyone finding out they found a skull. The two of them decided not to go to the police, not yet anyway. Matt was on board with seeing Mr. Lorenz first. He would know what to do, and when they saw Riley and Jimmy at school again, they could confide in them in secret.

In the meantime, Scott and Matt did all the Internet research they could on reported deaths in those woods but came up empty. There were several missing persons in Ridgeport's history, and with every one of those missing persons, a search was conducted in those very woods.

Scott wondered if the skull belonged to the mystery girl in his dream but couldn't help but think it belonged to Joe. Whoever it belonged to, there was a reason he went there that night. Scott endured many restless nights the rest of that week, and when he slept, he no longer dreamt of the mystery girl. He often referred to the notebook for what he had written down. He knew her description seemed familiar from his research - a blond girl with a sweater and ripped jeans sporting the gold necklace that read "Corinthians 13:4-13."

On the last day before school, her description again popped back into his mind. Something clicked. Scott rushed to his computer and looked up her description in Google. At first, some suggestive sites appeared. But then he narrowed his search by adding "Ridgeport girl who disappeared." Several articles popped up, with several of them with pictures. There she was. Mystery Girl. He had scanned over her picture like she was just another victim. He knew she looked like her but never connected the two. The answer was right in his face. Several articles described her wardrobe the night she went missing: wearing a sweater with ripped jeans and styling a gold necklace. That skull couldn't have been Joe. It had to be the mystery girl. It had to be. "Find Me. Find Joe," he wrote in the notebook. She repeated it in the dream and stood in the trench. That was why he had to go there. But what did that mean? Scott wanted to get to science class more than ever.

34

The next morning at school, the administration decided to conduct a random book bag check. They had been doing this at Ridgeport High School ever since the social norms

261

initiative passed in '83. The administration then wanted to make sure students were abiding by the code of ethics set by the town. Students marched in long, single-file lines off the buses and came to a standstill at the school entrances as teachers, deans, and security officers rifled through book bags and purses searching for illegal substances or anything "unsafe for the learning environment," as the town's rules stated. Scott couldn't understand why they chose to do this on a day that still was in the middle of a Polar Vortex but was sure they had their reasons. What had frustrated him more than that was of all the days for them to do this, he was carrying a skull in his backpack. You could get suspended or even expelled for having something they deemed illegal or unsafe.

"I have plenty of time to think about an excuse for this. Think Scott, think," he said to himself.

The students all walked like penguins toward the school, but before he knew it, only a few students separated him and his doom.

Dean Williams would be checking his bag. Of all the staff, why did it have to be him? He didn't like any of the students, and Scott wasn't even sure why he worked in education. Scott thought he was always out to get someone. Scott gulped. "Here we go," he mumbled.

"Open your bag," Williams said harshly.

"Yes, sir."

Williams shuffled through it with a metal rod and noticed the skull right away.

"Uh-huh. What is this, Casey?"

"Science experiment, sir, for Lorenz, sir."

"Uh-huh. Move along."

Scott froze. He bought it.

"Come on, Casey. You're holding up my line!"

He hurried through and almost tripped on a mat. He made it inside with a real live skull in his backpack. Ten periods to go, and he might have an answer. It was going to be a long day.

35

Scott did all he could to pay attention to his other subjects that day. Mrs. Harrington called him out for daydreaming. Mr. Ryan looked at him funny for constantly squirming in his seat, and his gym teacher, Mr. Dotson, made him run laps for not wanting to participate in the volleyball scrimmage. Scott made it to lunch in the middle of the day and found some relief eating with the band. The band hadn't been together since before the week off from school.

"Riley, Jimmy! Man, it's good to see you guys," Scott said.

"Oh, what am I? Chopped liver?" Matt asked.

"It's good to see you too, Matt. I just haven't seen them...you know what I mean."

"I'm just bustin' your chops."

"So, how have you guys been?" Jimmy asked. Jimmy grew up quite a bit over the last year. Now that he was a junior, he had really come into his own.

"Well, it's been an interesting break, to say the least," Scott said and looked at Matt.

Matt set his head down and bit into a piece of taco salad, the most loved food from the school cafeteria.

"What does that mean?" Riley asked.

Matt kept on eating, and Scott forced a slow grin.

"Are you ready for what I'm about to tell you?"

"Try me," Riley said.

Scott divulged the whole story, from the dream to last night when he had the epiphany that the skull could belong to Emma Ryan, the missing Ridgeport girl from 1986.

"So, let me get this straight. During the tundra weather this past week, you decided it would be a good idea to go dig the trench, which we haven't done since grade school, mind you, based on a dream you had?" Riley said.

"Well, yeah," Scott said.

Jimmy chuckled and then shoved in a spoonful of applesauce.

"I thought it was crazy at first, too. Up until we found the skull."

"And you think this skull belongs to Emma Ryan, the girl who went missing in '86, aka your mystery girl?"

"I'm like eighty-six percent sure," Scott said.

"Seems to weirdly make sense," Matt said.

Ever the skeptic, Riley furrowed his eyebrows, but Matt nodded at Scott and then pointed toward his backpack. If their word weren't enough, evidence would be. Scott unzipped the book bag and was careful enough that fellow students took no notice when he grabbed the Wrobel's attention.

"Riley, Jimmy - check it out."

Jimmy stopped chewing, and Riley dropped his fork. They could not argue with hard facts. That wasn't a skull from a Halloween shop. There were still specks of dirt on it, and a long crack ran across the top.

"I'm sorry, guys. You know how cynical I can get, and…."

"No need to apologize, Riley. We still love you, man," Matt said.

"So... the plan is to show this to Mr. Lorenz?" Jimmy asked.

"Yeah. He used to be interested in anthropology. I remember him saying that the first week of school," Scott said.

"Yeah. Scott's right. He did say that," Jimmy said.

"Well. We'll stay with you guys. We all have science together anyway."

"Why do you think I told you?"

Riley smiled, and Matt patted him on the back. The countdown to AP Bio began.

37

Mr. Lorenz was Scott's favorite teacher. He always conducted fun labs and seemed to enjoy coming to work every day. He always attempted to talk to every student throughout the fifty-minute period, checking in on how they were doing on an assignment and how their day was going. He cared, and it made Scott care.

The bell finally rang, and the band held back, like bowling pins in a row, facing Mr. Lorenz.

"Hi, boys. You know, you're going to miss your bus if you don't hurry."

They all looked to Scott to speak first.

"Mr. Lorenz. You said you had an interest in anthropology before becoming a science teacher, right?"

"Well, I'd say it was little more than an interest. I was an anthropologist. It just wasn't for me. I decided I'd rather teach."

The boys' faces lit up like a Christmas tree.

"What? Is it something I said?"

"Could you still perform your work, you know, if you needed to?" Scott asked.

Mr. Lorenz gave him a confused look and then saw Scott open the backpack. He mouthed "Where did you" when he pulled out the skull to show him.

"Matt and I found this in Spring Grove Woods. We weren't sure what to do with it, so we thought we'd ask you."

"Boys, I, this is most strange."

Mr. Lorenz gave the skull a quizzical look before questioning the boys.

"Did you call the police? They might want to investigate this."

"Well, no. We were interested to hear from you first," Scott said.

Mr. Lorenz nodded.

"Do you want to hold it?" Matt asked.

"Why don't we go back here?"

The classroom had a long closet in the back where science teachers stored supplies. Students never got to see it. It looked like the walls of a Halloween shop. Mr. Lorenz took the skull from Scott's outreached hands.

"Do you boys have someplace to be? I'll have to study it for a little bit."

"What are you looking to find out?"

"Well, I know it sounds crazy, but I think it belongs to Emma Ryan, the Ridgeport girl who went missing in '86. I just can't be sure. Any light you can shed on that would be great."

"What gave you that idea?"

"A dream."

"A dream?"

"Hard to explain now."

"I'll see what I can do. You can learn a lot from a skull - age, how they died. Give me until tomorrow."

"Thank you, Mr. Lorenz," Scott said.

38

Mr. Lorenz asked the boys to stay behind the next day after

class. They had been waiting for this moment since lunch the previous day.

"Come on in the back, guys. I have some information for you."

Sitting on a table next to some test tubes was the skull. If there was a perfect hiding place, it was here, in a science classroom's closet. The boys gathered round as if they were about to listen in on the presentation of a lifetime.

"Well, it's a girl, alright."

"It is? How can you tell?" Matt asked.

"See. I told you it was," Scott butted in.

"The jawline is less rectangular than men. I thought so yesterday but was so taken aback by your discovery; I didn't get a good look."

Scott felt his jawline, and Riley snickered. Mr. Lorenz continued.

"You see this small hole here on the frontal cortex?"

Scott nodded.

"It indicates blunt force trauma."

"Blunt force trauma?" Jimmy asked. "What's that?"

"Well...it could mean a lot of different things. But whatever it was, this girl was physically attacked or sustained an injury to her head. And it was bad enough to impact the skull."

"Oh wow," Jimmy said.

"Yeah, wow," Mr. Lorenz said.

"Mr. Lorenz, do you think it's Josephine?" Scott asked.

"It's probably not, no. It usually takes the human body years to decompose, so it could not be hers. Although, the skull is similar in age."

Mr. Lorenz pointed to the aging of the teeth and the condition of the skull. He said he estimated the skull to belong to a person before thirty-five years of age.

"Do you think it's Emma Ryan, Mr. Lorenz?"

267

"Well, we can't be one hundred percent sure. But if I were a betting man, I'd say so. You bring me a skull of a girl younger than thirty-five, found in an area she goes missing? More than a coincidence, wouldn't you say?"

Now, Mr. Lorenz could see the boys gathering around the skull, studying it. He handed it to them for another look. He watched as they re-examined the hole, the teeth, and the jawline.

"My young anthropologists," Mr. Lorenz said and laughed.

"You know, boys, we have to contact the police about this."

Scott's head shot up. He knew when they unearthed it, that's what they should do, but something held them back. It could have been that they illegally went to the woods after dark. But that wasn't it, not really. He thought it had something to do with the dream. He felt that if the police got involved, their investigation would be turned over to the police, and finding Joe could forever be lost.

"I know Mr. Lorenz. It is just...it is just this dream I had. Something is telling me we have to solve this case," Scott said.

"Uh-huh. And what's this dream?"

39

He listened in earnest. He couldn't tell most adults his dream, as they might wave it off and say, "That's nice." Not Mr. Lorenz. That's what made him such a great teacher. He treated his students like they mattered.

"That's quite a dream, Mr. Casey. And you think this 'Find me. Find Joe' thing means you can't contact the authorities?"

"I...I don't know. I'm pretty sure we found this mystery girl on our own. The mystery girl wants us to keep going. I don't know," Scott said.

Mr. Lorenz rubbed his stubble and adjusted his glasses. The boys could see he was thinking.

"Okay, but be careful. If you find yourselves getting into something you shouldn't be getting into, promise me that you'll call the proper authorities?"

40

The band thanked Mr. Lorenz and walked away from his classroom, satisfied. They at least mostly knew who it was. They knew it wasn't Joe. But what they didn't know was where to go from there. They weren't any closer to finding Joe. And did Joe even want to be found? Was Joe even alive? These questions have been running through everyone's head except Scott's, anyway.

Matt had to get to track practice; Jimmy left for basketball and Riley for chess. Scott was left behind at Ridgeport High. Unlike the others, Scott never took up a sport in high school, and though he took on his fair share of clubs the last three years, he quit most of them from a hard bout of senioritis. Also, after Joe disappeared, school took a back seat.

With everyone else occupied, Scott had a few choices to get home. He could brave the still-frigid conditions and walk the three miles home, wait until the four o'clock bus, or call from the main office and hope Loretta would come to pick him up. He chose the four o'clock. In the meantime, he had no place to go.

"Mr. Lorenz?"

"Yes, Mr. Casey?"

"Would it be alright if I hung out in your room until the four o'clock bus?"

"Well, as long as you don't mind if I grade some papers. I'm afraid I won't be much in the way of company."

"No, that's fine. Thank you."

He smiled, and Scott settled in his lab seat and set down his backpack.

Mr. Lorenz wasn't kidding. He had a stack of papers that mirrored the Leaning Tower of Pisa. And his concentration on each one was unflinching. Scott thought he couldn't even give one assignment that much attention. He admired him that much more. Scott turned his attention to the hand clock: 2:50. He had about an hour before he could even begin his way to the bus. After a long day of sitting, that extra hour would seem like torture unless he gave himself something to do.

Scott pulled out his journal. He had attempted to write in it daily since freshman year. That was the year his freshman English teacher had them write their own poems. Scott wrote one in the style of Wordsworth, relating it to the woods. He said how he wished he could just dig and dig and dig. He wanted to hide away from the world and create his world. His teacher thought it was dark but beautiful. She had encouraged him to keep writing, so he did, every day since. Lately, he wrote about Joe. He wrote down every detail he remembered about her because he forgot something about her every day that passed. He was forgetting how she looked, what her voice sounded like. He was afraid that there would come a time that he would forget about her entirely. He didn't want to move on from her. Joe was the greatest thing to have happened to him. And he hated the world for taking her away from him. In his last entry, he wrote, "I love you, Joe. I just don't know how to tell you."

Scott looked up from his journal and noticed that Mr. Lorenz had cut some fat off the top of his pile. Scott's eyes wandered all around the room. It was a typical male teacher's room. There were posters alright, but it didn't have that warm, fuzzy feeling of his female coworkers. There weren't streamers hanging from the ceiling. But he did have examples of student work, and he liked the interesting graphics and motivational quotes on the walls.

A quote from Einstein hanging over Mr. Lorenz's desk caught Scott's attention. "Imagination is more important than knowledge." Scott scribbled the quote down in his notebook and then underneath wrote, "Ha! A physicist speaks in a biology class." He heard the quote before and saw the poster but never thought anything of it.

He circled the words Imagination and Knowledge. Was his wild imagination leading him to the truth? Is that what Einstein meant? He unearthed a mystery based on a dream, an impulse. From that, he had accumulated knowledge. But...now what?

41

Scott wrote down everything he remembered from the night he last saw Joe. He remembered Joe talking him into going out at night. He remembered trying pot for the first time. He remembered roasting s'mores and staring at the fire. He remembered the strange rustling in the distance, running through the brush and winding up at the meadow where they'd slept the night away. He remembered waking up next to Joe and thinking that moment couldn't have been any more perfect. He remembered seeing her cuts and telling her men chased him, men with badges. He remembered finding the gold necklace he had intended to give to her.

Scott glanced at the clock, 3:22 p.m. Mr. Lorenz still had his face buried in papers. Scott read over what he had written. Then he read over it again, searching for a clue, any kind of clue. His eyes paused on "men with badges."

271

"Did the police know about her disappearance?" he thought. "Did they not see me in those woods? Is that why I don't want to go to them now about Emma Ryan?"

Scott thought back to Emma's story; how on the night she went missing, she wore a similar outfit that Joe wore, the one with the ripped jeans and a sweater. She also was out past curfew. He thought back to other Ridgeport missing person cases. They, too, carried some illegal activity or social blemish on their record.

He thought about the type of person Joe was. She was an influencer. At the wedding, it was her idea to drink. Did Ridgeport people know of that, like a *1984* Big Brother thing? Scott started to think that was crazy. Here he was, sitting in an AP Bio room in high school. They weren't in a dictatorship where a fascist mayor ordered the citizens to burn books. But there were weird connections in the disappearances.

Scott shook his head. He felt like he was grabbing at straws. The clock read 3:35. In another ten minutes, he could start his trek to the four o'clock bus. He stopped journal writing and began sketching a drawing of the bio room. Whenever Scott needed to take his mind off things, he sketched - mostly cartoons or pictures of nature. It helped him relax. He would never become Charles Schulz or Monet, but he didn't care. He stenciled in the lab tables, Mr. Lorenz's desk, the whiteboard behind him, the cinder block walls filled with inspirational posters, the door. Scott paused after finishing off the shading on the door.

"That's it. I know what I have to do."

Mr. Lorenz walked up in front of him.

"Mr. Casey, shouldn't you be running along? You'll be late for your bus?"

Scott looked at the clock. It said 3:55, and it left at four o'clock sharp.

"Oh. Thank you, and thanks for letting me stay."

272

"It's not a problem."

He grabbed his journal and backpack and ran like he was being chased by the coyotes again, out the door and through the hall.

42

The four o'clock bus sat at the opposite side of the school, and Scott barely got on in time. As he settled in his seat for the ten-minute drive, he gazed out the window toward the familiar sights and knew he should have used the last hour to work on his homework. He specialized in procrastination. When he got home, he scarfed down his dinner, hurried through his homework, and laid in bed thinking of his next base of action. He could not do this alone. He needed to talk to the band about this. Everyone needed to be on board for it to work.

43

Waiting for lunch the next day felt like torture. Mrs. Harrington made Scott stay after class for his daydreaming again.

"Young man, how can you be expected to learn when your mind is somewhere else?"

"I don't know."

"Well, you better think about why you are coming here, or you're going to be right back to failing like you were a couple of weeks ago, understood?"

"Yes, ma'am."

"You better run along now, or you'll be late for your next class."

Scott made his way out of the room and onto calculus. He never was a rule-breaker, but he could not concentrate on his studies right now. All he could think about was getting to lunch and talking with the band.

44

Scott thought through his conversation he would have with the band in bed last night. In total, he figured he slept for about four hours. All things considered, Scott surprised himself that he slept that much. And yet, he was as awake as a rooster at dawn. Carrying his idea with him this whole time left him restless, and he hoped the band would buy into it.

Scott showed up at their table in the cafeteria first. He brown-bagged it, and after sitting down, scanned the cafeteria line for Matt, Riley, and Jimmy. They were late, and Scott began looking around to see if he had missed them. The clock ticked down to one minute to go in the passing period, and after that, they'd be considered tardy. They were never tardy, not to lunch anyway. He looked from the clock and back to the line. Now he saw them, lined up together at the end of the line. Riley had his hands around his head and was red-faced and panting. Jimmy and Matt fanned their shirts as if trying to cool themselves off.

When they finally sat down, Matt spoke up first.

"Sorry, man. There was a fight, and all of A-wing was blocked off."

"Yeah, yeah. We had to use the stairs to go to the second floor, around to B," Riley said.

Scott realized they wanted to keep talking about the fight, but he cut them off.

"Well, glad you're here. Listen, guys, there's something that I've been meaning to tell you."

"Yeah? What is it?" Jimmy asked through a mouthful of pizza.

"I think I know what we have to do next now that we found the skull," Scott said.

274

Riley rolled his eyes, Jimmy glanced at a girl at another table and flashed a smile, and Matt looked up from his pizza, pretending to listen.

"What's your plan, Scott?" Matt asked.

Scott tapped his fork and exhaled as the band's eyes once again focused on him.

"Do you guys remember the door? The door in Matt's basement? I think the next answer lies in there."

Matt's eyes bulged, Riley resumed eating, and Jimmy excused himself to use the restroom. Scott hung his head and felt more tired than he had in a long time. He took a few bites of his peanut butter and jelly sandwich he made himself (Loretta gave up making his lunch years ago) and remained silent for a minute. Matt and Riley ate in silence too, and then it was Riley of all people who said, "If we're gonna get in there, we're going to have to put our brains together."

Matt nodded.

"She's got that locked like Fort Knox, but I agree. I think we need to go in there," Matt said.

Scott smiled and breathed a sigh of relief.

Riley called Jimmy back over. Even though Jimmy was a newly confident man, he still listened to his brother.

"Yes, Riley?"

"We're breaking in that door."

"We are?"

"Yes, and that means you are too."

Some of the old Jimmy the band knew returned, and his face turned a little white. The girl he was checking out got up to throw her tray away and moved to another table. Jimmy turned his attention back to the table and ran his hand through his auburn hair.

"Well, if we have to, we have to."

Scott set his hand in the middle of the table.

"All in, just like old times."

And they all connected hands and released. They were in this together, through the end.

45

The rest of the day was normal. Scott simultaneously wished he could crawl into bed and begin working on how to break into the door. Other than that, he didn't get called to stay after class and kept himself awake enough to learn his lessons. In AP Bio, Mr. Lorenz announced that it was dissection day.

"Today, we will be dissecting a frog. Now, as we have talked about before, one reason we dissect frogs is that their organs are laid out similarly to ours. So, you should see a blueprint on how body systems work."

A few groans arose from his class, but the seniors paired up in their groups without complaint. Of course, the band sat together. Even though Jimmy was still a junior, he got a waiver to take the senior-level course because of his early graduation track. Hence, the band still had their unofficial meetings throughout lunch and science. As the rest of the class joined together, Mr. Lorenz passed out the dissection trays with the tools of death - scissors, scalpels, forceps.

"Now remember, you are identifying the key organs on your worksheet. You only need to turn in one worksheet for your group," Lorenz said.

The formaldehyde overpowered the room, and Scott knew it might take multiple showers for the stink to rid itself from his body. When Mr. Lorenz placed their tray in the middle of their table, Riley placed his hand on the scissors first.

"Alright, well, guess we know who the killer of the group is now," Matt said.

Jimmy and Scott let out a good laugh. Riley quipped back, "How do you know I'm not?" But he laughed along with them.

Scott pinned the frog's legs to the dissection tray, and then Matt read the instructions to Riley. With the precision of a brain surgeon, Riley lifted the frog's skin halfway between its rear legs with the forceps. Then, with the scalpel, he cut along its center. Jimmy recoiled. Riley smirked as Jimmy held his stomach, and the rest of the band answered the question on the worksheet on the placement and size of the heart.

"Nice work, Squimmy Jimmy," Riley said and tousled his hair.

Jimmy squirmed away, embarrassed. He breathed in and out, trying to calm his uneasiness.

"Makes you think, doesn't it?" Scott asked.

"About what?" asked Matt.

"We just uncovered part of a dead body, and now here we are, cutting one open."

"Maybe we should become morticians," Matt joked.

Riley snorted and continued to use the forceps to move around the organs.

"All right, your turn, guys," Riley said. He handed the tools to Matt.

Mr. Lorenz made his way from table to table, and Scott noticed Mr. Lorenz had to stop by Johnny and Sam's table to tell them to stop playing hockey with the brain. Acting immature was their specialty. He never understood why they wanted to take an AP class if they just wanted to goof off.

"Do you think Emma was sliced open like this?" Riley asked.

"Do you mean like they do in the movies by some deranged serial killer? Is that what you mean?" Scott asked.

"Yeah. I mean, you said you dug her up in the trench and all."

Scott raised his eyebrows. He never considered that one person could be behind all the kidnappings and murders.

"Oh, I don't know. I thought that you're the murderer, right, Riley?" Scott said.

The band laughed again. Mr. Lorenz strolled by their table this time.

"How are we coming along, boys?"

The band turned back to the frog.

"Oh, very good, sir," Riley said.

"I see that you completed only a few answers on your sheet. You only have fifteen minutes left, so you better hurry."

"Yes, Mr. Lorenz," Scott said. Riley smirked at him when he walked away. Riley aced his classes his senior year but never cozied up to his teachers.

"Yes, Mr. Lorenz," Riley imitated.

"Shut up," Scott said.

"He's right. We need to get a move on. This is a big grade. You heard him at the start of class," Matt said.

Riley huffed and then started rattling off the parts on the sheet with the speed of an auctioneer. Riley had completed more than half of the sheet by the time he finished, and the rest of the group sat there flabbergasted. Jimmy patted him on the back.

"That's my smart big brother," he said.

Riley shrugged.

"I've been paying attention while you guys have been in your heads about conspiracy theories. Now it's up to the rest of you to finish. I know what the rest of the answers are."

"Well, if you know, can't you…." Jimmy started.

"No. You're not going to learn anything that way, little bro," he said.

So, the rest of the band hurried to beat the clock and finished labeling the liver, gallbladder, and the small and large intestines. They then had to answer the question, "What types of evidence can you gather to determine whether the frog is male or female?"

Scott finished answering the question just as Mr. Lorenz came by to collect their worksheet. He nodded and smiled at him. Scott smiled back.

"You're welcome," Riley said as he walked away.

"Thank you," Scott said.

"Yeah, thank you," Jimmy and Matt echoed.

The bell rang, and the day ended, but for the band, their education was about to begin.

46

The boys went their separate ways - Jimmy to track, Matt to basketball, Riley to math club, and Scott readied himself for the bus ride home. Scott wondered if he was still stuck in childhood - planning missions like an undercover spy while his friends engaged in the typical high school activities of playing sports and participating in clubs. He told himself no, not in this case. This case was all too real. This wasn't playing with GI Joes or playing Army. It was real-life detective work, and he just didn't have time for standard high school stuff. He only wished the rest of the band didn't either.

47

The band reconvened on the Saturday following Matt's basketball win against Naperville Central and Jimmy's placing first in the short distance in the Western Regional Invite. There were reasons to celebrate. The band met at The Ridgeport Diner, and Riley and Scott bought Matt and Jimmy the dinners of their choice: New York strip steak, medium rare for Matt and the "Works" Burger with everything on it, well done for Jimmy. The conversation flowed about Matt's impressive twenty-three-point finish to give the Warriors the three-point victory and Jimmy's photo finish over Pullman South High School runner Adrian Gerstner.

"I felt like I was really in the zone out there, yeah. I couldn't miss," Matt said.

Scott laughed.

"You can't miss any night. That's why you always get the ball."

Matt rubbed his hand through his hair and nodded.

"And you Speedy Gonzalez, what do you only get faster?"

"Yep," Jimmy said through a bite of his burger.

Jimmy was a little less modest in those days.

Riley grinned and shook his head.

Of course, the band knew why they were there. True, it was a special moment in Ridgeport sports history. But it was also a meeting of the minds. If they were going to do this thing, they needed to put all four of their heads together. The server came by their table and asked if they wanted the check.

"Um, not right now. Can I get some coffee?" Scott asked.

Matt cocked his head. He never knew his best friend drank coffee. Scott turned to the rest of the table.

"Would anyone else like some?"

"Nah," Matt said. Riley and Jimmy didn't say anything.

"One coffee then," the server said.

"Since when do you drink coffee?"

"Since now. I need something to help me think," Scott said.

"Interesting," Matt said.

Matt flipped the placemat over and whipped out a pen. He began drawing something.

"Whatcha drawing there, Matthew?" Riley asked.

A sketch of the basement and the exterior of the room.

"Oh," Riley said. He peered over, intrigued.

Riley turned to Scott, asking him to recall what he remembered about the room. He and Jimmy had never seen it.

"Well, it had a book of names, and certain names were crossed out," Scott started. He was deep in thought as if trying to piece together a puzzle.

"On the back of the list were signatures from the board of trustees and Mayor Goldman. There was a map on the wall, and books, lots of books. I can't remember what they were about, though."

"Huh. Weird stuff," Riley said.

"Yeah. Weird," repeated Jimmy.

"How's that sketch going, Matt?" Riley asked.

"It's going."

Matt looked like he was drawing with the intensity of a sketch artist. The band didn't say anything for a minute and decided to wait on Matt's artwork.

48

Matt revealed his drawing on the placemat. He drew from memory the inside of the room. He also drew the basement's basic layout, what surrounded the room, and what the lock looked like, and then jotted down a few notes on the bottom right corner.

"So, it's not all that big. It's more the size of a child's bedroom than anything, but it's crammed full of stuff. There's a skinny pathway in the room to maneuver around, but that's about it," said Matt.

"On the outside, there is now a camera watching the exterior of the room, which was not there when we broke in years ago. She must have gotten wise to the lack of security.

The band nodded as Matt pointed to his makeshift security camera.

"The lock is state-of-the-art electronic. I've been down to the basement several times since that day we went in there. She installed the lock before she installed the camera, so I inspected it. It's foolproof. It requires a fingerprint and eye scanner."

"Man. Total *Mission Impossible* stuff going on in there," Jimmy said.

"Yeah. The old door was wood, and we could have just knocked it in, but this one is steel. Good luck there," Matt said.

Scott sighed. He knew none of this. He did not dare go down there after the incident years ago, too afraid of what might happen to him if he was caught.

"The rest of the basement is still the same, no change there."

"And your notes there?" Scott asked.

The band hunched forward over the placemat, trying to decipher all his chicken scratches.

"One. She doesn't leave the house as much anymore because of being married to Peter. Two. Speaking of Peter, there are now two people in the house to deal with. Three. I'm pretty sure an alarm might sound if that door opens, or we try to penetrate the lock and fail, something like that. Four. I don't like to think about what will happen if we get caught. Five. My mom goes down there quite a bit to do 'laundry,' except we always have dirty clothes. Six. Is this really worth it?"

The band sat for a moment, feeling quite apprehensive. Scott sipped on his coffee and could see he had a good jitter going.

"It's worth it," Scott said.

Matt looked at the Wrobel brothers. Riley stared at the table like he was deep in thought. Matt knew if Riley said yes, so would Jimmy.

"It's worth it," Riley said in a whisper.

"What was that?" Matt asked.

"It's worth it. Okay?"

"Jimbo?" Matt asked.

"Huh?"

"I... I guess so. It's worth it. If that's what...what you guys want."

"Okay. So, it's worth it. Now what?"

49

"Now we say thank God for the Internet where you can research anything," Scott said. His whole body shook from the coffee now. He had called the server over for a pot of coffee, and then he just kept pouring.

"Maybe you should slow down there, killer. You look like you're gonna fall out of your seat, buddy," Matt said.

"I'm fine," Scott said, but his cup rattled as he brought it to his mouth.

"So, the Internet?" Riley asked.

"Yes, so we do some research on how to pick a lock like that and get past a camera."

"Well, the camera thing. We can just spray some silly string or something at it, I think. I've seen that done in movies," Jimmy said.

Scott nodded, but Riley winced, not sure if he was nodding in approval or nodding from the shakes of the coffee.

"Okay, research it, fellas," Matt said.

"Should we report back within a few days and see what we come up with?" Scott asked.

"Yeah. Here?" Matt asked.

"Doesn't have to be here. We could do it at lunch," Scott said.

"We'll figure it out," Riley said.

"Alright. Let's just keep each other posted and stick to the plan," Scott said.

Then they paid for their tab and left the diner.

50

Scott recalled *Mission Impossible* when Ethan Hunt broke into Langley to steal the NOC list. He considered using the same tactics - finding a way to get Mrs. Norris sick after she opened the door, but how reliable would that be? That was a movie. Nothing in the movies ever works in real life. He felt like Ethan, searching the World Wide Web for ways to break into a high-security room he wasn't supposed to enter. Scott searched "How to bypass a fingerprint scanner" on Yahoo and received thousands of results. Apparently, hackers have been through this territory.

The Internet has created a whole wild west for anything and everything, he said to himself.

Scott read article after article, amazed at how easy it looked to bypass a fingerprint scanner. And yet he believed it was hard because he was anything but an experienced hacker. Scott found a solution after hours of searching that involved a duster, a digital camera, an overhead projector, wood glue, graphite powder, and a lot of luck. He knew Matt had a fancy camera, and he was pretty sure they could find a way to convince Mr. Lorenz into letting them use his overhead projector.

"This just might work," Scott whispered to himself and smiled.

51

On the following day at the cafeteria, Scott asked the band if they had conducted any research yet. Matt chuckled and bit into his taco salad; Riley shook his head, and so did Jimmy.

284

"Well, I did."

"Okay, here it goes. Let's hear it, detective," Riley said.

"Detective? I thought we were all in this together?"

Riley shrugged.

"We are. It's just...I don't know, man. Are you sure you want to go through with this? You're talking jail time at best, having to face the wrath that is Mrs. Norris angry at worst," Riley said.

Matt laughed so hard he almost choked on his taco salad.

"I didn't stay up late again doing research just for the fun of it. Now, if you pansies don't want to do it, then I guess I'm going solo on this mission. Now, what will it be?!"

They quieted down, surprised to see the usual mellow Scott get all heated. Scott noticed a few other kids turned around in their direction.

"Okay, okay. Keep your voice down. We're in; we're in," Riley said.

Matt nodded, followed by Jimmy.

"So, what was your plan, Scott?" Riley asked.

52

"Okay, so I researched a lot of websites, and this was conceivably the easiest method I found."

"Well, let's hear it," Matt said.

"We dust something we know that Mrs. Norris regularly touches like a purse or a coffee mug or something. Then, we need to take a high-quality photo of it using a digital camera. We then project the image on an overhead, cover it with graphite powder, and then smear it with a thin layer of white wood glue. We have to wait until the glue is dry, and then we peel off the surface, and bingo, we have our print."

"Sounds simple enough, but who here has a digital camera?" Riley asked.

"I do," Matt said, rubbing his chin.

"And you're thinking that Mr. Lorenz will just allow us to borrow his overhead, aren't you?" Riley asked.

"Come on. He loves me."

Riley and Jimmy both smiled.

"I guess so," Riley said. "So, who's going to be our feather duster?" he asked with a grin.

"I'll do it. I live there, and I might as well get used to it, going into the whole criminal justice field and all," Matt said.

"Okay, so Matt is dusting and taking the photo," Riley said.

"Does that leave you doing the overhead projector thing, Scott?"

"Yeah. I'll take care of that."

"Beautiful. So, you won't need us."

"Not necessarily. We'll need someone to look at the photo with Photoshop to invert the direction and color. You know how to do that, Riley, right?"

All eyes turned to him.

"Well, don't you, Matt? You're the one with the digital camera?"

"Nope. I just shoot the pictures. Never learned how to edit them."

"Uh, fine. I'll look at it," Riley said.

"And Jimmy, we need someone to go to FedEx and print it on high-res tracing paper. Can you handle that?" Scott asked.

"Sure, sure I can do that."

"Good. Now everyone has a job. We work as one to get the job done," Scott said.

"Now, Matt, when can you get those prints?" Scott asked.

"I don't know. Give me a couple of days. I know my ma has a feather duster, but it's a matter of finding something she uses a lot and then making sure she and Peter are both out of the room to dust them and take the photo."

"Got it," Scott said.

"Okay, so once you get the photo, hand the camera over to Riley for the next step in 'Operation Mission: Impossible.'

"It is, though, isn't it?" Jimmy asked.

Riley shot his brother a look and shook his head.

Matt whispered, "It might as well be."

53

Matt thought about what he might tell his mom if she caught him snooping around her things or dusting them, for that matter. He figured he'd dust her favorite coffee cup, the one with the yellow smiley face on it. It was the safest bet. He had to wait until she had just finished using it, but before she washed it. That was the trick. Oftentimes, she'd leave it out for hours at a time before putting it in the dishwasher. Matt poured himself a cup of hot chocolate, and seeing that Peter and Sue Ellen were watching a movie (they often watched movies these days), he could convince them to have one.

"I'll just walk on in there with my hot chocolate, and Peter will notice it first. He'll say, 'Boy, that looks good. I think I'll pour myself a cup. He'll go in there, and then she'll yell from the living room for him to get her one.'"

He noticed his mom curled around Peter like a cat as he walked into the living room. They were watching *The Stepford Wives*; obviously, a Sue Ellen pick. Peter went more for either high-action or sci-fi stuff. When they heard Matt hit a creaky floorboard, they untangled each other with the speed of a high school couple caught by a parent.

"Matt, you startled us. What do you want?"

"Just thought I'd watch the movie with you if that's alright?"

287

"You want to watch the movie with us? You never want to do anything with us," Sue Ellen said.

Matt shrugged, careful not to spill the hot chocolate filled to the brim.

"Thought it might be nice to start."

Peter smiled and looked at Sue Ellen.

"It's okay," he said to his wife.

"Um, we would like it if you joined us, Matt," he said.

Matt waltzed over and plopped down on the armchair opposite the newlyweds. Matt took a sip of his hot chocolate, but now they paid him no mind, and their eyes fell back on the film.

"Mm. That is good hot chocolate."

"Shush now. We're right in the middle of this thing," Sue Ellen said.

They didn't notice the hot chocolate. Even Peter didn't take his eyes off the movie. Matt rolled his eyes and watched the film, hoping someone might look over. The town in the movie reminded him of Ridgeport, perfect on the outside but filled with dark secrets. He ended up watching the whole thing. He enjoyed it and didn't expect to. He only wished he watched it from the beginning but felt he grabbed enough of the storyline to understand the gist of it all. Peter outstretched his arms, yawning. Sue Ellen smiled up at him.

"Well, time to go to bed," Peter said.

"Yeah, I'll join you and Matt! You left your mug on our wood grain coffee table!? It's going to stain!" Sue Ellen screamed.

Matt's throat went dry before croaking out a "Sorry." He loved his mom but was scared to death of her. He never knew what kind of mom would show up - a sweet loving one or a mad rabid dog one.

"Baby, it's okay. I can figure out how to get that ring out. Come on, let's get you to bed," Peter said.

"It's just..."

288

"To bed, Sue."

Sue Ellen grabbed the mug and took it into the kitchen.

Matt hung his head, and Peter massaged his shoulders. But Matt never fully warmed up to Peter, which wasn't fair. He tried his best. Sue Ellen glared at him on her way back but stopped before heading up the stairs.

"I'm sorry. I got a little carried away. I love you, Matt." *Why'd she need to say that? I'm about to investigate you, so why couldn't you just stay mad at me?* Matt thought.

"I love you too."

She forced a smile and walked upstairs.

Matt sat back down and then remembered she grabbed the mug and put it in the kitchen. He had prints, her prints. He also had his prints on the mug. So, he had to be careful. He saw where she touched it, around the handle. He mostly cradled the body of it. If he could dust the handle and the body and see if her prints differed from his, he could be on to something. He heard the door to their bedroom close. It was time to dust.

Matt crept upstairs and walked out of his bedroom with the duster and his Canon Rebel in hand. He felt like one of those CSI guys, dusting and taking photos of prints. Matt just never expected to be playing detective for his mother. He felt uneasy like his mom was watching him with her door cracked, but no light shone through her closed room. Matt made his way to the kitchen, gathered the materials to dust for prints, and got to work.

54

Matt had watched one too many crime shows to know that dusting for prints wasn't as simple as tickling a microfiber duster over an area. So, after his conversation with Scott at lunch, he conducted his own research on the Net on how to dust, and so, there he was in the kitchen with gloves on, corn starch out on top of black construction paper, a small bristle paintbrush and clear plastic Scotch tape.

He poured a small hill of corn starch on the black paper and shook the starch over the mug. With the brush, Matt stroked every side and angle. He felt like an archeologist uncovering a dinosaur. Matt started to see the fingerprints. They were in the exact location he saw his mom carry it into the kitchen.

The grandfather clock chimed, and his heart almost leaped out of his chest. Matt closed his eyes before reaching for a piece of tape. He slid the tape over the cleanest print, and with all his concentration, lifted the print from the mug. He placed the tape with the print intact onto the black construction paper. And there it was, reflected and clear as day - his mom's fingerprint.

He picked up his Canon and snapped a few shots.

"Looks good," he said as he scanned through them in playback mode.

As he looked back at the mug, he thought the only thing missing was the yellow police tape. Matt grabbed the paper and ran the corn starch from the top into the garbage, careful that the print didn't fall along with it.

"Matt, what are you still doing up?"

Matt froze, standing over the garbage before turning and seeing Peter standing in the entryway.

55

"What?" Matt gasped.

"I said, 'What are you doing up at this hour?' It's pretty late."

"Oh. So, it is. What do you know about that?"

Peter made his way into the kitchen and started to look through the dusting materials.

"What's all this?"

"What's all what?"

"This?"

Peter pointed to the corn starch, the construction paper, the mug, the Scotch tape. Matt's mind raced, and he tried to think of something clever. Peter moved closer, noticing the print on the tape. Matt felt his hand twitch.

"I'm doing a science experiment for school. I was supposed to gather fingerprints and forgot until the last minute."

"Really? And whose prints are those?"

"Mine."

"Didn't your mother just use that mug, though?"

"Oh, well, yeah. But I washed it first," Matt lied. "I just grabbed the first thing I saw lying around in the kitchen after I saw the corn starch."

Peter nodded and smiled.

"Very detective of you."

He patted Matt on the back and moved toward the fridge to get a snack. Peter stuck his head in and examined each shelf before asking, "So, how does it work, the experiment?" But he heard no response. When he turned around, Matt was gone. Peter shrugged and resumed his search for his late-night snack.

56

Matt removed the camera strap from around his neck and prepared the area for evaluation. He set the construction paper with the taped print on his desk and placed the mug next to it. The only thing from his 'experiment' Matt left behind downstairs was the corn starch. He wasted no time getting out of there. His knees felt weak, and his palms dripped sweat. *How did I not hear Peter coming down the stairs?* he thought. At least it wasn't his mom. He didn't think he could have improvised as well with her.

Scott stared at the camera lying tilted on his sheets, picked it up, and looked once more through the photos in the camera playback. They looked good on there, but now it would be Riley's turn to take the memory card into Photoshop and transfer them into an electronic image.

Chapter 7: Ridgeport 2004

<u>Part Two</u>

1

The next day, Riley performed his Photoshop magic on what he considered the clearest image. He inverted the color a bit and adjusted the levels before printing it out and handing it over to Riley. If all went smoothly from there, he should have an image from FedEx that night on high-res tracing paper, ready to be cut out under Mr. Lorenz's transparency. Riley caught Jimmy coming out of the bathroom and handed him the print.

"Jimmy, run to FedEx and remember to print this on high-res transparency paper. Get this back tonight, and we can knock this thing out tomorrow," Riley said.

"Tonight? It's already eight o'clock," Jimmy said.

"They're open until nine. You should have plenty of time. It's just down the street."

Jimmy frowned but grabbed the paper from his hand.

"What kind of paper do you need to print it on again?" Riley asked.

"High-res tracing. Got it?"

Riley nodded his head as he walked away and headed back toward his room.

2

Jimmy stopped for gas and a Slim Jim before going the extra mile to FedEx. He felt that if the store closed before he got there, he could just say that he got a flat tire or something. But Jimmy knew the wrath that would await him at home if he didn't return with that print. He walked into an empty FedEx around 8:30 and asked where he might be able to copy on high-res tracing paper. The man at the counter directed him to the paper and a machine.

"Thank you, sir."

The man smiled.

294

Jimmy laid his tracing paper in the tray and made five copies. He figured that it never hurt to have some extra. Just as the machine started to buzz, a familiar voice said, "Hello." He turned his focus away from the copier and to the smiling woman standing right in front of him. It was Sue Ellen.

3

"I said hello, Jimmy. I didn't mean to startle you," she said through a light laugh.

Jimmy chuckled back, but no words came out.

"What brings you here?" Sue Ellen asked.

"Just making some copies."

"Oh, well, I can see that. For school? Don't you have a printer at school or at home?"

"Yes, ma'am. But we needed special paper for this project."

Sue Ellen nodded and then tilted her head to see what he was printing. Jimmy froze and could have sworn he turned as pale as a ghost. *Was this really happening?* he thought. Sue Ellen moved around the boy and grabbed one of the papers lying hot off the press. Jimmy swallowed hard as she began studying it. He noticed a look of bewilderment in her eyes, but he couldn't be sure. Before she could say anything, the friendly employee who helped Jimmy now approached Sue Ellen.

"Can I help you with anything, miss? We will be closing in fifteen minutes."

"Oh, yes. I wanted to print this on cardstock."

"I can show you where that is. Right, this way."

Sue Ellen turned to smile at Jimmy.

"Goodbye, Jimmy. It was good running into you."

Jimmy waved back to her but couldn't muster any words. Meanwhile, the fingerprint copies finished, and he couldn't rush out of the place fast enough.

When the boys asked Mr. Lorenz if they could borrow his overhead, he raised an eyebrow and asked if this was in any way related to the skull they showed him.

"No, sir," Riley said. But Jimmy always blushed red whenever he was caught up in a lie, and Mr. Lorenz noticed.

"Boys, now I'm afraid that I can't let you borrow that projector unless you tell me what's really going on."

Scott dug his hands deep into his pockets and rubbed the back of his neck. He hated disappointing his favorite teacher, and he hated getting caught up in a lie. He noticed the rest of the band looking his way. They knew he had the best rapport with the teacher, and they also knew they wouldn't be on this wild ride without his help. As much as he looked up to Mr. Lorenz, he worried that he could ruin everything. *That said, Mr. Lorenz did help them with the skull*, Scott thought.

"Okay, you might want to sit down for this, Mr. Lorenz. This is kind of a long story, and it's not exactly easy to believe," Scott said.

Scott divulged the whole story, starting from when they first entered the room as kids. The other band members chimed in from time to time, adding details as necessary.

"So, you see, after finding the skull, we sort of made this connection and knew we needed to get back in that room. That's why we need the projector."

Mr. Lorenz listened to every word, nodding periodically and waiting until his students finished speaking.

"That's quite a story, boys."

He leaned back in his office chair and adjusted his glasses.

"Do you believe us?" Scott asked.

"No, I think I do. But I need to be sure before I can let you borrow the projector."

"What do you mean?" Matt asked.

"Well, I never met Mrs. Norris nor talked with her on the phone. I'm not sure if she's the mastermind you say she is without getting to know her a little first."

Scott looked bewildered but nodded.

"Listen. Parent-teacher conferences are next week. Let me meet her then, and I'll get a better feel for your story. If I sense something is off about her, we'll meet again about this, okay? Until then, no projector. Got it?"

"Got it," Scott said, sounding disappointed.

"Now, you boys go on. I'm sure you have other things to do today."

"Yes, Mr. Lorenz," Scott said.

"See you, Mr. Lorenz," the rest of the band said.

He waved as they walked out and then rubbed his chin before heading out himself. He hoped their story wasn't true, but he knew in his gut that it was. He figured his meeting with Mrs. Norris would be very interesting. Very interesting indeed.

6

The band was nervous about the upcoming parent-teacher conferences, feeling like they would never come, particularly for Matt and Scott. Matt worried if Mr. Lorenz said the wrong thing to his mom and then imagined her catching on. If it hadn't been for Scott's resolve, the band might have called the mission off. Matt told Scott the day before the conference that he wanted to tell Mr. Lorenz to just forget it. He told Scott he wanted to tell him they wouldn't go through with it. He was the one who had to live with her, and he worried himself sick about what the backlash might be.

But it was Scott's reminder of why they were doing this and why they had to do this that prevented him from saying anything. Mr. Lorenz had to get a feel for his mom. They had to try to get a hold of the projector to complete the job. They knew that the day before conferences just might be the last normal day of their lives.

7

Sue Ellen strolled into Mr. Lorenz's room as the last parent of the night. She made it in time by twenty minutes, just enough for Mr. Lorenz to get a snapshot of the woman. She sported a red blazer black slacks, and her pearls matched her white teeth as she smiled.

"Good evening. I'm Mrs. Norris."

"Nice to meet you."

"Please, won't you sit down?" Mr. Lorenz said with a smile.

Sue Ellen complied.

"So, I see Matt's grades have been slipping lately. Why is that?"

"Well, he seems to be having a hard time concentrating in class. His mind is somewhere else, and that's leading to some missing work here, as you see on his progress report."

Mrs. Norris didn't look at the grade sheet but nodded.

"I've looked at the report, Mr. Lorenz."

"Oh. Well, then...so you know."

"He can still make up all his work, right?"

"That's correct. He can still make his work up from this quarter."

"And from last semester?"

"I'm afraid not. Those grades have already been finalized. I can't go back and change them now."

Sue Ellen frowned but then smiled.

"I had a hard time concentrating in school. I actually had a crush on my science teacher, Mr. Hardmon."

"Oh really?"

Mrs. Norris removed her blazer, revealing a low-cut blouse with significant cleavage.

"Sometimes it's hard to work when you can't concentrate. Wouldn't you agree, Mr. Lorenz?"

He blushed from embarrassment. He couldn't believe what had just happened. Never in his fifteen years of teaching had a parent tried to manipulate him like this.

"Yes, I agree."

Mrs. Norris scratched a space on her chest and continued.

"Well then, I'm sure you can produce some other way for Matt to make up those points. Extra credit, maybe? He's trying so hard to get into the Ivy League."

"Ivy League? He told me he's interested in a Big Ten school."

"Oh, I assure you. He wants to go to an Ivy League, as I did. I'm a Yale grad, you see."

Mr. Lorenz smiled weakly and grew impatient.

"I'll see what I can do. Matt has plenty of time to get an A."

"That's great news, Mr. Lorenz. I'm glad we had this chat."

"Sure. Me too. Well, it looks like we made it just in time before conferences ended."

"Oh, yes. Look at the time. I'd best be leaving. Please do not hesitate to call me should he not stay on top of his studies."

"Yes, Mrs. Norris."

Then she glowed from ear to ear, threw her blazer on, waved goodbye, and walked out of the classroom. Mr. Lorenz ran his hand through his salt and pepper hair. He knew the boys were right. He didn't even have to interrogate her.

8

Mr. Lorenz didn't go into the specifics with Matt or the rest of the band concerning Sue Ellen's actions. He still couldn't believe that a parent would use her sexuality like that in a town like this. When Matt asked him if they could borrow the projector the following day, Mr. Lorenz nodded, but no words came out.

"Are you all right, Mr. Lorenz?" Scott asked.

He rubbed his chin and stared off into the distance as if in deep thought.

"Huh? Oh yeah. I'm fine. Just fine."

"Mr. Lorenz? How'd it go with my mom?"

"Oh. Well, she just really wants to see you succeed," he said.

Matt looked at him funny as he saw his face flush red.

"So, is the projector just in the back room there?" Scott asked.

"Yes. Give me a sec. I will bring it out for you boys."

Mr. Lorenz shuffled into the back, and the band heard a few bangs and scraps against metal. Within a few minutes, he rolled out the projector with a wipe of his brow.

"Well, here she is."

"Boy, thanks, Mr. Lorenz," Scott said.

"Be careful, boys, and this is our little secret. No one knows you got this from me. Understood? I could get in a lot of trouble for this."

The boys all nodded in unison, and then Mr. Lorenz smiled. After showing them how to turn it on, he returned to his desk to grade papers. Jimmy took out the fingerprint on the tracing paper from his school folder. They set it on the projector screen. There was no going back now.

"Matt? Did you bring the graphite powder and wood glue?"

Scott thought he saw Mr. Lorenz look up, but he just flipped a worksheet over on his desk. Matt pulled the materials from his bookbag and placed them on the projector.

"Ready when you guys are."

They all stared at the two items for a second as if they didn't know what to do with them until Scott spoke up and said to pour the graphite powder over the print and layer it with the glue.

"Here. Why don't you do it then, Professor Science?" Riley said.

The three of them snickered, and Scott shrugged but grabbed the powder. Scott sprinkled the powder on top of the print as if he were adding salt to a steak. The rest of the band peered over his shoulder.

"Okay, I think that's good, man," Matt said.

Scott breathed out, opened the wood glue, and spread a thin ribbon on top.

"Now, we have to let it dry," Scott said.

He removed the tracing paper from the projector, and bits of powder ran over the sides and onto the floor. The glue began to run, but enough stayed over the print.

"Careful," Matt said.

"What am I supposed to do with this?"

Scott held the paper in mid-air for a second and thought the only way they could let the glue dry was if they were allowed to keep it on the projector overnight.

"Mr. Lorenz?"

He looked up from his stack of papers.

"Yes?"

"Do you think we can keep this paper on the projector overnight, please? The glue on our tracing paper just needs to dry."

"Yes. Just leave it there. I'll take care of it."

"Oh, thank you. We…"

"Go on now. You best be going home or to your after-school activities."

"Yes, sir," Matt said.

Scott placed the paperback on the projector as carefully as he had taken it off. The band gathered their things.

"Do you think he's upset with us?" Scott asked.

"Nah. He's letting us do what we asked. Isn't that what you wanted?"

"Yeah. I guess."

10

Matt insisted on going into the forbidden room alone, but Scott wouldn't hear any of it.

"I was there with you the last time we broke in, and I'll be there with you this time," Scott said.

Matt knew that Scott would pop over every day if he had to and gave in to the tandem break-in idea. Riley and Jimmy never so much as volunteered.

"We got you this far. You are on your own now," Riley said.

Matt and Scott waited for the day when Sue Ellen and Peter might slip out of the house and leave them alone. But when weeks went by, and neither of them made so much as a grocery trip together, the boys knew they might need to push them out. Sue Ellen had a birthday coming up, and Matt knew just the thing to give his mom: a much-needed date night.

11

Sue Ellen never made a big deal about birthdays anymore. She hated the thought of being another year older. She hated the fact that she could look gray and withered one day. Getting old was Sue Ellen's worst nightmare. She still had youth-like features, and when she overheard a teen in the grocery store call her a MILF behind her back, she didn't reprimand him but instead smiled and walked on. Yet, she sometimes noticed heavy bags under her eyes. She often felt tired, and she always preferred staying in to going out now, something that started after her second marriage to Peter. The day before her forty-fifth birthday, she noticed the first wrinkle on her forehead. She cackled at the mirror-like the Joker in the first *Batman* movie, and when Peter rushed upstairs to see what was wrong, he only made things worse.

"You can barely even see it," he said.

"Barely?! So, it's there?!"

"Well, I...I didn't notice it until right now."

Sue Ellen turned her focus back to the mirror, frowned, and reached for some Mascara to try to conceal the crooked line.

"Honey, you're beautiful," Peter said.

"Just give me some space," she said.

Peter took a step back and watched as she cupped her head in her hands.

"Just go!" she yelled.

About an hour later, Sue Ellen opened the bathroom door, made her way down the stairs, and wrapped her arms around her husband.

"I'm sorry. I don't handle getting old that well. Can you do me a favor?"

"Sure. Anything."

"Can we not make a big deal out of my birthday tomorrow, please? I don't want a cake, cards, anything. I don't even want to know I have a birthday."

"Oh, come on…."

"Peter! That's my wish. That's all I want for tomorrow."

He had already reserved a cake from the grocer, picked up a card from the drugstore, and had the massage chair he ordered ready to be delivered tomorrow. Now here she was, wiping tears away, demanding she didn't want anything tomorrow. Fantastic.

"What's a guy to do?" Peter thought. "Hon, I'm going upstairs. I need a shower."

He grabbed the cordless phone and canceled the cake reservation and the chair delivery. He hung up with a sigh.

12

Sue Ellen awoke on her birthday as if it was just another day. Strangely, she felt more refreshed than she had in a long time. Sue Ellen forgot about her slightly wrinkled forehead and resolved to forget that she'd gained a year. Peter traded in gifts for trying to be extra nice to his wife, but anytime he tried complimenting her, she rolled her eyes and laughed.

Apart from that, Peter felt as fine as he could, knowing that his wife felt as fine as she could. He cooked her favorite dish that night, grilled salmon with lemon green beans and Pinot Noir. Matt gulped the special dish down, with white sparkling grape juice as a substitute for the wine. Sue Ellen ate with a grin. No mention of her birthday came up all day, and that's just how she wanted it. At least that's how it was until Matt gave her his card filled with two tickets to see the band Air Supply.

Sue Ellen's eyes widened at the sight of the card. Peter's gaze froze on the card before lashing out at Matt.

"I thought we agreed, Matt, that…." Peter said.

"Honey. It's okay. He was trying to do something nice," Sue Ellen said.

Peter rolled his eyes and removed himself to wash dishes while Sue Ellen patted her son's hand. Upon opening the card, the tickets fell out right away.

"What's this?" Sue Ellen asked. And as she picked up the tickets, her eyes widened once again. This time, Matt could see a smile.

"Oh my God! Air Supply?! You got me Air Supply tickets?"

"Happy Birthday, Mom."

Peter swung his head around from the sink. He couldn't believe that Matt thought of such a gift and that the same woman who said she didn't want gifts would be so elated.

"What made you think of this, Matt?"

"Well, I knew this was one of the first dates you said you and Peter went on, and I know the two of you might need a much-needed date night, so…."

"Oh, honey. This is one of the nicest gifts anyone has ever gotten for me."

Sue Ellen reached over and hugged her son before addressing Peter.

"It would have been nice if you would have gotten me something too, dear."

"I thought you said yesterday that you didn't want anything?"

"You know I didn't mean that."

Peter shook his head and returned his focus back to the sink. He thought that he should do whatever is the opposite of what his wife says from now on.

"So, Peter, the concert is on the twenty-third. Set your calendar."

"The twenty-third? Of this month?"

"Yep."

"I don't think I can. I have a very important story due then."

Matt's heart skipped a beat. He didn't think about this loophole in the plan.

"Well. Get out of it. I want to go, and I'll ask Loretta if I have to."

Peter felt a chill run down his spine at the sound of her name. He didn't like the kind of person his wife turned into when Loretta came around. In fact, he wasn't sure he even liked Loretta. She was never there for Scott or anything.

"Fine. I'll see what I can do," he said through clenched teeth.

Sue Ellen gave Matt one last hug, and Matt breathed a sigh of relief. He committed the twenty-third to memory. In three weeks, "Operation Mission Impossible" could finally commence.

14

Date night finally came, and Sue Ellen was as giddy as a schoolchild. It felt like years since she went on a date, and Peter forgot all about her change in mood on her birthday. He was just content to see her in such high spirits. Sue Ellen even agreed to allow Scott to come over while they were gone, something she usually would not have done. She never cared for having anyone over without an adult present, but Matt thought he might be able to throw a kegger that night, and she might just say, "What the hell!"

Before they left for Air Supply, Sue Ellen pecked Matt on the cheek and tousled Scott's hair. Matt couldn't remember the last time his mother showed him any affection. He rubbed the spot of the kiss and furrowed his brow.

"I love you, sweetie."

Scott smirked and elbowed Matt as Sue Ellen turned to straighten her coat. Matt thought for a minute, and now he felt terrible for what they planned to do. He finally had the relationship with his mother he had always wanted. He turned his focus back to the skull and to the sketchy room. They wouldn't find anything there. *They were just overthinking this whole thing*, he thought. He really hoped so.

"Bye, guys. Don't get into too much trouble," Peter said.

Sue Ellen smiled, and with that, they opened the front door and walked out. The house was all theirs.

15

"Well? Should we get to it then?" Scott asked.

"No. Give it ten minutes. They may forget something. Peter tends to forget things. Let's watch some TV in the meantime."

The boys made their way to the living room, and Matt flipped through station after station. He thought about how relaxing sitting on the couch felt and that they shouldn't go through with it. Scott watched his best friend hesitating, getting a little too comfortable.

"Well, I think it's been about ten minutes."

"Uh-huh. Why don't we just watch a show first?"

"Matt. This is our shot. We worked too hard for this."

"Yeah."

"Oh, I see. This is about your mom tonight. Your mom who's hiding something weird in that locked room downstairs."

"Yeah. I suppose."

Scott jumped up from the couch and tugged Matt's hand.

"Come on already!"

"Okay! I'm comin'!"

As the boys started to make their way from the living room to the basement, the front door popped open, and Peter rushed inside.

"Forgot my wallet!"

They both watched the panic-stricken man dart into the kitchen and out back toward the front door.

"Bye, kids!"

"Uh, yeah. Bye!"

Matt glanced down at his watch.

"Took him about fifteen minutes this time," Matt said.

Scott nodded and opened the door to the basement.

16

Matt hid the fingerprint mold, a pair of scissors, and a small flashlight in a Ziploc bag inside the middle cushion of the couch downstairs. *Matt thought several scenarios needed to play out just right to arrive at this point.* And through it all, the band stuck together as it always had. The lights in the basement burned out months ago, and no one got around to changing them. So, the boys left the basement door open to cast just enough yellow light to find the zipper in the middle cushion. For a second, Matt felt uneasy that his mom knew the print was there and that when he'd open the cushion, it would be gone. But when he unzipped it, there sat the plastic bag with the print, scissors, and a flashlight safely inside. Matt breathed a sigh of relief.

"I guess I got to mold this thing on my finger now, huh?" Matt asked. "Turn that flashlight on, so I can make better cuts."

"Right," Scott said.

"Maybe you should cut it. You know that you're better with art stuff like that." Matt said.

Scott noticed Matt's hand trembling and frowned.

"Yeah, give me the print and scissors, you big baby."

"Hey! I just don't wanna mess it up, is all."

It was true that Scott excelled over the band in anything art-related. Matt watched Scott cut with the ease of an art teacher, and within seconds, a perfect print fell away from the paper.

"Well done, my man."

"Now, just shape it on your finger," Scott said.

Careful not to deform the print. Matt placed the print on his index, and even though it didn't cover the entire tip, the boys thought it just might get the job done. Matt held his finger high in the air as if testing wind resistance, and Scott helped guide him with the flashlight through the dark basement and toward the door.

17

"Wait a minute," Matt said.

"What?"

"Why in the world did we come down here without my camera?"

"Ha. I guess that would make more sense, huh? Why would we break in there and not have photographic evidence of it?"

"Think we were just in too much of a hurry to get down here after they left. Come on; I'll get it. Be right back."

"Oh, and Matt?"

"Yeah?"

"You have the silly string up there for the security camera, too, right?"

Matt paused and thought for a moment.

"Matt?"

"Yeah. I think so. I'll be right down."

Scott paced back and forth in the basement, hoping that Matt had both the Canon and the silly string. Breaking into the room wouldn't make much sense if it were all caught on camera. Scott looked toward the door when Matt tapped him on the shoulder, smiling. The camera hung around his neck, and he waved the can of silly string in his right hand.

"Nothing to worry about, man."

"Right. Yeah, nothing to worry about."

A mouse scurried along the floor in front of Scott, and the boys jumped back.

"When was the last time anyone cleaned down here? "Don't know if it's ever been cleaned. It's just a mouse. Not gonna hurt you. Come on."

The security camera outside the door stared the boys down, and a light on the camera blinked red. Matt shook the can of silly string and sprayed it all over the bulb.

"That should take care of it," Matt said. Scott nodded and then shone the light on the outside of Fort Knox. Matt's finger still hung in the air.

"This is it. Shine that sucker on the fingerprint scan, will ya?"

Scott did as he was told, and Matt moved his finger close to the imprint with the care of a bomb specialist. He felt like he was back to his youth, playing a game of Operation, and if he missed grabbing the broken heart, the buzz would sound, meaning game over. Matt pressed the print against the reader, and a warning sign lit up across the top: Warning! Incorrect Match. You have two more tries. The boys stared at each other, wondering. Would this really work? If they didn't get it, would the cops be called? Matt pulled his finger back, shook his head, and tried once more.

"Warning! Incorrect Match! You have one chance remaining."

"Scott. Do you think this will work? I don't know if we should go through with this. I mean, I don't know what will

310

happen if it doesn't go through again. Do we really want to sit around and find out?"

Scott looked from his finger to the reader and back to his finger.

"Scott?"

"Try rocking your finger left to right this time. I don't think you did it right."

"You sure on this?"

"No. But I got a feeling."

Matt's heart beat like a runaway train, and sweat poured down his temple. He bet his mom was having the time of her life at the concert, and here he was, breaking into her secret room. But he shook off his feelings of guilt.

"Okay. If you say so."

So once more, for the last possible try, Matt pushed his finger against the reader and, this time rocked it back and forth. The machine did not respond, and no sound emanated from its box. Then, after a few seconds, the boys heard a click.

"Welcome to the room, Mrs. Norris," the machine said in a robotic voice. It reminded the boys of HAL 9000, the computer from *2001: A Space Odyssey*. The boys watched in awe as the thick metal padded door opened. It worked. They were in.

18

As Sue Ellen belted out "All Out of Love" with the rest of the crowd, a message came across her beeper: "Warning! Incorrect Match! You have one chance remaining."

When the song finished and the applause died down, Sue Ellen and Peter returned to their seats. They smiled at each other the same way they had years ago when they saw Air Supply for the first time. What a perfect date. That was until

311

Sue Ellen noticed her beeper. Her eyes hardened with her heart, and she drowned out all the noise around her.

"Honey? Are you okay?"

"What?"

"You seem like something is bothering you."

"We have to go."

"What? But why?"

"We have to go, now!"

19

Matt flipped a switch, and the room looked just as it had when they first entered years ago: a large map of Ridgeport hung to their right, a bookcase faced the north wall, and a couple of binders lay scattered on a wooden table. The only difference they noticed was a large screen TV was fastened against the wall behind the table.

"Maybe she gets bored down here," Scott said.

"Maybe," Matt said.

Matt noticed the remote sitting on the table and switched it on. Instead of getting a TV show, the boys watched the drama of all things Ridgeport. Six screens split the TV into different sections of the town. One focused on the new district - in the parking lot of the mall, one focused on Ridgeport's downtown, one scanned Coleridge Park, another looked over a random street in a subdivision, one looked over the outside of the house, and to the boys' horror, one looked over Spring Grove Forest Preserve. A couple of cameras switched views, and the boys watched Ridgeport residents coming and going, unaware they were being watched. Matt's throat felt dry, and he now felt frozen to the spot.

"Matt! Take a picture of this. People are going to want to know about this."

"Right."

312

Just as Matt snapped a couple of shots, the door slammed shut, and the door's HAL robot voice said, "Room secured."

"Room secured? What does that mean?" Scott asked.

"Don't know. Try opening the door."

Scott gave the handle a good tug, but it wouldn't budge. He didn't notice any fingerprint scan on this side either.

"Room secured. Your request to keep the door open has passed. Try alternate exit."

"Huh? Are we stuck in here? What are we going to do, Matt?"

20

The Air Supply concert was about forty-five minutes away from home, but Sue Ellen's insistence that they arrive sooner motivated Peter to put the pedal to the metal. Sue Ellen shouted profanities at Peter any time she felt they were slowing down or if he made a lane change she disagreed with. He felt like he was driving an angry pregnant woman to the hospital.

"Who taught you how to drive!? Stella drove faster than you do!"

Peter bit his tongue, opting not to say anything. The last thing he wanted to do was to feed the dragon anymore. A traffic jam greeted Peter on Interstate 55.

"Take the exit! Take the exit!"

"Phew. Now. Can you reroute us to another highway or something?"

"Yeah. I suppose I could take side streets and get on at a different onramp."

"Okay. Let's do that."

Peter turned off near Kedzie Ave. and picked up again just outside the city. The jam was gone now, and nothing but free road lay ahead of them.

"Should be home in about twenty to twenty-five minutes. Just relax."

"I'll relax when I'm home."

21

"Alright. Just calm down. There's gotta be some way outta here."

"What if they come home, and we're still in here?"

Matt scanned the room, searching for an air vent.

"I don't know. We'll figure it out. Tell you what. Why don't you figure a way out of here, and I'll look through these binders?"

"But don't you think we should both look?"

"Scott, we came in here to snoop around, didn't we? Now take a few minutes and look, and then I'll help you."

"Well, okay. If you insist."

While Scott played with the door, Matt opened the red binder on the wooden table.

Ridgeport residents' names filled the binder, just as he had remembered, except he didn't remember so many names last time. Some names Matt recognized, such as Ms. Fink, his chemistry teacher. Her name was outlined in green highlighter. Matt flipped through the pages. The binder seemed so thick that all the Ridgeport residents appeared to be listed there. He saw that Scott's mom was highlighted in yellow, and with a couple more flips, Stella was highlighted in red. The names were in alphabetical order, and as Matt flipped, he shot a picture with his Canon.

Scott gave another tug at the door, but no luck, and that's when he heard the front door to the house open. He felt his heart leap out of his chest. Matt pushed Scott aside and tried the door himself. Scott stumbled backward into the bookcase, where a couple of books on Ridgeport history fell out. And as if from some haunted house, the bookcase swung

314

open to reveal a secret passageway. The boys' jaws dropped, but they broke off into a run down the dark corridor as soon as they heard Sue Ellen yell out their names.

Chapter 8: Ridgeport: 2004

Part Three

The bookcase slammed shut behind them, leaving the boys in total darkness. They kept running at full speed. Neither one of them wanted to think about what would happen if Sue Ellen caught them. Faint candlelight began to glow in the distance, and the boys noticed the tunnel begin to widen. They heard a bookcase opening behind them.

"Come out, come out wherever you are!"

Like running away from the coyotes, the boys felt like they were running for their lives. Hearts racing, sweat dripping from every pore, Matt and Scott pushed on through the winding path. The candlelight gave way to bright fluorescent lighting and a modern laboratory. White concrete walls extended high into what must have been a twenty-foot ceiling. The fluorescent lights beamed down upon men and women dressed in all white lab coats who wandered in and out of white doors. What appeared to be a nurse's station sat across from the row of doors, and in the middle of the lab lay a few open tables and desks. A few armored guards stood tall and unmoving at the opposite end of the lab.

"What the?" Scott whispered.

A steel staircase started at the front of the lab, running to a second-floor observatory, where no one seemed to be working. It was their only chance. The staircase stood just outside the lab, and to the boys' luck, was not protected by guards.

They tiptoed up the sixty steps as quietly as they could without being detected, and once they reached the top, they made sure to make themselves as small as possible. As they inched slowly across the observation deck, Scott noticed something or someone. His heart skipped a beat.

"Matt! Isn't that *Joe?*"

Matt turned to look down toward the middle of the lab.

"You bet your ass it is," Matt said. He snapped a few shots with his Canon.

The boys reached the middle of the deck when they had spotted Sue Ellen. She was talking to one of the armored guards downstairs.

The guard must have stood at least six foot three, with a body-builder frame, and flashed an MK47, but he looked frightened next to the furious Sue Ellen Norris.

"How could you not know where they are?! They came down this way! Where else would they go!?"

Back on the observation deck, Scott turned from Sue Ellen back to Joe. Joe appeared to be in a trance, sashaying back and forth, as if she were a model on a runway. She wore a modest summer dress with green and purple flowers, pearls, and a straw hat. A woman in a lab coat stood nearby, clutching a clipboard and taking notes.

"What is going on here?" Scott asked.

"Dunno. But we better get moving. We're gonna get found out any minute now."

"But what about Joe?"

"What are we going to do? March down there and get her away from everyone while she's playing Miss Model?"

Scott looked down at Joe again. She smiled and waved at an invisible crowd before turning and catwalking again. *Who was she?* he thought.

Matt felt a knot form in his stomach as he saw that the deck ended ahead and the steel staircase winded down into the lab this time, not outside of it. If there was an alternative exit, it had to come from the first floor of this insane facility. Sue Ellen started her way back to the passageway and then paused before heading out.

"Uh oh. What is she doing, Scott?"

She turned her neck toward the deck and smiled like the Grinch.

2

The boys broke out into a run. They stole the attention of the entire lab now, but their only chance of getting out of there was to outrace everyone. Sue Ellen climbed with the speed of a jaguar up the deck, and the boys swore they felt it tilt a bit as they made their way toward the descending staircase. Near the bottom of the stairs, Matt and Scott turned their heads back and saw Sue Ellen starting to descend, and that's when they ran right into the armored guard.

"Got ya!"

He grabbed them by their shirt collars like they were misbehaving toddlers. When Sue Ellen met them at the bottom of the stairs, she sounded winded and set her hands on her knees before straightening herself up. The armored guard held the boys high off the ground like punching bags. Sue Ellen's cold sapphire eyes burned into Matt and Scott's faces, and the warm mother Matt had just hours before was gone. Sue Ellen gave each of them a brisk slap across the face and kicked their groins without saying a word. The guard let them fall like dominoes on the concrete floor. The boys held their hurting bodies, made worse by the drop to the floor.

"And to think, I was fooling myself that I loved you, Matt. And that I trusted you, Scott. Was I not there for the both of you all these years? And this, this is how you repay me?"

The boys rolled in pain on the ground as Sue Ellen ranted, and the guard stood motionless and emotionless.

"You want to know what all of this is, do you? Well, what better way than to show you! You can even rediscover your friend Joe, or should you now call her Elizabeth. We renamed her once we brought her to our RCF, Ridgeport's Civilization Facility."

Sue Ellen bent down and picked up Matt's Canon.

"Pity. I remember when I bought you this camera for your birthday. Never thought you'd spy on me with it, though."

Sue Ellen smacked the camera against the concrete, cracking the lens.

"No more pictures with this."

Matt groaned, and she kicked him hard in the side.

"Shut up. You did this to yourself."

Tears ran down his face, and he curled into a tight ball.

"I think the rest of the weekend here might change their mind about doing anything stupid again. Arnold, why don't you get these two brats set up on the express package right away?"

"Yes, ma'am," said Arnold, the armored guard.

"I'll see you two Sunday night as two new men. Thanks, Arnold."

He nodded, and Sue Ellen made her way back to the passageway. She paused to admire Elizabeth's walk first and awarded her with some treat as if she were a dog. Then she patted her on the head and left the lab.

3

Arnold picked up the boys and carried them over to a man in a white lab coat.

"Dr. John Peterson orders from Mrs. Norris to give these boys the express treatment."

Dr. Peterson stood about as tall as Arnold, only much thinner and with a balding head and glasses.

"It would be my pleasure," he said with a wry smile.

Arnold again dropped Matt and Scott onto the concrete, this time at the doctor's feet, and then walked on to his post by the passageway's entrance. Despite wringing in pain, Scott still noticed Joe, or 'Elizabeth,' speaking with the woman with the clipboard.

"Joe! Joe!"

320

She didn't even turn around.

Dr. Peterson grabbed Scott by the arm and dragged him up.

"Come on. We got to prep, you boys. Time is money, as they say."

"Um, Elizabeth!" Scott yelled.

Elizabeth turned around this time, and Scott saw a hint of recognition in her face. She waved and then turned back to the woman.

"What?! What was that, Matt?"

"Elizabeth! Elizabeth!"

This time she didn't even stir.

4

Scott thought this was all a bad dream. She looked like Joe, but whoever was standing over there was not the girl he remembered. They had done something to her, and Scott knew they might do the same thing to him and Matt.

Dr. Peterson directed the boys to a desk with a polygraph machine.

"I know what that is, Scott. That's a lie detector test. They probably want to know how we got in here."

"Please, have a seat."

Two seats sat side by side next to the table. Matt decided to take the one closest to the polygraph.

"So, you've decided to go first, eh? Very brave of you, my boy."

"I didn't think doctors did this sort of thing," Scott said.

"We're expected to perform a great many roles that normal doctors don't do, Scott."

"How'd you know my name?"

"We know a lot about the people of Ridgeport, especially those closest to Mrs. Norris."

Scott folded his arms.

321

"You didn't know how we broke in here."

"Well, we're about to find that out, aren't we?" the doctor sneered.

Good thing Scott and Matt had watched a good deal of spy and cop shows over the years. They knew the key to passing the polygraph was to stay calm, no matter what. Matt appeared calm enough, which is why he volunteered to go first. On the other hand, Scott felt as shaky as a house of cards. Scott darted his eyes to Joe and the lady with the clipboard. The lady now walked Joe into a white, windowless room underneath the observatory deck. Scott's heart sank. He realized that Joe, at least as he knew her, could be gone for good.

5

Dr. Peterson ran off a series of questions, which started harmlessly.

"What is your name?"

"Where were you born?"

Questions like that gave way to some Ridgeport-specific questions:

"What is the motto of Ridgeport?"

"Who was Ridgeport's first mayor?"

Matt answered all questions without so much as blinking, and the spikes and waves of the polygraph stayed close together. The doctor seemed especially pleased with his knowledge of Ridgeport.

"Now, we will start the line of questioning of how you found this place. Understood?"

"Yes, sir."

"Good."

"Now. Why did you come here?"

"Why did you come here?" Matt asked back.

Scott smirked and noticed the spikes and waves remained unchanged.

"How did you get in here?"

"How did you get in here?"

Scott chuckled. He played the part of a toddler.

The doctor stopped the machine.

"I see. You're the calm one. Arnold? Come here."

"What!? What are you doing?" Scott exclaimed.

The doctor smiled and waved the former Navy Seal over.

"Arnold, Matt here is dodging my questions. Maybe you can help him find the truth?"

Scott's eyes darted from the doctor to Arnold to Matt. While Arnold appeared overconfident, so did Matt. Or at least, Matt seemed to be. He knew he must have been scared shitless. Arnold pulled out his .45 from his holster and pointed it straight at Matt's temple.

"Talk, kid."

But Matt sat still, and Scott could have sworn he saw him smirk.

"Do as he says, Matt. Come on, man."

"Better listen to your friend here."

Arnold cocked the trigger. Scott gulped, but Matt continued to sit still. It was at that moment Scott couldn't hold it in any longer.

"We stole her fingerprints! That's how we did it. We stole her prints."

"Scott...man, he wasn't going to do anything. I'm her son."

"Shut up!" Arnold shot near Matt's foot, making him squirm for the first time in the interrogation.

"Good, Scott. That's a very bright thing to do. Now tell me, how did you do it?" Dr. Peterson asked.

Scott looked at his feet and then backed up at the doctor. Arnold hadn't put his gun away yet.

"Well, it all started with an internet search."

323

Scott proceeded to tell them the whole story, or as much as he could, leaving Riley, Jimmy, and Mr. Lorenz out of it anyway. When he had finished talking, the doctor smiled and nodded to Arnold to put away his weapon.

"There. Was that so bad?"

6

Dr. Peterson walked the boys over to a nurses' station at the opposite end of the observatory deck. All of the nurses dressed in retro-style all-white uniforms with white caps, circa the 1950s.

Scott thought how anachronistic it was that these same nurses sat in front of state-of-the-art computers.

"Betsy, can you take Scott and Matt to the double Room 104, please?"

"Sure thing, doctor."

Betsy led them into an all-white hospital room on the west end of where Joe appeared to be staying.

"Okay, boys, in you go."

Nurse Betsy pointed at the beds with rubber straps dangling over the sides.

"I...I... can't go in there!" Scott cried.

"Oh, come on now, Scott. It's not so bad."

Scott broke into a run, but Arnold was waiting for him just outside the room.

7

"I see that we don't want to cooperate with Nurse Betsy, huh?"

Arnold pointed his MK47 at Scott's chest, and Scott threw his hands in the air.

"No, I'll cooperate. Promise."

"Good boy. Now get back in there."

When Scott reentered the room, Betsy already had Matt all strapped up. Scott noticed goosebumps forming on his arms.

"Why are you strapping us in?" Scott asked.

"So, you won't run away again."

"Oh," they said in unison.

"Okay, your turn."

Knowing Mr. GI Joe stood right outside, Scott hung his head and obeyed.

"That's it. This will just take a sec."

The nurse tightened four straps around Scott, one at his ankles, one at his waist, one at his stomach, and one at his chest. He felt like he was about to go on a roller coaster, except this ride would be much, much scarier.

8

Nurse Betsy drew the boys' blood pressure and took their pulse, but then the boys were surprised as the nurse came back with an 18-gauge, four-inch needle in her hand.

"What the hell is that for?" Scott asked.

"We're going to run some tests this weekend, and we want to make sure you have plenty of strength for them."

As the nurse made her way to Matt, he didn't flinch.

"Stick me, you sick woman."

"Ha! Oh, you. You know what? I think I'll get your friend first."

Matt shrugged and rolled his right sleeve back. Scott shuddered and noticed clear liquid spew from the tip of the needle.

"You didn't tell me what that was!"

"No need to worry."

"I don't like shots. I…"

Scott's head started to spin at the sight of the long, thin needle, and then everything went black. Nurse Betsy had gone when he came to, and he heard Matt faintly calling his name.

"Scott? You okay there, buddy? Scott?"

"Huh? What happened?

"You totally passed out."

"Did she give me a shot?"

"No. That's the funny thing. She didn't give me one either. She said I passed, and you didn't. Not sure what that was all about."

Scott rubbed his head. He still felt lightheaded.

"I didn't pass what?"

"Beats me, but you know what I think? I think all of this is just to scare us. She never meant to give us a shot. She wanted to see how we would take to being scared."

"Well, kudos to you then. What are we watching on the TV here, Matt?"

"Oh, crazy, Betsy flipped that on before she left. It's a program called "The Ridgeport Way.""

Scott nodded and stared fixedly at the fifteen-minute instructional video that reviewed the social norms and rules of the town, narrated by Mayor Goldman. She walked through various places in town - Coleridge Park, the grocer, the diner, the Historic District - smiling and pointing out how people should look and act. It all seemed very strange. No remote sat bedside to change the channel, so the boys were forced to watch Mayor Goldman say things like, "Notice how the men and women wear appropriate clothes per Ridgeport's dress code. In Ridgeport, it is not only important to be professional, but it is important to look professional at all times."

Matt rolled his eyes toward Scott, and Scott flashed him a faint smile.

"Matt, do you think that's why they took Joe?"

"Yeah, I'm afraid so."

"Me too."

326

After watching the video for the third time, the boys tried falling asleep but found they were more nervous and awake than ever.

"Matt, I can't sleep."

"Me neither."

"Must be the nerves."

"Oh shit. I gotta pee," Matt said.

Matt began squirming in the bed, trying to hold out. He looked to his left and right, but like the remote, a call button was missing.

"Think they forgot about us?" Matt asked.

Scott realized that he also had to pee but decided he wasn't about to wait around for the nurse to let him go to the bathroom, wherever that was.

"Nurse! Nurse!" Scott yelled.

But the only sound they heard was Mayor Goldman's voice reviewing social norms in Coleridge Park on the video.

"Nurse! Nurse!" Matt screamed, louder this time.

Nurse Betsy strolled in with a patient smile.

"Yes? What can I do for you boys?"

"We have to go to the bathroom."

Nurse Betsy let out a belly laugh, and the boys turned to stare at each other, not understanding what was so funny.

"Okay. Thought it was something important."

Betsy opened a closet and took out two long, clear tubes with white tips and two plastic bags attached.

"What are you doing? We have to use the bathroom?" Scott asked.

"You will be silly," Nurse Betsy said.

Betsy carried the tubes over and placed one on each bed.

"What are those for?" Scott asked.

"It will help you pee," she said.

"But we just have to go to the bathroom!" Scott snapped.

"Temper, temper. I told you boys that we don't want you going anywhere. It is mighty hard to trust boys who break in here, isn't it?"

Scott squirmed in his bed and pounded his feet against the hard mattress, but the straps didn't come loose. Nurse Betsy shook her head before approaching Matt.

"Seems like you're the more mature one. You'll have to calm your friend down there. He's not doing himself any favors. Now, let's give you some relief, huh?"

Nurse Betsy unbuckled the leather strap along Matt's waist. Matt's eyes widened, knowing full well what the tube and plastic bag were—a catheter. He'd only heard about these instruments of torture. Yet, he gave her no satisfaction in thrashing around or crying about it. Instead, he lay there like this was the way he always urinated. Betsy unbuttoned his jeans and slid down his boxers. Matt never had a woman touch him there before, making him genuinely uncomfortable. Here he was, in a strange lab, with a nurse about to insert a tube into his penis.

"Betsy! Stop! You...you...why are you doing this?" Scott asked, panicked.

Betsy turned away from Matt and asked, "Why did you have to do this to us?"

Then she turned her focus back to Matt, grabbed the tube, and with one quick, precise motion, threaded the catheter into Matt's penis. Matt flailed around like a fish out of water and clenched his teeth to avoid screaming. He didn't want to give her the satisfaction. The urine immediately splashed into the tube and emptied into the plastic bag. Betsy removed the tube about a minute later, and Matt laid his head back and closed his eyes. Scott noticed him wincing in pain and biting his lower lip.

When Betsy inserted the catheter into Scott, he screamed so loud that Sue Ellen heard him. And heard him, she did.

328

She watched him from security camera four. She had made sure the sound controls were working at full volume, and when she heard Scott's scream, it was music to her ears. Sue Ellen sipped on a glass of merlot, and toasted Nurse Betsy, who then turned to face the camera with a thumbs up.

10

No clock hung in the room, and even though Scott was both exhausted from being constrained and in pain from the catheterization, he felt uneasy about what was about to happen to them next. Scott stared at the ceiling, twiddling his thumbs and thinking of any way possible to escape their torture chamber.

"Don't you think your parents are worried about you?" Scott asked.

"Humph," Matt snorted, "No. I could be gone all week, and it'd be like a vacation for them."

Dr. Peterson pulled the curtain away and walked in with a clipboard. He smiled widely and asked each of them how they were feeling.

"Dr. Peterson, Nurse Betsy stuck a tube up our, up our penises to make us go to the bathroom," Scott said.

Dr. Peterson laughed the same belly laugh Nurse Betsy had.

"She did? Oh, well, it's just one of our tests, son. We're seeing how much pain a man can take. We want our Ridgeport men to be of strong mind and strength."

"What?"

"Seems like Matt here scored higher on the strength scale. Better step up your game, Scott."

"Huh? Step up his game?" Matt asked. "What does that mean?"

Dr. Peterson shook his head and stuck his palm out in the air.

329

"There will be time to address all of that later."

"Dr. Peterson, what's with Nurse Betsy coming in here with a long needle?"

"Oh, it's part of our tests."

"She said that Matt passed and I didn't."

"Again, just part of our tests," he said and smiled.

Dr. Peterson flipped a page on his clipboard and rubbed his chin.

"Right. Seems like you boys are scheduled for the mind test. We're going to escort you to Room 106. We'll take Scott first. There's not enough room for the both of you."

"The mind tests?"

"Yes. It shouldn't take long. An orderly will be in to take you in just a moment, and when it's done, I'll come back to check on you. Any other questions?"

Matt and Scott paused. Their lips were parched, and they couldn't remember the last time they sipped a drop of water.

"Can we get some water, please?" Matt asked.

"Not until you've completed the mind test."

Dr. Peterson turned to leave, but Scott spoke up.

"Dr. Peterson, wait. Have you heard from my mom or dad?"

He froze for a second, shook his head, flipped the curtain open, and walked out.

11

Jonathan came in about ten minutes later to unlock Scott and move him to Room 106. Even though he had no idea what was in that room or what he was about to do, it was somewhat of a relief to at least move from the same spot.

Jonathan seemed surprisingly friendly. He told Scott just to do as they said, and he'd be out of there in one piece. He said he overheard them saying he was in for the 'express

330

treatment,' which meant that he should be out in a couple of days if he complied.

"Jonathan, what's going on with Elizabeth?"

"Oh her? I don't think she's getting out of here for a while, son. They know it's too dangerous."

"How long has this place been here?"

"Well... let's see. I've been here thirty years now. I'm about to retire. Seen a handful of people come through here, and it's been around longer than that. I know that for sure."

Scott thought about all those that went missing in Ridgeport over the years. This is where they went missing.

"What happened to them all?"

"They didn't exactly work with our program, son."

"What does that mean?"

But Jonathan pulled into Room 106 without answering any further questions and greeted Dr. Ed Sievers: a tall, lanky man with glasses and dark wavy hair.

"Why, Scott, I presume? I bet you're itching to get out of that chair?"

Scott nodded vigorously, and Dr. Sievers just smiled.

"All in good time, son. All in good time. We won't leave you like that forever. We just need you in there for now for...your safety."

"But why?" Scott asked.

"Thank you, Jonathan."

"You're welcome, doctor," Jonathan said and made his way out of the room, closing the door behind him.

"Now, let's take your blood pressure."

The doctor hit a button on a remote, and Scott's bed rose. He placed a blood pressure cuff on and put the stethoscope in his ears.

"Okay. Good. One-ten over seventy."

He placed the cold scope on Scott's chest and moved it from side to side.

"You nervous, buddy?"

But Scott couldn't say a word.

"All healthy here, too. Must be nice to be young."

Dr. Sievers rose from his chair and walked to a sink to wash his hands. Scott noticed a few electrical pads attached to a rectangular white machine with radio-like nobs and a white rod with a magnet attached to its end. Scott wondered if Joe had been in this room and wondered if he would be like Elizabeth afterward.

"What's that machine?"

"That is what we are going to use on you today. It's called an ECT Machine, and it should help cure you of your mania."

"What!"

"Don't worry. It helps a lot of people. There is no need to worry."

Scott began thrashing in the chair again, just as he had when Nurse Betsy put the catheter in.

Dr. Sievers put on latex gloves and splattered some jelly on Scott's forehead. Scott tried to resist, but the straps were too tight. He swiveled around in his chair and grabbed the pads, placing them where the jelly had been.

"This will all be over soon."

"Aren't you supposed to knock me out or something?"

"Suppose to? Yes. Will I? No."

Scott opened his mouth to scream, but Dr. Sievers jammed a hard rubber bite block in his mouth.

"You'll want to bite down on this during the exam. You may have a couple of seizures. But not to worry, they won't last long," Dr. Sievers said with a chuckle.

Scott tried spitting the block out, but it was too thick. His thoughts raced, and his eyes shifted as he watched in horror as the doctor walked over to the machine.

"Now. I'm feeling in a good mood, so I'm going to ask you a series of true/false questions about Ridgeport. If the statement is true, you simply give me a thumbs up. If it's false, thumbs down. If you get the statement right, I won't shock you. Sound fair?"

Scott's eyes widened again, but he nodded, unable to speak.

"Good. Question one. Are you a good Ridgeport citizen?"

Scott put his hand in the air, paused for a second, and then flipped his thumb up.

"Oh. I'm sorry, that's a wrong answer," said Dr. Sievers and reached for a switch behind him.

A buzz radiated through Scott's brain, and he fell flat on the mattress. He felt like he had just been put in the microwave.

"Now. Are you a good Ridgeport citizen?"

This time, Scott's thumb slowly turned down.

Dr. Sievers smiled and marked something on his clipboard. This time, he moved his rolling chair closer to the table. He whispered his next question into Scott's right ear.

"Do you love Ridgeport?"

Scott shook his right hand. About thirty seconds went by, and he hadn't flipped his thumb one way or the other.

The doctor waited, then said impatiently:

"Last chance. Do you love Ridgeport?"

Scott flipped his thumb up.

"Oh, I'm sorry. You don't, but you will. Oh yes. When we're through with you, you will."

Dr. Sievers smiled maniacally this time and turned the knob up high, sending Scott into an epileptic fit. His body shook like a demon possessed him, and he foamed at the mouth. By the time Dr. Sievers lowered the knob, and Scott stopped shaking, he was a shell of his former self. His arms fell limp over the sides of the operating table, and his face was pressed against the pillow. Scott's body felt like all the bones were taken out and replaced with jelly.

12

Scott felt like all the life had been drained out of him when Jonathan, the orderly, came in to wheel him back. This time there was no conversation.

As Jonathan switched Scott and Matt, Scott tried to yell out for him to stop, but he couldn't get the words out. Always the fighter, Matt smiled and gave Scott the thumbs up. Scott didn't think he would ever be able to raise his thumb again.

13

Sue Ellen walked out of the secret room, happy after Scott's shock therapy. The express treatment was going according to plan. *Those boys are getting exactly what they deserve*, she thought. Peter was sitting on the couch, watching an old movie, when he saw Sue Ellen come in.

"Where have you been all this time?"

"Downstairs."

"What for?"

"Just playing around with the boys, you know."

"Oh. Are they down there?"

"Yeah. They wanted to sleep down there."

"Oh? Maybe I should say goodnight."

"No!"

Peter jumped back, and Sue Ellen stifled a laugh.

"No. They're already sleeping. It's late. Why don't we go to bed?"

"Alright then. Calm down, okay? Jeez, you alright?"

"I'm better than alright. I'm great."

14

Just before Sue Ellen and Peter walked up to bed, the phone rang. Sue Ellen stared at the phone with a quizzical look. It was eleven o'clock. She had no idea who could be calling now.

"Hello?"

"Sue Ellen? It's Loretta. Do you know when Scotty might be coming home?"

15

"Loretta! Hi. Sorry for not calling you earlier, but I was having so much fun with the boys tonight, I just lost track of the time."

"You did? I thought you went to see Air Supply?"

"Oh well, we did. But the concert ended early."

"I see. So...is he ready to come home?

"Well, Matt had asked if Scott could stay the night, and I didn't see a problem with it. They're actually asleep right now."

"Oh. Well, why didn't you just ask me first?"

"Oh, I didn't think that *you* would mind."

"What's that supposed to mean?"

"Oh nothing, nothing."

"So, I suppose I'll see him tomorrow then?"

"Huh?"

"Tomorrow? I'll see Scott tomorrow?"

"Mm hm."

"Are you okay, Sue Ellen? You don't seem yourself."

"Yeah, well, you know, you called me kind of late here, and I'm kind of tired. So, if we're done here, I'd like to go to bed."

"Okay...fine then."

"Good. Night, Loretta."

"Good..."

And Sue Ellen hung up on her and proceeded to bite her nails.

"Who was that?" asked Peter.

335

"No one. Let's get to bed."

16

Loretta paced around the house, holding tight to her portable phone. She rubbed her forehead, trying to piece together their conversation. Ever since Sue Ellen's wedding, she and Sue Ellen had drifted apart personally. They had more of a professional relationship now, serving as leaders in the Neighborhood Watch Committee. But they remained friendly, which made the phone conversation all the stranger.

Loretta knew Sue Ellen was hiding something from her but was unsure of what. She never played with the boys, and she always checked with her before Scott spent the night. Loretta knew she had failed as a mother, but she tried to patch things up with Scott, ever since her falling out with Sue Ellen. She just didn't know-how. John had been asleep for about an hour, and the only noise in the house was the hum of the dishwasher. She made too much of it. Maybe Sue Ellen was starting to change. Maybe. But Loretta knew her better than anyone and knew something was off, and she didn't like it, whatever it was. Not one bit.

Hours passed. Loretta tossed and turned next to John, got up, and tried to sleep again. The cycle persisted well into the night until she forced herself down for a few hours around four o'clock.

17

When Matt returned from 'shock therapy,' he looked like a dead fish. All his life had been sucked out of him, and had it not been for his will to survive and bring Joe and Scott to safety, he might not have had a pulse at all. Scott knew Dr. Peterson had shocked Matt more than necessary. He knew he must not have given in to questions as easily as he did, or else he wouldn't look as if he'd been struck by lightning. Jonathan parked Matt next to Scott and left without saying a word.

"Matt? You okay, buddy?" Scott asked weakly.

Matt's lips smacked, but he could hear no words come out. Scott wondered if Matt would ever be the same again.

18

Sue Ellen slept better that night than she had in many nights. She dreamed of a Ridgeport, a better Ridgeport, one that she made possible. They crowned her the new mayor and applauded her for all her good deeds. Matt was there, thanking her for fixing him, and so Sue Ellen put him in charge of the lab. Then he and Scott rounded up Riley and Jimmy and re-educated them. Sue Ellen had never been happier.

19

Scott realized he had barely slept in the last two days. He wondered how long they could keep this up, how long he could keep this up. The Ridgeport instructional video with Mayor Goldman played on repeat, and Scott imagined being back in town, in that diner, eating brunch, or at Ridgeport Park, playing a game of pick-up basketball. He imagined the wind blowing against his skin and the smell of fresh air. He must have watched the video at least fifteen times now and began memorizing each line, each movement Mayor Goldman made. He tried looking away from the TV, but as he did now, two days into staying awake, he began seeing spots, and so he turned his attention back to the mayor.

"In Ridgeport, we are committed to building a better future together, a brighter future. Wouldn't you agree?"

Mayor Goldman said with a bright smile as she walked along Coleridge Park.

Scott nodded his head in agreement while Matt laid his head backward, still knocked out from the electroshock therapy. Scott's stomach rumbled from hunger. He felt so weak that he wasn't sure he'd be able even to stand up if he ever did get out of his prison bed. Nurse Betsy strolled into their room with a water pitcher and a couple of plastic cups. She knelt beside Scott and tousled his hair.

"Boy, you want this, don't you?"

Scott's tongue felt like the Sahara but managed to croak, "Yes."

Nurse Betsy poured some of the water onto the floor next to him. Scott wished he could lap it off the floor, but he couldn't move.

"Say something from the video first."

She stopped pouring and waited for his response.

Scott tried swallowing to clear his throat, but any saliva he had was gone.

Nurse Betsy spilled some more water on the floor.

"In Ridgeport, we are...committed to building a future together. Wouldn't you say?" Scott choked out.

"Oh, good. Now that wasn't so hard, was it?"

Betsy filled Scott's plastic cup with the cool water and helped him drink.

It was the most satisfying drink he had ever had. He could feel the cracks in his mouth start to dissipate. He breathed out a sigh of relief.

"More, please."

Betsy frowned.

"Tell me something else from the video then."

She positioned the pitcher on its side as if to spill more water.

"In Ridgeport, we believe in rules and norms to make our town stand out in America," Scott croaked out weakly.

338

"That's what makes our town work. That's what makes our town perfect."

"Good."

Betsy gave Scott some more water, and he gulped it down. Then she tousled his hair again and walked over to Matt. She studied his unconscious face for a moment and poured the rest of the pitcher on his face.

"Wake up! You're fine!" she commanded, slapping his face.

Matt's eyes opened, shocked into consciousness, and his tongue sought to catch the rivulets of water running down his face. Betsy walked over to the sink, refilled the pitcher with icy cold water, and sat next to Matt.

"Now, Matt. You tell me something about Ridgeport, and I'll give you some more water. In your mouth this time."

"Screw you!"

"Come on! Matt!" Scott pleaded.

Betsy shot a stern look in Scott's direction and then turned her focus back to Matt.

"If that's how you want it."

Betsy unstrapped Matt's waist strap, pulled down his pants, and poured the icy cold water all over his boxers. Matt cried out and rocked from side to side.

His bed was now drenched in cold water, but Betsy once again returned to the sink for a refill.

When she returned, she asked him again.

"Now, just tell me something about Ridgeport, and you can have a drink."

"Love thy neighbor" and "Love thy Ridgeport."

Betsy smirked, and Scott thought she might pour more water on his bed, but she seemed satisfied.

"Not the best answer, but I'll accept."

She gave Matt some water, and he chugged it down.

"There. Was that so hard?"

339

Betsy offered him another cup, and he chugged that one, too.

Then she rose, and with the remaining half a pitcher, she poured it on Matt's chest for good measure.

"That's for being a snot-nosed punk. You think twice before giving me, or anyone else, a hard time. You understand?"

She turned, smiled at Scott, and walked out as if nothing had happened.

20

By the time Loretta finished her breakfast at around eight o'clock, and she still hadn't heard from Scott, she decided to make a second phone call. This time, the phone went straight to voicemail. Loretta stepped aside from the kitchen table and pulled the curtains above the sink away, the ones with the view of Sue Ellen's front yard. But there was no sign of Scott or Matt playing there. Loretta's eyes hung in bags from her sleepless night. She made herself a cup of coffee and cradled it in both hands as she walked back to the kitchen table. Her eyes rested on the Kitty Kat Wall Clock as its eyes moved from side to side, and its second hand moved steadily around. She perched herself on her chair this way for a while, sipping the cup with both hands and staring up at the clock.

Loretta checked the kitchen phone once more. It was now 8:30. She picked up and tried again, and still, the phone went directly to voicemail. She knew that either Peter or Sue Ellen should be awake by now. It was Saturday morning, and they were both morning people.

"Could it be that they were all out at breakfast?" Loretta whispered.

She shook her head and convinced herself that was it. She was being crazy. Loretta stretched out like a cat and trudged upstairs for a nap. When she awoke two hours later, she tried calling once more. Yet once again, the call went directly to voicemail.

21

Back at the lab, as painful as it was to be stuck here, at least Scott and Matt were left alone following Betsy's water torture. Their eyes were bloodshot from lack of sleep, and Scott's head twitched, hallucinating that Betsy had entered the room. Scott wondered how a place like this could exist. He wondered how long Sue Ellen could keep him there. She would have to return them for school, right?

"Matt? How are you doing over there?"

"Feel like shit. How are you?"

"Shit."

"Listen, Matt. I think you should ask for your mom next time someone comes in. Say you want to apologize. Maybe it can, you know, get us out of here."

Matt lay in silence and stared up at the ceiling.

"Matt?"

"It won't work."

"Come on! It's worth a shot."

"She put us here, remember? You know how she is. She doesn't care about us. She never has."

From her bunker watching the screens, Sue Ellen's heart sank. She grabbed a remote and rewound the tape to hear it again, just to make sure she heard it right.

"She put us here, remember? You know how she is. She doesn't care about us. She never has."

She hung her head and remembered Matt when he was just a baby, how his first word was "Mom," how he smiled at her, how he always reached out to her. She never remembered a happier time in her life than when he was that age and now wondered what went wrong. And then, from upstairs, she heard the doorbell ring.

22

Loretta stood right beside the entrance to the basement door, talking to Peter by the time Sue Ellen reached the top of the stairs.

"Loretta! What a pleasant surprise!"

"Sue Ellen? Are you alright? You look...a little winded."

"Yeah... I'm fine," she said in between heavy breaths.

Peter gave her a strange look and shrugged his shoulders.

"Just excited to see a friend, I guess?"

"Yeah. You got it, honey."

"Well, I'll give you two some space," he said.

Peter walked out of the kitchen and into the living room. Sue Ellen glanced over at the open basement door.

"What were you doing down in the basement?"

"Oh, you know, just some housekeeping stuff."

"Uh-huh. Where are the boys? I tried calling, but I just got their voicemails."

"They're out."

"Out?"

"Out."

"Out where?"

"The woods."

"The woods? But Scott should have known I was coming over to pick him up, right?"

Sue Ellen shrugged her shoulders.

"Boys will be boys."

"And you allowed this?"

"Oh, well, I didn't see how you would mind. You never have before."

Loretta eyed some black powder on Sue Ellen's fingertips. Strange, she thought. She was always so well-groomed, no matter what the time of day. Sue Ellen caught Loretta's stare and pulled her hand behind her back.

"Well, you better be going. I'll call you when they get back. I have a lot to do around the house, and I just can't entertain today."

This was also something she never said. She hated housework and found any excuse to get out of it.

"You're acting kind of funny, Sue Ellen. Are you okay?"

"I'm fine. I just have a lot to do, okay? I'll call you."

Sue Ellen began moving Loretta to the front door.

"Well, I will be waiting for that phone call. I'd like him home today."

"Yes, yes. Don't worry."

Sue Ellen opened the door, and with one last, quizzical look at her friend, Loretta walked herself out.

23

Scott had no idea what time it was. Neither of them had seen a clock or the light of day in what seemed like forever. The minutes felt like hours, and the hours felt like days. He wondered if Sue Ellen just forgot about them or if she had intended to leave them there permanently like 'Elizabeth.'

A new doctor with a clipboard strolled in the room. He towered over the beds with his tall, lanky frame and ran his hand through his dark hair as he examined whatever was on his clipboard.

"Scott, Matt, I'm Dr. Stevenson. I am taking over for Dr. Peterson this morning. You boys feeling okay this morning?"

"Well, actually, we haven't had much sleep with all the tests. We're exhausted!"

Dr. Stevenson nodded with a serious look on his face.

"Yes, well, you won't have to worry about that much longer. You'll sleep soon enough. Your next test is your sleep test."

"Sleep test?"

343

"Yep. We've been conducting experiments on mice to see if we can manipulate dreams, and we think we're getting close."

"What? Why? Why would you want to manipulate our dreams?"

"We believe you both have a behavior disorder that needs to be treated. Think of us as pioneers. We're curing you, and by the time you're out, you'll be stand-up gentlemen for Ridgeport."

Dr. Stevenson glanced back at the clipboard and flipped a page.

"Well, I'm going to have an orderly come in here to take you to your study. Don't worry. It will be good for you both to get your sleep."

"But, but Dr. Stevenson?" Scott asked.

"Yes, my boy?"

"Will it hurt?"

"It's sleep. Sleep has never hurt anyone. I'll see you when the study begins, okay?"

He walked out of the room, and while Scott was excited about sleep, he wasn't sure he wanted it in the way Dr. Stevenson was going to give it to him.

24

"Matt, do you think when we wake up from this sleep study, we'll be like Joe? Like a weird zombie?"

"Don't know. Hey, let's try to think positive here, huh? We're finally going to get to sleep."

"Yeah. I just don't know how you can be positive in a time like this."

"Well, I have to be. Not much we can do strapped down like this now, is there?"

"Do you think this was all worth it? Breaking in here? I mean, you don't seriously think when we get out of here,

344

they're going to let us remember that, do you? They'll probably wipe our memories like in *Men in Black* or something."

"It was worth it, man. I know that this sucks, but if we do get out of here, this whole place is going up in flames. I'll see to it personally."

And that was when a second armored guard entered the room. This one was just as tall and built as the other but wore nothing but a stoic expression. Scott gasped. Had he heard what Matt just said?

"Okay, time to go," the guard said. I'll take you first," he said, pointing at Scott.

"Me? Oh, okay."

He continued to wear an expressionless look on his face, and Scott could tell there would be no talking to this man like there was with Jonathan. The big man unlocked the bed's wheels, detached him from the IV bag, and moved him out toward the sleep study room.

"Bye, Scott. Remember, be positive."

"Thanks. I'll try."

25

Scott breathed a sigh of relief when he noticed a neatly tucked king-sized bed with several pillows in a dimly lit room. The thought of getting a good rest outweighed any ideas of what dreams they might manipulate. He didn't care at this point what they did to him. He wanted to sleep more than anything.

The guard placed Scott beside the bed, locked him in place, and walked out of the room. Scott's eyes wandered as he left him alone. Next to the bed stood a monitor of sorts, a white box with a screen, and a single knob. The monitor sent a chill down Scott's spine, making him think of the knob in the shock therapy room. After a few moments, a middle-

345

aged woman waltzed in with a smile on her face. Scott thought it weird how often people smiled in a place like this. He supposed it was because they didn't have to endure such torture.

"Scott, I'm Sarah. I'm your polysomnographic sleep tech, and I'll be getting you ready for your study. Have you ever had a sleep study before?"

"Um no..."

"Well, I bet you're nice and tired for this one, huh?"

"Oh yes, yes."

Sarah chuckled and walked over to a sink to wash her hands. From there, she walked toward a back room and rolled out a cart with a bunch of pads dangling from it.

Scott knew he should have expected it, but he took a deep breath anyway.

"I'm just going to put these on you. We want to check your brain waves, your breathing, your movement."

Scott felt like a science experiment, as the tech attached electrodes to his head, heart, and forearms. He watched as she placed a clip to his finger and these stretchy cloth belts across his chest. She connected all the wires to the box he saw before she entered the room, the one that reminded him of the shock therapy box. Then she inserted this plastic tubing inside his nose, one she said would measure airflow.

"Now, all you have to do is sleep. We'll take care of the rest. Is there anything I can get you to help you sleep?"

"No, I don't think I'll need any help with that, thanks."

Sarah smiled and walked back to the room where she wheeled the cart out and closed the door behind her. The lights in Scott's room dimmed, and he fell asleep within minutes.

346

26

Scott's dream brought him to a beach, but no one was there. The water was as grey as the sky, and a wooden pier led to a candy-striped lighthouse in the far distance. The light swirled across the water, casting a beautiful artificial light on an otherwise barren seascape. Scott walked toward it like a fly to a light trap. As he inched closer, he realized he wasn't alone on the beach. A girl about his age stood at the edge of the pier, looking out at the water. Her arms were crossed, and the wind threw her hair around in disarray. Her gaze remained fixed on the water, even as Scott crept toward her. The wind howled around the pier, and the water crashed against the wooden planks. Scott tapped the mysterious girl on the shoulder, and when she twirled around, his mouth dropped. There was Joe, just like he remembered her on that night in the woods.

"Joe!"

"Scott, listen. You can't save me. You have to get out of here before they...before they change you."

"Change me?"

"What are you talking about?"

"You have to get out of here."

Scott reached over to kiss her, but Joe disappeared and flew away with the wind. He thought he heard her breath howl against the water, "Wake up, wake up! Wake up!"

And then he realized someone was shaking him to wake up. His eyes opened to a blurry room and a blurry face as he continued to hear the "Wake up!" command ring in his ears. A moment later, his sight started to come to, and his mom hunched over him on the top of his bed.

27

"Mom? What are you doing here?"

"I've come to get you and Matt out of here."

"But how?"

"I'll explain later. Right now, you're coming with me."

Sarah walked out of the backroom, and Scott's eyes darted between her and Loretta. He thought for sure they might do the same thing to his mom now that she was found out.

"I'm so sorry that we couldn't complete the tests. But we trust they'll be in good hands with you, Mrs. Casey?"

"Of course."

Scott shook his head. He wasn't sure if he was so overly tired or if it would be just that easy for his mom to take them out of this evil lab.

Sarah unhooked the wires from the machine and removed all his electrodes, cloth belts, finger clip pulse oximeter, and nasal cannula. Scott felt like he had his body back again.

"So, how have you been, Sarah?"

"Oh, just fine. You know how it is raising kids."

Loretta laughed, and Scott wrinkled his brow. He couldn't remember the last time he heard his mom laugh like that. How did she know Sarah?

"Okay, you're free to go, Scott. It was good seeing you, Loretta. Don't be a stranger here."

"I won't. Good seeing you too."

Scott wondered if he was still dreaming. Was this part of the dream manipulation the doctor talked about? As Scott forced himself up from the bed, he nearly fell over. He hadn't stood on his own since being set into the bed with the leather straps. Loretta caught him and cradled him into her arms with a hug.

"There, there, honey. Everything's okay now. I'm gonna get you out of here."

"I love you, mom."

"I love you too, sweetie."

Loretta held on tight to Scott's hand to steady him, just as she had when he learned how to walk. Scott's legs felt as stiff as a dried piece of wood, and with his first few steps, he stretched his hands out like a toddler. Loretta steadied him, held his hand, and guided him toward the open door. Dr. Stevenson approached Loretta and Scott just as they made their way out of the sleep study room. He wore a skeptical expression on his face and held his clipboard tightly to his chest.

"Um, hi, Loretta."

"Dr. Stevenson."

Scott gave his mom another quizzical look. He knew he and his mom were never that close, but her interactions with Sarah and now Dr. Stevenson confirmed this. Loretta knew these strange people on a personal level.

"Did Mrs. Norris okay this?"

Loretta frowned and threw an arm around Scott.

"Let me remind you that Mrs. Norris and I are always on the same page, doctor. And if you have a problem with that, I'm sure I can make a note of it in your file."

"No, that won't be necessary."

Dr. Stevenson nodded and bit his lip. Loretta sighed, brushed him aside, and pulled her son with her.

"It's just strange that you should take him now, isn't it? Before his rehabilitation is complete?"

Loretta paused and then turned around with a look of disgust.

"I decide when his rehabilitation is complete, John. Not you, not anyone here."

Dr. Stevenson loosened his grip on his clipboard to let it dangle from his right hand.

"Yes, ma'am. You are the boss."

Loretta pretended not to hear him and ushered Scott along to Room 106 to retrieve Matt.

28

"Mom? What is going on? How do you know these people?"

"What is going on is I am getting you out of here. And I will explain everything later, baby, promise."

Scott's stomach felt like it was eating itself. He hadn't eaten in two days, and for fear of undergoing the terror that was the catheter, he pissed in his boxers just before he fell asleep. He felt like an old man. When Loretta entered Room 106, another nurse was unhooking Matt from the bed. The room smelled like a garbage dump, and that's when Scott found what appeared to be diarrhea stained on Scott's bed. A wheelchair sat next to his bed, but Loretta told the nurse it wouldn't be necessary.

"We're taking the alternate exit. Can't take the chair."

"Ah. Gotcha."

The nurse pulled the chair to the side, but as she tried to help Matt down, he slipped and hit his head against the side of the metal railing on the right side of the bed. He slid to the floor and wrapped his hands around his head.

"Well? Go grab an ice pack for him," Loretta said.

The nurse nodded and within minutes rushed back with one in her right hand. She blotted his head as he rocked back and forth on the floor in a tight ball.

"Are you all right, Matt?"

"Yeah. Just glad to be getting outta here."

After about ten minutes, Matt reached for the nurse's hand, and she pulled him upright.

"Thanks. You're about the only one here who actually cared for me."

The nurse patted Matt on the back, and Loretta grabbed his hand. She now held Scott in one hand and Matt in the other, like she was ready to walk a set of toddlers across the street. The boys gave the room one last disgusted gaze and then turned their heads, scanning for an exit. Neither of them minded holding Loretta's hand. It was comforting having someone there who cared for them. Loretta led the two of them past a row of closed rooms. Scott knew Joe was in one of them.

"Mom, we have to take Joe with us."

But Loretta ignored her son and pressed on past the rooms and toward the end of the staircase that led to the observation deck. Matt noticed that his smashed camera was still lying on the floor. He tried picking up what was left of it, but Loretta tugged at his hand and pulled him along. To the right of the smashed camera sat a four-person golf cart. Loretta knew that she would never get the stumbling teens who just underwent God knows what through the woods and to safety unless she had some help.

"Mom!"

"Shush. Be quiet."

"But Mrs. Casey…"

Loretta tightened her grip on the two of them. Neither of them had seen her take control like this before and fell silent. She led them to what looked like a golf cart at the end of the lab.

"Get in the cart," she ordered them.

"Huh?" Scott asked.

"You heard me. You're not gonna get very far dragging your feet. Get in."

The boys didn't hesitate and did as she asked. They had found Joe but would not leave with her. Loretta turned the key and made her way toward Arnold, waiting next to the exit with his rifle cocked across his chest. A look of suspicion crept across his face.

"Where are you takin' these boys, Loretta?"

"None of your damn business Arnold."

He snorted and tossed his gun across his right shoulder.

"Are you gonna let us through or not?"

Arnold looked at both the boys and smirked at their broken faces.

"I suppose that they've learned their lesson for now. You'll never be coming back here again, will ya, boys?"

They both nodded, expressionless, with the look of defeat. Then Arnold entered a code on a panel on the wall, and a steel door opened to reveal another tunnel.

"Have a good one, Loretta. I'll be sure to tell Sue Ellen you said hi," he said with a chuckle.

Loretta shook her head and yanked the boys through the door to freedom.

29

Loretta pushed the gas through a cave as the boys hung limp like dolls. The cave was like the one they entered to get there, but no lights were showing them the way out, and the air on this side of the exit felt dank and smelled musty, like an old basement.

"Mom, I can't see."

"It's okay; I know what I'm doing. We'll get there."

The cart hit a rock and tilted for a second. Loretta held firm to the wheel and steered it back on the dirt path.

After driving for about fifteen minutes, they found a dim light shining through the cave. As the team made its way closer, the light grew brighter until they found themselves at the cave's mouth.

"Okay, here we are, the mouth of the preserve. It shouldn't be much longer now," Loretta said.

"This whole time, the woods were connected to that lab?" Scott asked.

"Yes," Loretta said.

"Well, what if someone came upon this cave?"

"The tunnel runs pretty deep, but if they made their way in and got to the end, the door is disguised in hardened mud. Plus, you saw how it's pitched black in there," Loretta said.

"Yeah, who would think a re-education center is under our town," Matt said.

Scott shook his head and felt sick to his stomach. He couldn't believe that all these years of the town searching for missing children in these same woods, and all they would have had to do was walk through that cave and knock on a door. It was at that moment that the cart hit a mud patch.

"Damn it!"

One of the wheels spun, and Loretta got out and tried to push it out. But it would just rock back into the pit. After some time, she found a good piece of wood and set it under the tire. She tried the key again, and that finally got it out. Loretta could see her hands shake on the wheel. She knew it would only be a matter of time before Sue Ellen noticed what had happened. When she steered the cart right at a fork in the path, the boys knew they were not going back home, and they began to wonder if Loretta had forgotten her way back.

"Mom? Shouldn't we be going left?"

"No. We're not going that way. I drove here. The car's at the opposite end."

"Oh. But why would you drive here when it's right across the street?"

Loretta gave no answer, and Scott looked to Matt instead but just nodded. He figured they had gotten this far. So, she kept them going, down a hill and past a field of blue violets and Virginia spring beauties. A lonely oak stood tall here or there in the field. The boys rarely came down this way all these years, but it was quite beautiful. The field gave way to an overgrowth of young and old maples, oaks, and hickories. A few downed logs grew moss, and they sometimes heard chipmunks scurrying through the grasses. After some time, the trees thinned out, and a couple of picnic tables and grills sat among a large green field that gave way to the parking lot.

30

Meanwhile, Sue Ellen turned her attention to the security camera in her secret room and failed to see either boy. That's when she nearly froze to her seat. Her eyes shifted across the screen, thinking there might be a delay in the tapes or that they might be coming out of another room. When minutes passed, and still there was no sign of them, she began to squirm and then squirming led to pacing back and forth in the room.

"Maybe the cameras are off, or maybe they're just in an area where they're not picking them up," she said to herself.

Sue Ellen nodded, but with another look at the screen, and still no sign of either of them, she couldn't wait around any longer. She removed the *Ridgeport Welcomes You* book, and the bookshelf swung open, revealing the passageway to the lab. Sue Ellen exhaled, stepped through, and slammed the bookcase behind her. She knew the boys couldn't have gotten out, at least not on their own, and that last part of thinking scared her. Sue Ellen would have to reach out to Mayor Goldman if they did escape and explain. That was something she was not looking forward to.

She relaxed as she entered the lab, seeing 'Elizabeth' taking part in her afternoon tea exercise with Betsy. *At least she was still here*, she thought. Sue Ellen approached the two, smiling.

"Why, hello Elizabeth. Drinking tea, I presume?"

"Yes, ma'am, ginger tea."

"Very good. You are such a young lady. Now, doesn't it feel good to be a young lady?"

"Very much so, ma'am."

354

Sue Ellen turned her attention to Betsy, who stood up from her spot next to Joe.

"Betsy, have you seen the boys?"

Betsy gave her a quizzical look.

"Why, they left. They were discharged."

"Discharged! On whose orders?"

"On Loretta's, of course."

Sue Ellen stood frozen for a second and could feel her face growing red.

"Is everything alright, Sue Ellen?"

"Yes. Everything is alright. Everything will be just fine. You can continue your exercises. Goodbye, Elizabeth."

"Goodbye, Mrs. Norris."

31

Loretta parked the cart close to her Ford Explorer and helped the boys in. They didn't say a word. Loretta adjusted her rearview mirrors, and after seeing no one approaching, she pulled out of the lot and onto the pavement that led back to the street. As Loretta hit the open road, she pushed the pedal hard and weaved in and out of traffic like a madwoman. Just minutes in, flashing red and blue lights caught up with her Explorer, forcing her to slow down and pull over.

"Damn it."

Scott shook his head at Matt, but he just stared straight ahead.

The cop parked behind Loretta for what seemed like forever and then made his way to her window.

"Do you know how fast…"

Loretta flashed him a smile.

"Oh, it's you."

"It's me."

"Can I ask why you were going so fast today?"

"I'm in a hurry."

"I see. Well, you best be careful. Looks like you got two boys in the back there."

"I'm careful, Jerry."

Jerry nodded but tapped his fingers on the roof, unsure of what to say next. Loretta rolled her eyes.

"Can we go now?"

"Um, yeah. But just watch yourself? I don't want to clean up after an accident of yours."

"Will do."

"Have a good day."

"You too, Jerry."

Jerry smiled and then waved at Scott and Matt in the back, who both gave confused looks at him, followed by confused looks toward each other.

Loretta waited for the cop to pull out and drive ahead and then drove out herself. She pushed well past the speed limit again, without a care in the world.

"What just happened, Mom?"

"I'll explain later."

"But…"

"I'll explain later."

32

Despite getting out of a speeding ticket, Loretta appeared shaken up. She now white-knuckled the steering wheel and leaned forward in her seat. She narrowly missed hitting a van in the right lane, and the man shot a long beep her way as he maneuvered out of the way.

"Asshole!" she yelled out the window.

Scott had never seen his mom drive like this. She was the most cautious driver in the family. As he looked out the window, he noticed they weren't in Ridgeport anymore. He had no idea where his mom was taking them or what she was up to, or what had gotten into her. The boys let out a couple

356

of big yawns, and within minutes of each other, they fell asleep like babies. They could have fallen asleep in a Formula 1 racer that day, and the way Loretta drove, they did. Loretta woke them up with a thud of the car doors opening about ten minutes later.

"We're here."

They rubbed their eyes, and it reminded Scott of when Loretta woke him during his sleep study.

"Here...where?"

"Dad's office at *The Naperville Sun*. Come on, let's get inside. He'll know how to help us."

They crawled out of the car. Scott thought he knew the direction his mom was headed in, but he hoped it would work. Then she opened the doors, and she helped them walk in.

33

Sue Ellen marched toward Arnold, red-faced and hands balled into a fist. Arnold simply stood his post and gave her a questioning look.

"Arnold!"

"Yes, ma'am?"

"Where did Loretta and those two brats go?" she said through clenched teeth.

"You mean, you didn't know?"

"Did I know that Loretta kidnapped them out of here? No. No, I didn't know!"

"I thought you two were friends?"

"Never mind that, Arnold! Where did they go?!"

Arnold motioned his head and gun behind him.

"That's all I know. Said she was takin' the alternative exit. Didn't say anything else."

"You sure about that?"

"Yeah. I'm sure."

357

"Fine. Well, open up the door then."

Sue Ellen stole a look at Arnold's Glock in his holster. "And give me that."

"Excuse me?"

"You heard me."

He handed over the gun without another word and then punched in the code for the door.

34

Loretta had only been to John's work once. She tried to surprise him with a coffee and a breakfast sandwich from Dunkin' Donuts. That was before they moved to Ridgeport, before she met Sue Ellen, and before she and John drifted apart for so many years.

When Loretta walked into the newspaper office this time, she stood at the door, scanning the room for any sight of her husband. When she spotted John, he walked over to a man sitting at another desk, talking. She waited a few moments, and as he turned to walk back to his desk, she approached him with the boys in tow.

"John!"

"Loretta? Scott? Matt? What are you all doing here?"

John gave Scott and Matt a second look and noticed how all the life had been zapped from their bodies. He saw that they appeared so weak they could barely stand.

"What happened to you boys?"

"That's what I wanted to talk to you about. Do you have a minute?"

"Well, I suppose I could take an early lunch. Let's go into the break room."

John motioned Loretta and the boys out the door and into the breakroom down the right hallway. The room consisted of a single fridge with a few scattered round tables, a mounted TV, one microwave with a post-it that read "Please

Clean," and a box of opened donuts on a rectangular plastic table.

"Used to have a full-fledged cafeteria until the company had to sell it to keep some reporters on. It was turned into an office for an insurance company," he said while taking out his brown bag from the fridge.

Loretta reached out and grabbed John's hand. John looked at her wife's touch like it was a weird bug, something he had never seen before. It had been so long since they were even remotely intimate with each other. She pulled it away in embarrassment.

"Sorry."

"No. It's okay. That was nice."

Scott sighed and rolled his eyes. Even in his weakened state, he remembered how to be a teenager.

John unpacked his PB and J with chips and a cookie, the same thing he ate for lunch every day. Loretta couldn't help but smile, and for a second, she had forgotten why she came. Scott poked her in the side, bringing her back to reality.

"You're going to think our story is crazy, John."

"I've been in the newspaper business a long time, hon. I've seen a lot of crazy stuff."

"Yeah, but this one might take the cake."

John studied the boys' faces again and noticed the dark circles under their eyes this time.

"Why don't you boys tell it? I know it must be hard, but you have to tell me what happened to you."

Scott thought for a second, and even though his brain was half-dead, he wondered how his mother knew what they might have gone through.

"Do you have a recorder on you, John?"

John reached into his front pocket.

"Always do at work."

"Good. Take it out. Now, who's going to speak first?

The boys looked at each other.

"I will," Scott said.

35

Sue Ellen sprinted through the woods at a speed she didn't know she had. Every few hundred feet, she got terrible stomach cramps and rested against the trunk of a tree, but her adrenaline kicked in again and pushed on. When she reached the fork in the trail, she turned left without hesitating. She never considered the possibility that Loretta would be smart enough to park her car at the opposite end of the woods.

The alternate route from the lab to the Caseys was longer than going back through the secret room, but it was also the quickest trail in the forest. At Sue Ellen's pace, she made it from the start of the woods to the Casey's front door in just over half an hour.

Sue Ellen peered through the front bay windows, but no one seemed to be moving around, and after a few knocks on the door and a few rings of the bell, no one came to the door. Without thinking, Sue Ellen shot the lock off the front door and kicked it in like an old Western.

"Loretta! Just here to shoot the shit!" She gave the gun a sly smile and added, "Or shoot you," with a whisper.

"Oh, Loretta! John?!"

Sue Ellen made her way through the kitchen, sunroom, and the door for the attached garage. She kicked the screen door to the garage after seeing her Ford Explorer gone.

"Great. Now what?"

As she made her way back through the house, an old picture of Loretta and Sue Ellen posing for the camera at the Fourth of July barbeque hung atop the fireplace. She studied it for a second and then smashed it to bits on the hardwood floors. Shards of glass sprayed everywhere. She broke into a panicked run out of the house and onto the sidewalk. She

360

tried to think of all the places Loretta could have gone. Her head whirled, and the once calm domineering person was now in shambles. She thought of calling her but knew that was a stupid idea. She thought of searching the woods again but knew that would just waste more time. Sue Ellen looked back at the long sidewalk leading up to the Casey house. On the porch was a wrapped newspaper. She cocked her head to the side and remembered John worked for *The Naperville Sun.*

"That's it," she muttered. She darted across the driveway, opened the door to her Porsche, and sped off.

36

John eased back into his seat with his eyes wide after hearing Scott's unbelievable yarn about his kidnapping from their next-door neighbor in her underground lair.

"Did you know about this place before, Loretta?"

"I..."

"Did you know about this place before?"

Scott and Matt knew the answer but still waited in anticipation of John's question.

"I did. But I'll tell you about all that later. What is important now is keeping these boys safe and exposing that place once and for all."

John shook his head in disbelief, both at his wife for lying to him all these years and for the fact that a secret lab lay hidden under their neighborhood. He glanced up at the clock - five after twelve. His lunch ended five minutes ago.

"Shoot. I'm supposed to go interview the mayor for the story on severe budget cuts in Naperville."

"What about this story, John? What about your son? What about Matt? What about me?"

He hung his shoulders and drooped his eyes.

361

"Look. Once I get back, I'll go check it out. Right now, I would call the cops and wait until they get here. Your safety is what's important. Okay?"

Loretta frowned but nodded. The boys hung their heads, and John rubbed his hand through their hair.

"I'll be back soon. I'm sorry. It's not good practice to blow off an interview with the mayor. He's not the most understanding of people."

"No. I get it. I'll call the cops."

John forced a smile and made his way for the door.

"But John?"

"Yes?"

"What do I even tell the dispatcher?"

"Tell 'em...tell 'em that your boys were kidnapped, and you know where the kidnappers are."

She straightened up at this and tried a smile back. Then John hurried out of there.

Loretta knew about her involvement in the lab, but she didn't care at this point. She cared about what happened to Scott and Matt. Sue Ellen had gone too far. Her left hand shook as she pulled her cell from her pocket.

"Well, boys, here goes nothing."

She stared at the screen for a second and then dialed 9-1-1.

"9-1-1, What's your emergency?"

"Hi. My boy and his friend have been kidnapped."

"Okay. What's your name?"

"I'm Loretta Casey of Ridgeport."

"Casey. C-A-S-E-Y?"

"Yes."

"And the name of the children kidnapped?"

"My son, Scott, and his friend Matt Norris."

"Do you know who kidnapped them?"

"Yes. Matt's mother, Sue Ellen Norris."

362

"Sue Ellen, Matt's mother, kidnapped her own kid and friend? Is this a hoax call?"

"No, ma'am."

"Okay, then, do you have any idea of their whereabouts?"

Loretta took a breath. She knew that she sounded crazy on this call.

"They're...with me."

"Wait, a minute. I thought you said they were kidnapped with Sue Ellen Norris."

"They were. I rescued them, but now she's coming for them here, and she has a gun."

"She does? Are you sure about this?"

John looked at her in disbelief. He mouthed the words, "What are you doing?"

"Ma'am, are you sure you are not playing a hoax on us?"

"Yes! Please hurry. She has a gun, and she has come back for them."

"Okay. We will send a squad out."

"Oh, thank you."

"What is the address?"

"We're at 1500 W. Ogden Ave. It's *The Naperville Sun* Building."

"Got it. Be there soon."

Click. Loretta breathed a sigh of relief.

"What was that? Sue Ellen isn't here with a gun."

"She will be. She will be, John."

37

Right after Loretta hung up the phone, she jumped from the sound of a loud crash outside the front of the building.

"Wait here!" she yelled as the boys moved toward the door with her.

The entire newspaper staff gathered around Sue Ellen's wrecked Porsche, smashed inside the glass windows of the

363

front office. She was already out of the car and appeared unhurt. *Must have jumped out before it crashed into the glass*, Loretta thought. Sue Ellen waved her gun, and the newspaper staff inched backward in fear. Loretta stepped forward with her hands outstretched.

"Sue Ellen...be reasonable here!"

"Oh, my dear friend. Reasonable, you say? Reasonable? I'll tell you what's reasonable. You stabbed me in the back. You know we had an agreement, no matter how cruel it seemed. It was for the common good."

"I think this was different."

"Since when did you become the mother of the year?"

John inched closer to Sue Ellen's right, out of her line of sight.

Sue Ellen steadied the gun at her friend, urging her not to take another step.

"Just give me the boys. Give me the boys, and I'll be on my way. We'll pretend like this never happened, okay?"

"Sue Ellen, please."

But she fired a round at her feet. Loretta backed away, and the crowd backed up some more.

"Now. Go. Bring. Me. The. Boys. Loretta."

Knowing the cops should be there any second, Loretta did as she asked but made her way to the lunchroom as slowly as possible. Meanwhile, Sue Ellen turned around to see John only a few inches away from her. She fired two shots from the .45 without hesitation, both directly at his heart. He fell backward. She then fired a round into the air, bringing down pieces of the drop ceiling.

"And that goes for the rest of you. Not another step!"

John held his hand over his blood, and a staffer rushed to find an old newspaper to cover the bleeding. Another reporter rushed to find his wife. As Loretta approached with the two boys, she gasped when she saw her husband lying on the ground, with a woman reporter applying pressure with yesterday's copy of *The Naperville Sun.*

"John!"

"Dad!"

Loretta ran beside him and stroked his hair.

"I'm alright. I'll be okay," he said, smiling.

John laid on the floor, grunting as blood overflowed the copies of the newspaper. With as much strength as he could muster, he grabbed Loretta's shirt sleeve to get her attention.

"Loretta. My tape recorder is in my front pocket. Make sure you take it. It has the whole interview from the lunchroom on it. It also has these words."

John hit record on the tape.

"To...my wife: I know we didn't always have the best marriage, but I never did stop loving you, right up until the end. You will always be the woman of my...dreams," he said weakly.

"John? What are you saying? What are you doing?"

John waved Loretta off, and she tightened her hand around his.

"To my son...Scott: You are the man of the house...now," he croaked. "I love you more than life itself. I will be watching you grow even if I'm not here to see it. Make me proud, even though I know you already...have."

Loretta's tears streamed down her face like a waterfall, and as Matt and Scott came near, they both rushed to his side.

"Dad!"

"My boy!" he exclaimed with as much energy as he could muster.

"Are you okay?"

"I'll be okay. Don't worry about me. I'll be just fine, okay?"

"Take my recorder and give it to my editor, Julie Seehoffer. She'll know what to do with it."

"Julie Seehoffer? But why Dad?"

John patted his son's head and then kissed his wife's cheek.

"How sweet. Too bad you had to go and die," Sue Ellen said. She then pointed the gun at Matt and Scott, standing in shock beside Loretta.

"Now, come on, let's go. Both of you, and no one else, needs to get hurt."

Matt turned and balled his hands into a fist.

"I'm not going anywhere with you ever again! Do you all know what she did to us? Write this down in your paper, everyone! There's a secret lab…."

"Matt…I swear to God. I will kill every man and woman in this place."

"I hate you! I hate you!" he screamed and started tearing up.

At that moment, a male staff reporter threw a laptop at Sue Ellen but missed. Sue Ellen fired in his direction, grazing his arm. He fell back into a crowd of people.

"Now! Let's go! Don't make me kill anyone else!"

She waved her gun at the two of them, and they forced their way toward her.

"Scott! Matt! No!" Loretta cried out, looking up from John, tears streaming down her cheek. She pulled on Scott's shirt sleeve, but he resisted and moved on.

"It'll be okay, mom. We don't need anyone else getting hurt today."

"Yes, Loretta. We wouldn't want that would we?" Sue Ellen quipped.

"Take me. Take me instead. You know you'd like to take me instead," Loretta said.

Sue Ellen paused for a second but shook her head.

"Nah. I'd rather have your boy. I think that's better for the both of you."

Loretta screamed helplessly after the boys, but Matt and Scott walked out and over the shattered glass. As much as they hated the idea of giving into Sue Ellen, they hated more the thought of her doing further harm to any innocent people at the office.

"Oh, one more thing, dear. I'll need your car keys. I don't think I can get out now," she said through a laugh.

"You're not serious," Loretta said.

Sue Ellen pointed the gun at Scott's head, and Loretta gave her the keys.

"Thank you, dear."

"Had anyone called 9-1-1?" someone asked.

"I did...I just hope they're...." Loretta choked out.

"They're here!" a staffer exclaimed.

About six more squad cars, ambulances, and a fire truck pulled into the lot just as Sue Ellen closed the front door on the Explorer.

"Shit!" Sue Ellen yelled. She fired a round at one of the cop cars, busting a hole in the passenger side window and nearly missing one of the officers.

The cop in the passenger side drew his gun, and with one quick shot, hit a dart into Sue Ellen's driver's side rear tire. The Explorer careened to the right, hit a curb, and stopped in front of a bush. They surrounded Sue Ellen, and she came out with the boys with her hands thrown on top of the hood.

The cop who shot out the tire cuffed her, and as he did so, the staffers let out a collective cheer. The boys returned to Loretta, who was still kneeling beside John.

Before the paramedic could even kneel beside him, John was already dead on the floor where he had worked for twenty years. Scott tried shaking him awake, but all he felt was his dad's lifeless body in his arms. Tears now started streaming down his face. Matt stood beside him, with a hand resting on his shoulder. Scott threw it to the side. Loretta pulled Scott away, but he pulled free.

367

"He's not gone. He's just tired. He's just tired. He's just tired!"

It wasn't until the paramedic came over a couple of minutes later and officially pronounced him dead that Scott let go of his father. He wiped the tears from his eyes and felt so many emotions all at once: fear for living without a father, hatred for Sue Ellen, and the indescribable anguish from watching his father die. If gravity were a feeling, this was it. He remembered his father's wish to take the recorder to Julie Seehofer. He reached into his pocket and called out for Julie.

"Is there a Ms. Seehofer here?!"

"Ms. Seehofer?!"

A short blond woman who looked to be in her early forties came forward from the room.

"I'm Julie Seehofer, yes."

"It's my dad. He...wanted you to have this. But we need it back when you're done. He recorded some stuff for us on there too."

"Your dad was John Casey?"

"Yes, ma'am."

"Oh, I'm so sorry, Scott."

Scott hung his head, not wanting to hear those words ever again in his life. He knew people were sorry, but he didn't want to hear them. Hearing them meant he wasn't alive, and he didn't want to think about that.

"Thanks," he murmured.

Julie knelt next to John with a morose look on her face and started to tell Scott of the great reporter that he was. Scott smiled at first but then brushed away the stories with a wave of his hand.

"Thank you, but I just can't hear it right now."

"I understand."

Julie grabbed the recorder and smiled.

"I will be sure that we take care of this," she said.

"Thank you."

Julie smiled one more time and walked on back through the crowd. The cops marked the area as a crime scene and conducted interviews with people used to doing the interviewing. A paramedic wrapped up the one male staffer's shoulder wound and rushed him away to a nearby hospital. Another medic wrapped Loretta, Scott, and Matt in a blanket and found them a quiet place to sit and grieve.

38

The Ridgeport News   April 24, 2004
Ridgeport resident shoots up newspaper office

By Sally Weaver
Staff Writer

NAPERVILLE - Ridgeport resident John Casey was shot dead Saturday during a brutal attack on *The Naperville Sun* office in downtown Naperville.

Ridgeport resident Sue Ellen Norris drove her Porsche 911 through the glass windows of the paper's front office and demanded to retrieve Ridgeport teenagers Scott Casey and Matt Norris.

Newspaper staff members said she waved her gun around, forcing people to stay back. When *The Naperville Sun* reporter and Scott's father, John Casey, approached, she shot him twice in the heart.

"She killed my husband. I came back with the kids, but then she killed my husband. She killed him!" said Loretta Casey, Scott's mom.

Reporter Mike Avery said she then shot a fellow staff member in the shoulder when he tried to throw a laptop her way.

369

"She then pointed her gun at the kids and walked them out of there," Hughes said.

According to *The Naperville Sun* Editor in Chief Julie Seehoffer, Sue Ellen never worked at the paper, and she doesn't believe this was a targeted shooting on the staff or the paper itself.

Staff members said that after Casey walked out with the boys, she shot out a cop car's window to escape, but after the cop blew out her tire, the arrest was finally made.

Authorities are still trying to figure out the reason behind this attack. Sue Ellen Norris is Loretta Casey's neighbor, and they both serve on Ridgeport's Neighborhood Watch Committee.

The Naperville Sun   April 25, 2004
Ridgeport boys reveal town hides dirty secret

By Mike Avery
Staff Writer

RIDGEPORT - Just before *The Naperville Sun* reporter John Casey died, he gave his Editor in Chief Julie Seehofer a recorder. On the recorder, Ridgeport residents Matt Norris and Scott Casey exposed the dirty truth behind Ridgeport, America's sweetheart town.

In his dying wish, Casey handed over the recorder to his wife, Loretta, to give to Seehofer. He told her it was of the utmost importance that she got it. Casey served as a news reporter for twenty years on the paper and had covered some of *The Naperville Sun*'s most critically acclaimed stories. He reported on the kidnappings in Ridgeport, the lead water issue in Woodhaven, and the former Naperville mayor's racist comments. He was well-respected and was one of the most hardworking reporters the paper had ever seen. So, when he handed over a recorder filled with information that seemed more fiction than fact, we at *The Naperville Sun* took it as fact. Truth is stranger than fiction, after all.

Ridgeport resident and John's wife, Loretta Casey, drove the boys to the office on the 24 to escape Ridgeport resident Sue Ellen Norris, who, not even a half-hour later, smashed her Porsche into the front of the building.

As the tape would reveal, the boys escaped from a secret lab underneath Spring Grove Forest Preserve. The lab had a connection through Ms. Norris' home in Ridgeport's historic district.

The boys entered the lab through a secret passageway found through the Norris' basement. Matt Norris had admitted that he thought his mom was hiding something in there that needed to be seen.

Hiding something she was. When the boys entered her secret room, they found more than a room, but they found a passageway to a secret lab filled with doctors, nurses, and orderlies.

"They were running tests. We even saw Josephine there, the girl who was 'missing.' But she didn't go by that name anymore. She went by 'Elizabeth,'" Scott said.

Matt said that when Sue Ellen found out they were there, she admitted them into her lab, where they were tortured for two days.

"They tortured us. They shocked us, strapped us to a bed without giving us any food and water, physically beat us. It was terrible," said Scott said.

Norris said that the place had guards with semi-automatic rifles, and there was no way to escape.

"By the end of it, I could barely walk. I needed Mrs. Casey to help me out of there," Matt said.

The boys said they had taken photos, but Sue Ellen smashed their camera. This case is pending further investigation. Authorities have swarmed the Norris household, and we will be following up on the story.

The Naperville Sun April 26, 2004

By Julie Seehoffer
Editor in Chief

RIDGEPORT - Authorities have confirmed that the Norris household is the entrance for a secret underground lair for experimenting on 'socially misguided' residents of Ridgeport.

A team of doctors, nurses, secretaries, security guards, and orderlies have been placed under arrest for their involvement in the cover-up and mistreatment of Ridgeport human life. Josephine Barnes has been recovered, although she seems confused and refers to herself as 'Elizabeth.'

Authorities are currently confiscating personal lab files to confirm the torture experiments that Matt Norris and Scott Casey said they ran in the lab.

A secret passageway leads out of the lab and into Spring Grove Forest Preserve, where Loretta Casey said she helped the boys escape. Casey has since been questioned on her knowledge of the lab.

"I'm a committee member. I need to know these things. I'm not the only one, you know."

Casey has also been arrested for her apparent involvement in the cover-up.

A secret room, which begins in Norris' basement, leads into the lair. It is protected by a steel door with a fingerprint scanner.

The room contains several books, maps of Ridgeport, TV screens of the lab, and binders that contain names for all the residents in Ridgeport.

According to Sue Ellen Norris, the room served as a base of operations for the Neighborhood Watch Committee.

When asked about the binders, she said she was only following orders.

One binder contained names highlighted in red, yellow, or green. Those highlighted in red have been identified as either missing or dead. Those in yellow have marks below their name that display warnings for infractions on social behavior. Those in green are supposedly 'good citizens.'

"I'm not the one you should be talking to. I do what I'm told, just as every Ridgeport resident should do," Sue Ellen said.

Sue Ellen Norris' son, Matt Norris, said they found the room years ago but said they felt they should go back and check it out. They said something didn't feel just quite right at home.

"We made a molded fingerprint. We thought it was worth it. I knew it was a total invasion of privacy, but we wouldn't have done it if we didn't think it wasn't necessary," Matt said.

So far in this investigation, there have been twenty-seven arrests, including Sue Ellen Norris and now Loretta Casey. More arrests are expected as this case continues to unfold.

The Chicago Tribune - April 28, 2004

By Nancy Barr
Reporter

The ongoing investigation into the Ridgeport cover-up scandal produced more arrests this morning, with the board of trustees and Mayor Sheila Goldman being connected to the village's secret lab.

Mayor Goldman served as mayor of Ridgeport since 1980 and did not deny the cover-up.

"You got me. What took you so long?" she said. "But for all I did, I did it for the good of the town. I just hope everyone knows that. I love this place, and I made it a better place to live."

Ridgeport resident and Neighborhood Watch Leader Sue Ellen Norris said that it was Goldman and the board who oversaw the mysterious binder in the lab, which said who was a good resident and who was not. She claimed she was "only doing as she was told."

Now that the board members and Mayor Goldman are placed under arrest, the village manager will serve as interim mayor until the village can hold an impromptu election for new officials.

Ridgeport resident Tom Johnson said he could not believe that the town he grew up in could end up being so corrupt.

"I'm thinking of moving now, honestly. I stayed here because this was a place that worked. I feel betrayed."

Others felt there was something too good about the place.

"This place was a little too rigid. Too many rules, too many social norms. I mean, we never had crime or anything, but at what cost? And look what happened," said resident Jan Tyler.

Matt and Scott Casey have expressed that they will be going away to college.

"We'd like to get out of here now, but we'll be out soon. We're countin' the days," said Scott Casey.

39

When the dust settled following his dad's death, Scott made several stops to Sue Ellen's house, hoping to find Joe. Matt had taken up living with the Wrobels until he went off to school, so Scott's only motivation in going there was reuniting with his girlfriend. The house was always dark, and the curtains were always drawn. It reminded him of Boo Radley's place in *To Kill a Mockingbird*. He had a feeling

374

she was there, but no one ever came out. One day he thought he saw a figure in the upstairs bedroom staring down at him, but when he looked again, no one was there. One day, he caught Peter as he was opening his front door.

"Peter! Hi. Is Joe in there? I must see her. I have to…."

Peter rested one hand on Scott's shoulder and gave him a look that was filled with a thousand apologies.

"Son, the person you knew as Joe isn't alive anymore. Whatever they did to her in that lab changed her. I can't get her to leave her room much less…."

Scott's eyes darted from Peter to the cracked door. With all his muster, he pushed the much bigger man out of the way and threw the door open. He ran upstairs with the speed of a gazelle.

"Joe! Elizabeth! Joe!?"

"Scott! I don't think you want to go up there. Scott!"

Peter darted up after him, but Scott had already pushed Joe/Elizabeth's door open. Her hair was cut in a neat bob and dyed blonde. She sat cross-legged on her floor in a lovely polka dot dress and was combing the hair of a Shirley Temple doll.

Scott rubbed his eyes to make sure he had entered the right room. At least when he saw her last, she looked like Joe. Who was this? he wondered.

As he stood there panting, Peter caught up to him and put a hand around his right shoulder. Scott jumped, startled.

"You see, son? She's not the girl you thought she was."

"Hello, daddy. What a pleasant day it is, don't you agree? Who is this boy, daddy?"

40

"Joe…I mean…Elizabeth…you don't remember me?"

Elizabeth looked at Scott blankly and then smiled wide.

"Oh, I'm sorry, no. But it is a pleasure to meet your acquaintance."

Scott scanned the room. All her pictures of girl fem punk bands were gone. Her scattered books from the beat poets, gone. Her incense for 'purifying the room' gone. In its place was a tea set, pink wallpaper, and a poster that listed Ridgeport's old rules and social norms. A plaque that reads "Love thy neighbor" and "Love Thy Ridgeport" hung above her bed.

Scott turned to look at Peter with a worried expression on his face. He returned the look.

"Told you. Now, come on. It's best to get you home."

"Home? Do you mean living at the Wrobel's? I don't have a home, Peter, remember?"

Peter nodded nervously at this.

"Look, can I just stay here and have a moment of peace with her before I go? Please?"

Peter looked from Scott to Elizabeth and sighed.

"Sure. What the hell. Take a moment. I'll be downstairs."

"Thank you."

Peter closed the door, and Elizabeth resumed brushing the doll's hair.

"Joe?"

No answer.

"Elizabeth?"

She set the brush aside and put on a smile once more. He now noticed that she was wearing make-up and pearls to go with her formal dress.

"Yes? What can I do for you?" she asked with a smile.

Scott slumped his shoulders. He felt happy that he rescued her, but at what cost? *Who did he really rescue?* he thought.

Scott took a note out from his back pocket and handed it to her. Elizabeth gave him a quizzical look, but she took the note all the same.

"What's this?"

"It's just for you. I wrote it after seeing you again, and I have been meaning to give it to you since I got out."

Elizabeth smiled again, felt the note in her fingertips, and stared at Scott.

"Um, you can read it now if you want. It doesn't matter."

Elizabeth's quizzical look returned, and she unraveled the note and began reading.

41

Elizabeth,

First off, I want you to know that your real name is not Elizabeth at all. It's Josephine, Joe for short. I know you may think the contents of this note are hard to believe, but what I must tell you is true. You and I were boyfriend and girlfriend, and the last thing we did together was we stayed up past curfew in Spring Grove Forest Preserve, smoking pot and roasting marshmallows. It was the night I fell in love with you. It was the same night that you said men in badges were after you. It turns out that the following day you went missing. That's what led to this. You see, you were kidnapped, Joe. You were taken to that underground lab and changed into Elizabeth - the 'well-behaved' citizen they want you to be. But you're not that. You're much more interesting than that. You have a wildfire personality, and you light up anyone you encounter. You break all rules, but you have a kind soul. You're a tomboy, but you can be sensitive. You are a good friend and a good girlfriend. I know what kinds of things they do in that lab. I was there too. I think they changed your brain somehow. I just hope there is enough of Joe still in there that you can change back.

Anyway, I'm going to be going away to school, far away. I'm leaving for the University of Hawaii at Mānoa in a few weeks. I went out and got a cellphone since I'll be a college man now. My number is 708-399-3102. I know getting to Hawaii isn't cheap, so I'm going to give you a little money to get you started (if you want to come out and see me some time). So, that's it. I don't mean to alarm you, but I just thought you should know.

I love you, Joe,
Scott

42

When Elizabeth closed the letter, she noticed that Scott had dropped a wad of cash next to her, totaling a couple of hundred dollars.

"That's to get you started. And...if you don't want to come, consider it a gift."

Now it was Elizabeth's turn to carry a worried expression on her face.

"Who are you?"

"I told you...I'm Scott."

"Who sent you? What is this?" She shook the letter in her hand and tossed the money at Scott. He backed up and let it fall onto the floor.

"Daddy! Daddy! Help! This boy is saying strange things to me! Daddy!"

Peter rushed upstairs and grabbed Scott by the arm.

"But I…"

"Alright, son, it's time to go."

Peter dragged him down the stairs and shoved him out the door. When he returned to Elizabeth's room, she was back to playing with her dolls.

"Everything all right?"

"Yes; daddy. Everything is fine. Just fine."

43

Scott didn't see Elizabeth any day over the next few weeks. He tried day after day, but there was no answer at the door, and she repeatedly ignored any attempts for him to call her name at her window. When he got on the plane for Hawaii, he knew that the Ridgeport he knew and loved as a kid was truly gone for good. He would never have those moments back, and he would never have Joe back. A few days after Scott left, Matt flew off to pursue a degree in criminal justice at UCLA. The boys spent their last day together hiking through the woods, reminiscing of better days.

By the end of 2004, Scott had been at U of H for two semesters without so much as a text from Joe/Elizabeth, and Scott started to lose all hope that there would ever be a future there. That was anyway, until one day, he was studying late at night on a Friday, and his cell phone buzzed.

"Hello?"

Silence.

"Hello?"

No answer.

Scott hung up.

The phone rang a second time, the same number. Scott recognized the area code from back home, but he had been getting a lot of spam calls lately.

"Yes! What is it?"

"Scott? Is it you? It's Eliza...I mean Joe."

Scott nearly dropped the phone.

"Yeah. It's me."

"I'm in town. Do you want to meet up or something?"

Scott stared blankly at the time, 11 p.m. He was exhausted just a minute ago, but now he felt like he could run a marathon.

"Sure. Where are you?"

"Just arrived."

"You're at the airport?"

"Yes. Wanna pick me up?"

"Oh, well, I don't have a car here. It's Hawaii, so it's just cheaper to take public trans where I need to go. Plus, living on campus, I don't need one. Do you want to meet someplace?

"Sure, I suppose we can do that. Or, I could just come to your place. Where are you?"

Scott gulped. My place?

"I'm at Frear Hall; it's one of the dorms. The address is 2569 Dole St. in Honolulu."

"2569 Dole. Got it. See you soon."

Scott blushed and closed his flip phone. This was happening. He had no idea how, but it was happening.

44

When he saw Joe/Elizabeth again, she ditched the blond and was back in black, and she was starting to let it grow out again, too. It was shoulder length now. When he entered his single suite dorm room, she carried one bag and a smile with her. She plopped herself on his bed and immediately laid down.

"Well, yeah, just make yourself comfortable."

She laughed at this and yawned right after.

"So, Joe or Elizabeth, or where are we at here?"

"It's Joe. You were right."

"So...the letter? That's what did it?"

Joe nodded and stretched out like a cat.

"Yep. I reread that thing day after day and night after night. I tried to convince myself that it wasn't true, and then I discovered one of those punk posters under my bed. That's what did it for me. Patti Smith. Sue Ellen hated it when I played that music. When Peter came into my room one day and saw that hanging on the wall, he ran over and hugged

380

me. He was so excited. He kept saying, "I have my girl back."

Scott nodded and paced the small room, thinking about the transformation and trying to piece this magic moment together.

"And then you took the money and decided to just…."

"Scott…I just flew over eight hours to get here. Can't we talk in the morning? Why don't you just lay next to me for a bit?"

Scott blushed once more but had no problem with her request. They both lay there for a while, not saying anything, and then Joe fell into a deep sleep. They awoke in the morning, holding each other tightly as if they did not need their blankets. Then they kissed for so long that it seemed to transcend time and space. But when Scott tried to make any further moves, Joe brushed his hand away and rose from the bed.

Out of her suitcase, she pulled out a lovely gown that one might wear to a 19th-century ball. She stripped right in front of him, and Scott did all he could to keep his cool. Instead of moving toward the bed, though, she simply put on the dress as if she always dressed herself this way in front of men.

"What are you wearing?"

"This? This is how I always dress."

"Ha, no, it isn't. You dress in jeans and hoodies and t's."

"Oh, honey. That's so uncivilized. I may be Joe again, but Elizabeth taught me some things about how to live life properly."

As Joe applied some mascara, Scott rolled out of bed himself.

"Well, I guess I should get ready now too."

But as he started to strip, Joe stopped him short.

"What are you doing?"

"I'm changing."

"Don't you want to shower first?"

"I showered last night."

Scott continued to undress, but Joe stopped him once more.

"It's not polite to change in front of a woman, you know."

Scott stared at her unbelievingly and changed in his bathroom instead.

"So, where are you going today Eliza...I mean Joe?"

"Got a new job. I want to look sharp."

"A what?"

"Yep. I thought, why not work here as long as I'm going to get back with my old boyfriend."

"Oh...okay. Well, that's great! Doing what?"

"I'm a receptionist."

"Oh, good for you. Where?"

"Here, at the school. That way, I can keep tabs on you, ha-ha."

Scott froze in his tracks. He was more than happy to have Joe back but was worried that some of Sue Ellen got stuck in Joe.

"Well, I'll be. I'm so glad this is happening."

"Me too. We'll resume our snuggling later, k?"

Scott smiled at this, but he was worried at the same time. Who was he dating now? Who came to visit him?

Chapter 9: Ridgeport 2020

"For as crazy as that sounded, Julie, that's my story. The whole story. I hope it's a good story for your book."

"Thanks, Scott. I know it will do your dad a great service. I know this had to be hard for you to tell at some parts."

"Yeah, well, it was also fun to tell, too. Stories are like that. Not everything is bleak all the time. But you never know when things change or when people change."

"True. Very true."

"I mean, you seem like a good person. You always have. But who knows? You may have come here to kill me," Scott said with a laugh.

Julie Seehoffer laughed with him.

"So, how's Joe and the baby?"

"We're good. She's been back to being mostly Joe for ten years now. Occasionally she'll do something like act like she's walking down a runway, but after that, she's back to wanting to go on an adventure. And Danny is just fine. He's a little me. Curious about everything."

"And living in Hawaii. That's heaven, huh?"

"It is. Just wish it were cheaper. But I wouldn't want to live anywhere else."

"Don't you miss Matt?"

"Of course, I do. I keep trying to get him to move out from Cali, but I understand that he doesn't want to leave the mainland."

Julie nodded and scribbled something on her notepad.

"Well, is there anything else?"

Scott cleared his throat and looked to the floor.

"Yes, actually. There is."

"Well?"

"You remember Betsy? The nurse I told you about from the lab?"

"Yeah, mean one, right?"

"That's the one. She called me last week. Don't know how she found my number. But she called me. Didn't say who it was. She just said this is 'she.' I knew the voice. I knew it was her."

"Okay, weird. So, she's out of jail."

"Yeah, but that's not all. She said, "I'm the one that killed Stella. And the best part is, I was told to do it. And you'll never know who told me. That's the best part. You'll never know."

Julie put a hand to her mouth before taking more notes. Scott shook his head.

"Before I could get another word out, she hung up."

"Did you alert the authorities?"

"Yeah. But I haven't heard anything about it since. Not sure anything will be done. She didn't use a name, called from a private line or something."

"Want me to write it in the book or publish it in an article?"

Scott shook his head again.

"No. I want to move on. I just want to move on."

2

Loretta felt that she belonged in Birmingham Correctional Facility. She cried herself to sleep in her cold cell on top of her thin mattress every night. Loretta hadn't seen Scott in years, and as each day wore on, she felt that she never would. She mindlessly came out of her cell at lights up, folded the clothes in the laundry just so, ate her slop in the mess hall among the other innocents with displeasure, reveled in the few moments of sunshine in outdoor time, and always felt stabs of jealousy when others had visitors. She hadn't made friends there, either with the guards or the inmates. She gave in to talking to herself most times. Others called her Loony Tunes. Even those in for murder stayed away from her. They knew she was connected to that secret underground lab that was too much for anyone to wrap their heads around. At times, Loretta imagined Scott visited her and forced a smile. She even engaged in conversations with him.

"So nice to see you. I'm so glad you came."

"I just wanted to say I'm sorry, Mom. You really are a good mother."

"Oh, honey. Thank you. That means the world to me."

And then she would snap out of it at the sound of a guard's voice or an inmate snickering her way. The only comfort Loretta carried with her was knowing that she got Scott out and did the right thing after so many years of avoiding doing so. *But at what cost?* she would think. She often wondered if it would have been better if she didn't do anything. These are the thoughts that kept her up at night. These are the things that imprisoned her.

3

Peter Barnes was acquitted of all charges brought against him. He testified against Sue Ellen and cooperated with authorities regarding his wife. When Peter found out about the lab and what Sue Ellen was capable of, they divorced for a second time. That doesn't mean that he still didn't visit her from time to time at Cook County Jail. Sue Ellen both hated his visits and welcomed them. She had no one else visit, and although she made a couple of friends on the inside, she yearned for any news coming from the real world. When Peter saw her last time, he mentioned that Matt was still living in California but was thinking of moving back to live with him. Sue Ellen said she hated him after that and ended their visit. On today's visit, she hated other disturbing news he had to share with her.

Sue Ellen hardly looked like the put-together homemaker who oversaw the Neighborhood Watch in 2004. These days, her face had grown old, wrinkled, and tired with age. Her hair was still mostly blond, but it was tinged with grey and stringy. Her one-piece orange jumpsuit ran counter to all the stylish clothes she donned over the years. If Peter were just seeing her for the first time in sixteen years, he might not have recognized her, but he had been coming to the prison once a month since 2004 to torture her with news he knew she would despise.

Peter, on the other hand, hadn't changed much. He greyed, but his salt and pepper hair did not detract from his handsome face of his earlier days. His life outside of prison was much kinder to him as well. He continued to perform well in his business but started contributing to the community with volunteer work. He stayed in Ridgeport despite everything he had been through there. He called it his home, and those who remained his neighbors liked him.

As Sue Ellen parked herself on the other side of the visitor's glass to meet Peter on this day, he carried a smile like he usually had. She did not carry the same joy and kept wondering how she could kill this man if she ever got out.

"Sue Ellen. So nice to see you again."

"Pleasure is all yours, I'm sure."

"How have you been? Are they abiding by your social norms here?"

Sue Ellen rolled her eyes and grimaced as she saw her ex-husband smile.

"Out with it. What do you want to tell me?"

"Oh? Right to it? Sue Ellen, aren't you a little remorseful for what you did? A little at all?"

She cupped her head into her hands. When she brought them out to face Peter, her eyes were red.

"No. No, I'm not. I did it for the good of the town. Didn't we have a nice life? Wasn't the town safe? Sometimes people need to be taught how to behave. That's why little kids have timeouts, Peter."

"Ha, oh, I see. So now you're comparing your lab to time out."

"Forget it. You'd never understand."

"I loved you. Did you understand that? I loved you, and you betrayed that trust. You kept things from me."

"To protect you! I did it to protect you! Do you think I was the sole one behind that thing? Plus, would you have ever married me if I had said I was running a secret lab under my house?"

"You are really a piece of work." Peter shook his head.

"Thanks. You are so sweet."

"I wanted to tell you, darling, that they temporarily disbanded The Neighborhood Watch. They said it wasn't working to fight crime in town."

"They what?!"

"Yeah. That's what the mayor thought. I guess they are thinking of some other way."

"What other way? What? What are they doing?"

"Don't know, but I just thought you should hear it from me. The Neighborhood Watch is 'poof.' No more."

Sue Ellen's jaw dropped, and her heart sank.

"Peter, of all the disgusting things you told me all these years, this is the worst. The worst, Peter."

Peter felt a tinge of guilt at that moment. He did come to hate his ex-wife, but now he did figure that he went too far. As twisted as that program was for her, it was her life's work.

"Okay, it's okay. I'm sure they'll come up with something else."

"No. There isn't anything else. It worked. People may not have liked it, but it kept us safe. We were the safest town in America. Don't you get that!?"

A couple of guards came over to the booth now.

"Is there a problem here?" one of them asked Peter.

Peter shook his head no, but they kept a watchful eye on Sue Ellen. Sue Ellen brushed them aside.

"Go ahead! Take me. It's better than talking to this asshole. Take me!"

The guards did as she asked and pulled her up and out of the booth. She screamed as high pitch as anyone ever had and gave Peter a look that could kill on her way around the corner. He gulped and knew that he had gone too far. He just hoped that she would never escape.

4

There was a mass exodus out of Ridgeport following the underground lab conspiracy scandal. By 2020, about three thousand residents had left town. Ridgeport was no longer the safest city in America. It was no longer the safest city in Illinois. It was not even one of the safest cities. It's not as if there was a murder every week, but crime seeped into the city year by year as residents fled and businesses closed. Drug dealers hung on corners, theft increased two hundred percent (especially at the mall), carjackings were rampant, and assault and battery cases were also common. Following John's murder in '04, there had been dozens more. A couple of well-known places closed in town - The Ridgeport Egg and The Ridgeport Grocer were among them. A couple of places close to the mall decided to put up bars on their windows due to frequent theft cases in that area. An article in USA Today ran with the headline, "Ridgeport: America's bittersweet town."

By 2020, the crime had reached a level on par with the worst twenty-five towns in the state. In addition to the crime, the town seemed to just go into decay. The grass went uncut, sidewalks unfixed, graffiti unwashed from buildings. Some shops closed, and nothing was put into their place. That was how ghost towns started. That year, the village board decided to abolish The Neighborhood Watch because they didn't see a correlation between a decrease in crime and their efforts.

Mayor Jim Harding, a close friend of Illinois Governor John Martin's, visited Martin's office one day with a very unusual request.

"John, Ridgeport is in a state of emergency. We are bleeding residents. The Neighborhood Watch is no more. The town is riddled with crime."

"Uh-huh. And have you tried recruiting a more active police force?"

"Yes, no one wants to apply here."

"I see."

"John...I was thinking of a more experimental approach. It would be a huge favor."

The governor raised an eyebrow.

"What kind of favor?"

"I was wondering if you might pardon Sue Ellen Norris. We need to restructure The Neighborhood Watch. She's the only one who can do it."

"Are you kidding? It would be a PR nightmare. I'll never get re-elected."

"Not if we spin it right. Not if we spin it right. We can say that she has done her due time, learned her lesson, and that she will be under our watchful eye. We already disbanded The Neighborhood Watch. We'll say that 'wink' she is not in charge of anything... 'wink.'"

John rubbed his temple and sighed.

"What's the crime index in Ridgeport right now?"

"Ten. We're at ten, John."

"Ten!"

John sighed again and looked out his window. Clouds were gathering, and it looked like rain.

"I'll see what I can do."

"Thanks. You won't regret this."

As Harding left the room, the governor breathed out slowly, picked up the phone, and called Cook County Jail. Sue Ellen Norris stirred in her cell, thinking of all the ways to kill Peter Barnes.

Acknowledgments

This novel was a nearly three-year journey that involved waking up at four a.m. every morning to write before my newborn/turned toddler awoke and before I had to switch gears to go to work. I went through an excruciating editing process that I could not have done without my wonderful editor Alison Moran, who helped me tighten up several scenes throughout the story. I owe her so much for what became this finished product. I also would like to thank my grad school classmates and professor Seth Berg from my Story and Concept course for taking the time to further review and critique scenes and ideas in this novel. Thank you to William Jones for editing the sections in this text pertinent to journalism writing. Thank you to Codex Art & Apparel for your fantastic cover design work and the audiobook product. Lastly, thank you to all those who supported me in this process: my family. It would have been an even harder mountain to climb without your love and support. I hope this book has given you something to think about. Writing a novel starts with one person, but it takes a village to make it 'write.'